Praise for The Ravens series

'Enchanting.'
Kirkus

'An intriguing mystery built upon the
foundations of sisterhood.'
School Library Journal

'Wonderful worldbuilding, well-executed
plotting, and page-turning.' surprises.
Publishers Weekly

'A spectacular read for those looking to find a novel with
good representation, humour, magic, and just the right
amount of horror during the fall and winter seasons.'
The Nerd Daily

T0349934

THE
MONARCHS

KASS MORGAN
DANIELLE PAIGE

HODDER

First published in Great Britain in 2022 by Hodder & Stoughton
An Hachette UK company

This paperback edition published in 2023

1

A CIP catalogue record for this title is available from the British Library

Hardback ISBN 978 1 529 36387 6
Trade Paperback ISBN 978 1 529 36388 3
ebook ISBN 978 1 529 36389 0
Paperback ISBN 978 1 529 36390 6

Printed and bound in Great Britain by Clays Ltd, Elcograf S.p.A.

Hodder & Stoughton policy is to use papers that are natural, renewable
and recyclable products and made from wood grown in sustainable
forests. The logging and manufacturing processes are expected to
conform to the environmental regulations of the country of origin.

Hodder & Stoughton Ltd
Carmelite House
50 Victoria Embankment
London EC4Y 0DZ

www.hodder.co.uk

To our editorial coven: Lanie, Laura, Ellen, and Emilia.
Your words are magic.

— Kass

For my sister, Andrea. When we were small, I used to follow
you around like the sun. I love you, sis. I still would follow
you anywhere. And for Fi and Sienna, my little coven.

— Danielle

PROLOGUE

Long-dead eyes blink open in the crypt.

The first thing they sense is the absence of darkness. Light filters in through the tiniest of holes.

Lungs fill with air and ache with the pleasure of pain after so many years empty.

In and out.

A piercing scream erupts from a hungry throat, but the walls of the tomb constrain it. Hands claw at the sides of the box until bone and blood meet stone.

And then panic sets in as remembrance begins to take hold. Of what happened. Of who built the walls of this cursed prison. The witches did, of course.

The witches.

Where are they?

It doesn't take long . . . There it is. The sweet perfume of magic. The witches.

They are to blame. And they are still here. I can feel them.

One witch. Two witch. Three witch.

They've brought the wind. It howls overhead, an almost human, keening screech. It tears through the branches of the tree, whipping off limbs and leaves, tossing them like confetti to the ground below. It circles and rages, diving to the earth and destroying everything in its path.

They've brought the rain. A soaking, furious storm, shot through with thunder and lightning.

Amid it all, three girls. A Cups witch, a Pentacles witch, and most wicked of them all, a Swords witch, the one desperate to defy the laws of nature.

A tree falls. Glass shatters. One by one the witches fall to the ground — and the wicked one doesn't get up.

They've shaken the earth. It rumbles . . . and then everything just stops. The wind goes still. The rain vanishes as quickly as it appeared. The clouds part in the moonless sky.

The witches are too busy crying to notice anything but their grief.

No one feels it: the way the world split apart, a deep jagged cut in the beaten earth.

And no one sees it: the pale, dirt-covered hand that emerges from the deep, clawing its way to the surface.

"I am free. I am coming for them," a voice whispers into the dark. No one can hear. No one else knows. But vengeance is coming.

One witch, two witch, three witch . . . none.

CHAPTER ONE

Scarlett

"What you're suggesting sounds like you want to change what it means to be a Kappa witch," Eugenie accused Scarlett, passing their mother a serving dish of truffled mashed potatoes.

The end of winter break can't come soon enough, Scarlett Winter thought as she sat trapped at home between two Kappa alumnae who just happened to be her mother and sister at their last supper before she got to go back to Westerly College.

Scarlett took a deep breath to calm herself. Looking at Eugenie, Scarlett wished that she was back with her sisters again. Her real sisters: the Ravens. It had been three weeks since the Kappa girls bid one another farewell, after the most difficult term of Scarlett's life. And while they'd been texting constantly, it didn't feel the same. Sure, her mother, Marjorie, and sister, Eugenie, had been marginally *less* terrible to Scarlett recently, but . . . that was before Scarlett made her proposal at tonight's dinner.

"I'm sure that's not what your sister means. Right, honey?" Marjorie asked gently.

"Well, no—and yes," Scarlett said carefully, but just then her phone vibrated. It was tucked out of sight underneath her thigh, to avoid her mother complaining about phones at the dinner table. But she hadn't been able to resist smuggling it into the dining room tonight. Because of Jackson. Jackson, who she most definitely should not be encouraging. Or even texting. Jackson, who she'd cast a memory charm on to make him forget her.

"See? I told you. She's trying to tear Kappa down from within," Eugenie said with a smug look.

Scarlett took the opportunity to glance down at her phone.

She lives. When I didn't hear from you for a whole day, I began to worry . . .

Scarlett bit her lip to keep a smile from forming.

"Scarlett?" Marjorie pressed.

Scarlett shoved the thought of her complicated love life aside and folded her palms on the table. She needed her mother's approval tonight. But she wasn't appealing to her mother as her mother, she was appealing to her as the head of the Kappa alumnae council, the Monarchs. She was the crucial piece to getting the other witches to fall in line. Sometimes convincing one witch was the key to them all.

"I do want to change things, Mama, so that what happened last semester never happens again."

"And you think having every Kappa write down all her secrets accomplishes that? It exposes us to the greatest risk of all: discovery."

"I've thought of that. I've thought of everything. I am a Winter, aren't I?" At this, Scarlett sat a little taller. Truthfully, she *had* thought of everything. There had been nothing to do these past three weeks *but* think.

Marjorie sighed. "What happened last semester was an anomaly. But it is behind us. Let's leave the past in the past."

That was exactly what Scarlett was afraid of—that those who hadn't been there wouldn't understand what real danger truly felt like. What it felt like when your best friend went to the wicked side and killed three other witches just to make herself more powerful. "That's precisely the problem. The past isn't the past. The past is what came back to haunt us, and we didn't know about it. We weren't prepared for it. Because we don't know our own history." If only they'd known about the Henosis talisman, maybe they would have been able to stop Tiffany sooner. Maybe they could have saved Dahlia, their former president.

Her mother paused, considering.

"Tell me more about this *survey* you want to conduct." Marjorie Winters pursed her lips. Her emphasis on the word was slight enough that most people wouldn't have noticed. But Scarlett knew her mother well enough to hear the doubt.

"Yes, sister, do explain why you think invading our alumnae's privacy worthwhile," Eugenie butted in.

"Ignoring the skeletons in our own closet came back to haunt us last semester, and I don't want to let anything like that happen again."

"We can all agree there," Marjorie murmured, which raised Scarlett's spirits just a hint.

She squared her shoulders. "I want to ask everyone to submit a personal account of their time at Kappa. It doesn't have to include anything private; I'm not interested in a sordid history of hookups.

Just information about the spellwork they performed with the sorority, especially group workings; any historical information about the Kappa House or Westerly itself—"

Marjorie raised a hand, cutting off her daughter. "I'm sorry, honey, but Kappa Rho Nu has always placed a very high value on privacy."

"You really expect some of the most powerful women in the country to voluntarily hand you written proof they're witches?" Eugenie smirked.

"No, of course not," she replied, just as disdainfully. She had anticipated this objection too. She reached into the vintage Hermès bag her mother had gifted her over the holidays. Scarlett had always admired this bag, which her mother had gotten decades ago in Paris. It was enchanted to feel weightless on your shoulder.

An even better gift than the bag itself, however, had been the expression on Eugenie's face when Scarlett had opened it.

This bag was a reminder: Marjorie respected Scarlett now. Trusted her. After everything that happened last semester—*after seeing what Tiffany became*—surely her mother would see the wisdom in this plan.

Scarlett withdrew a leather-bound book. The cover had been embossed with two stylized tarot card images: the Moon and the Magician. As she flipped it open, she whispered under her breath, "I call to the Moon and to the Magician. Reveal the wellspring of my sisters' ambitions."

Eugenie sat back in her chair and crossed her arms, unimpressed. Marjorie, on the other hand, leaned closer. The blank pages bloomed with black letters so straight and solid they looked type-written. "Interesting. So the enchantment protects the anonymity of the contributors?"

Scarlett nodded. "And if the book detects signs of any non-Kappa witches attempting to tamper, it will wipe itself blank." She fanned through the pages, tightly blinking her eyes closed when she spotted Mei's entry about last semester. "I've already collected the current Kappas' memories, to demonstrate. My plan is to ask the Monarchs at the alumnae reunion to join us in a group ritual, to add any information they choose."

"Hmm. The spell is impressive." Marjorie tapped a nail on the hardwood as Scarlett snapped the book shut. She was quiet for a long moment. "Very well. We'll need to discuss this at the next council meeting."

Eugenie heaved a sigh. "I suppose we ought to put it to vote," she said.

Scarlett blinked, stunned by her sister's support. "Oh . . . okay. Well . . . thank you."

Then Eugenie grinned. "I do enjoy watching new proposals fail. Makes for such entertaining arguments at cocktail hour afterward."

Of course. Her sister would never truly back her, no matter how much she accomplished, no matter what strides she made. After all, her sister had come home for dinner tonight of all nights. The one night Scarlett specifically asked her mother if they could dine alone, because she wanted to talk Kappa business. Eugenie claimed it was because she wanted to spend more time with her younger sister, but Scarlett knew the truth. Eugenie was jealous. Worried

Scarlett might usurp her place as the most noteworthy Kappa president in the family.

Well, good, Scarlett thought with a tight smile. That was exactly what she intended to do.

"Besides," Eugenie continued, while she reached for the bell to call the housekeeper. "From what I hear, you won't need to dig around in ancient history for a fight. You've got your work cut out for you right here in the present."

"What do you mean?" Scarlett asked, forcing her expression to remain calm.

Eugenie flashed a smug smile. "Rumor has it Kappa won't be the only ones putting in a bid with the Panhellenic council to host Spring Fling this year. Theta's coming for you."

Scarlett actually laughed. "Is that all?" She'd been expecting far worse. Theta Omega Xi, the second-largest sorority on Westerly's campus, counterbidding Kappa for the Spring Fling wasn't exactly news. Their rivalry went back nearly as far as the founding of Westerly. "Maria begs the council to let her host every year," Scarlett said. "I wouldn't call one jealous sorority president a threat. Especially not after what happened last summer."

Even more than the other sororities and fraternities on campus, Theta historically took pride in adhering to practices like strict dress codes and rigid rules of conduct. Last summer, someone leaked sections from the handbook online, and it'd gone viral almost instantly. A graphic showing how to match different shades of white had garnered particular ridicule, as had a chapter on clothing styles and body types. It'd been a PR disaster. Everyone assumed it was a disgruntled Theta who leaked the book, but no one knew for certain.

"Underestimating your enemy is the first step toward failure," Eugenie replied as the maid entered. "Oh, Beth, darling, we're about ready for dessert."

Scarlett smiled icily at her sister as the new housekeeper entered with a cart carrying biscuits and clotted cream, placing one at each of their place settings. Scarlett took a bite of the biscuit and was immediately transported back in time. It tasted like her childhood, like safety and love and innocence.

It tasted like Minnie.

"Mama, how did you . . . ?" Scarlett turned toward Marjorie. Minnie, her beloved nanny, had passed away nearly a year ago.

"It's Beth. She's a Cups and an empath. We thought this dessert would be a nice treat," Marjorie said with a magnanimous smile.

Scarlett knew what her mother was doing. Marjorie Winter believed in throwing one of two things at a problem: money or magic. After what Scarlett went through last semester, her mother had been pulling out all the stops.

Scarlett pushed the plate away. Her mother was trying to be kind, but she didn't know her like Minnie had. Minnie would have known that there was no substitute for Minnie's cooking, just like there was no substitute for Minnie herself. Scarlett suddenly felt a strong and irrepressible urge to be alone.

"Actually, I've got some classwork to finish." She waited just long enough for Marjorie to nod in dismissal and then strode away.

Only once she was safely shut in her bedroom did she let the tears flow. A moment later, raindrops pattered against her window and thunder rumbled in the distance, summoned by her Cups magic, by her tears. Before she'd understood her special connection to water, she'd been scared of storms like these. She used to sneak into Minnie's room and curl up next to her, shaking.

"Don't be afraid, little one. The water is part of you. It is your magic," Minnie would murmur, wrapping an arm around Scarlett's shoulders. "It's funny, though, how something so destructive can be so beautiful at the same time." With Minnie, everything was part lesson, part protection, part love—and Scarlett was forever grateful for every word. They'd kept her alive. They'd kept her safe.

Scarlett thought about Tiffany, her best friend, who had caved in to her desire for power. Who *killed* people for it, her own sisters included. She was beautiful and destructive too.

"Don't be afraid, but be wary," Minnie always said when she sensed fear in Scarlett. "You are the storm. But there are other storms out there, too."

Over time, Minnie's words came to fruition. Scarlett's powers had grown over the years, and she had summoned a storm the night that Tiffany had threatened her life and Vivi's. Minnie had been right: She was the storm. But Tiffany had been one, too.

But then the thought brought a pang of guilt with it. Only her Kappas understood. They knew the real story. And they felt the same loss. Once they were back under the same roof, she'd feel better again. More grounded and centered. More at home. Yet another reason she longed to be back at Westerly again.

Scarlett rooted around in her bag until she found her tarot deck. Not the shiny new deck her mother had given her at the start of the school year. The old, tattered one Minnie had given her years ago. The edges on the cards were worn, and some had been bent or stained in places. But this deck knew Scarlett. Understood her heart.

It always gave honest answers. Even when those answers were hard to hear.

A distant rumble rattled the windowpanes. Scarlett held the deck in both hands and focused on the coming semester, on her new presidency at Kappa. On her and her sisters' chance to rebuild. Their fresh start after the horrors of the fall.

Spring brought new life. Rebirth, rejuvenation. They desperately needed that now.

"Show me what this semester holds in store for Kappa," Scarlett whispered to the cards. To Minnie, if she was listening somewhere.

Scarlett fanned the cards out across her bed, then ran her fingertips over them. Her skin tingled when she touched one card. She withdrew it from the fan and made another pass. The next card jumped from the deck of its own accord, before she even reached it. The third card followed. Scarlett swept all three up, laid them facedown before her, and took a deep, centering breath.

The first card represented Kappa's recent past. She turned it over.

The Tower. Danger, destruction, a sudden and terrible upheaval. *Well, that's certainly accurate.*

The second card would represent her and her sisters' present. She held her breath as she flipped it.

Three of Swords. The image depicted a bleeding heart, pierced by three swords. Grief, heartbreak, loss. Swords had been Tiffany's suit, Scarlett couldn't help but note. Each of the three swords reminded Scarlett of someone they'd lost: Tiffany, Dahlia, and Gwen, their former sorority sister.

Scarlett swallowed hard as she reached for the final card. The future. It would indicate what the Kappas should expect in the semester to come. *Please, give us some good news.* They needed it.

But when she saw the card, her heart sank.

The Ten of Swords. An image of a man lying face-down on the ground, ten swords protruding from his backside.

Betrayal. Enemies. Curses and attacks.

A flash lit up the bedroom, so blindingly white it seared the backs of Scarlett's eyes. A flash of anger followed. She shoved the cards so hard they spilled onto the floor. She paced over to the window and stared out into the storm. A storm nearly as violent as the one she and Tiffany had battled the night her best friend died, just a month ago.

It felt like years.

"I don't care what the cards say," Scarlett whispered to her own reflection. "I'll *make* this semester better. No matter what it takes."

Her only reply was the rumble of thunder overhead.

CHAPTER TWO

Vivi

"Oh, look, there's a spot right in front. That's a good sign, isn't it, sugar snap?"

Vivi shot her mother a suspicious glance from the driver's seat. Daphne Devereaux saw signs everywhere—omens of misfortune in tarot cards, portents of doom in tea leaves, and hints of danger in the cackle of crows—but she never, ever, saw *good* signs. Nor did she usually speak in the slow, overly cheerful tone people employed to soothe toddlers or disarm axe murderers.

Vivi knew her mother was trying to help alleviate her concerns about returning to Westerly College, and more specifically, Kappa House, the elegant Savannah mansion about a half mile from the spot in the woods where Vivi had nearly been killed last semester.

But while her brush with death had forced Vivi to accept that magic had a dangerous side, Vivi knew she could face any threat with her sisters by her side. After all, the Kappas were one of the most powerful covens in the country.

"Are you sure we'll fit there?" Vivi asked.

"You can't avoid parallel parking forever. We should've practiced more over the holidays," Daphne said with a sigh.

"I'm not *avoiding* it," Vivi said indignantly. "It's fine. I can do it." She took a deep breath, straightened out the car, and had just started backing up when she spotted three PiKa brothers coming down the block. Despite the fact that it was just after eleven a.m., all three were holding red Solo cups. Vivi rolled her eyes. *Frat bros.*

"Here we go, parking challenge commenced!" one of the boys shouted as he raised his cup in the air.

"The championship is on the line, but can the Americans pull through at the eleventh hour?" another said in a deep announcer's voice.

"Just ignore them, honey pie," Daphne said, suppressing a smile. She was generally deeply distrusting of men, but had a soft spot for boys with preppy swagger that Vivi had always found somewhat mystifying.

Her cheeks burning, Vivi grasped the wheel and whispered, "I call to the High Priestess and the Page of Swords. Lend me the skills that practice affords." The final syllable had barely left her mouth when her body began to fill with a comforting warmth, as if someone had wrapped her in a weighted electric blanket. All the tension drained from her shoulders, and almost without thinking about it, Vivi backed the car into the parking spot in one smooth movement, guided by muscle memory she hadn't before possessed.

She shot the boys a triumphant look. The one who'd taken out his phone gave her a thumbs-up. The other two had already lost interest and were walking down the block.

Daphne shook her head. "You're going to get spoiled. Using your magic for every little task."

"I thought you agreed that I need to practice!"

"I was thinking more about self-defense, sweetheart. Not parallel parking," Daphne said, glancing over her shoulder at the retreating PiKas. "And I *definitely* didn't mean you should practice in front of strange boys."

Vivi snorted. "Those frat bros wouldn't recognize magic unless their beer bongs came to life and started singing along to Florida Georgia Line. And even then, they'd probably blame it on bad weed."

"I wouldn't lump all fraternity boys together if I were you. I knew quite a few impressive ones in my day." Daphne's face turned slightly wistful, a rare expression that could only mean one thing —she was thinking about the one person they never, ever discussed.

"Was my father in a frat?" Vivi asked, careful to keep her tone casual, lest Daphne shut down or change the subject like she usually did whenever she felt Vivi pushing too hard.

"Of course. Vince was the quarterback. He joined the football fraternity."

Vivi froze. *Vince.* Her mother had always refused to tell Vivi her father's name, lest she "get any ideas about Googling him" or tracking him down.

It was by far the most information Daphne had ever divulged in one conversation, enough to make Vivi bold enough to ask, "So he went to Westerly with you?"

Daphne pretended to be too busy gathering her purse and unbuckling her seat belt to hear. "All set? Let's start taking these bags inside."

Although it was the third week of January, all the houses on their block still had their Christmas lights up, except for Kappa House, which had forgone decorations this year in the wake of their president's death. In the many other places she'd lived, Vivi had found holiday decorations in January rather depressing. They seemed to signal a dejected weariness that matched the dreary expressions of their occupants. But Savannah was an entirely different story. The elegant, slightly weatherworn mansions with Christmas lights peeking out from overgrown ivy reminded Vivi of an eccentric party girl who'd fallen asleep in her pearls.

"Do you want me to help carry this stuff up to your room?" Daphne asked from near the car.

"I'll be okay." Vivi whispered another spell she'd been practicing under her breath. The overstuffed duffle bag turned feather-light, and the suitcases on the steps levitated a few inches off the ground.

Without thinking, she glanced over her shoulder toward the forest behind Kappa House and shivered as she remembered the manic gleam in Tiffany's eye, the moonlight glinting off the dagger she held pointed over Vivi's chest.

For a moment, she was transported back to that clearing. She could hear the crack of thunder, the snap of shattered branches as the storm raged. The smell of rain-soaked dirt mingled with the scent of her own blood . . .

The ground beneath her trembled, yanking her back to the present. "What the . . . ?" She jerked her head from side to side, looking for the source. A huge truck rumbling down the street or a construction crew with enormous drills. But there was nothing —everything was still and quiet.

Daphne, who apparently hadn't felt anything, pulled Vivi in for a tight hug. "Take care of yourself, sweetheart."

"I will, I promise."

"I love you, darling," Daphne said, then released her.

"Love you, too." She smiled and waved as her mother turned back to the car, thinking how much had changed in just a few months. Vivi had arrived at Westerly desperate to start a new life away from Daphne and her constant premonitions of doom. But now she felt a pain in her chest as she watched her mother drive away.

However, her flicker of homesickness lasted just about as long as it took Vivi to turn around and see Etta standing in the doorway, a huge grin on her face. "You're back!" Etta said, pulling Vivi in for a hug. As usual, she smelled faintly of lavender and mint from all the time she spent tending to the garden and the more exotic plants in the greenhouse. "Come in. Do you need help with those?" She gestured toward Vivi's bags.

"I'm okay." Vivi snapped her fingers, and the suitcases began floating toward her.

"Wow," Etta said, impressed. "Someone's been practicing."

Vivi followed her into the foyer, smiling at the tea-rose printed wallpaper and the curved, mahogany table next to the brass coat-rack. The first floor of the house was glamoured to adapt to the seasons, time of day, or just the general mood of the occupants, but this iteration was her favorite.

"The first floor was all midcentury modern until about ten minutes ago," Etta said. "The house must've sensed you coming."

"There you are!" Mei said, coming down the wide staircase. Her wet hair was waist-length today and bright pink. "Did you wind up trying those charms I sent?"

Mei, the only other Pentacles witch in the house, had taken it upon herself to flood Vivi's inbox with spells that specialized in earth magic. "Yes, thank you! That last one was amazing." Mei had sent her a spell that allowed the user to summon stones from the ground to create a shield. Practicing it over and over in her mother's garden had made Vivi feel calmer and safer than she had since leaving the woods.

She'd be damned if anyone caught her off her guard again.

From somewhere inside the house, Vivi heard a muffled shout, and an instant later, a squealing mass crashed into her.

"I thought you'd never get here!" Ariana wrapped both arms around Vivi's middle and squeezed. "Did y'all *walk* from Jekyll Island? Or did you stop to see Mason first?"

"Yeah, you caught me," Vivi teased. "I decided to take my mother along with me to see my boyfriend." It was the first time she'd said the word *boyfriend* aloud to describe Mason. It was actually the first time in her entire life she'd called *anyone* her boyfriend.

"I knew I heard our favorite badass," Reagan said. She appeared in the hallway alongside Sonali, who rushed forward to give Vivi nearly as crushing a hug as Ariana.

"How are you holding up?" Sonali asked, stepping back to examine Vivi critically. She'd spent the break working at a hospital in a small Peruvian mountain town with terrible cell service and it'd driven her crazy not to be able to FaceTime with Vivi and track her recovery.

"Relax, Dr. Mani, she's *fine*," Reagan said, reaching out to fluff Vivi's hair. "She's never looked better. I'm the one you should've been worrying about. My mom's become obsessed with me dating a senator's son and dragged me to eight different DC Christmas parties. If I have to listen to one more Chad or Luke tell me about playing lacrosse at Dartmouth or rowing at Princeton, I'm going to hex my ears off."

"That should definitely solve the problem," Ariana said. "No self-respecting lacrosse bro is going to date a girl with no ears." She linked her arm through Vivi's. "Come on—there's iced tea waiting for you in the garden. I want to hear all about things with Mason."

"I'm not sure there's much to tell, but let me take my stuff upstairs and I'll meet you out there." Vivi smiled and headed toward the stairs, her enchanted bags drifting behind her. She and Mason hadn't been able to meet up over the break, but they'd spoken every day. It was delightfully strange that her former crush—and Scarlett's ex-boyfriend—was now the first person she thought to reach out to when she was panicking about course registration or simply wanted to share a silly dog video. However, there was a limit to how close they'd ever be able to grow, since there was a part of her life that had to remain hidden forever. Under no circumstances could Vivi reveal that magic was real and that Kappa Rho Nu was a sorority for witches.

She passed the second floor and paused to admire the deep blue walls hung with antique mirrors, candle sconces, and oil paintings of famous witches and powerfully magical sites around the world. Vivi loved the dramatic glamour of this floor, but no part of the house made her happier than the sunny third floor with its gabled ceilings and whitewashed walls, where she, Ariana, and Bailey each had one of the singles reserved for first-year sisters. But before she could slip into her bedroom, a voice caught her attention.

"It definitely wasn't like this earlier," Bailey was saying worriedly. "Do you think a bird flew into it or something?"

Bailey and Scarlett were standing in front of one the bay windows looking out over the garden. It had a window seat where Vivi had spent hours curled up reading, with a mug of tea bewitched to stay piping hot until the final drop.

"Everything okay?" Vivi asked.

"Vivi!" Bailey said. "You're back!" She gave Vivi a quick hug, then returned her attention to the window. She was fiddling with the hem of her sweater, like she always did when she was nervous.

"I'm back," Vivi repeated. "Hey, Scarlett." But to her surprise, her Big merely gave her a quick smile before leaning in to inspect the window where a huge, spiderweb-shaped crack filled one of the panes.

"I'm sure it's nothing," Scarlett said, running one of her perfectly manicured fingers along the crack. As usual, she was impeccably turned out in a tweed shift dress and pearls befitting the newest president of Kappa Rho Nu. "In old houses like this, the foundation settles sometimes."

It was true that the house often creaked and groaned, especially during storms, but Vivi couldn't imagine the foundation shifting enough to crack a window. "I thought I felt something out in the yard a few minutes ago, sort of a weird tremor."

Vivi could've sworn she saw a flicker of alarm in Scarlett's face before she smiled and said briskly, "There you go. It was probably one of the moving trucks passing too close to the house. Are you all right to fix it yourself, or would you like help?"

"I've got it," Bailey said confidently.

"Great. I'll see you girls downstairs in five. I'm calling a house meeting."

"Sure," Vivi said, about to ask how Scarlett's break had been.

But her Big was already hurrying down the steps.

The living room was full by the time Vivi stashed her suitcases in her bedroom and then ran back downstairs for the meeting. She smiled and waved at the Kappas she hadn't seen yet as she picked her way through the packed room toward Ariana, who scooted over to make room on a blue velvet footrest that matched the armchair in which Jess and Juliet were snuggled up.

The only person still standing was Scarlett. She stepped forward, and a respectful quiet fell over the room. "Welcome back, ladies," she said, her voice the perfect blend of warmth and authority. "I hope y'all had the relaxing, restorative breaks you deserved. Last semester, we faced the greatest threat in our coven's history, and we emerged even stronger for it. When Kappas stand together, there's nothing we can't do." She paused and rested her gaze on the one empty seat in the room, the red brocade chair next to the fireplace where Dahlia always sat during meetings. "But we also suffered tragic loss."

Vivi's throat tightened. In a just world, Dahlia would be here, welcoming the girls back to campus with one of her businesslike but still darkly funny speeches instead of lying cold and silent beneath a newly dug grave in Bonaventure Cemetery.

"Dahlia isn't here in body, but we all know she's here in spirit. We will continue to feel her presence. We will always feel her magic. Let's have a moment of silence for our sister . . . our *sisters*."

She's referring to Tiffany, Vivi realized as a few of the Kappas exchanged uneasy looks. Tiffany had been Scarlett's best friend before she'd become obsessed with the Henosis talisman, a legendary amulet she'd hoped to use to cure her mother's terminal illness. But while her intentions had been noble, the wicked magic had proved too powerful for Tiffany, sending her down a desperate, twisted path that resulted in her killing Dahlia to steal her magic.

In the end, Scarlett had been forced to battle her own best friend to save Vivi, a newbie witch who hadn't been strong enough to fight back. Guilt tugged at Vivi's chest. *It wasn't your fault,* she reminded herself.

The thought felt hollow.

She squeezed her eyes shut, but her mind continued to race. She saw the forest, the dark clearing. Her heart beat faster, wild and frantic, the same way it had that night. She could smell the storm coming, hear the crackle of electricity in the air and, above it all, Tiffany's laughter.

If she'd been a stronger witch, if she'd known more about this world, the way the other Kappas did, perhaps she wouldn't have fallen into Tiffany's trap.

No wonder Scarlett was angry with her. She should be. She'd been forced to kill Tiffany because Vivi hadn't been strong enough to fight back. Was she a burden on them all?

"Now, we have some minor housekeeping to attend to before we talk back-to-school parties," Scarlett continued.

"Oh good." Reagan perked up from the corner of the room where she was sitting with her back against the wall. "Can we do a French Revolution theme? I just inherited a bunch of antique jewelry from my great-aunt Sylvie, including a bracelet Marie Antoinette was wearing the night before she died."

Ariana rolled her eyes and whispered, "It's a good thing we don't guillotine people anymore for being out-of-touch one-percenters."

"That'll be up to our new social chair," Scarlett said. Her voice was steady, but Vivi could sense the effort required to maintain her composure. That had been Tiffany's old position. "I'd like to nominate a replacement. Someone whose hard work and dedication have already impressed many of us. Vivi?"

For a second, Vivi looked around the room, confused. Was Scarlett asking her for a recommendation?

Only when Mei raised a hand and said, "Seconded," did Vivi realize what Scarlett meant.

She's nominating me.

"Do we have any objections?" Scarlett scanned the room. Nobody spoke. Scarlett's smile widened. "Vivi, do you accept?"

Now she understood why Scarlett had been acting strangely—she hadn't wanted to tip her hand before the meeting. A flood of pride rushed through Vivi at this sign of confidence from her Big. *Scarlett believes in me.*

Around the room, the Kappas' faces conveyed a range of expressions from surprise to excitement—and in Ariana's case, elation. Etta and Juliet were exchanging pleased smiles, as if they'd known this was coming. Mei, too. Reagan looked vaguely annoyed, but when Vivi caught her eye, even she forced a smile.

Vivi cleared her throat. "Yes. Of course. Thank you."

"Great," Scarlett said. "Now, about those parties." She cast another glance at Reagan, who leaned forward, genuinely eager now. "We will be hosting the annual PiKa/Kappa welcome-back mixer here at the house next Friday."

Squeals of excitement broke out among the freshmen while the others watched in amusement.

"After all the shadows hanging over our house from last semester, we will need to put our best foot forward. Which is why I'm so glad Vivi has accepted her new post."

Some of Vivi's earlier excitement began to drain away. Social chairs were in charge of events. Which meant Vivi's first big test, as an officer of Kappa, was already nearly on top of her. She'd need to throw the biggest, most impressive mixer Kappa had ever hosted. And she had less than a week to prepare for it.

No pressure, right?

CHAPTER THREE

Scarlett

Something was wrong with Dahlia's grave. But as Scarlett stared at the Everly family tombstone with her Little Sister beside her, she couldn't place her finger on what.

"I just can't believe she's really gone." Vivi's voice sounded quiet in the hush of the graveyard. The same graveyard where, what felt like a lifetime ago, Scarlett had pranked Vivi and the other freshmen, in their first hazing rite as Kappas.

On the ground around the base of the headstone, heaps of flowers had been piled. Everything from expensive, professionally arranged bouquets down to little clumps of wildflowers, which Westerly students must have handpicked. Then she spotted what was wrong, between the lilies and carnations and other bouquets. Pink roses.

"She hated pink roses," Scarlett said, emotion rising.

"No one hates roses," Vivi said automatically, then opened her mouth to take it back. "I'm sorry, I didn't mean . . ."

But Scarlett didn't have time for Vivi's apologies; she was already dropping to her knees and pulling out the offending flowers. Vivi got down beside her and placed a hand on her elbow, stopping her.

"Hey, Scar . . . it's okay . . ."

She looked up at Vivi in surprise. Surprise that she had lost her calm and surprised too that somehow Vivi—the pledge she had dismissed at first sight—had become her closest confidant. The only best friend she had left. The lump in her throat swelled and ached. Scarlett tightened her jaw.

If Scarlett was being brutally honest with herself, it wasn't the fact that the wrong flowers were here; it was that Dahlia *wasn't*. Scarlett gripped the roses that she had gathered tight in a fist and rocked back and sat on the damp grass.

"Hey, we can put them on one of the lonely graves," Vivi said gently. As Vivi took them away, Scarlett stared at the sea of messages. There were thank-yous and we-miss-yous and we-love-yous from other students, sororities, cafeteria ladies. Everyone at Westerly knew Dahlia. At least they thought they did.

One note in particular caught her eye. It was next to a remaining clump of pink roses near her headstone. Scarlett picked it up. It was written on green stationery in elegant script. It only said *We know it was you*. Scarlett shivered.

Dahlia always put Kappa first. She'd been a great leader. Dahlia had used her magic all over campus in small ways to create good will for Kappa. Or influence. Or power. Maybe someone knew how cunning Dahlia could be, after all.

"Dahlia made friends with everyone not just because she liked them, but because she thought it protected us. *Being a good witch is good for all the witches.*"

"Oh," Vivi said, absorbing this, and then added, "She would

have done anything to keep us safe. And ultimately, she did." Vivi's hand came to rest on her shoulder. "She'd be proud of you right now."

"Would she?" Scarlett laughed, without humor. "I'm not sure she'd like the direction I want to take the sorority." Between her Big Sister Dahlia's ghost haunting her every step, and her mother and sister's constant pressure to be perfect, Scarlett's job felt impossible. Scarlett had been chasing perfect since she learned her first spell. And somehow as close as she came, it always slipped away. Somehow, she always ended up at almost. And never enough.

"She respected you. She chose you. And she would know better than anyone that things were far from perfect," Vivi protested.

Just then, a strong gust of wind picked up. Flower petals detached from the bundles at their feet and went skittering away across the gravestones. A few strands of Scarlett's hair pulled free of her ponytail and blew across her eyes. She reached up to brush them back.

At her side, Vivi gasped. "Look . . ."

Right in the center of Dahlia's nameplate, next to the feather, perched a butterfly. It was beautiful. Fat-winged and glossy in the sunlight, a deep purple, almost black, that reminded Scarlett of the Ravens themselves.

She swallowed around a sudden lump in her throat, as the butterfly's wings flickered, catching the sunlight. *Dahlia.*

A moment later, it took flight once again, drifting high up over their heads, and seemed to vanish against the cloudless blue sky.

"See?" Vivi smiled now, a real smile, the first Scarlett had seen from her since they returned to Kappa House yesterday. "Dahlia agrees. You're going to be a wonderful president."

~

Scarlett couldn't remember the last time she'd been nervous for a date. *Is this a date?* she wondered as she strode across campus toward the main green. Jackson hadn't been specific.

When Jackson had texted her two days into winter break to ask whose number this was, and why it was in his phone, it had felt like fate offering Scarlett a second chance. She'd lied and told him that it must have been there from a group text for philosophy notes, and he had bought the lie. And it should have stopped there. But Jackson texted again. And again. But the more they'd texted, bantering about her "snobby" sorority and the "moral implications of conformism," the longer the conversations had stretched on. And the flirtier the emojis became at the ends of their sentences, the guiltier Scarlett felt.

Let's grab coffee now that we're back on campus. That could mean anything. A coffee date, a friendly invitation to catch up.

Jackson had gone through so much with her last semester. Tracking a rogue witch, Gwen, uncovering the truth about what happened to his stepsister, Harper. Finding said rogue witch's murdered body, then helping Scarlett track down her killer. *Kissing Scarlett.*

Every night when she closed her eyes, Scarlett pictured it again and again. The bench overlooking the Savannah River. The way his lips felt, warm and soft against hers. The trusting smile in his eyes as he took a long sip of the tea she'd brought him.

Tea laced with a powerful potion to make him forget.

The guilt twisted again like a knife.

She paused to check her reflection in the window of the science building she was passing. She'd gone simple and classic today: a pleated mini and blazer, with a silk blouse underneath—cut low, but not *too* revealing. Coupled with her high pony and her armful of notebooks, she looked like back-to-school perfection. She might be on a date, she might not. Who knew? Who cared!

She was Scarlett Winter. No boy could rattle her.

With one last grin, Scarlett started back on her way. When she rounded the building, she spotted him immediately, a head taller than the group he stood with, his head tipped back mid-laugh.

Scarlett stopped for a moment and took him in.

Jackson looked somehow effortless and irresistible at once in a plain T-shirt and mildly torn jeans. His brown skin was warm in the sun, and his fade had grown out a little into tight curls—nothing else had changed since she last walked away from him.

Sensing her gaze, Jackson turned around. With one last word to the group, he jogged across the green to meet her.

Her heart kicked into higher gear. They'd been texting all break, but she hadn't seen him in weeks, and he didn't remember how close they'd gotten last semester. Would he hug her right now? Kiss her? Her lips tingled.

She still remembered their kiss, even if he didn't.

But when Jackson reached her side, all her worries melted. He leaned in, as casual as if he'd done it a million times, and kissed her cheek. "It's good to see you." His eyes, in the afternoon sunlight, looked light brown and warm and sweet.

"You too." She glanced past him. "Friends?"

Across the lawn, the group he'd abandoned were not-so-covertly staring, probably wondering why Jackson was talking to Scarlett Winter, of all people. She wiggled her fingers, and at least three of the guys jumped and looked away.

"The Young Philosophers Club I told you about," Jackson replied.

Scarlett arched an eyebrow and smirked. "How could I forget?"

"You know I'm heading it up this semester. We were just making plans for our first meeting." He fell into step beside her, leading the way toward the Grind, everyone's favorite campus coffee spot. "You should come. If you liked Follet's class last semester, you'll love our debates. It's this Thursday in the Taylor common room, after hours."

"Actually, the club sounds like fun."

Jackson looked genuinely surprised. "Really? Scarlett Winter joins the thinkers society? That has to be a first . . ."

"Because sorority girls can't be thinkers . . ." she said lightly.

"I did not say that. I just wasn't sure you'd have time, what with your busy social calendar and all."

Scarlett side-eyed Jackson. "Do you judge every sorority girl by your preconceived notions?"

"Only the most captivating ones," he replied with a wink that made her heartbeat stutter. Then he added, "But there's something suspicious about how perfect she always seems."

Her mouth went dry.

They had wound toward the center of campus, where rows of tables had been set up alongside the green. Each one advertised different events and activities in the coming semester. She spotted a crew table with an entire boat propped up, and another group passing out free muffins to advertise their baking club.

"Oh, I don't know about perfect," Scarlett said, her voice as lighthearted as she could manage. "I had a bad hair day once."

He burst into laughter. "Ah yes, my mistake. Let's settle on nearly perfect, then. Ninety-nine percent."

She smirked. "Of course, if we're talking grade percentiles—"

"If this is about you scoring higher than me on the semifinal *again,* I swear . . ." But he nudged her shoulder playfully as he said it.

"It's not my fault you couldn't remember your Kant."

"Well, since I *Kant* wait for Young Philosophers Club"—he snickered at his own joke—"I'd love to find some other time to pick your brain. Maybe over dinner?" He eyed her again, and once more, her pulse skipped.

Okay, that was *definitely* a date.

Before she could reply, he held up a palm.

"Hey, before you say anything, there is something you should know," Jackson said, suddenly serious. "When I first started texting you, my motives weren't exactly pure. When I first found your number in my phone, I thought it was some kind of fate. I wanted to know more about Kappa."

Scarlett exhaled a breath she didn't know she was holding. "We don't allow boys to join, not yet, anyway," she said, trying to lighten the moment. Jackson gave her a small smile.

"I wanted to know about Kappa because it was where . . . what I thought I lost my sister to . . ."

"Jackson, I can explain . . ." she began.

He shook his head. "Something came over me. Some kind of peace. It wasn't Kappa's fault—it was an accident. And it was wrong for me to be angry at Kappa or suspicious of Kappa. And then I realized you weren't Kappa, you're you. You're Scarlett, and all I want . . ."

"What do you want?" she echoed as he stepped forward, getting closer to her.

"Is to attempt to make dinner for you and watch a really good bad movie . . ."

"I want that too. Except for the dinner part. Let me help, I know my way around the kitchen."

"Because of Minnie."

"Yes." She beamed, delighted that he remembered from her texts. "But tell the truth. You don't want to be seen in public with me because you don't want the thinkers to see you with me."

"No, it's not that. It's just that I'm saving up every spare dollar at the moment."

They fell into step again, and she watched him from the corner of her eye. "Are you? What for?"

"Road trip next summer," Jackson replied. "My sister, Harper, and I had planned it, back before . . . uh. Well, you knew her, I think, right? Your freshman year?" He rubbed the back of his neck.

Scarlett flinched. "I did," she managed to reply.

Harper had died their freshman year, in a terrible accident at Kappa House. Tiffany and Scarlett had been there—inadvertently caused it, in fact, a secret Tiffany had made Scarlett swear to take to her grave.

Last semester, Jackson had finally learned the truth about Harper's death. Gotten closure. But now . . .

So many secrets. How could anything possibly work between her and Jackson, when she had so much to hide?

Jackson was shaking his head. "Anyway, I still want to go. For her, you know?"

"I get that." Scarlett looked away toward the clump of tables they were nearing. The rest of the students bustled around campus, seeming totally unaffected by last semester, by all the death and pain. But Scarlett had been changed, irrevocably. The same way she imagined Jackson must have been, after Harper's death.

"Hey." Scarlett glanced back over at him, an idea forming. "Don't you cater events?" That was where she had first spoken to him outside of class. He had worked an event Dahlia threw at Kappa, what felt like a lifetime ago.

Jackson lifted an eyebrow. "Why? Are you in the market?"

"Actually, yes. Pretty often, in fact. We have a mixer next Friday. If you need more shifts to pick up or anything . . ."

His expression brightened. Scarlett could get lost in those eyes. "Okay. I might take you up on that."

"Welcome-back mixer, next Friday!" someone yelled, and Scarlett was shaken back to reality.

Theta Omega Xi had rented two folding booths and pushed them together in the middle of the green, draped in their sorority's colors: green and pink. The whole thing looked so preppy and put together, Scarlett might've mistaken it for a Lilly Pulitzer pop-up shop.

They'd set up a dry ice machine in a pink cooler, and girls kept reaching into it with dramatic flourishes like they were performing a magic trick, pulling out reusable water bottles monogrammed with WC—Westerly College—and handing them to passersby. Scarlett would have bet money they were filled already, and it sure as hell wouldn't be with water.

"Are they serious?" she murmured under her breath to Jackson, just as one of the girls in a tight plaid skirt caught sight of her. Kappa had already announced their welcome-back mixer for the same night.

Scarlett remembered the girl. She'd tried to pledge Kappa the same year as Scarlett. She had managed to light a sparkler, barely, but failed the second initiation test. Not enough magic in her to make a full witch. Scarlett remembered every girl who ever pledged but especially those with a little bit of magic. But this girl's name escaped her. Katie? Katheryn? Something like that . . .

"Scarlett!" the girl cooed, and shouldered through a gaggle of freshman boys trying to talk Maria, Theta's president, into giving them a second round of not-water bottles. "I'm so happy to see you. We wanted to invite you and your Kappas especially."

She held out a leaflet done up in a pastel version of the colors on the table.

WELCOME-BACK PREGAME.

"We didn't want to impinge on your party or anything," the girl was saying—*Cait,* that was her name. "It's just, Theta hasn't hosted anything big in a while, and we thought, since your party doesn't usually start until late, we'd give everyone a pregame spot to head beforehand."

"Did you," Scarlett replied, her tone as cool as her stare. *Or is it to try and smooth over your bad reputation while messing with ours?*

Cait's gaze jumped from Scarlett to Jackson and back. Then the girl peered more closely at Jackson and batted her lashes. "You're welcome too. Are you new on campus? I haven't seen you around before."

Scarlett battled an instant, bone-deep dislike.

Jackson, however, looped an arm around Scarlett's waist, and some of her defensiveness melted. "Nope. Been here since freshman year. It's a big campus once you step off Greek Row, y'know."

Scarlett fought to keep a straight face and passed the flyer back to Cait. "I'm afraid Kappa will be busy getting prepared for our own event that night. Tell Maria we're sorry to miss it."

"Tell me yourself," replied Maria, over Cait's shoulder. Theta's president wore the same plaid skirt as her girls—had they gotten uniforms this year? How 1990. But she'd paired it with a gray sweater that set off her dark hair and pale complexion well. Maria was one of those pretty girls who knew it and took full advantage.

"Maria." Scarlett regarded her coolly. Jackson's arm, still wrapped around her waist, tensed. "I was just telling Cait that we won't be able to make your party. Since, as I'm sure you recall, we have our own event to prepare for that evening."

"Well, that is a shame." Maria's smile was all teeth. "We hoped to get the whole campus involved. You Kappas get such a great turnout, but last year I heard a few people saying they weren't sure if they could go. Plus others said they wished parties started earlier, so they could last a little longer. I thought, *brainstorm,* why not fill those voids?"

"Yes, well." Scarlett's jaw tightened. "I'm sure your party will be so much fun." *Here's hoping they don't get the whole campus drunk before ours even starts.*

"Of course it will. After all, haven't you heard? Exclusivity is out. Westerly's going to be all about *inclusion* now, which means Kappa — the *most* exclusive sorority on campus — is out."

The words stung. And they didn't ring true. The Kappas were the most diverse sorority on campus, except for one thing. They all had magic.

"Still carrying a torch for Kappa I see?" Scarlett snapped back.

Maria laughed. "I prefer roses to feathers now. I don't know what I was thinking. Feathers are so last year."

Scarlett's eyes traveled to a pink rose pinned to Maria's lapel. It was the identical shade to those on Dahlia's grave. Next to the note: *We know it was you.*

"Maria, who leaked your handbook last summer?" Scarlett asked, feeling bold.

Maria's smile froze over. "Karma's a witch, Scarlett Winter. You'll see."

Witch. Scarlett's heartbeat quickened. Surely it was just a botched attempt at a turn of phrase.

Before Scarlett could reply, Maria spun away, waving a flyer like a battle flag.

So Eugenie was right. Theta really was coming for Kappa with a vengeance. And whether or not Dahlia really was responsible for Theta's fall from grace, there was one thing Scarlett knew for certain. There would be hell to pay.

CHAPTER FOUR

Vivi

V ivi smiled as she slid into the chair Mason had pulled out for her. Before moving to Savannah, she would've cringed at these gestures of chivalry, especially from a guy her own age. Mason held doors, stood up whenever a woman left the table, and would have given his jacket to the ghost of Lizzie Borden if she'd looked cold. Yet Vivi had come to realize his behavior stemmed less from adherence to old-fashioned gender norms than from a genuine desire to make life more pleasant for everyone around him.

"Did I already tell you how beautiful you look tonight?" he asked, brow furrowing with mock consternation as he sat down and placed his napkin in his lap. He'd taken her to a French bistro with outdoor seating along the river. The trees were wrapped in fairy lights and lanterns hung from the boughs like oversize versions of the fireflies glowing around them.

"You did," Vivi said, pleased that it was warm enough to forgo a sweater. She'd borrowed a romantic pale pink dress from Ariana and didn't want to cover up the flattering sweetheart neckline. "But I won't object to you saying it a few more times."

"Noted. I'll set a reminder for every twelve minutes," Mason said as he pretended to reach into his pocket for his phone. Vivi laughed and leaned across the table to smack his arm playfully, accidentally knocking over a bottle of balsamic vinegar in the process.

"Oh, shoot," she said as a stream of dark brown liquid began to stream off the edge of the table onto her dress. But instead of seeping into the fabric, it skimmed right off as if Vivi were wearing a raincoat.

"Is your dress okay?" Mason asked as a busboy came and wiped off the table.

"Totally fine," Vivi said with a relieved smile. Sonali had performed a fixing charm on Vivi before she'd left, to ensure her hair, makeup, and outfit stayed perfect throughout the date. "I love this spell so much," Sonali had said. "Though it always drove my teammates crazy when I'd leave the pool after a long swim meet with my eyeliner still in place." Vivi appreciated all the help she could get; this was her first time alone with Mason since before Christmas, and she didn't want any mishaps to spoil their evening. She'd been weirdly nervous about meeting up, convinced that despite all the time they'd spent on the phone, they might not have the same chemistry in person. But her nerves had drained away the moment she opened the door to Kappa House and saw him grinning at her on the front steps.

"So, how is it being back?" he asked. "I'm sure it's tough, being in the house."

According to the press, Dahlia and Tiffany had both been killed in a freak tornado that'd swept through the woods behind Kappa House. It felt both comically far from the truth and somehow perfectly apt at the same time, a heartbreaking, violent tragedy that extinguished two young lives. Mason knew that Vivi had been out in the woods as well, and while she obviously couldn't tell him that she'd been kidnapped by a demonic witch who'd tried to remove her heart, it'd been a relief to be able to talk about the traumatic events in more general terms—how terrifying it'd been, how helpless she'd felt against that kind of power, how guilty she felt for surviving when others didn't.

She'd been honest about the emotions, at least, if not the exact details.

"It's hard," Vivi replied, after a long pause. "Every time I walk past either of their rooms, or visit Scarlett in Dahlia's office . . ."

Mason nodded sympathetically. "I can only imagine. How's Scar doing?"

Vivi tried not to bristle at the implied intimacy. Mason and Scarlett had parted on good terms last semester—at least, until Scarlett had caught him and Vivi kissing way too soon after their breakup. But Scarlett had forgiven them, and to judge by the breathless recap she'd given Vivi of her date with Jackson, she was already moving on.

"She's doing as well as can be expected, I guess."

Mason shook his head wearily. "Losing your two best friends at once—it's beyond cruel. Maybe she should've taken the semester off or something?" Vivi raised an eyebrow, and Mason laughed. "That doesn't sound like her, does it? No, you're right. It's probably good for her to keep busy."

"She's already tackling the presidency with her usual force of will. It's nice to see her back in action." Scarlett's main focus right now was Kappa's alumnae reunion next month celebrating the 150th anniversary of the house's founding. The alumnae were flying in from all over the world and included a Pulitzer Prize winner, a supermodel turned start-up founder, a former secretary of state, a famous actress, and two senators. The current Kappas were in a frenzy of excitement, especially the seniors, who knew that this would be a once-in-a-lifetime opportunity for networking.

However, Vivi could barely think about the reunion right now. She still had so much to do for the welcome-back mixer, her first big responsibility as social chair. Her first chance to prove to everyone that Scarlett had made the right choice. Or prove that she was in over her head . . .

"Vivi?" Mason said. She shook her head and saw the waiter staring at her expectantly.

"Oh, sorry." She glanced down at the menu she'd forgotten to peruse. "I'll have the . . . the . . . bouilli . . . baisse, please."

"The bouillabaisse," the waiter repeated, his lips twitching as he corrected Vivi's botched pronunciation. "Very good, mademoiselle."

Vivi's cheeks flushed. Apparently, all the magic in the world still wasn't enough to keep her from embarrassing herself. Before she could stop herself, she cast the memory-wiping spell she'd been practicing—one of the few she could cast without speaking a word aloud. If all went well, the waiter would never remember her blunder.

"Sorry," Vivi said after the waiter had wandered off, a slightly dazed look on his face. "See, this is why Scarlett was nuts to make me the social chair. I can't even order at a restaurant. How am I supposed to plan fancy parties? I'm still so new to wi—" She caught herself just in time to swallow the word *witchcraft*. "To sorority life. And now I'm supposed to be running things?"

Mason reached across the table and squeezed her hand. "Come on, Vivi. Scarlett's a perfectionist control freak. She wouldn't have chosen you if she didn't know you could handle it. So when's the party?"

"Next Friday. I've got the first planning meeting with the other girls tomorrow." Vivi had recruited the other freshmen to help. She wanted the party to be a surprise for the older girls.

Reagan had been all in from the start and had already sent Vivi a bunch of ideas, most of which seemed designed around specific items in her wardrobe. Bailey had worried they might need more experienced witches to help, but Vivi had promised they'd ask the upperclasswomen if they needed it.

Mason ran his finger along the inside of her wrist, sending shivers down her spine. "Between your brains and your sisters' help, I'm sure you'll knock it out of the park. And you know you can always call me if you need help with anything. I'm up for waiting tables, even."

"Please. I'll need you to do the most important job of all. Hang out next to me and keep me sane all night."

"That I can definitely do." He winked, then unwound his grip, nodding at her empty glass. "Should we get some drinks?" He turned to catch the waiter's attention.

Shit. Judging by the way the waiter's gaze drifted over their table, not noticing Mason's full-on wave, the memory-wiping spell had worked *too* well.

While Mason's back was turned to her, she whispered under her breath, "I call upon the Ace of Swords. Your attention to him soars."

The waiter snapped to attention and beelined in the direction of their table. After Mason ordered, the waiter bowed his head deeply and then took off so quickly, it looked like he was about to break into a run.

"They're very, uh . . . attentive, here," Mason said, looking slightly perplexed.

"Must be your irresistible charm."

"I guess." Mason glanced over his shoulder, a crease appearing between his brows, as if something were bothering him.

Vivi cleared her throat. "So what about you? How was your first week?"

He blinked and seemed to refocus on Vivi. "Great, actually," he said. "My adviser told me she's preparing a proposal to officially invite me to study under her!"

"Don't you do that already?" Mason had spent the past year as a part-time research assistant, helping his professor with her book about women in colonial Savannah. Vivi had occasionally met Mason outside City Hall, where'd he emerge from a full day in the windowless basement archive room, eyes shining like a kid in from Santa's workshop.

"No, I mean to become a PhD candidate at Georgia Southern after I graduate from Westerly. You need an adviser to sponsor you, and normally they won't even offer until you've already finished a master's program, but she said we've been doing such great work together that she doesn't want to risk me accepting an offer from another school."

"Mason! That's amazing, congratulations!" She raised her water glass. "To the future Dr. Gregory. Have you told your parents yet?"

Mason shook his head. "No, not yet." Vivi knew that his parents had both been pushing for him to attend law school and join the small firm his father owned. Actually, "pushing" was a bit of an understatement. There was already a cubicle with Mason's name on it at the office downtown, and his parents had made it very, very clear that if Mason chose to "waste his time reading diaries and recipe books," they were going to cut off all financial support.

"Do you want me to be there when you tell them? For moral support?"

"That's very sweet," Mason said with a smile. "But I think this is something I have to do on my own."

Vivi nodded, though she couldn't help but wonder how things would be different if Mason were still dating Scarlett. If the perfect daughter of the revered Winter family told the Gregorys that she supported Mason's plans, would his parents take them more seriously? Scarlett naturally gave everything she touched an air of credibility. Her family had been prominent members of Savannah society for generations, whereas the closest thing Vivi had to an ancestral home was the Wendy's drive-through.

Unless, that is, her father had ties to Savannah. Ever since her conversation with her mom, the name Vince had been stuck like a burr in Vivi's mind. But every time she had almost worked up the courage to Google some combination of "Vince football Westerly College," she froze, terrified of what she might find. What if he had a whole new family? Did she really want to read about the kids he'd chosen over her? What if he turned out to be a criminal? Or some nutty online conspiracist? Daphne must've had her reasons for wanting to keep Vivi in the dark. Did Vivi really want to open some Pandora's box that could never be closed again?

She shivered as a cool breeze swept over her bare shoulders. Vivi glanced up and saw that the star-filled night sky had grown hazy, the glowing yellow moon now blurry and indistinct. "Would you like my jacket?" Mason asked. His voice sounded faint and fuzzy, as if he too were being obscured by the thick clouds.

A loud, sharp *crack* sounded above her. Vivi jerked her head up to see a large raven perched on a low tree bough, staring down at her with unblinking yellow eyes. She normally felt an affinity with the birds for obvious reasons, but something about this one sent a chill through her. It swiveled its head to the side and then held it unusually still, as if fixated on some object behind Vivi.

No, *pointing* at it.

Slowly, Vivi looked over her shoulder and suppressed a gasp as her eyes settled on a tall, blond figure.

Tiffany.

Every muscle inside Vivi went ice cold and clenched. She stared, transfixed, at her tormentor. But no, the white girl standing there with a couple friends, waiting for a table inside, looked nothing like Tiffany on closer inspection. And her blond ponytail had bright neon pink streaks dyed throughout it.

Suddenly, as if sensing Vivi's stare, the girl turned. Looked right at her.

Her pulse picked up, skittered along her veins. She'd expected to feel better that it wasn't Tiffany, but something unnerved her.

Mason tapped her arm, startling her back to herself. "Any more bread?" he asked, with a suppressed smile and a glance at the basket.

With his hand still touching her arm, his skin warm and electric, she could hardly say no. "Please," she said with a grin.

When she turned around again, the pink-haired girl was long gone and the waiter was hurrying over with their food. And yet Vivi couldn't shake the sensation that she was missing something important. Why had that girl been staring so intently? Even without the attention spell, it seemed odd.

"You should dig in before it gets cold," Mason said as he gestured toward Vivi's bouillabaisse.

"Oh, right." She took a spoonful of the seafood stew and closed her eyes, savoring the rich blend of flavors. This was well worth the embarrassment of her botched pronunciation. The spices cleared her mind, and for the rest of the meal, she was able to focus on Mason instead of worrying about pink-haired girls or oddly behaving ravens.

"You know what else my new PhD means?" Mason asked after he'd paid the bill and they'd started walking back along the river.

"What?"

He took her hand and pulled her in for another kiss. "It means I'll be spending the next few years in Savannah . . . with you."

Her stomach flipped like she'd just missed a step. Then she wrapped her arms around his neck and stopped thinking altogether.

CHAPTER FIVE

Scarlett

The hum of anticipation in the common room did little to ease Scarlett's distraction. She couldn't stop thinking about her date later. Dinner at Jackson's place. He told her to meet him on campus first, so they could walk to his off-campus apartment together.

He'd also insisted she didn't need to bring anything but herself, but she'd brought wine anyway. A special bottle, selected from Marjorie's secret reserve stash under the house. Scarlett figured they deserved it, after everything they'd gone through.

Even if Jackson didn't remember half of it.

"Madam President," Etta cooed, interrupting her thoughts. "Where do you need these?" Scarlett glanced over at her friend, currently balancing a stack of seeds on a tray. Etta grinned. Etta was a Cups witch, and her magic aligned with all things that grew. Scarlett knew that as important as the herbs she grew for their spells were, sometimes Etta felt overshadowed by the other flashier powers. She hoped her idea today would help Etta see just how vital her skills were to the sorority — and to her.

"Right by the pots will be fine." Scarlett pointed her to the far wall, where Mei was organizing a series of ceramic pots by color and size and snapping photos for her million-plus followers.

The freshmen were already seated cross-legged on the common room floor, which had been transformed into a sheet of plastic, rather than the usual Persian carpets. Easier cleanup.

"Wait! So how is this spell going to help us take down the Thetas?" asked Hazel Kim, a sophomore Wands, who sat sprawled out on the ground, stretching for her track meet later.

Every girl had heard about the Theta pregame, and everyone had assumed that that was the purpose of the meeting.

"Will the seeds grow into plants that will make the Thetas sleep through their pregame?" Reagan offered her hand up like the overachiever she was.

"We'll get to the Thetas later. Right now, there is something much more important for us to focus on."

The girls looked at one another, confused.

"What could be more important than crushing someone who is insulting us?" asked Reagan.

Scarlett centered her gaze on Reagan. "What's more important than the Thetas' crude happy hour? We are. I thought you'd all be interested in learning some new magic."

Twenty sets of eyes snapped to focus on her. She had their attention.

Scarlett swallowed hard. Maybe she'd oversold it.

"Yes, please," Vivi said, winking supportively at Scarlett.

"Okay, well, it's a new ritual," Scarlett replied. "Well, actually, an old one. I borrowed the idea from one of the old alumnae journals I've been reading in the library." In fact, it used to be a house tradition, several generations back. "It's Pentacles magic." She glanced at Vivi, who straightened. "Each of you will decide something you want to grow in the coming semester — your GPA, your athletic skill . . . your love life." A few girls tittered. "Whatever you decide to focus on. Then you'll select the right plant to go with that desire — Etta will help with the herbology there."

Etta waved from where she'd finished arranging the seed packets next to the pots.

"And we'll all cast a growth spell on your plant. As it grows over the coming months, your goal will flourish too." Scarlett smiled, pleased with herself.

Reagan rolled her eyes, but at least didn't comment out loud. Sonali bent her head toward Reagan, whispering.

"Wait, are we Goop witches now?" Reagan quipped, eliciting some laughter from Jess and Juliet.

Scarlett would have laughed herself, if she weren't the object of the joke. It's something she might have whispered under her breath to Tiffany back in the day. Now, though, it stung.

"Ha," she said out loud. "We should always consider ourselves lucky to work at that level of business."

"Wait — are you saying Gwyneth is a Kappa—"

"I'm saying that being open is the first step to any success. Here and beyond. And that isn't about the past, that's about the future."

"I love it," Vivi piped up, with a glare at her fellow freshmen.

"Me too." Ariana beamed. Beside her, Bailey nodded, although she didn't seem like her usual enthusiastic self.

"Is this required?" Juliet asked. She was currently standing behind Jess's chair, gathering her girlfriend's twists into a thicker braid. "I've got a thesis draft due next week already . . ."

"If you don't want to participate, you don't have to." Scarlett bristled. "But it will be our first house-wide ritual since we've returned to campus."

Juliet flashed her a sullen look. In the end, though, the senior shrugged and remained where she stood.

Scarlett cleared her throat. "Let's all take a moment to think about the goal we're choosing." She already had hers picked out. She'd plant a seed for leadership ability—maybe an iris for wisdom, or hawthorn for power and energy.

Or would you rather plant violets for love? a little voice at the back of her head whispered.

She ignored that voice. Leading Kappa was more important.

A murmur caught her attention. Juliet and Jess, their heads bent together. "Dahlia would never be so kumbaya, though," were the only words Scarlett picked out, and yet they were enough to make her breath catch in her chest.

Were they right? Was this a bad idea?

Dahlia *wouldn't* have worked a ritual like this, true. But Dahlia's rites had always been about power, immediate goals. Scarlett was sure this was the better approach. *One less likely to lead to a Tiffany situation.*

Scarlett had said she'd take Kappa in a new direction this semester, and she meant it. No more abusing their powers.

"Are we all ready?" Scarlett waited for everyone to nod. "Great. Now, Etta, would you like to walk us through the herbs we have to choose from and the best uses for each?"

She was gratified to notice Bailey and Ariana sliding out notebooks to write in as Etta started to speak.

Still, she couldn't quite shake the nagging sensation that somewhere up above, Dahlia was looking down in disapproval.

~

By the time Scarlett made it onto the campus greens, she was running late. Jackson had asked her to meet him outside of Hewitt fifteen minutes ago, but she'd spent more time on the ritual than she anticipated. Her concentration had been scattered, her mind only half on the task at hand. She kept stopping to check on the other girls, to make sure the freshmen were all doing it correctly — and, yes, to eavesdrop on Juliet and Jess again, to see if they or Reagan were complaining anymore.

No one else said anything negative, but Scarlett caught a few sideways glances she couldn't interpret.

What is wrong with me? She picked up her pace. Normally she was so confident, so sure of her decisions. Ever since they got back to Westerly, though, she'd been acting like a jumpy freshman again, second-guessing herself at every turn.

She checked her phone again. Still no reply from Jackson. Her last text, *Running a few minutes behind!* had gone unread.

She quickened her pace, then something to her right caught her eye. A boy fighting with a giant paper map of the campus.

He was a white guy about her age, dressed in jeans and a blue cashmere sweater. He looked up and looked around, his face full of frustration. Then his eyes fell on her and he broke into a smile. His face was flushed with exertion, sweat glistening along his brow. Beneath it, he was handsome. Strong, square jaw, baby blue eyes, and a swoop of thick, dark hair she'd bet anything he normally styled to perfection.

"Didn't mean to startle you." He ran a hand through that hair, ruffling it a little, and the edge of his sweater rode up just high enough for her to glimpse well-defined abs. "Sorry, sorry. I don't mean to stare. It's just that you're so . . . You're just the first person I've seen on campus in a few minutes. And I'm . . . a little lost."

Scarlett glanced around her, realizing he was right. For this hour on a weekend, it was strangely deserted.

Scarlett held up her phone. "Where did you even get a real map? You know that we have a really great app with a map function?"

"Ahh . . . right," he said, sheepishly. "I still need to download that. This just came with my welcome packet."

"But that map is totally working for you?"

"It will once I figure out which way north is."

Scarlett laughed and put her hands on his shoulders and turned him in the right direction.

Every witch knew their directions in case they needed to cast in one of them.

"Thank you, you are saving my life. I'm already late."

"Which building are you looking for?" she asked, leaning in to the map. She was taken, or she wanted to be once Jackson caught up with her. But there was no reason to let a hot guy go to waste. Mei had been woefully single last semester. Maybe Tall, Cute, and Lost was the cure for that—she should invite him to the mixer.

"I need to find the head office. I'm new." He grimaced. "Supposed to pick up my transfer papers." He rose up onto the balls of his feet, obviously waiting for her to make conversation. Ask where he transferred from, or why.

To judge by his smooth Southern drawl, he couldn't be moving from *too* far away. Still, Scarlett was already running late. She couldn't afford to humor him.

"You'll want the admin office." She pointed across the greens, at the building with a tall clock tower attached. "But I'm not sure they're open on weekends."

"Alas," he said, looking not disappointed in the slightest. "Well, that's all right. I'll just have to come back."

"Mm." She started off again toward Hewitt. But this guy did not take the hint. He fell into step beside her.

"I've seen you around, haven't I? On Greek Row. Which sorority do you belong to again?"

She fired him a cool side-eye. He was cute, in a bad-idea sort of way. But she had enough on her plate already. Not to mention a much more deserving candidate for her attention. "Kappa Rho Nu."

"Oh! We're siblings." He stuck out a hand. "I was in PiKa at

Vanderbilt. Just moved here, and, lucky me, a room opened at the house."

Mason's old room, she couldn't help thinking as she shook his hand.

"I hate to be rude, but I have somewhere I need to be," Scarlett said. She turned to go and then paused. "I'm Scarlett Winter, by the way." She gave him a short smile.

"Xavier," he said. "See you around, maybe?"

She offered a halfhearted wave — she could practically feel his gaze tracking her across the greens anyway, and she considered turning back. What harm would it be to bring Mei or one of her sisters a new romantic prospect?

"Hey, Xavier . . ."

He smiled, expectant.

Scarlett surprised herself. "Avoid Professor Grant's history class. The PiKas will try and convince you it's an easy A, but it is brutal."

Xavier tipped an imaginary hat toward her as he turned away.

Scarlett had the invitation to the mixer on her lips, but something held her back. He was a stranger. And after last semester, the idea of inviting someone new anywhere near her sisters made her hesitate. No matter how cute he was.

Mind your business.

Then she forgot all about Xavier, because she was rounding the corner to face Hewitt, and . . . no Jackson.

Shit.

Scarlett pulled out her phone again and tapped his number to call. While it rang, she paced around the building. Just as his voice-mail was picking up, she heard laughter coming from the rose garden, a little alcove tucked behind Hewitt.

She hung up and followed the sound.

A few steps later, she recognized Jackson's voice. "You're kidding!" he exclaimed.

She rounded the corner, smiling, an apology ready on her lips. In the garden, Jackson stood in the midst of his circle of friends, the same philosophy club group she'd seen him with last time.

"Sorry I'm late," she called, breathless.

Jackson looked up, a frown creasing his forehead.

"Hi, everyone." Scarlett kept her smile plastered on, even though it started to feel fake and forced. "Mind if I borrow your fearless leader? We had dinner plans."

But Jackson wasn't even looking at her anymore. He'd turned back to the group. "Matt, you were saying we should pick up Butler for next week's meeting?"

Scarlett stood frozen by the entrance, heart thudding in her eardrums. Surely, he was just finishing up the meeting. Surely, he wasn't blowing her off just for running a few minutes late.

But Jackson stubbornly ignored her, making plans for the time the group would next meet, and the location.

Scarlett frowned. Of all the ways she'd imagined their first date going, this hadn't been it. *Scarlett Winter does not wait on any man.* Yet here she stood, doing just that.

"Jackson?" This time a sliver of an edge crept into her tone.

The group he was with knew the score, at least, even if Jackson didn't. The Young Philosophers began to peel off to exit the garden, some waving at Jackson over their shoulders, others openly gawking at Scarlett on their way out. When the last one had departed, Jackson finally faced her again, unable to avoid it. "Scarlett. Good to see you." His voice sounded stilted, almost forced.

He'd dressed well, in slacks and a button-down shirt, which was fancier than she'd ever seen him wear. Something glinted around his neck—a silver chain necklace.

She tried to broaden her smile, even as her heartbeat picked up. "I'm sorry I was late. Got caught up in some Kappa business."

"Yeah, well, don't worry. As you can see, I can entertain myself just fine without you." With that, he shouldered his backpack.

Her heart rose into her throat. "So . . . you don't want to do dinner anymore."

"I can't."

"Why can't you? You asked me. Remember?" she blurted, feeling hurt and confused and defensive at once.

"I just can't . . ." He started for the exit, but she stepped into his path. He met her gaze, jaw set. "See you in class, Scarlett."

"You can't be serious."

His forehead scrunched. For a moment, he seemed conflicted. Yet eventually, he shook his head, that same distant look in his eyes. "I thought I could, but I can't. You're a Kappa. And I can't be with a Kappa. See you around, Scar."

Her heart sank as she watched him walk away. She felt stung, more than she had any right to be. Somehow, she'd deluded herself into thinking that Jackson really cared about her. That some gravitational pull in the universe was bringing them together time and again.

Sure, they'd started to flirt again over break, but it was only that. Text flirting. She thought they'd had chemistry when they hung out the other day.

But he didn't remember last semester. Charging into danger side by side. *Kissing.*

Or maybe he just doesn't like you, she thought, watching him cross the green in the late afternoon sun. He never looked back, not once. If he didn't like Scarlett for who she was without their shared history . . .

Well. That only made his rejection hurt all the more.

CHAPTER SIX

Vivi

The Thirsty Scholar was a favorite among Westerly students because it stayed open late and the bartenders didn't card as long as you tipped well. It was why the five freshman Kappas had gathered in a corner booth here, far from the attentive ears of their sisters back at the house.

But that also meant they needed to be careful that none of the other Greek life members milling around the low-ceilinged, wood-paneled pub could overhear their discussion. As soon as Sonali—the final one to arrive—slipped breathlessly into her seat, Bailey slid her tarot deck from her bag and began to sort through the cards, half hidden beneath their booth table, in case anyone walked past. Once she'd chosen the correct card, Bailey pinched it between her fingertips and reached over to grip Sonali's hand.

The rest of them formed a chain and whispered the words along with her. "I call to the Queen of Air. Let no one here of our presence be aware."

Vivi focused on channeling her power to Bailey. A moment later, she sensed the shift in the room. Faces turned away, curious eyes snapped back to their own tables.

Bailey smiled with satisfaction and released Sonali's hand. "Done."

"Thank you," Vivi said, making a mental note to study Bailey's technique. It seemed a lot more effective than Vivi's attempt on her date with Mason.

"I'm sorry I'm late," Sonali said with a sigh as she gathered her thick, wavy black hair into a messy bun. "Mistakes were made."

"What happened?" Ariana asked. "Are you okay?"

"*I'm* fine. But there's this obnoxious mansplainer in my public health class who never lets anyone else talk, and I guess I just wasn't feeling it today so . . ." She paused, blushing. "I cast that charm that makes someone's tongue swell up. Everyone thought he was having an allergic reaction and kept crowding around him so I couldn't cast the countercharm before the paramedics arrived, and it was a whole thing."

"Oh my God, that's amazing," Reagan said with a laugh.

"Is he going to be okay?" Bailey asked worriedly. "I mean, I'm not saying he didn't deserve it, but . . ."

"Yeah, he's fine. I finally cast the charm once he was on the stretcher, but it took a while. Anyway, so about this party!"

Vivi nodded and opened her mouth, but before she could speak, Reagan leaned forward, causing her striking red hair to spill over the shoulders of her sheer black blouse. "I have a few ideas, Devereaux," she said.

"Why don't we let Vivi tell us what she was thinking first?" Ariana said. Her voice was sweet, but with a hint of warning.

"Yeah, Reagan," Bailey teased. "You'd better watch out, or Vivi will take a page out of Sonali's book."

"Sorry, sorry," Reagan said, raising her hands into the air. "Proceed, Vivian."

Vivi flashed Ariana a grateful smile. "I'd love to hear your ideas afterward, Reagan. But I do have some initial pitches." She reached into her bag to retrieve her phone, opened the video file Ariana had helped her create, then withdrew her own tarot deck and flipped over the top card. "I call upon the Moon, creator of tricks and confusion. Lend your strength to this illusion."

Her phone screen lit up, and a 3D image of the Kappa living room appeared above it, almost like a hologram, rotating slowly. "I thought we could do an Alice in Wonderland theme," Vivi said. "See?" She tapped the couch, transforming it into a large mushroom, then swiped across the ceiling, revealing a chandelier made out of teacups. "The living room could be the Mad Hatter's tea party, and then we could do something with the Red Queen and croquet in the garden."

"Whoa!" Bailey leaned forward to see better while Sonali nodded, looking impressed.

"I've marked each glamour with the spell I thought we could use," Vivi continued. She zoomed in on the refreshment table, which was covered with oversize cupcakes and impossibly tiny sandwiches. "I think a basic illusion glamour would work here."

Reagan raised an eyebrow. "Um, yeah, maybe if you're not

worried about it wearing off halfway through the party and freaking out all the guests."

Bailey nodded. "You'll need a much more powerful charm to avoid rousing any suspicion. Did you think about using an alchemical illusion charm? They were very popular during the Renaissance. Juliet and I have been experimenting with them during our tutoring sessions."

Vivi's cheeks warmed. She'd never even *heard* of an alchemical charm. And she and Scarlett had never restarted their tutoring sessions after the Tiffany crisis last semester. "I'll take that under consideration." Reagan and Sonali exchanged a look Vivi couldn't quite read.

What am I doing? She wasn't ready for this job. If she couldn't even get the freshmen on board, how in the world was she supposed to impress the older girls?

Vivi knew how important this welcome-back mixer was. "This will set the tone for the whole semester," Scarlett had told her at breakfast that morning. "Not to mention, we need to show the Panhellenic council that Kappa is still the best choice for the Spring Fling. Theta's gunning for it hard. In fact, I think they may be trying to get back at us—Dahlia leaked that stupid handbook online. Or at least, they're blaming her. Let me know if you need any hand-holding on this."

Hand-holding. Vivi had shaken her head, insisted she was fine. She couldn't stand the thought of asking for help so soon, letting her Big down right off the bat.

Under the table, Ariana nudged her leg.

Vivi cleared her throat. "Right. So, I'll need each of you work-ing on spells for the different elements. Reagan and Bailey, do you want to handle the lanterns and candles?" As Wands witches, they were particularly suited to magic involving light and flames.

"Etta showed me a Cups trick that might be helpful too," Ariana said eagerly. "It's a potion that lets you feel the effects of any alco-hol you drink, but staves off the hangover completely."

"I love it." Vivi grinned. "Now, is that something we should reserve for Kappa use only? Or should we share our magic with the less fortunate?"

"I'm for it if it prevents anyone from puking on our lawn. The-ta's throwing that stupid pregame," Reagan said, shooting a glare toward the far end of the bar. "Everyone's going to be trashed before they even get to our party."

Vivi followed her gaze and spotted the Thetas in question, a cluster of girls near the bar. Although the sorority claimed to have changed its tune, she was amused to see that every girl still sported one of the three approved hairstyles from the now-infamous Theta handbook, and that they all wore ballet flats and carried Long-champ purses.

Just then, another girl in ballet flats strolled over to join the Thetas, although her pink hair made it clear she wasn't constrained by the old rules. It was the same girl Vivi had seen at the restaurant the other night. She shivered again, remembering when she had mistaken her for Tiffany, then spun back to her sisters.

"Listen, I don't mean to be a bitch," Reagan said in a tone that suggested just the opposite. "But I think this plan might be a little . . . ambitious. I mean, you don't want to bite off more than you can chew, right, Vivi?"

"Um, excuse me," Ariana cut in. "Were you not there in the tomb that night when Vivi saved all our asses? I didn't see *you* stop that tidal wave, Reagan."

"I never said she wasn't *powerful*." Reagan widened her eyes and looked wounded. "But I think Vivi would be the first to admit that she still has some catching up to do in terms of spellwork. I mean, if the glamours wear off during the party, we're going to be in serious trouble." She paused to take a sip of a drink, then grimaced and spat it back into her glass. Her vodka soda had turned thick and brownish gray.

"Who turned my cocktail into gravy?!" Reagan shrieked.

"I guess you have some catching up to do in terms of protective spells," Bailey said sweetly. There was a tense moment of silence, and then all five girls burst out laughing.

"Okay, okay, I deserved that," Reagan said, wiping her mouth with her napkin. "But how the hell am I going to get another drink? No way I'm going up to the bar and making small talk with the Thetas."

"Why do you think they're suddenly being so competitive with us?" Ariana asked. "Haven't they always kind of understood that Kappa's out of their league?"

"Scarlett told me that Maria blamed Dahlia for leaking the handbook," Vivi said.

"Seriously?" Reagan said, rolling her eyes. "She's just using that as an excuse to usurp our position as the most prestigious sorority on campus. Talking about inclusivity like it's some marketing strategy. It's literally the most delusional plan I've ever heard."

"What are her plans?" Bailey asked, surveying Maria curiously.

"Besides posting a million selfies alongside quotes about 'positivity'?" Reagan shrugged. "I don't know. But she seems to think she's campus royalty just because she's dating Vince Lee's son."

"The football player?" Ariana asked. "Wasn't he some kind of Westerly legend?"

Vivi's breath caught in her chest. *Vince?* That was the name her mom accidentally let slip the other day. Vivi's father's name. She'd been able to resist looking him up until now, but if he had a son on campus, that meant Vivi could have . . .

Trembling slightly, she reached for her phone and searched for "Vince Lee Westerly." There were hundreds of hits, but one number jumped out at Vivi: 1998. He'd graduated just a year ahead of Daphne, which meant they'd been on campus at the same time. How many other Vinces could there have been on the team?

Reagan was nodding. "And his son, Tim, is supposed to be even better. He's probably going to drop out early and go straight into the NFL, and then Maria can live out her life's dream of being a WAG." The other girls looked at her blankly. "That's what they call wives and girlfriends of professional athletes . . . especially the ones who spend all the player's money on, like, jewelry and blowouts."

Vivi tried to keep her face neutral, but her heart was pounding as she searched the Westerly football roster for the years her mom had been in college. Vince Lee was the only Vince on the team. That was her father; it had to be.

"Like you're one to judge," Sonali said with a smile as she reached out to tug a strand of Reagan's impossibly glossy hair.

"I didn't *pay* for a professional blowout," Reagan said indignantly. "Mei did it for me."

"Vivi, are you okay?" Bailey asked. "Why are you staring into space like that?"

"Sorry, it's nothing." Vivi shook her head, but the motion did nothing to dispel the question expanding in her brain, pushing aside all other thoughts. Did she have a *half brother* at Westerly?

Vivi's lonely childhood flashed before her eyes. The long, empty afternoons in an endless procession of sparsely furnished apartments where Vivi would wait for her mom to come home from work. She'd always fantasized about having a sibling but had given up on the idea long ago.

"I know what she's thinking about," Ariana said with a grin. "It just walked into the bar."

Vivi followed Ariana's gaze to see Mason scanning the crowded room. Based on his bulging messenger bag and the folders under his arm, he'd come straight from the library and seemed slightly bewildered to suddenly find himself somewhere so crowded and loud.

"Don't pretend to be a mind reader, Ari," Vivi said with an affectionate smile. "We know it's not your strong suit. Literally." As a Cups witch, Ariana was a gifted empath, but the mind-reading spells that came so easily to Wands witches like Reagan generally stumped her. "I'll be right back."

Vivi stood and waved, briefly breaking through their distraction spell. When Mason's eyes met hers, his face broke into a huge grin that sent a warm, fizzy feeling through her entire body. He walked over to their table and dropped his bag on the seat next to Vivi. He kissed her on the cheek, then turned to greet the other girls. "Can I get anyone a drink? I can wait at the bar while y'all finish up your meeting. I know I'm not supposed to be privy to state secrets."

"It's okay," Ariana said sweetly. "We can always wipe your memory."

Mason laughed while Bailey shot Ariana a look of warning. "Fair. But not until after I order you ladies another round of drinks."

"I'll take another vodka soda," Reagan said in the easy manner of someone accustomed to others paying for her drinks. She glanced at the bar, then turned back to Vivi and Mason with a mischievous smile. "Actually, I'll come with you. The hot guy from my anthropology class just walked in."

"Sure," Mason said, exchanging an amused look with Vivi.

"He's a keeper," Ariana whispered as Mason and Reagan made their way to the bar. "I want one for myself. I wonder how well cloning spells work?"

Their server appeared at their table with a smile. "Are y'all interested in ordering some food? Or maybe some refills?"

The Kappas stared at her, startled. Bailey's distraction spells *never* failed.

"Um . . . I think we need a minute," Vivi said, as Sonali and Ariana exchanged worried looks.

"No problem. I'll be back after I get rid of this," the server said, gesturing to the tray of dirty glasses balanced on her hip. But before she turned away, something crashed into her, and the tray went flying.

Vivi's vision blurred as something wet and cold streamed down her face. She gasped and looked around wildly while Ariana, Bailey, and Sonali did the same. Their table was suddenly covered with puddles of beer, and each girl was soaked in sticky liquid.

A second later, a muscular arm swung over their heads as a large blond guy with a buzz cut threw a punch at an even beefier guy with black hair.

Bailey leaped from her seat and darted to the other side of the table, away from the line of fire, while Sonali flattened herself against the wall.

"Hey!" the server shouted. "Cut that out *right now.*"

But the guys ignored her as a third well-built man joined the fray, and within seconds they were on top of each other.

"Fight! Fight! Fight!" A crowd had formed around them and no one seemed the least bit worried that this fight was taking place *on* their table. A fist came flying toward Vivi and brushed against her cheek. She jerked reflexively to the side, more stunned than hurt.

"What the hell, man?" she heard Mason say as he pushed through the crowd and wrestled one of the guys off the table.

The blond guy sat up and aimed a fist at Mason. "Why don't you mind your own business, Gregory?"

Mason raised up an arm to block him. "Well, my girlfriend is my business. And it looks like you just hit her." She had never seen that fierce look in his eyes.

The blond guy looked Vivi up and down, then let out a nasty laugh. "I'm sure she did something recently to deserve it."

Mason's voice went quiet and cold. "You do *not* talk like that to anyone. *Especially* not my girlfriend. Now apologize."

There was a thud as the blond guy's fist met Mason's stomach. Vivi shot to her feet and stood on top of the booth, but her view was limited by the crowd, which seemed to have doubled in the last minute, everyone standing up to get a view of the fight. Some people even stood on chairs or tables to watch.

Without thinking, she squeezed her eyes shut and whispered under her breath. "I call to the Empress. Alleviate my distress." It was a catchall spell Scarlett had taught her last semester, for emergencies. "I call to the Emperor and the Empress," she repeated, louder. With her free hand, she reached into her purse, scrambling for her cards. Her fingers brushed the deck. "Alleviate my distress."

The pink-haired girl looked across the room and caught Vivi's eye. She looked perfectly serene, despite the chaos unfolding in front of her. Startled, Vivi turned away, though not before she saw one of the fighters crack Mason across the jaw. *What was* wrong *with these guys?*

Vivi looked down, and two cards were sticking up from her deck. She snatched them free. Sure enough, the Emperor and Empress gazed up at her, serene in the face of the chaos, a matching pair. She squeezed her eyes shut, concentrating with all her might. "I call to the Emperor and the Empress. Alleviate my distress."

A sudden, tense silence descended over the bar. A few people murmured, but she didn't hear any more slaps or grunts.

Vivi's eyes snapped open.

Mason's opponent stumbled into a chair and fell into it. The spiky-haired guy swayed on his feet, and Mason caught him just in time, helping him to lean against the bar before he fell.

The blond guy had one hand clamped over his bleeding nose. But he didn't try to attack Mason again. He just stumbled toward the exit, swaying the whole way. The crowd parted to let him pass, no one willing to get much closer with all the blood on his shirt.

Vivi was still watching him go when suddenly, the entire bar *shifted*. Instead of the wood rafters and cozy pub-style tables, branches sank from the ceiling. The floor turned to mud underfoot, and the tables and chairs grew vines, snaking toward her. Vivi felt something curl around her ankle and stifled a scream.

What is going on? She tried to shake her foot lose but found she couldn't move. Her feet were rooted to the floor. Vines wrapped around both her legs. Curled up her calves, tickled the backs of her knees.

The air had changed, too. The stale air-conditioning had turned into something damp and humid. She heard flutters, wingbeats. *Moths?* she wondered. *Or butterflies . . .*

"Vivi!" Mason shook her elbow.

A blink, and the bar crashed back into place. Normal ceiling, normal floor. Regular crowd, all returning to their own tables and drinks, now the show had finished.

Vivi gulped in deep breaths, trying to steady herself and calm her racing heart.

For a moment, it had felt like she was back in the woods again.

Lost in the dark, with a storm approaching. She shook her head. It was just a bad memory. That was all.

"Are you okay?" Mason asked. Only then did she register his face, the bruise on his cheek, and the ball of ice wrapped in napkins he clenched in one fist.

"I'm fine," she said, touching her jaw. She barely felt anything. "It's you I'm worried about." Vivi reached for the ice, held it to his cheek.

He forced a smile, which came out more like a wince. "It's nothing. Not compared to Dante." He glanced back at the spiky-haired guy leaning against the bar. To judge by the swelling, Dante was going to have a black eye soon.

"You know him?" Vivi glanced from the fighter to Mason.

"He was in PiKa with me." Mason's old frat, which he left last semester. Vivi knew most of his closest friends were still members. "He's one of the gentlest guys I know." Mason shook his head. "I don't understand what got into them."

"Were they drunk?"

"I'll say." He sighed, and Vivi could hear the worry in it. "But I've never seen them like that before."

On impulse, she wound her arms around his waist and buried her face in his chest.

He's okay. Everyone's okay.

But she still couldn't get the forest out of her head.

CHAPTER SEVEN

Scarlett

G otta hand it to you, Little Sis. I never would have thought of this one. Kappa Wonderland . . ." Scarlett gazed out at the transformed Kappa living room. In place of the usual antique couches, there were glamoured toadstools and squishy mushrooms. The carpets looked like grass to match, and funhouse mirrors around the edges of the room made the whole space seem even larger than it already was.

Vivi looked up at her, expectant.

"I thought there would be more Red Queens and Alices," Scarlett said, smoothing down her gown. The crinoline beneath it bounced back, giving Scarlett the satisfaction that only a fabulous costume could.

"Are you kidding? No one would dare. They value their heads. You are our Red Queen."

And Vivi was definitely their Alice. The wonder that Scarlett was afraid that her Little had lost was back in force and in every detail of the party she had created.

Guests wove through the party dressed as the Cheshire Cat, the Dormouse, the March Hare. By the backyard entrance, a fountain made of delicately balanced teacups flowed with champagne, and nearby a handful of Kappa sisters and PiKa brothers were taking turns stepping in front of a wall of clocks. A sign nearby explained the clocks would reveal the birthdate of your one true love, but Scarlett knew they'd really just been spelled to show the birthdate of the person standing closest to you.

Mei called it the hookup wall. Vivi had named it the Wall of Hearts, which Scarlett surmised the author Lewis Carroll would've preferred. Scarlett watched Mei react with elation as the clocks displayed a series of numbers for a cute PiKa guy that she'd had her eye on since last semester. And who somehow was making his Tweedledee costume look hot.

"Hey, that's my birthday," the unsuspecting PiKa proclaimed, and winked at Mei.

"No shit, Sherlock," Mei replied.

"No, I'm Tweedledee," he deadpanned.

"Of course you are."

Not sure if he's the one, Mei, Scarlett offered apologetically in Mei's head. He clearly had one too many at Theta's little pregame.

Hot Tweedledee is just so wrong that he's right . . . after I get him, like, a dozen cups of coffee, Mei said back in Scarlett's head.

Watching Mei toss her long pale curls over the shoulder of her White Queen dress, and flirt with her new match, Scarlett felt a pang. She couldn't help but think of what Dahlia would be wearing if she were here, or what Tiffany would be murmuring in Scarlett's ear.

Probably some sharp commentary on the theme. Tiffany always had disliked themed parties. Scarlett repressed a smile at the thought, conflicted.

I shouldn't miss her after what she did. Scarlett took a deep, cleansing breath.

At Scarlett's elbow, Vivi was still blushing over Scarlett's compliments. "I know you told me not to overdo . . ."

Scarlett side-eyed her Little. "It *is* a lot." She'd been worried when Vivi had started setting up today. Spells ran everything from the glamours to the self-serving drink bar — not to mention made the whole house spillproof, since, college party. "But you pulled it off."

Vivi straightened, obviously pleased, and Scarlett felt an answering swell of affection.

She was proud of her Little. And pleased her first party as president was going so well already. This would be Kappa's year. She'd make sure of it.

Even Theta's irritatingly timed pregame party hadn't proven *too* much of a problem. Juliet and Etta had worked together on a spell at the door, which automatically repelled anyone who'd already partied too hard for the night. It gave them the sudden, irresistible desire to turn around and go sleep it off at home. Mei's Tweedledee seemed to be the exception, not the rule.

"Oh, and . . . sorry about that." Vivi glanced past Scarlett.

Far below, a handful of servers wove through the crowd, their trays heaped high with canapes and cocktails in specialty glasses.

It took Scarlett a moment to realize who Vivi was looking at and why.

Jackson held a champagne tray, offering it to a cluster of juniors near the fireplace. Scarlett's body went hot and cold at once.

Even in the over-the-top Mad Hatter suits Vivi had given the servers to wear, Jackson looked good. He had a slim chain around his neck, and his hair was slicked back under his top hat, yet he wore the ensemble with the same confidence as his usual jeans. Like he didn't care what anyone thought about him.

Least of all me.

"I forgot to cancel him. We can send him home. I can go over there right now and cast a—" Vivi whispered, clearly about to offer a leaving spell.

"It's all right," Scarlett replied, her voice stiff. "He needs the money. I don't want to begrudge him a job just because he isn't interested in me."

Beside her, Vivi huffed. "If he wasn't interested, he could have just told you. He didn't need to lead you on and then stand you up in front of people. What was that?"

"I don't know, and I don't care. I don't know what I was thinking. We never would have worked . . ." Scarlett realized she was using way too many words for someone who was pretending not to care, and she stopped herself. Scarlett turned away from Jackson, nose held high. "Onward and upward." Yet for some reason, this rejection felt harder to shake off than usual. Maybe because her emotions were already running high from last semester. Or maybe because she couldn't help but wonder if things would have turned out differently if she didn't have Kappa's secrets to guard.

As if he sensed her gaze on him, Jackson raised his head to scan the balcony, and Scarlett quickly stepped back.

Vivi was still standing beside her, straight-backed, awaiting marching orders. Her eagerness made her Alice costume—with the pretty blue dress and matching innocent bow in her glamoured blond hair—even more convincing.

Scarlett resisted the urge to laugh. "Go on." She shooed her Little toward the steps. "Go enjoy your party. You've earned it."

She watched her Little descend to join her cluster of froshlings, then followed more slowly, trying to summon her usual energy. Normally Scarlett adored parties. Seeing and being seen. Impressing the whole campus.

Tonight felt different. Maybe it was because she was the one responsible for everything. Or maybe it was just the fact that, as she descended the steps, only a handful of faces followed her movements.

She'd gone all out on her Red Queen costume. The gown was an update of one that Beyoncé had worn in a video that she had just dropped for yet another surprise album, only Scarlett had changed the color from platinum to red. Her hair was a confection of soft strawberry curls that piled high toward the ceiling. And her makeup had been glamoured by Mei with Marie Antoinette in mind—red lips, red cheeks, and little shapes drawn in eyeliner that were supposed to signify passion. She was a vision, objectively, so why then didn't the whole room see it?

Across the living room, another girl had gone several steps farther: a taller wig, which somehow seemed to be blooming with roses, and a red ball gown made entirely of leather but still somehow contorted into the neoclassical ballroom style. Scarlett was a vision, but this girl was a spectacle.

Tacky, she thought. And yet a crowd of people was oohing over the other girl instead of her.

The bad taste in Scarlett's mouth only soured more when said other girl turned, and Scarlett realized it was Maria. She should have known by the tall, mustached guy on Maria's arm, wearing rabbit ears and a Flavor Flav–worthy giant pocket watch around his neck. Tim and Maria were one of the OG couples on campus. In fact, Scarlett and Mason had double-dated with them a couple times when they were all freshmen. But once Scarlett got the black feather and Maria got none, they never really went out again. Scarlett had seen her at parties. But now it seemed she was seeing her everywhere. Well, she wasn't going to let Dahlia's actions and Maria's petty revenge plot get in the way of her manners.

Scarlett glided over to their side with a forced smile. "Tim. Maria. So glad you could make it. I wasn't sure you'd be able to, what with hosting your own party before this."

Maria's smile tightened at the edges. "Of course! We wouldn't miss your little after-party for the world." Maria winked. Scarlett bristled, but Maria was already gesturing between their outfits. "And, I guess great minds think alike, hmm? What a coincidence!"

Scarlett bit the inside of her cheek, resisting the urge to point out that her custom, designer-worthy dress had nothing in common with Maria's shiny pleather one. "Well, you look great," Scarlett said, as graciously as she could muster. She must not have successfully concealed her irritation, because Maria reached over to pat her forearm.

"Oh, honey, don't worry, you look adorable too."

Scarlett shrugged her hand off, resolving not to let this girl get under her skin anymore. After all, Maria was just a girl. And she was Scarlett Winter.

"And I am so glad that someone had the bravery to bring back the meat dress."

Maria's smile dropped, and she dug her nails into Tim's arm.

Tim laughed. "Ouch, babe."

"I've got to mingle," Scarlett said, sidestepping her. "Enjoy the *after-party*."

Maria stopped her with an outstretched hand. "Next time I hope you can make it over to Theta! We're planning another mixer next weekend."

"Hey," Tim interjected. "Maybe you can convince PiKa to come too. If you and Mason wanted to—" He cut off when Maria elbowed his side. Mason apparently had not kept in touch with his former PiKa brother since dropping out of the frat. Otherwise Tim would have known about Scarlett and Mason's breakup. Maria most definitely knew otherwise—her smirk was wider than the Cheshire Cat's.

"Mason isn't a PiKa anymore. And he and I aren't together anymore," Scarlett replied coolly. "*And* I'll have to check my calendar.

After all, some of us still have schoolwork to attend to." With that, she gave Maria another nod, and excused herself.

Damn it. Eugenie was right. The Thetas really were gunning hard for Spring Fling this year. There was no other reason Maria would host events two weekends in a row, especially a first event that conflicted so directly with Kappa.

She should have sent a couple girls to Theta's pregame tonight. Seen if it had actually been decent—the kind of competition Kappa needed to worry about. She found it hard to believe, considering Theta's long-standing reputation as second-best—and the little fact that Kappa had *magic* at their fingertips.

The house hummed with chatter and the clink of glasses. As she drifted up the hall, she spotted the boy who'd waylaid her for directions the other day—Xavier, was it?—dressed head to toe in black. He lurked near the entrance, standing out like a sore thumb. What was he doing here?

The crowd parted easily as Scarlett made her way toward him, the way crowds always did for her. "You realize this is meant to be a costume party, right?" she said when she reached his elbow.

"I am wearing a costume," Xavier said.

"It's not a costume if you have to explain it."

"I disagree. Those are the very best kind, Ever hear of the Knave of Spades?" he said, with a flourish of his arm. "The Red Queen sentenced him to death. But it turned out he wasn't the Knave of Spades, he was the Knave of Clubs."

"Does Lewis Carroll know about this knave?" she asked.

"He was a lesser-known knave." He pulled a card out of his pocket and handed it to Scarlett. It was the Jack of Clubs. She felt herself smile wide; it felt good to be surprised.

"You are still not winning our costume contest, but you can stay."

He bowed his head to her. "Thank you, Your Highness."

"You really never should bow your head to the Red Queen," she said lightly.

"I don't mind a little danger. I think the queen might just spare me."

Scarlett felt herself relax a little. It felt good to be able to talk to someone who didn't know anything at all about any of her troubles.

"So how does our party compare to yours back in—" Scarlett lifted her chin, not wanting to give the impression that she actually cared about his response.

"Vanderbilt," he finished for her. Xavier paused to take a long, slow look around the room. "I'll tell you over coffee, if you'll meet me for one tomorrow."

Scarlett scoffed. "Has anyone ever told you you're extremely persistent?"

"It's my middle name." He bowed as if thanking a crowd. "Nine a.m. at the Grind." The campus coffee shop. Personally, Scarlett preferred the upperclassmen-only lounge in Taylor. But how was he to know? He was new.

"I never said yes," she said, considering him again. After a bruising day, where life was all showers and thunderstorms, Xavier definitely was a bit of a rainbow.

"You didn't say no, either."

She couldn't help it. Her gaze shifted back toward the crowd. Toward the servers weaving through it. She couldn't find Jackson from here, yet Xavier read the look easily enough anyway.

She rolled her eyes. "*No.* There, I said it. Happy now, Xavier?"

"Ah, I see." His demeanor shifted all at once, his spine straightening and his hands drifting to his pockets. "The lady is otherwise engaged. Not to worry, I can take a hint." With that, he strolled away, hands in his pockets.

Scarlett watched him go. At the same time, she caught more than a few other girls watching, too. She wrenched her attention back to the party. *What was I doing?* Right, making a scene. She'd thrown out a perfectly good boy for one who wouldn't even give her a second look.

Scarlett hadn't wanted to brave facing Jackson again. Not so soon, not when he'd made his disinterest clear. But knowing he was this close, Scarlett couldn't resist. She couldn't shake the instinct that something was wrong. There was something about their last exchange that seemed out of character. Even if he wasn't into her, she would expect him to tell her so. He'd always been a good communicator.

And what if he remembers more than he should?

She didn't know what she'd do if the memory spell failed. Try it again? She hated the idea. But nothing had changed. Her loyalty must be to Kappa, first and foremost.

Suddenly, as if she'd conjured him, Jackson's familiar curls appeared close by. Disappearing around the corner of the foyer. The sight made Scarlett's pulse kick up. The hallway he was headed up had been strung across with velvet ropes and an enormous, impossible-to-miss sign: KAPPA ONLY.

What's he doing?

She sidled out of the common area and stepped over the ropes to follow him. Maybe he'd gotten lost on his way to the bathrooms.

She wheeled around the next corner, where the storage pantries and the back stairs into the basement were located. She *really* didn't want someone as insightful or tenacious as Jackson nosing around back here. But the moment she rounded the bend, she froze, her breath seizing. She felt like someone had punched her in the gut.

Jackson leaned against the basement door, in full view. But he wasn't alone. A girl in a shiny plastic skirt had her fingers clutched behind his neck. She whispered something. Then his lips collided with hers.

For a split second, the girl glanced over, and Scarlett's stomach performed an unpleasant somersault. It was a Theta girl. *Cait.*

Then Jackson kissed her again, and Scarlett spun away, her heart breaking in two.

CHAPTER EIGHT

Vivi

Vivi smiled as two girls—one dressed as a sexy White Rabbit, the other dressed as what Vivi assumed was a sexy Caterpillar, although she looked more like a sexy frayed garden hose—stared awestruck at the refreshment table.

Pride rose in Vivi's chest as she admired her handiwork. The table was covered with platters of pastel-colored pastries. There were enormous pink-and-white cupcakes the size of basketballs and tiny, bite-size lavender éclairs no bigger than a matchbox. At one end, a huge, whistling silver teapot emitted puffs of steam.

"How did they *do* that?" the sexy rabbit asked, leaning toward the teapot for a closer look.

"Careful!" The caterpillar tugged on her friend's puffy white tail to keep her from singeing her pink-painted nose. "I heard they hired some special effects expert from LA. It must've cost a fortune."

Above their heads, small teacup-shaped lanterns drifted through the garden, to match the glamours she'd put on the chandeliers inside. It looked like an enchanted tea party come to life—all except for the corner of the yard they'd reserved for a chessboard-painted dance floor.

Every one of her sisters had done an incredible job on the magic. And it had been Vivi's hand directing them.

Scarlett's praise from earlier in the night echoed in her thoughts. *It looks incredible.* Vivi had to agree.

At her elbow, Mason grinned, the flicker of the floating candles reflected in his eyes. "You Kappa girls certainly have a flair for the dramatic."

Vivi huffed in mock outrage. "*Us?* Dramatic? Never." She leaned in to run a fingertip up the center of his chest. Mason had gone all out with his Mad Hatter costume and looked surprisingly sexy in his purple frock coat, bow tie, and oversize top hat. "But you have to admit we're good at it."

Mason caught her in his arms and spun her to face him. "Very good." He bent close, until his forehead came to rest against hers. She leaned up to kiss him then pulled away with a smile.

"Come on. There are still a few guests I haven't met yet. We should mingle."

Mason shuddered. "You realize I left Greek life for a reason, right?"

"I gave you an out! I said that you didn't have to come tonight."

"What? And miss the chance to witness your triumph?" Mason looked around admiringly, then held out his hand. Vivi reached for it, and he spun her around, the skirt of her blue dress swirling around her.

"You two are sickeningly cute," Bailey said, rolling her eyes as she approached. "You should have to get a permit before you're allowed to appear in public."

"Uh-oh," Mason said. "Does this mean your date didn't go well the other night?" After hearing Bailey complain about how hard it was to meet guys as a French literature major, he'd offered to set her up with a friend of his.

Bailey shot Mason a withering look. "You should've warned me about the Adam Sandler impressions."

Mason shook his head. "I *told* him that wasn't first date material. Sorry, Bailey. But he grows on you, I swear."

Ariana skipped their way, drinks in hand. She never spilled a drop, no matter how wildly she moved. The benefit of being a Cups witch, she claimed. "Okay, punch has been sufficiently spiked with hangover-proofing."

"You're a hero." Vivi accepted the drink Ariana passed her, then grinned over her head at Reagan and Sonali, who were standing nearby. "Great job with the lanterns, by the way. And Sonali, people are losing their minds over the flamingo holograms."

Sonali executed a skilled curtsy. "Stole that trick from my mother's dinner parties."

Vivi was about to ask what kind of dinners her mother threw, when Reagan suddenly scowled at something in the distance.

"Heads up," she said, just before Vivi heard someone clearing their throat behind her.

She turned to find a vaguely familiar girl dressed as a Red Queen — Scarlett wouldn't be too happy about that — with a dark-haired guy holding an oversize pocket watch on her arm. Behind the pair stood the pink-haired girl from the Thirsty Scholar.

"Vivi, right?" the Red Queen asked with a wide smile. "I hear you're the one to congratulate on all this." She stuck out a hand. "I'm Maria. This is my boyfriend, Tim, and Rose, one of my Thetas."

Tim. Vivi's breath caught in her chest as she surveyed Vince Lee's son, the boy who might be her brother. He looked like a caricature of a star quarterback, with a square jaw and rectangular face that gave him a passing resemblance to Gaston from *Beauty and the Beast,* though his expression looked more bored than menacing. Apart from his dark brown hair, there was nothing about him that bore any resemblance to her. But they were half siblings, after all —perhaps Tim took after his mother.

"Um, thank you." Vivi cast a quick look at her friends. Reagan was glowering, but Ariana, Bailey, and Sonali looked merely curious. After a moment's hesitation, she took Maria's hand.

The other girl shook with professional precision. Vivi was reminded of the practice job interviews they'd done in an econ class at one of the high schools she'd attended. "You're a skilled planner, to pull all this off," Maria said as she released Vivi's hand. "Too bad we didn't have your help earlier. Our party tonight could've had better turnout."

"Maybe you should have thought of that before you double-booked against Kappa," Reagan said sweetly.

Maria raised an eyebrow and looked meaningfully at Reagan's wineglass. "There's that famous Kappa hospitality I've heard so much about."

"Have you all seen the dessert table?" Bailey said quickly. "You should check it out before all the éclairs are gone."

At that, Tim perked up slightly. "Éclairs?"

Maria shook her head sadly. "I'm doing Whole30. And Rose is gluten free."

Tim's face fell, and Vivi saw her moment. "Well, *you* shouldn't miss them. They're amazing. Come on, I'll show you!" Her sudden burst of excitement prompted a bemused look from Mason, but she ignored it. There was nothing wrong with the Kappa social chair taking care of her party guests, even if it meant guiding them a grand total of ten feet to the refreshment table.

"Here we are!" Vivi said brightly, handing Tim a plate. "Are you enjoying the party so far?"

"Huh?" Tim said, his attention clearly focused on loading his plate with pastel-colored treats. "Yeah, it's good."

"What else do you have going on this weekend?"

"Not much. Some other parties, I guess." He took a huge bite of cream puff, sending a spray of powdered sugar through the air. "And the game Sunday, of course."

"Of course," she echoed, feeling a faint twinge of disappointment. If she and Tim were truly long-lost siblings, then surely there'd be some sort of connection between them—a natural rapport, or sense of familiarity and comfort. This was awkward. "Your dad went to Westerly, right?"

Tim glanced up from his towering mound of pastries and looked at Vivi with surprise. There was a dusting of sugar on his nose that reminded Vivi of a dog that'd just been caught with its head in the fridge. "You must be a big fan of college football."

"Oh yeah, huge. I love . . . sports," Vivi said weakly, knowing that there wasn't a spell in the universe powerful enough to make her pass as a football aficionado. "Actually, no, not exactly. I . . . um . . ."

To his credit, Tim seemed nonplussed by Vivi's stammering. He took a bite of éclair and looked at her placidly, as if perfectly content to munch on pastries while this awkward freshman figured out exactly what she was trying to say to him.

"I don't know much about my father, if that's what you're getting at," Tim said, not unkindly.

"So you're not . . . close?"

"My mom doesn't talk much about him. I didn't even know he was this big football star for a long time."

"Me neither!"

Tim stared at her blankly. There was no way she'd be able to play this cool. She'd never been able to play *anything* cool. If she didn't come clean now, Tim was going to write her off as a creepy weirdo and spend the rest of his time at Westerly avoiding her. "Okay, this is going to sound really random, but . . ." She took a deep breath. "But I grew up without my dad, too. I didn't even know his name until a few weeks ago when my mom finally let it slip. She said it was Vince and that he played football at Westerly. She graduated a year after your dad."

Vivi braced herself for incredulous laughter, or a defensive *what kind of joke is this?* But instead Tim simply stared at her for a long moment, his expression inscrutable.

"Wow," he said finally.

"Yeah," Vivi said. There was another awkward beat of silence.

"I'm sure this wasn't what you were expecting to hear tonight. My mom said that he played football at Westerly, which makes me think . . ." She trailed off, not quite able to say the words aloud.

"That we might be siblings or something?"

"Yeah." She was relieved that he'd said it first. "Or something."

"That'd be pretty wild," he said, smiling for the first time.

"Just regular wild," Vivi said quickly, lest he think she was getting too worked up. "Not, like, you get a book deal and a reality show wild."

"I guess. Sorry, what'd you say your name was again?"

"Vivi."

"Vivi," Tim repeated, as if he liked the sound of it. "It's nice to meet you, Vivi." He shook his head and laughed. "Sorry, what a weird thing to say to your maybe sister."

Vivi grinned. "It's a pretty weird situation. So where did you grow up?"

"I was born outside of New Orleans, but we moved to . . ." Tim trailed off, distracted by one of the floating lanterns drifting overhead. Vivi had tried to make sure they didn't float too far from the big oak tree out back, so as not to draw suspicion. Now, though, the globe seemed suspended in midair, nothing above it but stars.

Vivi's heart plummeted toward her toes. "Invisible wire," she said lightly.

"Cool," Tim said. "How'd you—" His words were drowned out by a deafening crash from somewhere inside the house.

Vivi turned to exchange a startled look with Ariana, who was still talking to Mason and Bailey a few yards away. *Fireworks?* Ariana mouthed. But Vivi had specifically told Reagan no fireworks tonight. And the crash had come from inside the house.

"I'm sorry," Vivi said to Tim, forcing a smile despite the prickle of dread in her stomach. "I have to go check on something. I'll be right back." She'd only started to turn around when, to her horror, the floating globe exploded like a popped balloon, sending sprays of shattered glass in all directions. Everyone near the drinks table shrieked and ducked for cover, including Rose, who yelped as glass rained down into her hair.

"Don't move!" Vivi shouted, running toward her. But Rose was already swatting at the glass shards that had nicked her skin, leaving small pinpricks of blood. Before Vivi could reach her to help, Rose spun around and began to run away, clutching her arm.

"Rose, wait!" Vivi called. If she could just reach Rose, she'd be able to cast a healing spell and a memory-wiping spell. But her voice was drowned out by more smashes as, one by one, all the other hovering glass globes exploded.

"What do we do?" hissed Ariana at her side.

"Go find Scarlett," Vivi said as she desperately jammed her hands into the pockets of her costume. She hadn't been able to fit her whole tarot deck, but she'd selected a few cards to bring, in case she needed to redo a spell.

Ariana nodded and took off into the house just as Sonali returned. "The bonfire—" Sonali panted. "Help."

She followed Sonali's gaze and saw Reagan and Bailey on either side of the fire pit, where the flames were stretching toward the sky, impossibly high, and had started to leap outside the ring of stones. The tallest flames were nearly the height of Kappa House itself, despite the fact that there was hardly any wood left on the pile they'd lit.

"Oh my God," Vivi whispered in horror as red-hot embers began to fall onto the wooden balconies.

She and Sonali broke into a run and reached Bailey and Reagan just in time to grab their hands while they chanted breathlessly, "We call to the Queen of Wands and Fire. Help us to extinguish this pyre."

Vivi whipped around. They were being too loud—anyone could hear them. But another glance around showed the garden in total chaos. Sorority girls stood on picnic benches to avoid the piles of broken glass on the ground. Frat boys were carrying their girlfriends from the scene, and others were fleeing across the grass toward the road.

Nobody was paying attention. At least, she prayed they weren't. She took a breath and joined in the spell. "We call to the Queen of Wands and Fire. Help us to extinguish this pyre."

She could feel the magic. It raced along her shoulders, down her arms, and flowed into the energy emanating from Reagan, Bailey, and Sonali. But instead of the surge of power that normally came from casting spells with her sisters, Vivi felt a jerk of painful resistance, like bashing her fists against a solid brick wall. Almost like their spell was backfiring.

And still the flames grew higher, hungrier, licking at the wooden siding of Kappa House.

"We call to the Queen of Wands and Fire." Vivi was practically shouting now. She couldn't hear the others. All she could hear was the roar of fire; all she could feel was heat, and the pressure of that other mind, warring against theirs.

And then faint and distant, just along the edges of her perception, she could have sworn she heard another sound.

Laughter.

"Vivi!"

Someone grabbed her shoulders from behind, startling Vivi so badly, she dropped her sisters' hands and felt the surge of magic go out like a light.

Scarlett was muttering something next to her, and a moment later, Mei and Etta skidded to a stop, breathing heavily. In a blink, the bonfire went out, as quickly as if it had never existed. Even the flames on the siding of Kappa House vanished.

"Thank you," Vivi said hoarsely and let out a long breath. But her relief was short-lived. The garden had been nearly destroyed, the grass covered in a blanket of broken cups and plates.

Glass glittered on every surface, remnants of the floating chandeliers. The partygoers who remained looked shell-shocked, eyes wide and mouths agape as they stared at the damage.

Through the back patio doors, Vivi could see the house hadn't fared much better. The walls and carpets were all stained, and someone had broken the dining room table in half. To top it all off, in the distance, sirens wailed down the street. Someone had called the police.

The remaining dazed guests staggered away, leaving only the

Kappas behind. Finally, Vivi turned slowly to face Scarlett, bracing herself for a look of rage or disgust. Or both.

Yet Scarlett only set her jaw and looked away, surveying the destruction for a moment before she began barking orders. "Jess, meet the police at the door. See what you can do to convince them we're fine here. Sonali, go with her. Reagan, Bailey, clean up this." She gestured at the fire pit. "Mei and Etta, I'll need you inside. Juliet, Hazel, you're on yard cleanup—"

"What about me?" Vivi asked softly.

Scarlett flashed her a smile so cold, Vivi shuddered in the warm Savannah air. "I think you've done enough for one night."

CHAPTER NINE

Scarlett

I t was three in the morning by the time they got the house back into working order. Thanks to Mei and Etta, the living room sparkled once more, every surface power-cleansed of all the punch and food that had spilled in the mad rush to flee. The police had let them off with a warning, since it was the Kappas' first offense —Kappa Rho Nu did *not* get the police called on their parties.

Scarlett could already envision the phone call she'd be getting from her mother in the morning. But it didn't matter right now. Right now, they needed to focus.

"Everyone understand their part?" Scarlett asked quietly. The coven was kneeling on the living room carpet around a bowl of bay leaf and cedar incense, for purification and protection. Each girl had her tarot deck set before her, a single card turned upright, each a different card in the Swords suit.

"Maybe we should just do it in the morning," Etta murmured. "They're all exhausted, Scar."

"Dahlia would've let us get some rest first," Reagan added, with a pointed look in Scarlett's direction. Scarlett gritted her teeth against a surge of annoyance. Dahlia had never needed to alter the memories of half the student body at once. It was one thing for the sisters to complain when she was trying to teach them something new. It was another for them to balk at their most essential duty: protecting their coven.

"You're right. We should all get some sleep, and in the morning when someone graffities *witch* on our front door, people will start to believe them because they remember that time they saw the Kappa House light on fire and then mysteriously go out," Scarlett bit back.

Mei piped up. "Memory work is time-sensitive."

Scarlett thanked Mei in her head, not wanting to further cement the idea in the others that Mei was always taking her side.

"Scarlett, shouldn't we be asking a Swords witch to lead this, then?" Reagan persisted, nudging Sonali at her side. Sonali didn't seem quite as confident. She ducked her head and shook it.

Scarlett sighed. "I understand we're all stressed right now. But things are only going to get worse if we don't stick together. So." She held out her hands to the girls on either side of her. "Are you with me or not?"

Reagan held her gaze, chin raised in defiance. But one by one, the other girls joined hands. Eventually, after a long pause, Reagan looped one hand through Sonali's, the other around Vivi's.

Scarlett tried not to let her relief show. She didn't know if they could do this with even one Raven missing. Memory work was never easy, and to perform it on this scale . . . Scarlett just couldn't believe that, in light of what had just happened, she faced any resistance at all. What had gotten into Reagan lately?

Across the circle, movement caught Scarlett's eye. Vivi, shifting in her seat, worrying at her lower lip. She'd been like this all night, ever since Scarlett's rebuke earlier. Guilt trickled through Scarlett's chest.

It hadn't been very presidential of her, blaming Vivi like that. But she'd been flustered, not to mention scared. She'd never seen magic go so wrong, not at their own hands. Inside the house, the teacup fountain had boiled over, the matching chandeliers had exploded, and the mirrors had warped and melted in on themselves as the glamours failed.

There was no normal way to explain to the partygoers how a plush toadstool chair had suddenly morphed back into a velvet settee while they were sitting on it. Or why the grassy carpet had suddenly changed both color and texture at once.

All Scarlett could picture was the horrified expressions. Horror would turn to disgust and fear if they learned who—and what —the Ravens really were. This was the closest the Ravens had ever come to being discovered. And it had happened on her watch.

She shouldn't have entrusted such a big undertaking to a freshman, let alone such a new witch.

"What happened tonight," Scarlett said slowly, realizing she needed to own up to that fact. "It's my fault. As president, I'm supposed to keep you safe, and to protect our secrets. I failed you, and for that, I'm sorry."

Vivi shook her head. "No, Scarlett, it was my job—"

"A job I gave you," Scarlett interrupted. "I take responsibility for that. But right now, we need everyone's help in order to fix it.

Ravens, let's make sure we're all focused on what's important: setting this right."

She waited for everyone to nod once more before she bowed her head. And they got to work.

~

Scarlett couldn't sleep. After they finished the memory charm, the other girls trickled off to bed one by one, but she retreated to the kitchen to finish washing dishes from the party. She could have simply magicked them all clean—or hired the caterers to come back and cart the extras away in the morning. But the simple, repetitive motion relaxed her.

"Being president isn't what you think, Scar," she remembered Dahlia telling her. "It means that as close as you are to your sisters you have to stand a little apart. You have to see what they cannot. You have to be their friend but also their guide. You have to say the tough thing as well as the encouraging thing. And if you really want them to pay attention, you have to scare them a little . . ." Scarlett thought of her time with Dahlia and all that she had learned from her Big, believing that she would take Dahlia's place as president one day. Just not this way. But unlike Dahlia, Scarlett was determined not to lead with fear. But her new way to build a witch wasn't exactly working, was it?

Scarlett couldn't—wouldn't—lead with fear, but what if the distance part was true? If she had stepped back tonight, she would have seen that Vivi had bitten off way more witchcraft than she could chew. If she hadn't been so worried about improving the girls with the intention spell, maybe she would have listened to the girls about the Thetas. If she hadn't been thinking about Jackson. If. If. If. All the ifs added up to this. She wasn't paying attention. And that was on her. Not Vivi. Not her sisters.

She kept on washing the dishes, but she couldn't wash her guilt away. She was bent over the stove, rinsing a champagne flute, when a soft footfall on the tiles made her tense.

"It's just me," Vivi murmured, low enough to avoid startling her. "I can help, if you want."

Scarlett stared into the sudsy sink for a moment, collecting her thoughts. Then, without replying, she shuffled to the left, and let Vivi step up to the counter with a drying towel.

For a few minutes, they worked in silence. Scarlett scrubbing and rinsing, Vivi drying and replacing the dishes in their proper cabinets.

Eventually, Vivi cleared her throat. "I'm sorry."

"I know." Scarlett sighed. "I'm sorry too. I shouldn't have chewed you out in front of everyone. And I was the one who gave you the party . . ."

"I just wish I knew what went wrong," Vivi groaned. "I don't know which spell backfired, or even *how*. All that damage . . ."

"You should have asked me for help," Scarlett said. "After what we've been through together, that shouldn't be a question."

When Vivi spoke, her voice came out small. Younger sounding. "I wanted to impress you."

"And for that, we might have exposed ourselves to the entire campus," Scarlett replied, anger flaring back up in her chest. She felt for Vivi and she was mad at her at the exact same time.

She reached out to the tap and turned the hot water on higher. Thoughts of her mother, of what she'd say when she found out what a disaster Scarlett's first event as president had become, made her annoyance build. "You need to learn to prioritize, Vivi. Being impressive is not as important as being safe."

"I know that," Vivi said quietly, tears springing to her eyes.

The sink groaned.

"We don't cry over spilled magic. We clean it up and we move on. Together. And we tighten the cap so there is no next time. We were lucky this time."

There was another sink groan.

Scarlett ignored it. "I assigned you the position of social chair because I thought, after last semester, you'd be a good fit. You were levelheaded in a crisis. After tonight, I'm worried I made a mistake. And I'm worried about you, Vivi. We have the one hundred fiftieth anniversary reunion coming up soon, which just about every Kappa who was ever anyone will be attending. Not to mention Spring Fling after that, assuming Theta doesn't steal it from us. Maybe you're not ready. Maybe this was too much too soon . . . after . . . everything. If you can't handle this, then I need to find someone else."

Vivi flinched. "No, I can handle it, I promise. I just . . ."

With a rattling sound, the faucet burst off the sink. Both girls leaped backwards, cursing, as ugly red-orange water gushed from the broken pipe. The stench of rotting eggs filled the kitchen.

"Of course." Scarlett flung her hands up. "What else wants to blow up tonight?" she yelled at the house in general.

Beside her, Vivi glanced upward, no doubt thinking about their sisters, asleep somewhere overhead.

"I'm going to shut off the water." Scarlett stomped toward the basement stairs. Tomorrow she'd have to call facilities. Great. More people poking around in Kappa House.

"Let me help." Vivi followed.

Scarlett ignored her and stomped past the back room.

At the top of the basement steps, Scarlett wrenched open the door, and Vivi ducked past her to turn on the light.

Or she tried to, anyway. Vivi flicked the switch back and forth a few times, then shook her head. "Dead." Past Vivi, the darkness was so complete, she could only make out the first step. The rest was silent. A void.

"Damn it." Scarlett groped around the supply closet for the stock of candles Etta kept. When she had one in hand, she whispered, "I call to the Queen of Wands. Show me your might by giving us light."

The candle sputtered to life. Cupping one palm around the delicate flame, Scarlett led the way down the steps. The flame in her hand hissed and climbed higher. Hotter.

With each step she descended, the air grew hotter. Muggy and thick as soup.

"Vivi, you reset the basement breaker." Scarlett pointed her Little toward the deepest, darkest corner on the far side, near rows upon rows of carefully labeled ointments — and more than a few vintage bottles of wine. "I'll handle the water."

Vivi shuffled away from Scarlett, her breathing heavy. She turned back.

"Scarlett, the water . . . Is it you? I know you are mad at me . . ."

Scarlett shook her head. She was mad . . . but this wasn't her.

"Not me. It's an old house," she offered up, but something in her didn't like this. The Kappa House was a gazillion years old, but it was slathered in magic; like a woman who had used La Mer all her life, it was very well preserved. Scarlett could not remember ever having to call facilities, except to keep up appearances, in all her years here.

As for Scarlett, she approached the boiler, nestled between the laundry machine the girls almost never used — it was far easier to clean their clothing magically — and the external pump for the garden hose, which fed most of the greenhouse.

This side of the basement, unlike the other half, was all cobwebs and empty space. It was huge down here. Scarlett knew there had been petitions over the years to renovate it, add more bedrooms or maybe work areas. Yet they all fell through eventually, higher-ups at Westerly denying the motion in spite of Kappa's considerable influence. So the basement sat empty, gathering dust. No one even used it for storage space.

Part of her wondered why. But then again, it *was* eerie down here.

With every step she took toward the boiler, the heat increased.

Her face itched, reminding her of earlier, when she'd raced to contain the bonfire. It had felt the same way, flames licking inches from her nose.

Behind her, she heard muffled curses, as Vivi attempted to switch on the lights. But Scarlett had eyes only for the far wall.

She could have sworn she heard something else. Not the creak of the house overhead or the occasional gust of wind from a drafty doorway. It was more rhythmic. Steady and deep.

A whoosh and a gust. Almost like . . .

Breathing.

Scarlett's foot sank into something soft, and she inhaled sharply. But when she lowered the candle to look, it was just an old piece of carpet someone had discarded, soggy with damp. She grimaced. She'd have to clean up down here soon. Maybe she could get the froshlings to do it, as penance for the way their party turned out.

Inching around the carpet square, she kept going toward the back wall. Upstairs, the house had felt chilly for a Savannah evening. Now sweat beaded on her skin, trickled along her spine. When she reached the knob to shut off the water and touched the metal, it *burned*.

Cursing, Scarlett jerked her hand away. *What the hell?*

She whispered a command, and the candle flame climbed higher, illuminated a wider circle. The wall looked normal. Stone, with wires along it. Yet when Scarlett brushed a fingertip along the stone itself, it was hot enough to make her flinch.

Electrical problems?

She frowned. That was when she heard it again. The soft in and out, louder now. Closer. Like someone was asleep, mere inches away.

"Hello?" she whispered. She expected Vivi to reply. Yet no one spoke.

The breathing stopped. For a moment, she felt sure she'd imagined it.

Then the whispers started.

Jumbled, hissing. A dozen voices all speaking at once, in a language she didn't recognize. Yet even if she didn't understand the words, Scarlett could grasp the feeling.

Fury.

Every instinct in her body screamed at her to run. But Scarlett Winter didn't run from a fight. Especially not a fight with her own imagination.

"Cut it out," she snapped. Then, before she could second-guess herself, she whirled back to the valve and wrenched it hard, ignoring the sear of pain in her fingertips. She needed to turn it off before the whole kitchen flooded.

She pushed hard, yet the wheel resisted. Then she wrapped her hand in the hem of her shirt and gave it a hard yank toward the off position.

The whispers got louder. Closer.

Breath tickled the nape of her neck. Something slithered through her hair. Wind? *Or fingertips . . .*

"Come on." She gave one last hard tug, and then everything happened at once.

The lights came back on, flooding the basement in bright fluorescence. Across the basement, Vivi let out a triumphant *whoop*.

Above Scarlett, the ceiling gave a horrible groan — and exploded.

Sulfurous, stinking water poured onto Scarlett's head, extinguishing her candle. She screamed and leaped backwards, but it was too late. She was drenched, head to toe. Her eyes watered and stung. *Rust*. The water was a hideous orange-brown color.

At least that explained all the whispering. *Water rushing through the pipe*. She felt like an idiot. A wet, thoroughly disgusted idiot.

"Scarlett?" Footsteps thundered her direction. Vivi stared at her, wide-eyed. "Oh my God. What happened? Please tell me what spell fixes this."

Scarlett laughed at the irony that was Vivi. She really was still a baby witch in so many ways even though she'd already experienced more things than most witches had ever had to.

"Some things are beyond spells. I think we need to find a plumber . . ." After everything they had been through this evening, Scarlett had been sure this night couldn't get any worse. But as she wrung out her ponytail as best she could, she was pretty sure it just did.

CHAPTER TEN

Vivi

Vivi woke up after a restless night plagued by visions of flames and echoes of their guests' terrified screams. But even those images didn't weigh as heavily as the memory of Scarlett's face as she said, *If you can't handle this, then I need to find someone else.*

Maybe that would be the responsible move. Not only had she ruined the first party of the year, the event that was supposed to reestablish Kappa's place at the top of the Westerly hierarchy, she'd nearly exposed the Ravens' secret.

The knot in her stomach tightened as she forced herself to accept the reality of the situation: she needed to resign.

Someone knocked softly on her door. Vivi groaned and burrowed into her pillow, wishing she could just vanish into thin air. There was definitely a spell for that, but knowing her, she'd probably botch it and end up trapped in some magical no-man's-land for the rest of time.

The knock came again, slightly louder this time. "Come in," Vivi called with a sigh as she swung her legs over the side of her bed. She was wearing her rattiest T-shirt and embarrassing Hello Kitty pajama shorts, but that hardly seemed to matter compared to the mortification she'd endured last night.

The door opened revealing Ariana and Bailey, each carrying a tray.

"We thought you'd be feeling off, so we brought you breakfast," Ariana said cheerily as she carried the tray inside and placed it on Vivi's bed. There were pancakes, sunny-side-up eggs, bacon, and fresh-squeezed orange juice. Then Bailey walked over carrying two different pots and a mug.

"We didn't know whether you'd be in the mood for coffee or tea," she said, setting everything down on the comforter. "Ari wouldn't let me make you the invigorating ginger punch I've been working on."

Ariana rolled her eyes. "Bailey, you found the recipe in a spell book from 1688. Half the ingredients are borderline poisonous."

"I *told* you I'd found a substitute for arsenic," Bailey said with a huff.

"Coffee is good, thanks," Vivi said. "I don't need any reminders about my way-too-mad tea party. This was really sweet of you, but I'm not sure I can eat right now."

"Good. More for me, then," Reagan said as she barged inside, Sonali on her heels. They were carrying dessert: a huge tub of ice cream and an ornately decorated chocolate cake.

"You made a *cake?*" Vivi's eyebrows rose.

"Didn't you see the chocolate soufflé she made when she got an A minus on her midterm?" Bailey asked.

Sonali shrugged, a little sheepish. "I bake when I'm upset."

Vivi winced as a new wave of guilt crashed over her. "I'm so sorry about last night. I shouldn't have pushed you all so hard. Clearly we tried to do too much at once."

"It's not your fault," Ariana said firmly. "We all worked together on everything. Whatever happened to the spells—"

"It wasn't our magic," Reagan interrupted, her mouth still full of the ice cream she'd already dug into. "I've done that fire spell a dozen times."

"We did it exactly right," Bailey added. She had bags under her eyes and looked nearly as exhausted as Vivi felt. "We did *every-thing* right; there's no reason why the fire should have gotten out of control."

"It's possible I made a mistake with the Swords magic." Sonali exchanged a meaningful look with Reagan before she spoke again. "At the end of the night, when we were trying to contain the bonfire, I felt something . . . like another type of magic, pushing back."

Vivi had felt it too. Almost like their magic had a mind of its own. If someone else had intervened, then perhaps this wasn't entirely her fault, after all. But then again, if this *wasn't* her fault, they had much bigger problems at hand.

"I don't know . . ." Vivi said uncertainly.

"We should talk to Scarlett," Ariana said as she perched on the edge of Vivi's bed. "She needs to know if someone's trying to sabotage us."

The girls fell silent and avoided one another's eyes as the room grew still and charged, all of them clearly thinking about what

Tiffany had done right under their noses. Was it possible that someone *else* in the house could be a traitor?

"I'll talk to Scarlett," Vivi said finally. "But I don't want to leap to conclusions. We're all jumpy after last semester, and it's entirely possible we did just mess up last night." Reagan opened her mouth to protest, but Vivi cut her off. "I'm not saying *you* did, Reagan. But we cast a ton of spells. There was a lot of magic to balance. Who knows what could've gone wrong."

Witchcraft was powerful. Unpredictable. The far more likely explanation was that Vivi overreached. After all, surely one of the upperclasswomen would have spoken up if they'd sensed some wicked magic at work.

"Either way," Vivi continued, "whatever happened, the blame is on me."

"Don't beat yourself up." Ariana pushed a plate of pancakes she'd stacked in Vivi's direction. "It was your first big event. And right up until the end, it had been going amazingly, right girls?"

Everyone nodded. Even Reagan, although she glanced at Sonali again while she did. Vivi wondered what the two of them said about her in private. If Reagan was still upset about Vivi being chosen as social chair. Reagan and Sonali had more experience than she did, since they'd both grown up with witchcraft. Not like Vivi, new to everything at once.

"Don't give up," Ariana said softly. "You're just getting started. Everyone stumbles a bit at first. But you're going to be a great social chair. I know it."

While Vivi got dressed, she practiced what she was going to say to Scarlett. But as she trudged downstairs, the thought of facing her Big made Vivi's legs feel too heavy to navigate the final steps.

Maybe it was better to give Scarlett a day or two to cool off first.

To Vivi's relief, Kappa House was quiet that morning. She normally relished the noise and bustle that came with twenty college-age witches living under one roof — the joyful yelps celebrating a successful glamour, the ominous booms of spells gone wrong, the clatter of coffee cups in the kitchen, the thud of impromptu bedroom dance parties, the chirp of birds in the aviary — but today she was happy to avoid the pitying or chilly looks of her sisters.

She grabbed her book bag from its hook in the front hall and carried it into the library — one of her favorite rooms in the entire house. It was one of the few that hadn't been glamoured, and Vivi could see why. It'd be criminal to tamper with the floor-to-ceiling shelves of antique, leather-bound books, the large wooden cabinets with apothecary-style drawers for dried potion ingredients, and the gorgeous blue ceiling emblazoned with a gold-leaf elemental compass.

Vivi settled into her favorite armchair and took a deep breath, inhaling the comforting scents of leather, furniture polish, candle wax, dried herbs, and the faint, smoky scent of spellwork. The act usually filled Vivi with a sense of reverence, as if she were actually breathing in generations of magic — a rich legacy to which she now belonged. But this morning, it simply made her feel like an imposter. How many of the spells in these books would she ever be able to perform without hurting people?

She pulled her neuroscience textbook out of her bag and opened it to that week's chapter, but no matter how many times she forced her eyes to travel over the opening sentences, she couldn't get anything to stick. There didn't seem to be room in her brain for anything other than her shame and regret. She winced as she recalled the expression on Tim's face as he'd helped Maria guide the frightened Thetas to safety. Her story about them being half siblings sounded outlandish enough on its own; her erratic behavior at the end of the party would hardly make her seem more credible. In addition to ruining Kappa's reputation, she'd probably also destroyed any chance she'd had at getting to know her brother.

With a sigh, Vivi rose to her feet and began to pace. A patchwork of ivy covered most of the windows, filling the room with dappled green-tinged light that enhanced the room's otherworldly quality, as if the library had been transported from a fairy lair. She ran one hand along the leather spines, some cracked with age, some still resplendent with their gold lettering. There were glossaries of herbs, historical records, manuals on astrological birth charts, atlases of ancient maps, and countless spell books.

Perhaps if she could figure out what went wrong last night —whether it was interference or just a spell that backfired—she could at least ensure that it never happened again.

The answer had to be here somewhere. Buried amidst the collected knowledge of every sister who had ever lived in Kappa House and all the witches who'd come before them.

She made another loop around the room, examining the titles more closely this time. A breeze tickled the back of her neck, and she glanced around to examine its source. The library windows were rarely opened, but it wasn't unusual for odd breezes to circulate through Kappa House on occasion, a product of rain-warped shingles, the constant flinging open of doors, and the lingering aftermath of Wands magic.

The sensation came again, more like a puff of breath on her neck than a breeze.

She shivered and turned her attention back to the books. There was a large dark blue clothbound book sticking out over the edge of one of the shelves, as if someone had read it and replaced it carelessly. *Llewellyn's Guide to Protective Garden Construction.* Curious, Vivi pulled it out and gently opened it, taking care to support the fragile, cracked binding.

The cover fell open easily, and to her surprise, Vivi found another smaller book tucked inside. This one was thin, little more than a notebook, really, though an expensive-looking one. The kind Vivi's mother used to buy her on her birthdays, embossed leather with thick, unlined pages, which she was always too nervous to write in, afraid she'd ruin the pretty notebook with her childish scrawl. They always wound up at the back of her closet, collecting dust.

The dark brown leather cover was embossed with an ornate pattern of silver leaves with symbols tucked inside, the most prominent of which was a circle with a crossed pattern in the center. It almost looked like a pentagram.

Vivi felt a small tingle of excitement as she ran a fingertip along the smooth leather. A pentagram for a Pentacles witch? Some instinct made her glance up, check that the library door was still shut, the room empty, before she removed the hidden notebook.

She replaced *Llewellyn's* on the shelf, then carried the notebook back to her chair to examine it more carefully. The paper was so old it had gone brown in places, like parchment. It was handwritten, too, although whoever had created it had excellent penmanship. Vivi could almost have mistaken the elegant cursive for a script font, if not for the occasional shift in tone, as if the ink, too, had dulled with time.

It was a grimoire, she realized, a book of spells. Some pages bore illustrations done by hand, intricate renderings of altar setups and tarot card layouts. Other pages contained what appeared to be notes—first a spell, then a few pages of description, advice from the author on testing the spell.

There were countless spells she'd never even heard of. A recipe for "siren honey" that, when added to lavender thistle tea, would produce a singing voice so beautiful, it'd hypnotize any listener. A charm that allowed one to understand birdsong and send messages through willing larks.

But it was the author's preface that really caught Vivi's attention, a short manifesto on the dangers of focusing on magical suits:

> *Young witches are often initiated into the magical community through tests that identify the source of their powers—Wands magic, Cups magic, Swords magic, or Pentacles magic. This custom only*

dates back to the seventeenth century and was popularized by those
who sought to limit the power of individual witches. The concept of
a rogue witch was so threatening that the establishment chose to pro-
mote the falsehood about magical suits to encourage the formation
of covens, which were easier to track, monitor, and influence. The
intent of this modest volume is to help witches remove the shackles
of this unjust restraint and embrace the full scope of their magical
abilities.

Vivi's mind raced. If she could learn some of these spells, perhaps she'd be able to unlock her full potential. She could dazzle
Scarlett and her sisters and make them forget all about her mistakes
last night.

Her fingertips began to buzz, as if magic was already building
up within her. Perhaps she could try one of the simpler spells now,
just as a warm-up. She riffled through the notebook carefully until
she came to a header that said "Convenient Vanishing Spell," with
a short summary underneath:

> *This highly adaptable spell should be considered foundational magic*
> *for any witch. It can be used to disappear simple objects, and under*
> *the right circumstances, is a useful tool for vanquishing one's enemies.*

Vivi frowned, wondering what exactly "vanquishing" meant in
this context, then decided not to worry about it. The only person she'd ever wanted to make disappear was her old roommate,
Zoe, but now that Vivi had moved out of the freshman dorms into

Kappa House, Zoe's snide comments and passive-aggressive jabs were no longer an issue.

A simple object. She reached for a pen and played with it absent-mindedly as she read on.

> *Vanishing spells require equal parts air and earth magic. Instead of calling the Empress of Swords and/or the Queen of Pentacles, which dilute a witch's power with clumsy incantations, it is far more elegant to clear one's mind and tap into these two sources of energy that always surround a talented witch, regardless of classification.*

Vivi frowned. Magic was hard enough without trying to follow vague instructions like "clear your mind," but she supposed there wasn't any harm in trying. She stared at the pen intently and tried to imagine it disappearing. Nothing happened. She tried again, squeezing her eyes shut. This time, she felt the familiar buzz of magic in her chest, but when she opened her eyes again, the pen was still in her hand.

She sighed. Great. Her brilliant plan to up her magical game and impress all her sisters had lasted for a great total of about ten minutes. She glanced back down at the grimoire and skimmed the notes written in the margins.

> *Blood, which acts as an amplifier with most spells, can be especially useful with vanishing spells. Just a few drops can have a dramatic effect.*

She rooted through her book bag until she found a small safety pin, unfolded it, then pricked the pad of her thumb. Just hard enough to draw a single drop of blood.

She squinted at the pen, ignoring the faint sting of pain.

This pen isn't here anymore. She willed herself to imagine it vanishing, melting into the air.

A thin line of sweat prickled along her scalp. She tried to ignore it, but the itch grew into a burn, until she finally broke and reached up to rub it.

When she looked back, the pen was gone.

The spell had *worked*.

With a satisfied smile, Vivi leaned back in her chair and closed the small volume. When she looked up, she was surprised to glance out the window and discover that it was already late afternoon. Through the ivy, the neighbors' porch lights glowed golden yellow in the dusk.

But it had been time well spent. She had been desperate, lost, in need of guidance. She'd been on the verge of giving up, of letting her Big Sister down even worse. Just when she'd needed it the most, Kappa House had provided.

This time, when Vivi faced the portraits of former Ravens, their gazes no longer seemed foreboding, but encouraging. Like they were silently telling her, *You can fix this.*

For the first time all day, Vivi believed it.

CHAPTER ELEVEN

Scarlett

The main green was packed for Tuesday movie night. Every sorority had their own territory staked, and Kappa, as usual, had the place of honor: dead center on the green, far enough back from the big projector that they didn't need to crane their necks for a view, yet close enough that the light from the movie reflected on their blanket and allowed everyone on campus a view of the Ravens in all their glory.

Tonight, however, the energy felt more subdued than usual. They were all still reeling from the party on Friday, although they'd done their best to disguise it.

Scarlett was especially on edge.

Why is #ThetaforSpringFling trending on campus Twitter? Eugenie had texted her almost first thing the next morning.

Later that night, she'd dealt with a furious Marjorie over the phone. "I hear the *police* came to the house?" her mother had thundered. Underneath her anger, Scarlett could tell Marjorie was afraid, too.

Afraid they'd be exposed. Afraid Kappa would be in even more danger than they'd already faced last semester. It had taken all of

Scarlett's powers of persuasion to reassure her mother that she had things under control. She explained that the police coming by was an isolated incident, one they'd handled.

She hadn't described how far out of line the party had really gotten. If Marjorie caught wind, she'd really blow a gasket. But to judge by the feelers Scarlett had put out in class on Monday, tentatively asking a few other sorority and frat presidents how it had gone, their memory spell had done its job.

Nobody remembered much about the Kappa party. Just some cool décor and too-strong cocktails. Everyone seemed to be chalking it up to drinking too much at Theta's pregame. And the entire campus was buzzing about how much fun Theta's impromptu after-party had been—apparently Maria had managed to set up an entire buffet, complete with a beer pong tournament and craft beer kegs, all on a moment's notice.

It made Scarlett's blood boil, to be outshined like that. Yet she couldn't exactly complain. It would be far worse if anyone knew what really happened.

Scarlett shifted on her signature chair, a big white beanbag disguised as a swan. Tiffany had bought it for her their sophomore year. It had been a joke at first, but they'd enhanced it with magic, made it as comfy as reclining on a bed of feathers.

Ever since Scarlett had started using it at campus movie nights, she'd spotted lookalikes popping up among all the other sororities. Girls with hot pink flamingoes or inflatable swans, trying to compete.

She spotted one now, over on Theta's blanket. A girl named Deylin, lounging with a Gamma girl on a half-deflated pink swan that seemed to glare at Scarlett. Taunting.

Because right next to them were Cait and Jackson, cuddled up on a paisley quilted blanket Cait must have brought.

In the flickering light of the movie — an old classic this week, *Psycho* — Scarlett could see just well enough to make out Jackson's arm wrapped protectively around Cait's shoulders.

It sent a pang through her, and she forced herself to look away. It was a double pang because it was one of *their* movies, only he didn't even know it. They had bonded over their mutual love of horror movies when they were on their way to confront Gwen, when they thought she was the one who was trying to hurt the Kappas. But that memory was gone just as surely as Gwen was. And Scarlett was here in the dark, still reliving it all on her own.

She sighed and looked away from the screen. She couldn't even bring herself to enjoy the part when Norman Bates first mentions his mother.

"Don't look now," murmured Mei softly, from where she lay on her own cushion next to Scarlett, a simple Moroccan-style pouf glamoured to match the bohemian silk pants and crop top she wore tonight. "But Tall, Dark, and Cheekbones over there has *not* stopped looking at you for the last ten minutes."

Mei nodded in the direction of Theta's blanket. Xavier lounged beside a Theta girl. He hadn't brought a blanket, just spread out his PiKa hoodie to sit on.

Sure enough, he was staring right at Scarlett. The moment she made eye contact, he waved, a jaunty little smirk on his face. The girl beside him looked up, offended.

She had a sudden urge to roll her eyes. And yet . . .

She glanced at Jackson again, surreptitiously. She considered Xavier and then Jackson. It would be a test. Like when you flip over a card and feel in your gut what you really want. If there was any part of Jackson that still felt the way she thought, when he saw her with someone else, she would elicit a response. She hesitated thinking about the Xavier of it all. How he'd feel if he knew he was being used. But then Jackson drew Cait even closer after she jumped to a loud moment on the screen.

So she looked back at Xavier, grinned, and lifted a hand. Beckoned him over with one finger, curling upward.

That was all it took. He leaped to his feet, scooped up his hoodie, and picked his way over toward their blanket.

Closer to hand, Mei flashed Scarlett a quick wink. *Enjoy,* her sister whispered directly in her head, a playful grin on her brightly lipsticked mouth. Then Mei shuffled her pouf over to make room for Xavier at Scarlett's side.

All around her, her sisters were lounging comfortably. Vivi was lying with her head on Mason's chest, her arms folded over her stomach. Scarlett shifted her view to Juliet beside them, Jess's head in her lap, absentmindedly toying with her girlfriend's braids. Etta and Ariana were both enraptured by the movie, making eyes at each other and whispering between creepy moments, and Reagan kept shushing them.

Who knew that horror films were such a turn-on?

Just then, Xavier blocked out her view of the screen and the mushy display before her. She was grateful. She smiled up at him.

"Permission to approach Her Highness," he offered.

Xavier did a double take, hesitating before he actually plopped down next to Scarlett. Kappa had spread out a big comforter underneath all their chairs, decorated in moons and stars.

Xavier raised his eyebrows, patting the fabric. "How is this thing so comfortable when I know for a fact this lawn is ninety percent rocks and ten percent old tree branches?"

Scarlett laughed under her breath. "After a few years, you learn how to work with the terrain."

"So I hear I owe you an apology," he said, and Scarlett's eyebrows rose.

"For what?"

He winced, sheepish. In the flickering of the movie screen, the shadows around Xavier's sharp features stood out even more. "I have to admit, I left your party early."

She sighed. "Let me guess. You fled to Theta?"

Xavier shook his head. "Actually, I went to bed. What can I say? I'm ancient at heart."

She laughed again, and Reagan spun around, shushing. But when she noticed it was Scarlett talking, she flushed red and silently turned back to the movie. Scarlett stared at her back, remembering how angry Reagan had seemed during the party cleanup. Did she still feel that way? Like Scarlett wasn't as good of a leader as Dahlia had been?

Beside her, Xavier bent in close. "I'm going to grab some popcorn," he whispered. "Want anything?"

She was about to ask for a Coke when motion caught her eye: Jackson, disentangling himself from Cait and heading toward the snack booth set up on the far end of the green. "I'll come with you," she murmured, before she had a chance to think better of it.

Xavier offered her a hand, and she let him pull her up off her chair. His hand felt surprisingly rough against hers, calloused, as if he worked with it a lot.

It didn't match the rest of his demeanor, which was carefree frat boy to a T. Curious, she fell into step beside him. "So, how are you liking Westerly so far?" she asked. "Is it living up to your old school's standards?"

"And then some," he replied, his eyes lingering on hers. "Oh, I'm sorry, did you mean academically, or in terms of the dating pool?"

She snorted and rolled her eyes. But she couldn't help smiling, just a little. At least if nothing else, flirting with Xavier tonight provided a much-needed boost to her ego. "Why did you transfer? Besides for the dating pool, I mean."

He grinned. "So curious. Do you always give new arrivals the third degree, or am I special?"

"I'm just making conversation," she protested. They neared the line for the snack bar, and she spotted Jackson two people ahead, his hands in his pockets, head tilted to one side.

Scarlett followed his gaze and realized he was staring straight across the lawns back at Cait. As if he couldn't bear to be away from her for one more minute.

What is so freaking special about her? Scarlett couldn't help wondering. Jackson had always been so adamant about his dislike for sorority girls. It had taken Scarlett weeks of texting to wear down his defenses enough for him to ask her out.

Then he blew her off days later, only to fall head over heels for the polar opposite of what he'd wanted?

The line moved, and Jackson took a step forward without so much as blinking. Under the concession stand lights, she saw he was even dressing differently, in a button-down shirt and slacks. It looked wrong on him. The Jackson she knew barely ever wore a shirt that didn't have a face or a slogan on it.

"If I'm intruding . . ." Xavier said, startling her back to the present.

Her cheeks flushed, and she caught him looking from her to Jackson, a knowing look on his face. She forced a laugh. "Sorry. Lost in thought. It's been a busy week."

"It's Tuesday," he pointed out.

"You were saying, you transferred because . . ."

"You really don't let people change the subject, do you?" He ran a hand through his hair.

Scarlett peered at him more closely. Why was he so on-edge all of a sudden? "If you don't want to talk about it . . ."

"No, it's fine. It's just a bit of a sore spot with my family, that's all." He laughed again, but it sounded weaker this time. Forced. "My parents . . . They have pretty big expectations. Of who I'm supposed to be, what path I'm meant to follow."

Scarlett's throat tightened unexpectedly. She could understand that. Her mother's rebukes over the weekend were far too fresh in her mind. "They made you transfer?"

"They didn't *make* me," he said, with a wry twist to his mouth that told her that was exactly what had happened. "They were just very clear about all the reasons I should do it, and also that they wouldn't continue to help out with my tuition if I refused."

Scarlett sighed. "Sadly, that sounds all too familiar."

Xavier grimaced. "I'm sorry to hear that."

"Eh." Scarlett raised one shoulder, halfhearted. "It could be worse. Don't get me wrong, I love my family."

"Oh, same." He cast her another look, longer this time. "I just sometimes wish they loved me as much as they love their traditions."

Scarlett looked up at him, feeling a sense of kinship suddenly that had nothing to do with their frats being siblings. It felt some-how like the first true thing he'd said.

"The queen has rethought her position about costumes. She thinks that she prefers you with yours off," she said with meaning.

"I think that can be arranged," he said sincerely.

Someone bumped into her, pushing her forward.

"Hey, watch it," Xavier said to the guy behind them, putting his hand protectively on her back. She didn't move it, but when she faced forward, she realized they were already at the front of the line. Jackson stood off to the side, waiting for his popcorn. Talk-ing to Xavier had almost made her forget, almost distracted her enough.

And yet . . . something was *off* with Jackson, she just knew it. Not just the Cait thing. He had this look in his eyes, far away and lost. She'd never seen him like this. Normally he paid attention to everything and everyone. When she'd met him, he'd been annoyingly observant. At first she found it unnerving, then she found it charming, then she found it kind of irresistible. Now it was just absent.

She had to talk to him. She had to try. Trying to make him jealous was stupid, childish. All that mattered was that he was okay. It wasn't about getting him back, she told herself. She almost believed it.

"Excuse me one second," she said to Xavier. Then she peeled out of line.

"Jackson." He didn't react. Didn't even look up or acknowledge her presence. Resisting the urge to shout, Scarlett touched his shoulder instead, lightly. *"Jackson."*

He jumped almost a foot in the air. But finally he looked at her. Kind of. More like looked over her shoulder, as if he couldn't quite focus on her face. "Hi."

"Are you okay? I mean really okay?" Scarlett blurted.

Normally Jackson made her feel analyzed, picked apart, *understood* straight down to her core in a single glance. Right now, he barely registered her presence.

"Stop looking at her. Look at me," she commanded. She almost reached for her magic, but she stopped herself. Jackson was the one part of her life that she had wanted to be magic free.

He frowned. A hard crease appeared between his brows. The Jackson she remembered didn't frown this much, either. She was more accustomed to cocky grins and sarcastic taunts. "I'm fine," he said, in the same deadened voice she'd been hearing from him all week. "I just need to get drinks for me and Cait." As he spoke, he reached up to rub the back of his neck, making the chain he wore rotate back and forth.

"Right." Scarlett cleared her throat. Here went nothing. If she didn't at least *ask,* she'd never know. "About Cait . . ."

The first spark she'd seen in days appeared in Jackson's eyes. "She's wonderful."

"Okay. I mean, that's good. I'm happy for you, but I . . . When did you get together with her?" Her heart rate picked up, no matter how many times she tried to remind herself. *It doesn't matter. He was never mine to begin with.*

But if they'd been together the whole time she was texting with him over break, or before Scarlett was meant to go on a date with him . . .

"This weekend," Jackson said. "At Theta's pregame party."

Relief flooded through her. At least he hadn't been leading them both on all winter break. *Still.* "So . . . it's pretty new, between y'all?"

He nodded. "I suppose it's new. It feels like I've known her forever. She's wonderful."

Hurt opened up inside her chest like a chasm. "Listen, Jackson—"

"I have to go." He reached out for a couple of sodas and then paced away across the lawn.

Scarlett watched him go for a moment, heart sinking. *Let him go.* He was clearly just fine. Head over heels, in fact. Whatever she'd thought about the two of them, it wasn't meant to be.

At the very least, she'd assured herself he didn't have any idea what they went through last semester. That was a good thing. *You should be happy about this,* she scolded herself, as she rejoined the line at Xavier's side.

Xavier shifted in place. "How long ago did you break up with the cater waiter?"

"Don't call him that."

"So recently, then?"

"Not exactly. I thought we were something. But he didn't agree," Scarlett said, the words tasting bitter in her mouth.

"Then he's an idiot. You know . . . some guys can't see a great thing, even when it's right in front of their faces."

"Not you, though?" she fired back sarcastically.

Xavier smirked. "No. I have perfect vision."

"Does that seriously work on anyone?" she teased.

"It hasn't yet. But I'm an optimist."

Popcorn and drinks in hand, they were almost back to the Kappa blanket when she heard it. It was quiet at first, almost a whisper, at the edge of her perception. Scarlett assumed it was just one of the many couples they were weaving their way between, murmuring sweet nothings, especially since the movie was reaching its romantic conclusion.

Then it grew louder. Closer.

Beside her, Xavier stopped in his tracks, head canted to one side. "Do you hear —" he started to ask.

Someone screamed.

And not on the screen. Hitchcock had nothing on this one. This one was real. A high-pitched, panicked scream, the likes of which Scarlett had never heard before, not even in the midst of her fight with Tiffany. Every hair on the nape of her neck rose.

All around them, people sat upright, bewildered.

The shrieks continued, hysterical, growing in volume. And it was coming from the middle of the green. *Kappa*.

Forgetting all about Xavier, Scarlett broke into a run. She had to dodge other sorority and fraternity clusters, as everyone jumped up from their respective blankets and chairs. But finally, she spotted the commotion.

Bailey was writhing on the blanket. Reagan and Sonali were trying to grab her arms, but every time they did, Bailey would lash out. Scarlett watched Reagan flinch and pull back, a red line on her arm where Bailey had clawed her.

In the split second that she freed herself from Reagan, Bailey grabbed a chunk of her own hair and pulled as hard as she could. Even from several paces away, Scarlett heard it rip free.

A moment later, she reached Mei and Etta, who had their eyes half closed, murmuring something already.

"Hey, Bailey! It's me! I'm here. You have all your sisters here with you . . ." she yelled from a safe distance. Then she closed her eyes and talked to all the sisters at once in their heads.

Calming spell, Scarlett thought, projecting it to every Kappa present. *Now.*

And then she followed her own advice, dropping to her knees beside Bailey and holding out her hands. All the Kappas followed suit, kneeling around her.

Bailey looked bad. She'd scratched her own face and throat, and streaks of blood stained her white dress.

Somewhere in the distance, floodlights snapped on. Scarlett heard murmurs and shouts, a wail of an ambulance siren.

Beside her, she heard Mei mutter a distraction spell and felt a faint twinge of relief coupled with distress. She should have thought of that herself, the second she saw Bailey. Around them, people's gazes went unfocused, turned away. But the spell wouldn't last for long, and the bystanders had already seen too much.

Scarlett gripped her sisters' hands. "Two of Cups and . . ." *Crap, what was the second half?*

Her breathing hitched, panicked, her mind still spinning with fear. Bailey looked so vulnerable, curled in on herself, streaked in red. Scarlett couldn't stop thinking about Tiffany, the woods. The way she'd looked when the storm swallowed her whole.

The other Ravens watched her for a moment. Finally, Etta squeezed Scarlett's shoulder and took charge. "Two of Cups and Star of the Wheel . . ."

At last, Scarlett found her voice. "Let this child by your light be healed."

"Two of Cups and Star of the Wheel," everyone echoed. "Let this child by your light be healed."

The fight went out of Bailey's limbs. She sagged against the blanket, her eyes falling shut. But the bloody streaks remained on her face and throat, a huge chunk of her hair still missing.

Bailey was in trouble. And their magic wasn't reaching her. She was still. Why was she so still? She was still breathing, though.

"Two of Cups and Star of the Wheel, let this child by your light be healed." Scarlett's voice rose in frustration, as did her sisters'.

"It's not working," Reagan hissed.

Then Mei gasped. *Distraction's failing. Nothing is working. Why is nothing working?* As soon as Mei's voice whispered that in Scarlett's mind, she felt the scene shift again. People started to notice them once more. A few PiKa brothers had wandered over.

"Why are you guys just crowdng around her? Why aren't you helping her?" someone asked.

"Does she need help?" someone asked Mason, standing beside Vivi.

Maria's boyfriend, Tim, shouldered around him. "I'll get her," he said. "Ambulance is over by the parking lot." He knelt down and looked to Scarlett for permission.

Scarlett stared at him. Then at Bailey's limp, bloody form. She nodded.

Tim scooped Bailey up as if she weighed no more than the dress she wore. Vivi stepped away from Mason to Tim's side.

"I'll go with her," Scarlett's Little offered. "Make sure she gets to the hospital okay."

"Me too." Reagan leaped up.

Scarlett watched them cross the lawns toward the flashing red lights in the distance, her body numb. *What happened?* Minutes ago, Bailey had been fine. Enjoying the movie alongside her sisters. Hadn't she?

Was there a warning sign? Had Scarlett missed it because she'd been too busy trying to make Jackson jealous with Xavier?

She didn't even remember Xavier until Mei nudged her and nodded his direction. Only then did Scarlett turn to find him staring straight at her, a look of bewilderment on his face.

Shit. How much had he seen?

CHAPTER TWELVE

Vivi

"M ugwort?" Vivi called from behind one of the stacks at Cauldron and Candlesticks, the shop in downtown Savannah where the Ravens purchased most of their magical supplies.

Scarlett withdrew a hefty compendium from the shelf and fanned through it. "Pretty sure there's still a fresh bundle in the pantry. Did they restock the incense cones, though? We're running low on dragon's blood."

"I'll see what they have," Vivi said, then inhaled deeply, letting the heady mixture of dried herbs, pungent incense, and old books wash over her. The scent of magic cleared her head and slowed her pulse. It was the first time she'd felt truly relaxed ever since the disastrous party.

"I've been thinking about the mixer," Scarlett said slowly, as if reading her thoughts. "The way all the spells backfired at once . . . What do you think went wrong?"

Vivi stiffened, her relaxation short-lived. Was this a genuine question or some kind of test? "Reagan and the others think someone else interfered," Vivi said carefully. "They said they felt another type of magic when we were trying to repair the spells."

Scarlett nodded, then rose onto her toes to reach for a whorled blue agate on the top shelf. "And you?"

The guilt and dread that'd been festering in her stomach crept up her throat.

"I thought it was me."

"Why?"

"I was . . . distracted during the party." Scarlett raised an eyebrow and waited for Vivi to continue. Vivi knew the time for vague excuses had passed, so she took a deep breath and said quickly, "I think I met my brother."

"What?" Scarlett blinked rapidly, uncharacteristically startled. It took a lot to make Scarlett Winter lose her poise, but this revelation had done it. "What brother?"

Vivi relayed her strange conversation with Daphne and what Vivi had gleaned about Tim. Scarlett's shocked expression gave way to sympathy as she listened quietly. But there was another expression hiding just behind it, something that looked almost like pity.

"So you're talking about Maria's Tim?" Scarlett asked after Vivi finished.

Vivi nodded.

"Wow, I mean . . . I don't know what to say."

Vivi shifted uncomfortably, wishing she'd thought this through a bit more.

"Well, I'm here for you, if you need anything," Scarlett said slightly awkwardly, as though Vivi had lost, and not gained, a family member. Was having a long-lost brother something to be embarrassed about? Until this moment, Vivi hadn't realized that to someone like Scarlett—with her perfect pedigree—having a brother from another mother might be looked down upon.

"Thanks," Vivi said, ready to change the subject. "But right now I'm focused on the family I know. The Ravens. I promise."

Scarlett nodded. "So *do* you still think that it was a Kappa spell that failed at the party?"

Vivi shook her head. "I don't know. After what happened to Bailey on the lawns, I didn't *want* to believe it, but what if someone *is* out to hurt us? I can't go through another semester like the last one."

"I know." Scarlett let out a long, slow breath. She replaced the agate on the shelf. "But if someone is targeting Ravens, we need to put a stop to it."

"Something happened at the Thirsty Scholar too. There was a fight that broke right through our distraction charm and landed on our table. It came out of nowhere."

Scarlett hesitated. "It could be nothing. Alcohol *does* tend to fuel stuff like that."

"Sure, I know but . . ." Vivi paused, unwilling to share anything else that might be treated with pity. "I've been having these strange . . . visions. Like I'm still in the forest with Tiffany. One moment everything feels normal and then it shifts. It feels so real that I almost believe I'm back there with her."

"I'm sorry." Scarlett walked over and wrapped her arm around Vivi. "I get flashbacks like those too. It's awful."

"I think it might be more than that," Vivi said quietly, almost afraid to say the words aloud. "What if she's not really gone?"

Scarlett was already shaking her head. "I saw her. Her family collected her . . ." She couldn't bring herself to say *body*. "She's gone, Vivi. But if someone else got ideas from her . . ."

Vivi tensed, suddenly aware that Scarlett might've purposely brought Vivi here to have this conversation. Off campus. Far from prying eyes and ears. "You don't think it's another Raven, do you?"

Scarlett pressed her lips together for a moment before speaking. "I hope not. I trust my sisters. But I can't help thinking that I trusted Tiffany, too."

Vivi closed her eyes as a wave of nausea crashed over her. If there was another sister that was wicked, how would they ever be able to trust each other?

"Listen." Scarlett shook Vivi's shoulder lightly. "Let's not try to freak ourselves out. Not until we have something concrete. Agreed?"

Vivi opened her eyes. "Agreed."

After all, we need to focus on making the hundred and fiftieth celebration of Kappa a smashing success, don't we?"

Vivi smiled at her Big and nodded with more confidence than she felt. This event had to be perfect. It just had to.

Later that afternoon, Vivi leaned back against a tree, the grimoire balanced on her knees. It was dark enough in the forest that she could barely make out the writing anymore; the sun had begun to set, and whenever the wind shook the boughs, black, spidery shadows scuttled across the pages. Just a few days ago, she would've balked at the thought of going near the forest where Tiffany had lured her to remove her heart and steal her magic. Yet after her conversation with Scarlett, she'd needed a private place to think —and to practice her new spells—so she'd found herself drifting toward the woods behind Kappa House. Holding the grimoire, she felt powerful and safe for the first time in months. The book contained magic that seemed to leap straight from the page into Vivi's veins. It made spellwork feel so easy, so natural, that Vivi felt ready to face the demons lurking in the forest, whether real or imaginary.

And this was just the beginning. If she could master the glamours in the grimoire, Vivi could prepare the entire reunion party with one single spell and wouldn't need to rely on anyone's help but her own. This time, if anything went wrong, she'd have no one to blame but herself. If there was a rogue witch in their coven—Vivi shuddered—they wouldn't have anyone's magic to tamper with but her own.

She'd entered the forest in the late afternoon, and at first, everything had seemed fine. She could hear the road from the spot where she sat, the cars passing every so often a comforting hum, even if she couldn't see them through the thick underbrush.

But as dusk fell, part of her couldn't help but cast nervous glances as the shadows lengthened and twisted, reminding her of the birds Tiffany had summoned out of the smoke. Her heart began to race, and she brought her hand instinctively to her chest as she remembered the pressure building behind her breastbone, sharp and cracking.

Vivi forced herself to take a deep breath. Nothing could happen to her here. They'd defeated Tiffany and destroyed the Henosis talisman.

And Vivi would never, ever allow herself to be that weak or vulnerable again. For her own sake and for her sisters'. She was going to read the grimoire from cover to cover, absorb its secrets, and become the type of witch people admired—not one they worried about or pitied.

She tapped the flashlight setting on her phone, then got back to work.

She could have sworn that the spells came easier out here in the forest. But then again, Vivi was a Pentacles witch. Maybe that made a difference, being closer to the earth, to the trees bending overhead and the roots creeping through the rotten undergrowth below.

She shifted, stretched her arms over her head, then took a deep breath, inhaling the scent of the forest: the damp ground covered in rotting winter leaves and the piney spice of the trees above.

Then she removed a pin from her pocket and pressed the point against the sensitive skin just between her wrist bones, digging in until it made her gasp.

"Show me what I want to see." She barely even recognized her voice. It rasped in her throat, scraped at her lungs. She tipped her head up, watched through the tangle of her hair, as the woods *shifted*.

The trees moved first, arching their limbs up and away from Vivi like supplicants raising their arms in prayer.

Vivi rose slowly to her feet.

She could see the stars now, millions of them, far more than Savannah's lights normally allowed. The longer she stared, the more the sky seemed to lower toward her, like a curtain, fluttering within reach. She extended a hand, mimed grasping that curtain with her fingertips, and pulled.

The sky fell apart.

Or at least, it appeared to, collapsing like fabric onto the forest floor, blanketing the ground until she couldn't see the earth or the leaves anymore, only stars underfoot. Overhead, the sky itself had gone black, a nothingness that yawned over the treetops.

Around her the trees stood like strange sentinels, rising up out of the starry ground. Then something caught her eye. A flash of movement between the trees.

Someone was watching.

She felt a jolt of anger; she'd come out here for privacy, for space, so why the hell couldn't people just leave her alone? But the magic sizzling in her veins burned her resentment away, leaving her suddenly eager to test her new skills. So what if someone was spying on her? The energy building in her chest made Vivi certain she could perform whatever spell she needed to. She could wipe someone's memory. She could conjure an image so terrifying, the intruder would be too frightened to speak of it again.

Vivi flung both hands upward. In a blink, the real world returned: normal stars in a normal sky. Normal trees no longer melting into puddles of gold.

The figure in the distance had shrunk to a shadow. Vivi raced after it anyway, racking her mind for a spell to slow whoever it was down.

"I call to the Queen of Earth," Vivi panted as she ran. "Show me your power over death and rebirth." The ground trembled slightly underfoot, as roots unraveled to follow her command. They burst up through the forest floor, reaching for the spy, snatching at their heels.

It's working, she realized with pleasure as she watched the shadow ahead of her stumble to a halt. Vivi tried to speed up, eager to confront the intruder, but her legs felt suddenly heavy. A moment later, every inch of her body went cold, as if she'd just been plunged into an icy sea. The air around her turned sharp and biting, and her breath came in visible puffs. She'd never felt a chill like this, not even the winter she and her mother had spent in North Dakota.

She wrapped both arms around herself and tried to speak through chattering teeth. "I call to . . . the . . . Queen of Wands. Show me your might . . . give me light."

She waited for the familiar sizzle in her fingertips, but they remained cold and dull. She'd always struggled with Wands magic, but she should've been able to cast a simple warming spell. "Show me . . ." She was panting now, shivering so hard speaking was a struggle. "Your might . . ."

Then as quickly as it had arrived, the cold snap broke. Vivi gasped in relief, rubbing her arms hard, her fingertips and toes tingling as blood rushed back into them.

Up ahead, the figure had vanished.

"Damn it," she whispered, jerking her head from side to side before something caught her eye — something fluttering on a bush with a few broken branches, like someone had barreled through it recently.

A hair.

Vivi reached over and plucked it out. It was blond at the root, but an inch along, the strand shifted into a brilliant, neon pink.

Rose.

Oh, God. This was bad, this was really bad. A non-Kappa had seen her working magic—and not an easily explained away little spell, either. Big, impossible magic. She'd have to figure out another memory spell. But they'd already wiped Rose's memory of the party.

Vivi's phone buzzed, and she let out a startled yelp before tucking the strand of hair into her pocket and pulling out her phone. "Mason, what's up?" Her voice shook. She cursed herself. *Act normal, Vivi.*

Mason didn't seem to notice. *"What's up?* Where are you, Vivi? I've been waiting for almost an hour already." In the background, she could hear soft music playing, and the low hum of chatter.

She blinked a few times, and then she drew back to check the time on the phone: 7:47. *Shoot.* How had it gotten so late? She'd been planning to head back to Kappa House long before her date with Mason. "I was studying, and I completely lost track of time. I'm so sorry."

"Vivi." He sounded tense and irritated, a rare combination for him. "This is the first time we've seen each other in days. I've been looking forward to this, and now—"

"I know, and I'll be right there." She glanced down at herself and cringed at the mud streaking her jeans. "Just give me a few minutes to change."

There was a long pause on the other end. "Forget it, Vivi."

Her stomach sank. "Mason, I'll make it up to you, I promise. I've just been really stressed between school and Kappa—"

"I know, Vivi." He sighed. "Just, try to remember that other people's time matters too? You aren't the only one juggling a lot right now. And I miss you. We need to make time for each other."

"You're right. I'm sorry," she said again, with more feeling this time. But when she glanced at the screen again, he'd already hung up.

CHAPTER THIRTEEN

Scarlett

For the most part, Scarlett had left Dahlia's office unchanged. It was fairly common practice — most of the décor was accumulated from Kappa presidents past. Everything from the heavily stocked shelves to the enormous desk and the globe in the corner that secretly opened to reveal cut crystal glasses and a decanter.

But it did make Scarlett tense for a split second every time she walked in here. Memories always flooded through her. The long hours she spent on the side of the desk where Vivi perched now, taking mental notes on Dahlia's instructions.

Every now and then, it gave her vertigo to view this room from the other side. To think of it as *hers*.

This afternoon, though, Scarlett pushed the nostalgia aside. Something was very wrong, and she needed to think. Though she didn't mention it to Vivi in the magic shop, Scarlett was beginning to fear that someone *was* interfering with Kappa's magic. But who?

She'd visited Bailey in the hospital after the attack, with Vivi and a few of the younger girls. No matter how hard she tried, Bailey couldn't remember what had caused her fit — or even the rest of the night. She remembered waiting for the movie to start, sharing a popcorn with Ariana, winking at one of the boys sitting on the Theta blanket, and then . . . nothing. Until she woke up in the hospital covered in bandages.

Bailey was back at the house now, her wounds magically healed, her lost hair regrown. But for something like that to have happened to one of Scarlett's sisters, on her watch? It was unacceptable. Distressing even.

It's like Scarlett doesn't even know what she's doing, Reagan had said.

The words had rankled. Mostly because they were true.

She cleared the desk — scattered with her textbooks and laptop, the notes she'd been magically transcribing from paper to computer for a few of her classes. Time for a little scrying.

Scarlett set a crystal ball in the center of the desk and pulled the curtains. She sat down at the desk and inhaled slowly, held it for a heartbeat, and let it go just as slowly. The sound of her breaths filled the room, slowly crescendoing until it seemed the whole office breathed around her.

The air felt thick. Hot. Scarlett half expected to start seeing steam rise off the crystal.

She let her vision haze. Her focus slipped sideways, until the room took on a dreamlike quality. She felt as if she had one foot in the office, and the other in another realm. Somewhere far off and peaceful. Somewhere nobody could touch her . . .

That's when the whispers began. Soft at first, faint enough Scarlett mistook it for the sound of water in the pipes, or her sisters chatting several floors below.

Scarlett didn't blink, didn't take her gaze from the crystal ball.

And then she saw it, too. Faint at first, and growing clearer by the second. It looked like *hands,* dozens and dozens of them, pressing against the inside of the crystal ball, desperate, shoving. Trying to claw their way out.

The whispers grew louder. A hissing, right up against the nape of her neck.

Bang bang bang.

With a shout, Scarlett cursed, and the room snapped back to normal. The crystal was just a crystal. The whispers vanished.

Bang bang bang.

Scarlett resisted the urge to smile. It was just a knock at the door. "Who's there?"

Mei stood in the hallway, her hair an uncharacteristically messy tangle of auburn curls. "Emergency meeting," she panted, breathless. "Panhellenic . . . council. Gym."

Scarlett rose at once. The Panhellenic council governed all the sororities and fraternities on campus. Emergency meetings usually dealt with big issues, things the dean needed to supervise. The last one Scarlett attended was when a former fraternity was accused of spiking the punch at their parties. They'd been stripped of their letters and house. When she passed the living room, she saw Vivi slouched in an armchair in the corner.

"Vivi, come with us." As the social chair, she needed to attend too.

Scarlett followed Mei and Vivi out of the house and across Greek Row toward the gym. She stayed behind them a few paces, forehead knit. She had seen hands. A lot of them. Although she wasn't sure what it meant. She'd have to look it up later.

Her mind raced, and she quickened her pace to catch up with Mei and Vivi. Scarlett was anxious to figure out what this meeting could be about. Had something else happened? Another fight like the one in the Thirsty Scholar? Or maybe people were worried about Bailey . . . But why call a whole meeting to discuss what had happened to her?

Inside the gym, the council had been set up in the usual fashion: a half circle at the front for the presidents of each sorority and fraternity, then a few rows of folding chairs for the other officers. Dean Sanderson stood behind a podium in the center, overseeing.

Mei took her place in the front row, as alumni liaison, with Vivi at her side as the social chair. As usual, the Kappas were among the last to arrive, although today, Scarlett felt an uncharacteristic twinge of anxiety about that.

Every eye in the place followed their procession. Normally Scarlett was accustomed to this type of attention and welcomed it. Lately, though, Kappa seemed to be attracting all the wrong kinds of stares.

Scarlett coasted into her seat near the center of the table.

Maria, seated to Scarlett's left, looked suddenly serious. "About time you joined us," Maria told Scarlett sotto voce.

Scarlett eyed the enormous clock over the auditorium door. Without her needing to ask, she noticed Mei twist her hands in a complicated motion, and the minute hand on the clock ticked back two paces. "Last I checked, I'm right on time," Scarlett replied once Mei had finished.

Maria wrinkled her nose.

Scarlett glanced at Vivi, remembering what she'd told her about Tim. Scarlett whispered in Vivi's head, *I don't know what your maybe brother sees in this witch*.

Vivi pursed her lips, stifling a laugh. Scarlett returned her attention to the dean.

"Yes, well." Dean Sanderson cleared his throat. "Let's get straight to business. I think we all know why this meeting was necessary."

Scarlett folded her hands primly in her lap and took in the auditorium.

Everyone was still watching her. Only her. Her heart picked up pace, rising toward her throat.

"As we all know, last weekend, the police were forced to visit our campus in response to a drunk and disorderly complaint at one of our houses."

Drunk? Scarlett's shoulders tightened. Surely he couldn't mean . . .

"I have seen the police report myself," Dean Sanderson continued, "and it is unacceptable behavior, especially from a sorority that we have always venerated at this school."

Oh, God. Scarlett peeked at Maria, who sat ramrod straight beside her, a faint smug smile curling the edges of her lips. *Did our memory spells backfire?*

Scarlett had watched Jess enchant the two officers who stopped by. Jess had told them word for word what to write in their warning. There had been nothing about alcohol, just a noise complaint, and barely one, at that.

"In addition, we have received complaints from several other members of this council who were in attendance that evening, about the complete disregard for safety at this particular . . . *event.*" Dean Sanderson's lip curled with disdain.

"But—" Scarlett blurted before she could stop herself. She clamped her lips together, hard. *But no one should remember,* she'd been about to say.

The dean stopped speaking, and turned a cool, assessing look on her. "Ms. Winter, please wait until your turn to speak."

Her pulse beat so fast Scarlett saw spots at the edges of her vision. *This can't be happening.* Kappa never got into trouble. Especially not trouble of this magnitude.

What is my mother going to say? Her head swam, helpfully conjuring up a mental image of a furious Marjorie, a taunting Eugenie.

The dean kept talking, reading out a list of their sins, but all Scarlett could hear was the white noise in her ears. Finally, he gestured her way. "Ms. Winter, if you have anything to say in defense of Kappa Rho Nu, in the face of these allegations, now is the time to speak."

"I . . ." Her throat tightened. Threatened to close.

You can do this, Vivi's voice suddenly sounded in her ear. Scarlett glanced down at the front row, where her Little flashed her a thumbs-up. Beside Vivi, Mei nodded, eyes wide.

Scarlett drew in a deep breath and squared her shoulders. "We did host a mixer at Kappa Rho Nu House last Friday evening. We also received a noise complaint from the police, which two officers delivered in person, and for which I am deeply sorry. But this was Kappa's first ever offense of this magnitude, and as far as I was aware, the noise was the only issue. This is the first I am learning of any alcohol complaints or additional safety concerns. I will of course do everything in my power to address any such problems in the future—"

"Assuming you *have* a future," Maria murmured.

Scarlett resisted the urge to scowl. "But I can hardly address concerns of which I was not made aware, Dean."

Dean Sanderson glowered at her. Scarlett raised her chin and stared right back. She'd spent enough of her life being intimidated by Marjorie Winter. This man didn't frighten her. She'd been off her game when she first came in here, thrown by the allegations.

But Scarlett was a Raven, damn it. She could turn this around.

Still holding the dean's gaze, she focused on the spell. An influence spell, one that, strictly speaking, she shouldn't abuse. But a tiny nudge in the right direction couldn't hurt . . .

I call upon Justice and Temperance, she thought. *Let this judge view us with deference.*

Dean Sanderson broke her gaze and shuffled a stack of papers on his podium. He was quiet for a long, long moment, during which Scarlett held her breath. It seemed as if the whole room held with her, everyone poised on the edge of their seat to find out what would happen.

Everyone except Maria, who lounged beside Scarlett, relaxed and smug. In the audience, the few Thetas she'd brought along with her — Cait, a girl named Deylin, and that pink-haired fresh-man, Rose, was it? — all appeared equally excited. Kids on Christmas morning, about to open a gift.

They know something, Scarlett realized.

Finally, the dean huffed into his microphone. "I am afraid we are going to have to put Kappa on notice," he said.

Scarlett's heart sank all the way down into her stomach. *"What?"* she yelled, at the same time Maria blurted out, "Excuse me?"

Scarlett looked at her, startled, and Maria flushed. Then the other president balled her fists. "Notice is hardly sufficient." Sororities or fraternities on notice could still operate as usual, pending any further injunctions. "They should be suspended," Maria said. "They put people in danger."

"This is our first offense," Scarlett argued, standing up. "And what *danger* are you talking about?"

"You know *exactly* what I mean," Maria retorted, her jaw set hard.

How much does she remember? Scarlett's pulse quickened.

The dean cleared his throat. "Ladies. This is not proper council behavior from either of you. Ms. Winter, you especially should be careful just now."

Scarlett sat back in her chair and resisted the urge to cross her arms in a huff. In the front row, Mei and Vivi watched her with concern.

It'll be okay, Mei said.

But Scarlett couldn't help but think that it wouldn't be okay.

Kappa was falling apart. And it was her fault. Tears pricked at the corners of her eyes.

"Kappa Rho Nu will remain on notice for a period of one month, pending any further complaints or injunctions."

"But—"

Dean Sanderson held up a hand to stave off Scarlett's protest. "In the event that your house manages to behave itself for this time span, the notice will be removed, and you are free to resume your usual operations. But I warn you, any more behavior like this will *not* be tolerated at Westerly. By any of you," the dean added belatedly, glancing around at the remainder of the presidents arrayed across the stage.

Andrew Haight, president of PiKa, caught Scarlett's attention and mouthed, *Sorry*.

Scarlett wondered if he'd known this was coming, too, and failed to warn her. *Screw them all*.

Next to her, Maria stuck a hand in the air. Scarlett ground her molars to avoid commenting. The dean actually rolled his eyes. "Yes, Ms. Grimaldi?"

"What about the Spring Fling?" Maria folded her hands in her lap. "It's the biggest Greek event of the semester, and as I understand, it is traditionally hosted by the sorority house in the best standing with the Panhellenic council. If Kappa Rho Nu is starting the semester out on notice . . ."

"Ms. Grimaldi, the Spring Fling is not until April. Doesn't it seem a bit early for—"

"With all due respect, Dean, planning typically begins by the start of the semester. For an event that large, of course. If one wants to throw it . . . *safely*." Maria side-eyed Scarlett, who clenched her jaw so hard she could hear it crack.

Dean Sanderson sighed. "Fine. For the moment, Theta Omega Xi may begin plans for the Fling—"

"Are you *kidding* me?" Scarlett blurted.

"*And* when we draw nearer to the date, we will review the respective houses' behavior records at that time."

"So we're supposed to start planning a party that someone else might eventually get credit for?" Maria clenched her fists, clearly not pleased either.

"That depends, Ms. Grimaldi." Dean Sanderson eyed her over the rim of his glasses. "Do you intend on Theta incurring any behavior injunctions this semester?"

Maria's already red cheeks darkened. "Of course not, but—"

"Good." The dean slapped one palm on the podium, miming a gavel. "It's settled, then. Unless anyone has any additional business to discuss . . ."

The rest of his words vanished again, drowned out by the roaring in Scarlett's ears, the stark and painful realization. Maybe she'd been grasping at straws earlier with Vivi. Maybe there was nothing wrong with the magic at all, nobody else out there to blame.

Maybe it was her.

I am officially the worst president in Kappa history.

CHAPTER FOURTEEN

Vivi

Vivi sighed as she sat on the stone steps of Westerly's alumni center, burrowing deeper into the camelhair coat Scarlett had given her for Christmas. When she'd balked at the extravagance—even to Vivi's highly untrained eye, it was clear that the silk-lined, fawn-colored coat was incredibly expensive—Scarlett had rolled her eyes and claimed that the gift was more for herself than for Vivi, as she wouldn't have to look at Vivi's "depressing" parka anymore. First semester, a comment like that would've stung, but Vivi was now sufficiently fluent in Scarlettspeak to know what it really meant: *I want to do something nice for you without it being weird.*

Today was the first truly cold day Savannah had had all winter, and the crisp air felt energizing compared to the glumness of Kappa House in the wake of being put on probation.

Vivi clutched the hot cider in her hand more tightly, relishing the warmth spreading through her skin, almost like the sensation of magic. At the last minute, she'd added a vanilla latte to her order. She had no idea what Tim liked to drink, but based on his reaction to the dessert table at the Kappas' party, it was clear he had a sweet tooth.

She and Tim had agreed to meet at the alumni center to explore the Westerly Hall of Fame and see what they could learn about Vince together. She thought it could be a nice way to bond with her sibling. Still, the whole thing felt a little awkward.

Vivi took a sip of her cider and tried to steady her nerves. She was surprised by how badly she wanted this to work out. She hadn't even known of Tim's existence until a week ago, but the fact that she had a brother had turned her world upside down. For her entire life, Daphne had been Vivi's family—her *only* family. But now the universe had brought her this gift—a half brother—and she didn't want it to slip away.

Her phone buzzed in her pocket. It was a text from Mason:

What are you up to? Still on for coffee later?

She stared at it for a moment, then slid the phone back into her pocket, feeling a prickle of guilt. She hadn't told Mason about Tim yet, and she felt weird keeping such a big secret from him. But every time she tried to bring it up, words failed her. The situation sounded so ludicrous, even to her. But she'd called her mom a few nights ago and confirmed: Daphne had a fling with Vince in one of the many cities she was passing through after college.

"Hey," Tim said, slightly breathless, as he jogged up to the steps. "Damn, it's cold today." He bounced in place and rubbed his hands together.

"Maybe you shouldn't have worn shorts?" Vivi said with a smile as she handed him the latte. "Here, this one's for you."

"Wow, that's really nice of you," he said, sounding surprised.

Good surprised, Vivi thought. He took a big gulp, then held the cup up to examine it. "What *is* this?"

"A vanilla latte. Sorry if I got it—"

He took another long sip. "It's amazing!"

"Okay, you can knock it off," Vivi said, convinced he was making fun of her. She supposed in the world of college sports, where star players like Tim were regularly given extravagant gifts, a latte would seem like a silly offering.

"No, I'm serious. I've never had one of these before."

"You've never had a *latte?*"

Tim smiled sheepishly. "I guess I always thought it was, like, kinda a girly drink."

Vivi shot him a look. "Really?"

"I know, it's ridiculous. But you're in a sorority, you know what it's like to feel you have to project a certain image."

"Kappa's not really like that, actually. No one's going to write me up for wearing the wrong shade of white after Labor Day." She flushed, remembering that Tim was dating the president of the sorority she was making fun of. "Sorry, I know Maria's trying to change all that."

"It's fine," Tim said. "I know what kind of reputation Theta used to have, but Maria's trying to make it better." He looked up at the alumni center, an elegant brick building with white shutters and ivy growing up the side. "So you think this place has information about Vince?"

"I think so. Pretty much everything I found on Google was related to college football. Do you know much about him?"

Tim snorted. "Nope. He was even better at vanishing than he was at football. He walked out on my mom before I was born. I never even met the guy. Last I heard, he was somewhere in Canada. Honestly, it was a little weird showing up at Westerly and hearing people talk about my dad like he was some kind of god. I know he was a football legend and everything, but to me, he was just the bastard who left us."

"Yeah, that makes sense," Vivi said, feeling suddenly awkward. "So why'd you agree to meet me here?"

Tim shrugged. "I don't know . . . It seemed important to you."

"That's really nice of you." Vivi exhaled. "So, do you still want to go inside?"

"Let's do it."

As they headed up the stairs, the door opened and a girl came hurrying out. From her blazer and gold name tag, Vivi guessed she was a student employee at the alumni center. When she saw Tim, she came to an abrupt stop and gasped, eyes widening. "Oh my God, hi!" she said, then shook her head. "Sorry, that was weird. I always forget that you're, like, a real person on campus. You were amazing last weekend, by the way."

"Thanks . . . Amanda," Tim said with a warm smile as he peered at her name tag. "I appreciate the support. We couldn't do it without the fans."

As Amanda walked off, beaming, Vivi turned to Tim. "What were you saying about Vince being 'treated like some kind of god'?" she asked wryly.

The inside of the alumni center looked more like the lobby of a boutique hotel than a college administrative building. Elegant upholstered chairs and leather couches were arranged around glass coffee tables sporting vases of flowers and stacks of upscale magazines. There were dishes of fruit and candy scattered throughout, and Tim wasted no time helping himself to a handful of pillow mints.

"Hi, there," a cheerful blond woman called from behind a large mahogany desk. "Can I help y'all with anything?" Tim flushed and shoved his hand into his pocket to hide the mints.

"Yes," Vivi said. "We're looking for the Alumni Hall of Fame. It's in this building, right?"

"Just down that hall. I'll show you."

"Thank you," Vivi said, motioning for Tim to join them. Once the woman's back was turned, he took one more handful of mints, then jogged to catch up with them.

"Are y'all undergrads?" the woman asked pleasantly. When they nodded, she continued, "That's wonderful. We wish more of you would come visit us here." She led them down a hallway lined with rosebud wallpaper and into a long gallery-type room full of glass display cases. Portraits of Westerly alumni lined the walls, the oldest of which wore top hats and frock coats. "Are you looking for information on anyone in particular?"

"Yes, um, Vince Lee?" Vivi said.

The blond woman's face lit up, and her eyes flickered to Tim. "Absolutely. I'll show you our athletics section." She led Vivi and Tim to the far side of the room, where an enormous display case filled an entire wall. There were trophies, black-and-white photos of men in old-fashioned leather football helmets and cheerleaders in long pleated skirts, old pennants, and lots of signed bats and balls. "There he is," she said, beaming at a glossy photo of a handsome, square-jawed young man. His short dark hair was slicked with sweat, but his expression was triumphant as he hoisted a large trophy into the air. "That's from the end of his junior year, when he led Westerly in their first of two undefeated seasons."

Vivi thanked the woman and waited until she'd left.

"You really look like him," Vivi said, nodding at the photograph. Tim shrugged and then looked away. His eyes widened as something just behind Vivi caught his attention. "Whoa, look at that."

Vivi followed Tim over to a huge glass case full of mannequins in all sorts of outfits: tuxedos, ball gowns, judges' robes, military uniforms, and others. "This is incredibly weird," Vivi said, leaning in to inspect a mannequin in what appeared to be a figure-skating dress. "But kind of delightful."

"'What they wore,'" Tim read from a plaque on the wall. "'This collection celebrates the accomplishments of Westerly's most esteemed alumni through the ensembles they wore during their finest moments, whether accepting an Academy Award, a Nobel Prize, or a Purple Heart.'"

"Cool! So which future outfit of yours do you want here someday?" Vivi asked, wondering which of Mei's fabulous ensembles would end up here. Her makeup tutorials on YouTube regularly got half a million views, and there was no question she'd make her mark on the fashion or cosmetic world soon. Or perhaps both.

"Should they save room for a mannequin holding the Stanley Cup?"

"Not unless I suddenly get really, really good at hockey."

Vivi let her head fall into her palm. "Right. I knew that. So, what would be in the display case?"

"I don't know . . . I guess probably my jersey," he said flatly.

"You don't sound too excited about that prospect."

"No, I mean, it'd be an honor and everything. I'm just getting a little tired of the whole football star thing. But, whatever, it's fine. I think everyone knows what it's like to be scrutinized or pigeonholed all the time. It's just the way the world works these days."

"Sure." Vivi started to nod automatically, then paused. "Actually, no, not really. I moved around a lot growing up and started a new school every year. Sometimes more than that. So I'm more used to feeling invisible, I guess."

"Wow. That sounds pretty tough. Did you . . ." He frowned and shifted his weight from side to side before continuing. "Did you ever blame Vince for any of it? Like, did you think anything would've been different if he'd been in your life?"

Something in his voice tugged at Vivi's heartstrings, and for a moment, the football star in front of her disappeared, replaced by a little boy longing for a father who never came home.

"Not exactly," Vivi said gently. "It was different for me. My mom refused to tell me anything about my father. I didn't even know his *name* until a few weeks ago."

"I'm almost jealous," Tim said bitterly, then shook his head, "Sorry, I know I sound pathetic."

"What? Hardly." Vivi hesitated, then reached out to give him an awkward pat on the shoulder. "You got a raw deal. It's normal to feel angry."

"Thanks. It feels good just to talk about it. Whenever I bring it up with Maria, she always tries to bring out her healing crystals or whatever to 'chase away the bad vibes.'"

"I guess she's just trying to be helpful . . . in her way."

Tim smirked. "Listen, you shouldn't let Scarlett turn you against Maria. She's really nice once you get to know her."

"Sorry, you're right," she said, blushing. Maria was Tim's girl-friend, and Vivi needed to get along with her if she was going to have any chance of making Tim a part of her life. "She seems to be doing a great job as president."

"Yeah, I'm happy she got the position. She's always kind of felt like number two, you know? She hasn't had many opportunities to shine until now. I think this is going to be good for her."

"Trust me, I get it. Except that I always felt like number, I don't know . . . seven," Vivi said with a laugh. "Maybe the three of us can hang out next time?"

"Definitely." Tim pulled out his phone and frowned. "I need to get to class. Which direction are you heading in?"

"Barbiea Hall. I need to pick up a study packet at the copy center."

"Cool, my class is right next door. Want to walk over together?"

"Sure," Vivi said. They made their way back to the reception area, where Tim grabbed one more handful of candy before heading outside. As they walked, Tim kept surging ahead, clearly eager to limit his time in the cold, but whenever he realized he'd left Vivi behind, he'd turn around and wait for her.

"Sorry," he said sheepishly. "I always walk too fast."

"No worries," she said, just as her phone buzzed. *I'm in line at the café. What do you want?*

Vivi's stomach sank. The café was right next to Barbiea Hall, which meant that Mason might spot her with Tim, which would raise many more questions than she was ready to answer right now.

"Sorry," Vivi said to Tim. "I forgot a book I need at home, so I actually need to head in the other direction."

"No worries," Tim said. "Talk to you soon?"

"Absolutely," Vivi said with a smile.

He broke into a jog, then spun around and called, "Thanks for the coffee!"

"Anytime!" Vivi shouted back, then flinched when she saw a missed call from Mason.

I'm so sorry, she texted quickly. *Scarlett needs my help with something at home. Can we meet up later?*

It was nearly five minutes before Mason's response came through. *What's going on, Vivi? Why are you avoiding me?*

Her stomach twisted. She knew it'd be simpler to tell Mason about Tim, but she was already at a disadvantage, following in Scarlett's perfectly pedigreed footsteps. Mason's family was more like Scarlett's than her own. Even though Mason was kind and open-minded, would he ever want to introduce his parents to a girl with a deadbeat father who had a bunch of kids with different women? Vivi still remembered the look that Scarlett gave her in the magic shop — *pity* — and she feared that Mason would have the same reaction.

I'm not! she texted back. *I swear, things are just really hectic right now. I'll call you later.*

She held her phone for the entire walk back to Kappa House, waiting for Mason to respond, but her phone remained still and silent.

CHAPTER FIFTEEN

Scarlett

The Thirsty Scholar hummed with life. Yet when Scarlett shouldered through the entrance, she could hear conversations stutter as people gaped at her or broke off to whisper. She didn't need magic to guess what they were saying. They were all gossiping about the fall of Kappa.

She marched to the stool in the far corner, head held high.

So word had gotten around about Kappa's notice and losing Spring Fling. At least they wouldn't have to break the news to anyone.

She slid onto the barstool, shoulders tense, spine stiff. She refused to give anyone any more to gossip about. She'd come here for a drink. She wouldn't leave until she'd had it, no matter how uncomfortable she might feel.

She needed the breather from Kappa House. The stares of random Westerly students in here didn't bother her nearly as much as her sisters' side-eyes and murmurs. With the big alumnae reunion coming up in just a few days, they were all at their breaking points. The sorority would still be on notice during the reunion, which was awkward and embarrassing, and could even affect the futures of the current students. How could the girls impress the powerful, influential alums when, at the moment, their biggest claim to fame was putting Kappa in severe jeopardy?

It was a particular blow to the seniors. Mei, who'd spent weeks preparing her portfolio to show a legendary costume designer, had gone sullen and quiet. Jess's frustration was even more palpable, since she'd already received a sternly worded email from the Pulitzer Prize–winning journalist she'd been hoping to intern for that summer. Scarlett felt like this was all her fault. Kappa was crumbling around her.

Vivi kept insisting she had the reunion plans under control, that she didn't need Scarlett's help. But all Scarlett could think about was the welcome-back mixer. If things got out of control again . . .

She lifted a hand from the bar top and waved, at the same time employing a subtle Swords spell.

The bartender glanced her way, nodded, then went back to a conversation he was having with another girl. Scarlett couldn't be sure, but she thought she recognized her as one of Maria's younger Thetas.

Great. So even off campus, Thetas beat out Kappas.

She slumped in her seat, posture forgotten. Naturally, Xavier chose that exact moment to appear at her elbow. "Rough week?"

"You don't know the half of it," she muttered.

He raised a hand. The bartender peeled away from the Theta to head over. Scarlett was too tired to feel insulted. "How is that girl doing? Bailey, was it?" Xavier asked, after ordering them both the house special, some sort of whiskey drink Scarlett would usually avoid.

Tonight, it seemed fitting.

Scarlett sighed. "She's feeling a lot better, thankfully."

"Do the doctors know what went wrong?" Xavier slid her drink over, his hand brushing against hers.

She ignored the tingle that raced up her arm. "They said it was stress-induced. Which, with everything that happened at Kappa last semester, I could understand." But would *stress* really make a girl hurt herself like that?

Scarlett took a sip of whiskey. Then a longer drink, because the burn in her chest helped. "I just can't help feeling like I'm the worst president Kappa's ever had."

"There are worse legacies to have." Xavier raised his glass to tap hers, before he took a healthy swig as well.

She snorted under her breath. "Such as?"

He grinned. "Such as never being president at all."

Scarlett grimaced. "Six months ago, I would have agreed with you. Now . . . I'm not so sure." She watched the ice melt in her glass for a moment. "Everything used to be so simple. I knew what I wanted, and what I needed to do to get it."

"You're too young to be having a quarter-life crisis." Xavier nudged her. "Besides, something tells me you still know what you want."

Jackson. She pushed the thought from her mind. He'd made his choice. Besides, Scarlett wasn't one to lose her head over a guy. She had more important priorities. At least, that was what she told herself.

"I wanted to be president so that I could continue my family's legacy," she said. A rueful smile touched her lips. "Or, honestly, so I could improve on it. I wanted to be the best president in Kappa history, to make a name for myself, instead of always living in my family's shadow. Why am I the screwup, the only one who can't hack it?"

"Well . . ." Xavier swirled his own drink for a moment. "It's kind of hard to stand out from the crowd if you do the same thing they all do."

She glanced at him.

He shrugged. "What? I told you before, you aren't the only one with family issues."

It reminded her that the last time they'd talked, she'd not only been using him to try to make another guy jealous, but she'd also abandoned him in the middle of their conversation.

"Hey, sorry about . . . er, running off, the other night."

Xavier waved. "Already forgotten. I'm just glad your friend was okay."

"Me too." Scarlett let out a bitter laugh. "Is it just me, or has everything seemed upside down this semester?"

"You mean your campus isn't always a living soap opera?" Xavier peered over his shoulder pointedly, and the couple next to them at the bar quickly looked away, pretending they hadn't been eavesdropping.

"You mean your overachiever parents didn't study the social situation here in depth before they made you transfer?" Scarlett fired back.

"Shockingly, they do not appear to care about my extracurricular life whatsoever." Xavier winked. Then he shifted, leaned his elbows on the bar top. "Can I ask you something?"

"Shoot."

"Would you have wanted to be president of Kappa, if your mother and your sister hadn't done it before you?"

She frowned. She didn't remember telling him exactly which members of her family had been presidents. *Stop being so paranoid.* After all, it was common knowledge. If he was a PiKa, he could have learned it from any of his brothers. She let out a slow breath. "I . . . don't know how to answer that."

The longer Xavier held her gaze, the quicker her heart fluttered against her rib cage. He wasn't Jackson, but he was handsome in a different way. And he clearly had a similar family to hers, understood her dilemma right now. The pressure on her shoulders.

"Do you ever imagine what it would be like not to be a legacy, not to be a Kappa? To just be a regular girl, just living her life, no pressure . . . Just you, being you?" he asked.

"Never. Who wants to be regular?" she replied automatically with a chuckle.

He smiled, looking a bit surprised either by her response or Scarlett herself. "I don't think you could ever be regular, Scarlett Winter."

"What about you?" she said. "You don't seem the frat type. Why did you join?"

He caught a glimpse of her expression, and he raised his

eyebrows. "Believe it or not, it isn't easy to change schools." He shrugged. "But I wouldn't break my back to be their president. Too much responsibility."

"Ahh, I see. You're one of those do-the-bare-minimum-to-get-by types, then?"

He leveled her with a direct stare. "Oh, not at all. I just have other priorities."

Her face tingled. The sensation spread along her neck, trickled down her spine as he continued to stare. She knew she ought to look away, break his gaze . . .

But he was easy to talk to. And charming enough, with his thick Southern accent. With the whiskey flooding her body, Scarlett couldn't deny, he was tempting. And definitely into her.

Xavier reached over to let his fingertips brush along the back of her wrist, and sparks danced in his wake. Her heart beat so fast she wondered if he could see it pulsing in the hollow of her throat.

Before she could say anything, before she could reach out to return the touch, he turned back to the bar and scooped his drink up again. "My studies, for example, are a big priority."

She laughed. The corner of his mouth twitched, but he only raised an eyebrow and took a sip of his drink. "What are you studying?"

"Economics," he replied, and Scarlett couldn't help her instinctive groan. "What? It's a lucrative industry."

"So *that's* your motive. Money."

Xavier wagged a finger at her, like a scold. "Don't be so hasty to judge, Ms. Winter. You've barely begun to scratch the surface of my motives."

But I could. The thought rose, unbidden, in that moment, powered by the whiskey already trickling through her veins. One touch, a few words, and she could know *exactly* what his motivations were. What drove him.

What intentions he had with her.

He might seem flirty, but she needed to know. She couldn't let herself get caught up in another Jackson mess again. Her heart couldn't handle it. Not after last semester.

Just a little peek, she told herself. A quick glimpse into Xavier's mind. Normally Scarlett refused to use magic like this, especially on a boy. On principle, Scarlett Winter did not need magical assistance to win over men.

This is different. This was more like . . . self-defense.

With one more sip of whiskey for courage, Scarlett reached up, before she lost her nerve. She brushed a fingertip along his temple, lightly, just once.

Just enough contact to let her slip into his thoughts . . .

Queen of Swords and words; show that for which he yearns, she recited in her mind. Focused hard.

Yet all she found was a blank wall. Nothing. Not even a stray thread of emotion—amusement, annoyance, anything. She blinked and let her hand fall back to her side with a frown. Swords magic had never been her specialty, but she was normally good at reading people's emotional states, at the very least.

She caught Xavier eyeing her strangely and forced a smile. "You had a bit of fuzz."

He smirked, a little too knowing. "Thanks, then."

"Anytime." Her head swam. She'd had too much to drink.

What the hell am I doing? Spying on a guy's thoughts, feeling insecure. All because one boy rejected her? *For a Theta,* she couldn't help adding, salt in the wound.

Scarlett pushed her drink back across the bar top. Cute as Xavier might be, she shouldn't be doing this. She already felt tipsy enough for the room to waver at its edges, and the last thing she wanted to do was give all the staring people in this pub the satisfaction of seeing Scarlett Winter off her game. "I should get going."

"Let me guess: Kappa business?"

"No rest for the ambitious," she replied, scooping up her purse.

"I thought it was the wicked."

"None for them either." She winked, then strode toward the doors. She didn't need to look back to know he'd be watching her go. Everyone in the bar was, after all. Scarlett raised her chin; a queen never disappoints her subjects.

Never let them see you sweat. That was what Minnie would have advised. Her mother, too. One of the few areas where those two were in agreement.

She did, however, allow herself one small amusement when she reached the exit. "I call to the Queen of Wands and the Ace of Cups," she murmured while she pushed open the door. "Show me your powers are true by ruining those brews."

Before the door even finished swinging shut behind her, she

could hear a few frat guys groaning in complaint, spitting out their beers. "Gross, this tastes like piss," one called.

Then she reached the main lawn and took a deep breath of fresh air. For a moment, she felt just the tiniest bit better.

~

The path Scarlett normally took to Kappa House from campus looked darker than usual. She blamed that on the new moon tonight, combined with the thick clouds overhead. They blocked out any remaining starlight, and the campus's few lampposts did little to illuminate the spaces between.

Still, Scarlett usually liked nights like these: heavy with the potential for a storm. She felt closer to her own emotions anytime the sky hung with unshed rain.

Tonight, though, she kept pausing in her tracks. She kept hearing a noise in the distance. A faint, susurrous hiss, as if something were dragging along the pavement. She stopped, and the noise stopped, too.

Every few paces, she checked over her shoulder, a chill passing along her spine. But no matter how often she looked, the path remained empty. Deserted, actually, which was strange for this time on a Thursday night, when the other students should have been filing back to Greek Row.

She started to walk again, and the noise started back up.

This time, Scarlett didn't turn around. She dug in her purse for a compact mirror and used it to pretend to check her makeup, flashing it over her shoulder all the while.

Nothing.

With a deep breath, she began to move again, quicker this time, her legs flashing, heels clicking on the hard ground.

Another noise. Not the hissing, whispering sound, but harder, more concrete. Footsteps, behind her.

Just another Greek student, she told herself. After all, she'd just been wondering where everybody was.

Trying her best to ignore her spiking adrenaline, she picked up her pace. At the same time, she said softly, "I call upon the Queen of Cups."

High above, thunder rumbled.

It didn't start to rain. Not yet. But she could feel the closeness of the storm, its readiness to unleash at a word from her. If something —or some*one*—really was out there in the dark, trailing her, Scarlett would be ready.

She'd almost made it to the next streetlight when the thunder rumbled again. It was loud. But not quite loud enough to drown out the other sound.

The footsteps were getting closer.

Scarlett scanned the woods to either side, the pavement ahead. Nobody in front of her. She was under the streetlight now, its orange glow granting her courage. With one last steadying breath, Scarlett whirled around, fists balled, ready to defend herself.

Only to watch Xavier raise his palms in surrender, about ten feet behind her. "Whoa, don't shoot."

"Are you *following me?*" She crossed her arms, glaring.

He wore the same infuriating little half smirk as always. "Not everything revolves around you, you know, Scarlett." Then he pointed past her. "PiKa House is about five doors down from Kappa, remember?"

She scowled. "You could have said something instead of creeping up on me."

"I was about to. Not my fault you've got supersonic hearing."

She huffed out an annoyed breath.

"And," he added, looking a little sheepish, "part of me wanted to make sure you got home okay. You seemed a little put out at the bar."

"Well, word to the wise. The way to put a girl at ease is *not* to creep up behind her on a dark path." Still, she fell into step beside him. "And I can defend myself, before you get the idea you need to play gallant knight."

He eyed her fists, still clenched. With effort, she smoothed her palms against her skirt.

"I can see that. My apologies."

Much as she hated to admit it, she *did* feel safer with him beside her. If for no other reason than that it made her stop focusing on every tiny noise in the surrounding woods. Listening for the snap of a twig or the scrape of a foot on muddy ground.

They reached the main road, and Xavier actually dipped into a bow. "My lady. Your gallant knight has delivered you safely."

She snorted and rolled her eyes. But she was smiling, too. "Have a good night, Xavier."

"You, too, Scar." He searched her face for a moment, as if about to say something else. In the end, he only waved and jogged off into the light mist that had begun to fall. Scarlett watched him go, rain hovering around her shoulders, not quite touching her hair or her clothes. Cups witch, after all.

She had to admit . . . it was getting harder to keep her distance from that boy.

CHAPTER SIXTEEN

Vivi

By the time Vivi met up with Mason on Friday evening, the cold spell had broken and the evening air felt almost balmy. They'd arranged to meet by the river, at one of the benches overlooking the docks. She walked past bars and restaurants festooned with fairy lights that reflected off the dark water, giving the scene an otherworldly quality that would've normally seemed dreamy and romantic. But she and Mason had barely spoken since their tense text exchange two days ago, and Vivi was too on edge to appreciate the ambience. She had to make things right before they spiraled out of control.

When she spotted him sitting on a bench, she forced herself to smile warmly despite her nerves. "Hey!" she called. She felt an urge to break into a run and throw herself into his arms, but decided that might ruin the effect of her sophisticated outfit. She'd gone out of her way to dress for the date, borrowing a miniskirt from Sonali and a pair of heels from Reagan again. She'd tested out her new glamouring ability too, giving her eyes a smoky shadow and contour to her cheeks.

She could tell by Mason's quick double take that her efforts had paid off. But instead of standing to kiss her, or telling her how great she looked, he simply nodded and said, "Thanks for showing up this time."

Vivi winced. She knew she hadn't been the best girlfriend over the last few days. Weeks, maybe, if she was being honest. She had so many secrets, so many parts of her life Mason could never understand. She and Tim had been texting a bit since their visit to the alumni center—they'd even ended up swapping baby photos that looked remarkably alike, and Tim had already broached the idea of having Vivi and Daphne over for Thanksgiving. Vivi couldn't imagine her mother accepting the invitation, given how hard she'd tried to erase Vince from her past. Still, Vivi couldn't help fantasizing about having a real Thanksgiving for once—a cheerful dinner with turkey, stuffing, and laughter instead of the vegan stew for two Daphne usually prepared.

She needed to figure out a way to tell Mason, but didn't know how. Vivi just wished she could wave a magic wand and have him accept this new part of her, no questions asked.

Well, she could do that, actually. No wand required. A few whispered words, and she could ensure Mason wasn't angry anymore. She could ease him into forgiveness, make him perfectly content with her sometimes cagey or callous behavior . . .

No. No way, she told herself sternly. Using magic on him would be crossing a line Vivi refused to go anywhere near.

After a moment's hesitation, she perched on the bench. Close enough to catch the scent of his cologne, a spicy, piney smell that made her want to lean into the crook of his shoulder and just breathe him in. But she could tell by his rigid posture that he wasn't exactly in a cuddly mood.

"I'm sorry about the other day," she said, eager to clear the air. "I treated you horribly."

"Yeah, I know," he said, staring out at the river. His tone was cold, almost mocking. She'd never seen this side of him before.

"How can I make it up to you?" Vivi said, shifting on the edge of the bench as she tugged at the hem of her now too-short skirt.

Mason sighed, and when he looked at her, his expression was more sorrowful than angry. "It's not just about last night, Vivi. It's . . . I want us both to be honest with each other. I've been in relationships before where I was always on the outside looking in, and I hated that feeling."

He was talking about Scarlett, of course. He and Scarlett had broken up because Mason felt they weren't connecting anymore, that they had nothing in common. But she and Mason were different; they had a special connection. She just needed to make him see that. Vivi angled her body toward him. "I feel the same way. I want to be partners, real partners."

"Then tell me why you've been so distant lately. Why do you keep avoiding me?" His voice cracked slightly, and Vivi's heart twisted.

"I don't know," she said, reaching for his hand.

His face hardened and he jerked his hand away. "So you're really just going to sit here and lie to me. Do you really think I'm that stupid?"

"What . . . what do you mean?"

"Come on, Vivi, don't do this, please." He groaned and then buried his face in his hands. "I *saw* you."

"Saw me do what?" she asked as her pulse started to race. Had she been foolish or careless enough to reveal a hint of witchcraft?

"I saw you with Tim Lee. Right after you texted that you couldn't meet for coffee because you were busy at Kappa House."

"What? Oh, God, Mason, no. It's not like that, trust me. I just ran into him and we talked for a few minutes. It's nothing."

He raised his head and stared at her wearily. "Then why the hell did you lie about where you were?"

"It's . . . complicated," she said. The moment the word left her lips, she realized her mistake.

"Complicated," Mason repeated. "Well, why don't you try explaining, and I'll do my best to follow along." When she didn't respond, he snorted. "You decided you preferred the star quarterback to a nerdy history major. Doesn't sound all that complicated to me."

"Mason, you're being ridiculous! I'm not cheating on you."

He was silent for a long moment, then he slowly nodded once. "No, I don't think you are. But I know you're thinking about it."

"So, what? I'm not allowed to have male friends?"

"Of course you can have male friends! But you've been weird and distant since the party, and then you stood me up and then *lied* about what you were doing. What the hell am I supposed to think?"

Just tell him, Vivi thought. But as her brain raced to find the right words, that sinking feeling of dread returned to her chest. In some ways, she and Mason were a lot more compatible than Mason and Scarlett had been. But by all outward appearances, Mason was slumming it with her. Scarlett was beautiful, intelligent, confident, glamorous, and came from one of the wealthiest, most respected families in Georgia. And although Mason's parents lived right here in Savannah, he'd never invited her to meet them. Was it because he knew they'd find her uncultured and uncouth? Was he already that embarrassed by her?

"Tim is my . . ." The words died in her throat. Mason's face sank, his eyes full of hurt. No, she couldn't let him suffer like this. Not when it'd be so easy for her to take away his pain.

I call to the Moon, she thought, *provider of wisdom and clarity. Please guide him through suspicion to charity.*

The clouds above them thinned, revealing a faint silver glow. Mason leaned back against the bench with a sigh and rubbed the bridge of his nose. "I don't know why I'm acting like this. It's just that I really care about you Vivi, and I want this to work. So you know what? You're right. I trust you. If you say there's nothing going on between you two, then I believe you." He smiled and reached for her hand. "I'm sorry for freaking out. Will you forgive me?"

Relief flooded through her as Mason smiled hopefully, but it was tinged with guilt that made it a little difficult to smile back. She had treated Mason poorly, and now here he was asking *her* for forgiveness. To say nothing of the fact that she'd used magic to manipulate him. It was a minor spell, but there was a reason witches were not to interfere with free will—it was a dangerous, slippery slope that had all sorts of unforeseen consequences.

I won't do it again, she told herself. *It was just this one time.*

"I'm sorry, too," Vivi said truthfully, although Mason would never know the full extent of her apology. "I've just been under a lot of pressure lately. I thought I could handle this social chair position, but it's so much more work than I expected it to be, and I made a huge mess of the stupid mixer, and now we have the reunion coming up and we're on notice with the council and it's all on me to make things right. And on top of that, school hasn't been going well . . ." As the words tumbled out of her, she felt tears prickle the corners of her eyes. It was true—despite her frenetic childhood, Vivi had always gotten stellar grades. But now she could barely keep up with her reading, let alone study for exams. Even Bailey hadn't been able to help her during a "pre-midterm check-in" in art history the other day. She'd caught sight of Vivi's terrified face and tried to send her the answers, but it turned out that the professor had given everyone a slightly different version of the test.

"Oh no, babe," Mason said, wrapping his arm around her. "It's going to be okay, I promise. You're going to pull it off. Look what you did with the Alice in Wonderland party. It was the event of the season!"

"Yeah . . ." *Until somebody almost got killed,* she thought miserably. Vivi wiped her nose with the back of her hand, then laughed when Mason passed her a handkerchief. "Sorry, I know that was gross."

"Don't worry about it," Mason said, pulling her closer to him.

Vivi exhaled slowly and rested her head against his shoulder. "I'm sorry, Mason. I know I've been a crappy girlfriend lately, but I'll do better, I promise."

"Nobody said *crappy*," Mason teased.

"Well, absentee, at least. So what's been going on with you? Did you tell your parents about your plans for next year?"

"Not yet." Mason turned to stare out at the water. "I wanted to this weekend, but Mom kept talking about the law firm, how they'd won a bunch of important new clients, and saying how they'd have plenty of work for their interns this summer, hint, hint. I lost my nerve."

"You'll figure out how to say it." Vivi slid closer to him along the bench, until their thighs pressed together. "You just need a little time."

"I don't *have* time." He tilted his head back and sighed. "I've got to give my adviser an answer in the next couple of weeks."

"Would it help if I went with you? For moral support?"

He laughed, then tilted his head to the side and surveyed her quizzically. "You really want to meet my parents for the first time during a dinner where they might murder me?"

"Well, with a neutral third party there to witness, at least it would be harder for them to get away with it, right?"

"You'd really do that for me?"

"Of course." She caught his hand, wove her fingers through his. "Isn't that what non-crappy girlfriends are for? Besides, I can always talk up the job opportunities for historians. Or maybe start rambling about how I'm going to major in basket weaving and start a vegan commune after graduation. You know, make your plans look solid by comparison."

He snorted. "I know you're joking, but that might actually work."

"Great, I'll prep my portfolio. Unrelatedly, know anywhere I can buy a few baskets to photograph?"

"You're amazing, you know that?" He leaned in to kiss her.

But Vivi drew back before his lips reached hers. "Uh-uh. First, we settle this date. You said you only had a couple weeks to do this, so . . . what day will the parental news be broken?"

"Taskmaster," he teased. "Well, you have the alumnae reunion tomorrow, right?"

"To which you will be my world's most handsome date."

"So, how about Sunday morning?"

"Define morning . . ." Vivi had a pretty good idea that, if things went well, the reunion wouldn't end until the wee hours.

"Brunch?" he clarified. "I'll set it up with my parents."

"Perfect."

"Just like you."

She rolled her eyes. "You're so cheesy."

"You love it." He kissed her again, and this time, neither of them pulled away.

CHAPTER SEVENTEEN

Scarlett

The dining hall had been transformed. When Vivi first suggested it as the perfect location for the 150th alumnae reunion, Scarlett had been dubious. The building itself was handsome: stone walls, high ceilings with wooden beams, big glass windows that overlooked campus. But when push came to shove, it was still a school cafeteria. Scarlett found it hard to imagine throwing the sort of soiree they'd need to impress the Kappa alumnae *here*.

Yet Vivi had found a way to surpass even Scarlett's wildest expectations.

The moment guests set foot inside, they found themselves transported into a near replica of the palace at Versailles. Enormous antique floor-to-ceiling mirrors lined the wall opposite the windows. All the regular tables and chairs had been replaced by high-top cocktail tables in gold filigree, with a few clusters of settees and poufs in the corners for guests to sit.

The floors, normally simple vinyl, now resembled black-and-white marble threaded with veins of rose gold.

And the coup de grâce: a single glance in the mirror made Scarlett gasp. Because she didn't see herself reflected there—at least, not in the dress she'd come wearing, an emerald green empire-cut gown with a carefully placed slit to show off her legs and matching high heels.

Her reflection wore an eighteenth-century gown worthy of Marie Antoinette herself. Puff sleeves, an enormous bell skirt. The reflection even added a small beauty mark near her lip and a curled wig effect.

At her side, Xavier cut an equally handsome figure. He wore a standard suit, pressed to perfection, but his reflection sported full French court attire. In the mirror, he lifted an eyebrow. He turned side to side to admire his own outfit. "I knew Westerly had a good programming department, but these special effects could rival the pros."

"Welcome to a real Kappa event," Scarlett replied, grinning. She'd had her doubts about inviting him as her date, but she had to admit, he looked the part.

"Now I understand the hype." Xavier executed a little bow, then held out a hand. "Care to dance, *mademoiselle*?"

She was about to accept when another figure joined them in the mirror, wearing an even more elaborate headpiece than Scarlett's.

"I have to admit," said Marjorie Winter in a low voice, "you've done passably well."

Scarlett released Xavier's hand and forced a tight smile. "It was all Vivi, my Little." And that was true. Vivi had refused even the tiniest offer of help from Scarlett in the lead-up to this. Truth be told, Scarlett had been nervous about tonight too.

Scarlett tried to temper her relief. The last mixer had started well too. Still, she wanted this to work, for Vivi and for all of Kappa.

"Scarlett's being modest," Xavier interrupted, startling her. She'd expected him to do what all her past boyfriends did around Marjorie—linger quietly on the sidelines until introduced. But Xavier stuck out a hand, all charm. "Xavier Hunt. Pleasure to meet you, Mrs. Winter."

Despite herself, Scarlett wondered how Jackson would behave in the same situation. She imagined he would be equally direct but a lot less polished. More funny, perhaps. But who was she kidding? Now there was absolutely no chance of her ever having to introduce Jackson to her mother. At least that was a blessing.

Marjorie stared at Xavier's palm without moving a muscle. She hated people who made their own introductions.

Xavier took it in stride, reaching up to run his hand through his hair instead. "Anyway, if you ask me, half of leadership is good delegation skills."

"I didn't." Marjorie pursed her lips and glanced at Scarlett. "But you make a point there. Well delegated. I harbored concerns for this event after hearing about your latest fiasco."

Scarlett stared at her mother. Marjorie had been all over her with texts and phone calls ever since Kappa had been put on notice —because *of course* Eugenie had heard about it within ten minutes and gone straight to her.

Scarlett could just picture how excited her sister must have been to be able to rub this in.

But at the end of the day, Scarlett *had* screwed up. "I'm going to put things right," she said, after a long pause. "I just need a bit of time, that's all."

Xavier rested one hand on the small of her back, lightly, a silent gesture of support.

"Time is a luxury we can't all afford."

"It was just a warning, Mama." Still, Scarlett lowered her voice. On the off chance that *some* of the alumnae weren't as plugged in to the current events of Kappa as her mother, Scarlett didn't want to cue anyone else in to how badly her presidency was starting off.

"Kappa Rho Nu has never been *warned* in the entire one hundred fifty years of its existence." Marjorie peered past Scarlett at the crowd. "I know you wanted to make an impression with your presidency, Scarlett, but I must say, this is not the one I expected."

Scarlett's cheeks flushed. Before she could argue further, Xavier broke in. "Actually, that's not strictly true."

Both Marjorie and Scarlett stared.

He furrowed his brow. "I figured I should brush up on some history for tonight, since it's an anniversary . . ." He glanced Scarlett's way quickly. "In 1974, Kappa received a citation for disorderly conduct. Same again in 1987."

Scarlett looked at her mother, surprised. "Wouldn't you have been on campus that year?" she asked.

Marjorie pursed her lips, ignoring her daughter. "Thank you for that lesson in my own history, but I'm perfectly aware of those incidents, and they were minor. Certainly nothing of this magnitude."

Scarlett could tell by the irritable spark in her eyes: Marjorie was both impressed and annoyed by Xavier.

Still, Scarlett waited for her mother to drift away toward a cluster of her school friends—a writer shortlisted for the National Book Award and a director whose most recent film had become the top-grossing movie of last year—before she actually laughed. "That was poetry." She side-eyed Xavier and let him draw her onto the dance floor this time. "Did you seriously read Kappa history just for this?"

"You seem like the type of girl who appreciates detail," Xavier was saying. "I wouldn't want to disappoint, after you finally took me up on that date."

"This is a date, is it?" Scarlett arched a perfectly manicured brow.

"Call it what you want, but if the suit fits . . ." Xavier grinned, and spun her as the music picked up.

Scarlett couldn't deny, Xavier holding his own against Marjorie Winter made him more attractive to her. Not to mention, it made her eager for the next step of the evening.

If Marjorie was already upset, she'd be even more so soon. The thought made Scarlett strangely giddy. Perhaps it was due to the cavalier, handsome boy spinning her on the dance floor.

Her mother still hadn't signed off on Scarlett's plan to collect the alumnae's previous spells and Kappa memories in the book she'd created. At the last council meeting, Marjorie claimed she hadn't had time to raise the question. So Scarlett planned to force her hand, whether the council approved or not.

Scarlett eyed the clock above the doorway, enchanted to look made of gold and silver tonight. Vivi really hadn't missed a single detail.

"I should go and find Vivi." Scarlett released Xavier's hand, although not before he raised it to his lips to kiss the back of her knuckles. Her breath caught, but she extricated herself before she had too much time to think about it.

It still unnerved her that she'd been unable to read his thoughts back at the Thirsty Scholar. And while it flattered her how eagerly he'd accepted her invitation tonight, she couldn't shake the feeling there was some other reason for it.

With one last glance, Scarlett drifted away to find her Little and the podium Vivi had promised to provide.

She only made it a few steps across the slowly crowding hall, however, when she spotted a familiar tousle of curls. *Jackson.* Wearing the same catering uniform—although tonight, his reflection wore a full-on eighteenth-century brocade jacket and breeches tight enough to show off . . . well. Tight enough.

Scarlett grimaced and looked away. She couldn't afford to be distracted. Not right before she gave this speech, which would require a careful spell along with it, so the dates of the Kappas in attendance wouldn't understand some of what she said.

But another glance at the mirror made her pause midstride.

There was something wrong with Jackson. In person, he wore his usual easy smile as he offered a tray of canapes to a passing cluster of alumnae. His reflection, on the other hand, wore a haunted, terrified expression.

Startled, Scarlett glanced around at the other partygoers. Everyone else's reflections, aside from the elaborate attire, looked normal. Vivi had done such a good job on the spell, in fact, that Scarlett had overheard the PiKa guy who had come with Hazel begging to know what CGI company they'd hired to build the mirrors.

Only Jackson's reflection seemed messed up. *Wrong.*

Her heartbeat sped up.

Scarlett sidestepped a dancing couple and wound through the crowd, following Jackson as he headed toward the kitchen for a refill. The next time she glanced at his reflection, it noticed her. She watched with growing horror as mirror-Jackson reached out a hand to Scarlett and opened its mouth in a silent scream.

She grabbed the real Jackson's arm.

He stumbled, tripping, and his empty tray clattered to the floor. "What the hell?" He jerked free and whipped around to face her.

As he did, something fell loose from his vest. The silver chain he'd been wearing the last few times she'd seen him. She'd never seen him wear jewelry before, but this he never seemed to take off. And now she could see the full necklace.

At the end, dangling around the middle of his chest, was a double-pointed rose quartz.

The crystal most commonly used in love spells.

"You again," Jackson said with a scowl. "Stop following me. How many times do I have to tell you I'm not interested?"

"Just one more should do the trick," Scarlett replied, sidling up to him. "Sorry about this," she added. Then she grabbed the chain and *yanked.*

Jackson shouted in pain.

Scarlett's hand felt like she'd just submerged it in ice. Her fingers went numb, and pain shot from her elbow all the way up to her shoulder. With a yelp, she released the crystal. The stone left an angry red burn mark in the center of her palm.

Worse, it remained attached to Jackson's neck.

He tucked it back under his vest angrily. "You have no right. This is *private*." But she could hear it now. The monotone in his voice, the glazed look in his eyes. He was only capable of saying and doing what the witch who cast that love spell wanted him to say or do.

And Scarlett had a pretty good idea who to blame. After all, he'd been hanging all over Cait for weeks.

But did that mean . . . Scarlett didn't know how Cait could've managed a love spell this strong. Scarlett remembered Cait from her own rush party at Kappa. She'd lit a sparkler, barely. When it came time for the entrance exam, she hadn't been able to produce so much as a spark during the tarot ritual.

Magic was a finite resource. Whatever amount you had, you could hone. Cait could have studied on her own, like Minnie or Gwen, and become a solitary practitioner. Yet she should only be able to cast simple charms, something like encouraging a plant to grow or lighting a candle flame. No way could she cast a love spell strong enough to break another human's willpower. Much less a love spell a Kappa witch couldn't remove.

It didn't make any *sense*.

"I'm going to fix this," Scarlett said firmly. Even though Jackson continued to glare, she hoped the real him, the Jackson trapped inside this enchantment, could hear her. "I'm going to save you."

"The only person who needs saving here is *you,* from your own delusions," Jackson muttered. He bent to pick up his tray.

Only then did Scarlett notice the cluster of bystanders watching. With a deep breath, she forced a broad smile and spun away. She couldn't fix it right this second.

Right now, she had to focus on Kappa. Both their future, and their freedom from the past.

Her Little was waiting with a confused look next to the platform she had erected. "What was that all about?" Vivi asked when Scarlett reached her.

"Later." Scarlett bent to give her a quick one-armed hug. "You did an amazing job, by the way. Everyone's gushing. Even my mother, though she's too angry about the council warning to say so."

"We'll get Spring Fling back. Don't worry." But from the way Vivi worried at her bottom lip, Scarlett could tell her Little was only trying to comfort her. She didn't actually know they would.

Neither did Scarlett.

Still, she accepted the flute of champagne Vivi passed her. "If we tackle it with the same skill that you tackled this?" Scarlett gestured at the resplendent room. "Then you're right. I have no doubts."

Feigning more confidence than she felt, Scarlett gave her Little one last reassuring squeeze and stepped onto the podium.

The room quieted at once, a swell of shushes and whispers

crossing the floor with lightning speed. Looking out at the crowd, Scarlett was struck by the sheer amount of power in this room— and not only because of their magic. The Ravens and the Monarchs were unstoppable because of their sisterhood. A stray Theta witch like Cait might pick up enough tricks to enchant one boy, but she was no match for this coven.

"Kappas," Scarlett said, her voice magically amplified to carry across the high-ceilinged hall with no effort. "Sisters both past and present, friends and honored guests, welcome to our humble reunion." A chuckle passed through the crowd. She allowed herself a small smile. "All right, so humility might be one quality we *aren't* known for."

A louder laugh this time.

"Can we give a round of applause to our social chair, Vivi Devereaux, please, for making this *enchanting* event a reality?" Scarlett grinned at her blushing Little and clapped harder than anyone. Once the noise died down, she continued. "I want to sincerely thank you all for coming, and for supporting us after everything we went through last semester."

A few murmurs of agreement passed through the crowd. Scarlett noticed more than a few older relatives of current Kappas grip their daughters' shoulders.

"It means the world to us current members to see how many of our former sisters came tonight. We hope y'all are having fun." Scarlett raised her champagne, and a cheer rose in response. "And while y'all are here enjoying yourselves, we have one small request.

We'd like to ask you to share a little more of your wisdom, regarding Kappa's history."

With that, she glanced to the side wall, where Vivi had moved to stand beside Etta, Mei, Jess, and Juliet. At a nod from Scarlett, her sisters' lips began to move. Mouthing the words of the spell they'd planned out ahead of time.

When Scarlett faced the crowd once more, she noticed the non-Kappa guests—the dates and catering staff in attendance—all wore blank, glazed expressions. For a moment, it reminded her uncomfortably of the way Jackson had just looked at her.

She shook it off. *This is different.* They weren't influencing anyone's free will. Just enticing the non-Kappas in the crowd to stop listening for a few minutes, while Scarlett addressed the Kappa alumnae.

"My sisters and I have a new project," Scarlett said. "We have crafted this spell book—" She gestured to Vivi, who held it aloft. She fought back a smirk when some of the older attendees startled and glanced around, worried, only to find their dates in a trance. "To compile a collective history of Kappa's coven.

"It's enchanted so as to protect the anonymity of all contributors. What we ask is simple: we want to know about your time at Kappa. Your memories, both good and bad. And especially any spells you worked with your sisters when you were at Westerly. How they went, whether they worked as intended, or if there were any . . ." She hesitated. "Unforeseen consequences."

She'd worded this part carefully. She didn't want to give her mother any *more* reasons to worry. Not when she wasn't even sure what was happening on campus, or why.

Magic is acting weird wasn't a good enough reason to frighten the alumnae. Just because a weak witch had worked one powerful love spell, a Kappa glamour had backfired, and another Kappa girl had had a screaming fit in public, it didn't have to mean anything . . . necessarily.

Scarlett scanned the crowd, which had gone silent. She caught her mother glaring, and her sister watching in openmouthed shock. Eugenie probably hadn't thought Scarlett would go through with this. Not without their mother's approval first.

Watch me.

Last semester, after Dahlia's death, Scarlett had promised to do things differently around here. And she would. Starting now.

"Given what happened to my predecessor," Scarlett said, more softly, "how she was killed by one of our own . . . I want Kappa to learn from our history. To ensure we never again repeat it. And become the strongest coven we can be."

When she stopped speaking, the room remained dead silent. For one heartbeat, two, three.

And then an older woman Scarlett recognized from some of her mother's dinner parties began to clap. Slowly at first. Another woman joined in, and another.

Soon, every Kappa in the room, past and present, was applauding.

Scarlett's gaze darted back to her mother and Eugenie again. Eugenie's nose was wrinkled in disapproval. But even Marjorie had begun to clap, slow and purposeful. Oh, Scarlett would get a lecture after this. Definitely. But it would be worth it.

She raised her hand to acknowledge the room. Then, just as she was about to give Vivi the order to revive their guests, her attention snagged on one more person. Xavier.

Since he wasn't a Kappa, Xavier should have been just as out of it as the rest of the bystanders. But when Scarlett's eyes locked with his, she could have *sworn* he stared right back. Awake and aware.

CHAPTER EIGHTEEN

Vivi

"T his is *wild*," Mason said, sounding slightly dazed as he lifted an arm to spin Vivi on the dance floor. "A week ago, you were freaking out because you hadn't done enough party planning, and then you pulled *this* off?" He smiled and shook his head while doing his best to help Vivi move in time to the music. When the string quartet—all wearing powdered wigs and eighteenth-century costumes borrowed from Westerly's theater department—had struck up a waltz, Mason had grabbed Vivi's hand and said it was time to put his cotillion classes to good use. "I've never seen a Kappa event like this. I don't understand. Where did the money come from? Who'd you sell your soul to in order to make all this happen?"

"A social chair never reveals her secrets," Vivi said with a coy smile. "But really, do you think people are having fun?"

"Are you kidding?" Mason tightened his hold around Vivi's waist and gently moved her to the right, just in time to avoid bumping into another waltzing couple. "People are going to be talking about this party for years."

As if on cue, Ariana broke away from her date and skipped over, holding her phone in the air. "Have you seen this? Photos from the party are already all over Insta, and we were trending on Twitter for a minute. People who don't even go to Westerly are talking about how jealous they are. The Thetas are going to lose their minds!"

"The ultimate sign of success," Mason said with a laugh. "Have you met any of the alumnae?"

Ariana nodded. "I just spent twenty minutes talking to this graphic designer who builds websites for female entrepreneurs in India. She said I could intern remotely for her next semester, if I wanted."

"That's great!" Vivi said, motioning for Ariana and Mason to follow her to the edge of the dance floor so they wouldn't create a waltz traffic jam. She looked around the room and felt a swell of pride. Everything was going according to plan. Jess was deep in conversation with the journalist she admired; Mei, Etta, and Reagan were dancing with a group of alums that included a biologist rumored to be in the running for a Nobel Prize and a famous Hollywood director; and Scarlett seemed to be on cloud nine, watching the festivities with a contented grin.

Off to the side, Vivi's own mother was speaking animatedly with a few women from her own Kappa pledge class. This was the first alumnae function Daphne Devereaux had attended since she vanished from Westerly without a backwards glance almost three decades ago.

"Your mom seems to be having fun, too," Mason said, following Vivi's gaze. "You should've seen her face when Scarlett thanked you in her speech. She's clearly very proud of you. As am I."

"As am I," Ariana repeated solemnly before turning to grin at Mason. "Sorry, you know I love you, Professor Gregory. Even if you do sometimes talk like a sexy Victorian ghost."

Mason laughed and shook his head. "You're right. I guess that's what happens when you spend too much time in the archives. Maybe you should start sending me a vocab word of the day to keep me up to date. That would be pretty . . . fire."

Ariana groaned then looked up and mouthed something to her date, who was still standing where she'd left him on the dance floor, smiling stiffly as he swayed in time to the music. "Oh my God, that boy is so adorably awkward. I gotta go save him."

Vivi felt less adorably awkward as she watched Ariana go. She was thrilled that her boyfriend and best friend had such a great rapport, but she was weirdly envious of how easy it was for Ariana to toss out a playful *I love you* when it took all of Vivi's self-control not to let those three loaded words slip out when she was with Mason. She knew she loved him, but the prospect of being the first to say it was too terrifying.

"Do you want to head back out there?" Mason asked, extending his arm. Vivi stole a quick glance down at her hands. She'd had to glamour them to hide the marks all this magic had left. It had started with pinpricks along her fingers, then the backs of her hands. But some of the bigger spells had left deep welts, wounds that burned whenever she moved her fingers too quickly.

It's fine. She'd get some of Etta's ointment from the kitchen later tonight to soothe the injuries, just as she'd been doing all week.

She'd spent every free minute of the last week practicing for this night. Every spell at the event she'd learned in the grimoire, and it had cost her. She'd awoken this morning with bloodstains on her sheets, small cuts on her hands broken open in places, and bags so dark under her eyes it had taken her three tries to cast a glamour to disguise them.

This magic was different from Kappa magic. More malleable, once you got the hang of it. Only, she *hadn't* gotten the hang of doing these spells without the pinpricks. But if this fabulous event came at a minor cost to her comfort, well, she could deal with that.

She tightened her grip around Mason's shoulders, concealing a faint wince as he swung her around. From this angle, she could see the mirror, her favorite creation. In it, she and Mason looked like a prince and princess, surrounded by courtiers at an elegant royal ball. She nudged Mason until he twirled her again, just so she could watch the period dress in the mirror swirl in time with the real dress she wore, a deep V-cut with a corset waist and a trailing lace hem that flared around her knees.

His forehead came to rest against hers as the music shifted to a slower song. His arms went around her waist, and the warmth of his body seemed to sink all the way into her bones.

Mason had a way of making her feel so safe and protected.

Even so, she still didn't expect it when he whispered, "I love you, Vivi."

Sparks raced over every inch of her body, so intense she half worried the glamours of the party would explode into glitter around her. She noticed the mirror shift and shimmer for a second, out of the corner of her eye, before she willed it back into place.

Mason's thumb slipped down her cheekbone to press against her lips. "You don't have to say it back if you aren't ready. I just couldn't hold it in any longer."

She pressed a kiss to the pad of his thumb. "I love you too, Mason."

A radiant smile spread across his face, as if she'd just made him happier than he ever thought possible. She knew how it felt, because the same feeling was welling up with her. Fizzy excitement mixed with pure contentment. She felt like she could do anything—like *they* could do anything, together.

"Hope I'm not interrupting you two lovebirds." Daphne had a wineglass in one hand and a flush in her cheeks Vivi had never seen before. "I just wanted to congratulate my daughter, if that's all right with you, handsome?"

Vivi never realized she could go from elated to wanting to melt through the floorboards in two seconds flat. "Mom, please."

But Mason only laughed. "Fine by me, Mrs. Devereaux."

"Oh, please, call me Daphne, sugar snap. We'll be back in a moment." She looped her arm through Vivi's and began to drag her away.

"You've got the worst timing in the world, you know that, right?" Vivi said.

"You've got all night to smooch your boyfriend. I want to tell you and Scarlett what a great job you've both done."

Vivi shot Mason an apologetic smile over her shoulder, then allowed her mother to drag her through the press of bodies toward the snack table. Along the way, she spotted Sonali and Bailey talking to some older alumnae, and Hazel in a deep blue gown with an older guy on her arm. Everyone was enjoying themselves. Some a little *too* much, she thought, with another glance at her mother.

But as they neared Scarlett, who was standing near the snack table, deep in conversation with Xavier, the handsome new PiKa transfer she'd brought as her date, Vivi's sisterly senses tingled. Judging by the hardened expression on Scarlett's face, this was *not* the sort of conversation they should be interrupting.

"Mom, hang on." She made a grab for Daphne's hand, but her mother was too far gone after who knew how many glasses of champagne she'd shared with Marjorie.

"— thought we had something. Why did you *invite* me, if you weren't interested?" Xavier was saying, his voice restrained, his jaw tightened with anger.

"I thought I made it clear we were here as friends," Scarlett said, her voice pitched low, although Vivi detected an undercurrent of distress from her too. "I'm sorry, Xavier, but I don't see this going anywhere."

"Unbelievable," he spat just as Vivi's oblivious mother reached their side.

"Scarlett, love!" Daphne's tipsy voice really carried. Vivi hurried to catch up to her mother. "This party is *amazing*. Oh, and who's your handsome boy here?"

"I'm not," Xavier replied, whirling away. Vivi watched him go, her eyes jumping from his clenched fists to his scowl.

You okay? she asked Scarlett quietly, using Swords magic to ask her Big directly so Daphne wouldn't overhear.

Fine. Clearly, he was a bad idea anyway. Scarlett's reply sounded normal, tinged with amusement, even. But her gaze lingered on Xavier's retreating backside, her expression torn between irritation and worry.

"I'm so proud of you both." Daphne squeezed Vivi's wrist, reached over to catch Scarlett's too.

"Sorry," Vivi murmured, but her Big only laughed.

"It's sweet." She wrapped her free arm around Vivi's shoulders and squeezed. "I'm glad *some*one's mom approves."

"Is your mom not having a good time?" Vivi asked worriedly, looking around the room in an attempt to locate Marjorie.

"She thinks the party's great. But she's furious about the warning we got."

"Don't worry about Marjorie." Daphne leaned in conspiratorially, swaying a little. "She's *very* impressed by tonight. She just doesn't want to admit it. She won't stay angry long, honey." She winked at Scarlett, and Vivi watched a little of the cloud on her Big's face dissolve.

All right, so maybe drunk Daphne wasn't a *complete* disaster. Still, she stayed long enough to embarrass Vivi at least half a dozen more times over the course of the night before Mason swooped in and convinced Daphne to let him call her a cab. While he waited with Daphne outside, Vivi ducked into an alcove in the corridor next to the dining hall to take a breath and rest for a moment before she began making her final rounds to say goodbye to all the alumnae.

She'd been on a high all night, buoyed by her success, but she was starting to feel the toll of so much socializing.

Her phone buzzed with a text from Tim. *Photos from your event are everywhere—congrats! Is Scarlett thrilled?*

Vivi smiled, touched by Tim's excitement for her. He was nothing like the self-centered, cocky football star everyone thought he was. *I think so. She's not someone who overdoes it with praise, you know?*

She and Coach Carver have that in common. Do you think Scarlett was a football coach in a past life?

Unlikely. That wouldn't explain her natural gift for walking in heels.

Why can't Coach Carver rock a pair of stilettos? Your bias is showing.

Says the guy who was afraid of lattes.

Toosh.

Vivi laughed out loud. They'd hung out again yesterday and spent nearly three hours sharing embarrassing stories from their childhood. Tim had admitted that, all through middle school, he'd mispronounced *touché* as "toosh."

Vivi slid her phone back into her purse. From her perch, she could see a sliver of herself in one of the mirrors she'd enchanted; she'd placed one right by the door to the dining hall to set the scene when the guests arrived. Her reflection looked exhausted, the kind of bone-deep tired that showed in every line of her face, every hollow around her eyes and under her cheekbones.

Her vision grew blurry, and Vivi blinked rapidly, assuming that her eyes were giving out from fatigue. But then she realized that it was the mirror that'd turned fuzzy, and she watched with a twinge of alarm as her reflection was obscured by a cloud of gray smoke. "What the hell?" she whispered as she rose to her feet and inched toward the mirror. The corridor was dark and empty, and the sounds of music and laughter drifting from the main hall had become distant and dim, as if it were all happening very far away. Vivi shook her head, trying to dispel the strange, heavy silence that'd settled over the corridor, thick and suffocating.

She crept toward the mirror, her skin tingling in response to magic that hadn't come from her or her sisters. She felt like an animal who'd caught the scent of a predator, a dangerous, hungry presence lurking in the shadows. "Who's there?"

She'd meant to shout, but the words came out whisper-thin.

The smoke in the mirror swirled, then thinned slightly, revealing Vivi's reflection once again. Except that it wasn't her reflection, not quite. Vivi brought her hand to her neck and saw the Vivi in the glass do the same. But where Vivi's fingers brushed only bare skin, the Vivi in the glass touched a familiar blue pendant on a thick, ornate gold chain.

It was the Henosis talisman.

Vivi gasped and tried to yank it off — she could feel the heavy weight on her neck, crushing her windpipe — but her fingers were clawing empty air. It reminded her too much of the woods, the chains around her wrists, the pressure behind her rib cage as her own heart betrayed her, fought to break free. And all the while, Tiffany, wearing the Henosis talisman, laughing as she lured Vivi to her death.

Just when her head began to swim, the image once again

disappeared into the dark smoke, and the weight around Vivi's neck vanished. Gasping, she placed her hands on her knees and took a few deep, greedy breaths. She didn't know who was doing this or what they wanted, but the last time she'd gotten into a magical fight, her opponent had nearly killed her. Vivi needed to be stronger this time.

A new image began to materialize in the mirror, and Vivi braced herself for whatever was coming next. She was stronger than she'd been last semester, capable of fighting back. This time, it was a gray Victorian farmhouse perched on a tall hill next to a single willow tree. There was something vaguely familiar about it, from the wrought-iron gates framing the drive to the black birds perched on the widow's watch at the top of the peaked roof. Were they ravens?

Despite her better judgment, Vivi tilted forward for a closer look, then gasped as an invisible force pulled her slowly toward the mirror. The surface began to ripple as if it were made of liquid instead of glass. Vivi tried to plant her feet on the ground but scrambled to find her footing. Her face was just inches from the mirror now; she could smell damp grass and could hear wind rustling the trees. A sign creaked on the swinging gate. LONE WILLOW FARM.

The air felt warm and welcoming, and for one brief moment, Vivi closed her eyes and imagined sinking all the way in. A raven called in the distance, but it sounded much more human than avian. What was it saying? She just needed to get a little closer . . .

No.

Her eyes snapped open.

I won't let you control me.

Vivi clenched her fists and dug her nails into her palms, hard. She felt a couple old cuts split open. The sting and ache made her feel alive and alert again. "I call to the Moon, destroyer of illusion. Give me the strength to resist this confusion."

The force pulling on her disappeared for a moment, but before Vivi could catch her breath, it returned, even stronger than before.

"No," Vivi groaned, leaning back with all her might. Pain shot up her arm and raced along her nerves as she repeated, "I call to the Moon, destroyer of illusion. Give me the strength to resist this confusion."

The force disappeared so suddenly, Vivi flew back and nearly slammed into the wall behind her. She took a few deep breaths and waited for the panic to subside. She felt shaky and drained, but somehow strong at the same time. Whatever that was, it hadn't gotten her.

Yet it almost felt like someone was trying to *show* her something. Something to do with the Henosis talisman.

Vivi shivered as she remembered the look of manic cruelty in Tiffany's face as she clutched the pendant. They'd destroyed the talisman, taking care to ensure it'd never hurt anyone again. It was gone forever.

Wasn't it?

As she made her way back toward the party, she smiled and tried to regain her composure. She needed to discuss what had just happened with Scarlett, but for now, her one job was ensuring that nothing ruined the end of the party.

She remembered the call of the raven through the mirror, only now realizing what the noise had sounded like.

It'd been calling her name.

CHAPTER NINETEEN

Scarlett

T his calls for champagne," Scarlett announced when the
Ravens finally all made it home from the alumnae reunion,
well past midnight and with a litany of successes under their belts.
It wasn't just the party. Jess had scored the summer internship
she'd been gunning for; Mei had been invited to understudy with
a Broadway costume designer over spring break; Juliet was in the
running for a postgrad position at one of the best microbiology
programs in the country. Everyone had succeeded tonight.

Especially Vivi, who'd pulled off the party of the decade, and
Scarlett, the president responsible for it all.

But their night wasn't over yet. Not with what Scarlett had
planned.

"*Just* champagne?" Etta asked, in a lighthearted teasing tone that
Scarlett hadn't heard in weeks. As she spoke, the senior wiggled her
fingers, and a few of the houseplants in the foyer perked up, curv-
ing toward her obediently. "Or something more . . . magical?"

"Ooh, come on, Scar, we haven't done a house-wide ritual in so
long," Mei added.

Even Reagan looked interested, although she didn't actually
voice it.

Scarlett glanced across the living room at Vivi. Was it her imagination, or did her Little look more tired than the rest of the girls? Then again, according to her sisters, Vivi had cast all of the glamours for the event herself. That *would* take it out of you. "If everyone has enough energy left, after tonight . . ." she began.

Vivi was staring off into space. But the moment she saw Scarlett staring, she perked right up with a wide smile. "Sure, I'm in."

Scarlett glanced around the sitting room. They hadn't turned on all the lights yet, and in the dim, the antique furniture and solemn portraits of sisters past that lined the walls gave her an idea. "Well. Since tonight was all about meeting our predecessors and securing Kappa's success . . ." she said slowly.

In the corner, Juliet nudged her girlfriend. But for once, the whispers weren't negative. "That's Scar's plotting face," Juliet murmured with a grin.

"This will be good," Hazel agreed from nearby.

Their excitement buoyed Scarlett's. "I was thinking we could call in a little favor with Kappa's founder and get her opinion on how we can put Theta in their place once and for all. I want to perform a séance."

A hush fell across the room. For a moment, she worried she'd misread the night. But then Etta gasped and bounced onto the balls of her feet and Ariana reached over to squeeze Vivi's hand as a few other girls let out excited squeals.

"Yes! That's perfect," Mei declared.

"Yaaaaaasss," Reagan declared tipsily. "Finally!"

Vivi stood up, her eyes mischievous. "I have something that

might help. Wait right here." Her earlier tiredness forgotten, Scarlett's Little bounded up the steps.

While she was gone, Scarlett and Etta raided the storeroom for supplies—plenty of black candles, curtains to black out the windows, along with salt and thyme for extra protection.

By the time they made it back to the living room, Mei and a few other girls had doled out glasses of red wine—better for scrying than champagne, Scarlett noted with approval—and some of the chocolate cake Sonali had baked the day before, as well as various leftover hors d'oeuvres from the party.

They arranged the food and wine in the center of the circle, and then Scarlett walked the perimeter with the salt and thyme mix, careful to leave an opening for Vivi when she came back.

A couple minutes later, her Little bounded down the steps two at a time, beaming and clutching a slim leather-bound book. "This is where I found the spell I used for the reunion," Vivi declared when she reached the circle, kneeling on a pillow left free for her.

"Ooh! Revealing your fabulous secrets, are we?" Ariana cooed.

Scarlett reached over to tilt it up so she could read the cover. Nothing but a pentacle design embossed in the leather. "Where did you find it?"

"In the library when I was researching." Vivi fanned through the pages. "I've been studying it in my spare time; some of the spells are really unique, and . . . here!" She laid the book down flat on the ground, so they could all bend closer and read.

Sure enough, it was a séance ritual, although unlike any Scarlett had seen before. This ritual didn't mention anything about salt or protective circles, or even food and drink to offer the spirit as thanks.

In fact, it looked surprisingly simple. Scarlett pursed her lips. "Are you sure this will work?" She ran a finger over the page, reading the words a second time.

"So far, they've all worked for me," Vivi said with a hopeful expression.

This melted Scarlett a little. It was clear that Vivi wanted to impress her—and was excited to share something new. Still, she caught Reagan side-eyeing Sonali, and Hazel sighing in exasperation as she considered what to do.

Scarlett wouldn't make the same mistake twice. She'd said she wanted this semester to be about Kappa working together, trying new things. If Vivi wanted to do a new spell, well, then . . .

"All right," she said definitively. "Let's do this." She nodded to Vivi, who passed the book around the circle.

Meanwhile, Scarlett rose and approached the ornate gold-framed mirror over the fireplace. A normal sorority would have probably needed two burly PiKa brothers at least to lift the thing. Luckily, the Ravens weren't normal.

A few whispered words from Scarlett, and the mirror practically floated off the wall. She guided it to the center of the circle with her fingertips, and let it sink to the carpet.

Then she retook her position, kneeling at the head of the mirror. "Everybody got the words down?" She waited for a nod from every girl present before she clapped her hands together. "Good. Wands witches, a little light?"

Reagan, Hazel, and Bailey lifted their hands in unison, and the black candles Etta had placed around the room flared to life. In the same motion, the overhead lights died.

With only the candles for light, the room plunged into dim. It took a moment for Scarlett's eyes to adjust.

"Should we call the quarters?" Mei asked quietly.

Scarlett hesitated. Normally she always began a group ritual that way. Especially something like a séance, involving potentially disgruntled spirits. But Vivi's grimoire hadn't said anything about doing that first, and if Scarlett had learned one thing over her many years of practice, it was never to veer off-book for a spell you were trying for the first time.

"Not this time," she said. "But join hands, to create the circle." She waited for everyone to link up.

Across the mirror, Vivi's eyes reflected the firelight, wide with excitement. When she noticed Scarlett watching, she grinned back.

"Now we'll invite our desired guest," Scarlett said quietly. Through her sisters' clasped hands, she felt a shiver of anticipation pass between them.

Scarlett shivered, too. Was it her imagination, or did it already feel cooler in the room? But that couldn't be the spell. They hadn't even started yet.

She took a deep breath. "We Ravens of Kappa Rho Nu call upon our ancestress. The founder of our house, the original Raven.

Pearl Johnson. Visit us here, in the coven you built, and share with us your wisdom. We beseech thee."

"Pearl, we beseech thee," her sisters echoed, a beat later.

The candles along the walls flickered, ever so slightly, in an imperceptible breeze.

Now for the spell, taken word for word from the grimoire. She spoke slowly, careful not to make a mistake with the unfamiliar phrasing. "We are power, vision, sight. We demand to part the veil of night."

On the second chant, her sisters joined in. "We are power, vision, sight. We demand to part the veil of night."

Their voices rose higher, toward a crescendo. "We are power, vision, sight. We demand to part the veil of night."

The candle flames cast shadows on the walls. At first, Scarlett could trace each shadow to a girl kneeling in the circle. But then . . . were there *more* shadows than girls?

"We are power, vision, sight. We demand to part the veil of night."

She wasn't imagining it. Strange shapes appeared along the walls of the room. Stretching fingers and limbs bent at odd angles.

Scarlett shuddered and looked away. Down at the mirror between them.

She could see a shape forming. Still hazy and indistinct, but with every breath, it drew closer. Dark hair, a pale oval of a face.

Pearl.

"We are power, vision, sight. We demand to part the veil of night."

The air went cold. So cold Scarlett's breath fogged at her mouth. At the same time, wind stirred their hair, sending Mei's long strands nearly flying into the candles, until her friend glamoured her locks shorter at the last instant.

Scarlett tightened her grip on her sisters' hands. They couldn't break the circle, or they'd risk letting whatever unseen spirits lurked beyond it inside. "We are power, vision, sight. We demand to part the veil of night."

Reagan locked eyes with her, a determined expression on her face. Bailey looked terrified, yet she kept hold of their hands, continued to chant. "We are power, vision, sight. We demand to part the veil of night."

Vivi caught Scarlett's eye, and nodded down.

The face had almost crystallized. Pink lips, wide eyes. It could be the face of Pearl Johnson, whose portrait hung upstairs in the gallery hall. Then again, it could be anyone else with her complexion and long dark locks.

"Pearl?" Scarlett whispered.

Bailey gasped. The rest of the girls tensed, but they kept chanting anyway. "We are power, vision, sight. We demand to part the veil of night." The face was getting clearer. She looked young. Then again, maybe they were summoning her as she looked when she'd attended Westerly. Scarlett couldn't be sure.

Pearl's mouth began to move. One syllable, over and over.

On the walls, the false shadows solidified. Other figures rose around them, until it looked as though there were dozens of Kappas packed into the room, all howling and chanting. Distant voices

Scarlett couldn't understand. It jumbled together into a babble, like water in a stream.

But closer, in the mirror, the figure reached up. Definitely a woman, her hair raven black and waist length. She touched a palm to the mirror, and suddenly Scarlett could see her skin vividly. Every inch of the outline of her fingerprints, as if the mirror weren't a mirror at all, but a window, and she was a solid figure, pressing a hand to the other side.

"Sisters." That voice sounded clearer and louder than the rest. Goose bumps raced down Scarlett's arms, along the back of her neck.

"Sister," Scarlett replied. She spoke louder to keep the tremble from her voice. "We ask your guidance and wisdom. How may we overpower our enemy? Please, sister, show us how."

"The enemy is at hand," Pearl whispered.

"Yes, sister," Scarlett said. "Please guide us."

"The enemy is at hand," Pearl shouted. "Remember who you are. You are the Ravens."

A deafening crack, like thunder, shattered the room. In the same instant, all of the candles snuffed out.

Bailey shrieked and tore her hand from Vivi's. Next to them, Reagan started to curse. Someone gasped.

Scarlett's heart raced, her skin crawling, because she could swear . . . *something was in the room.*

She heard it underneath the gasps and cries of her sisters. Fingernails, raking along the ceiling. A rattling, painful-sounding breath somewhere high over their heads.

Scarlett rose to her feet, banishing her fear. "Begone, spirit," she said, her voice as forceful as she could make it.

A blinding light flooded the entire room.

Mei stood next to the light switch, eyes wide, hands trembling.

Scarlett scanned the ceiling, but she couldn't see anything out of place. No more shadows lurked along the walls, either.

"Well *that* was clearly a terrible idea," Reagan grumbled. Then she reached out to one of the nearest candles. But it remained dead in her grip. The freshman frowned and spoke aloud. "I call to the Queen of Wands. Show me your might by giving us light."

No flame touched the wick.

"What the hell," Reagan murmured, just as the other girls began to speak up.

"I call to the Queen of Earth," Mei was whispering, hands cupping her cheeks. Scarlett watched in growing horror as Mei's usual glamours shrank away: her hair growing back out to simple, shoulder-length waves, faint bags appearing under her eyes, and a zit alongside her nose.

Not a stitch of magic.

Nearby, Etta seemed nearly as panicked, a glass of wine in hand. Whatever she wanted it to do, it wasn't.

What was going on? She found Vivi sitting on the floor, flipping through the grimoire, looking for an answer to the question no one dared say out loud.

Scarlett looked back at Mei's bare face. *Not a stitch of magic,* she thought again.

Scarlett reached down deep, for the true well of her strength.

Cups magic. "I call to the Queen of Water," she whispered. "Heed the call of your true daughter."

Normally at those words she would feel a surge of energy. Cups magic willing to do whatever she bid it.

Yet she felt nothing. No power. No storm.

Her pulse began to race. *No*.

Scarlett had made mistakes with spells before—every witch had, when they first started out. But she always *felt* the magic. Regardless of whether the spell worked the way she intended, *something* happened when she cast it.

Now . . .

Scarlett surged to her feet. She heard shouts of protests from the other girls, but she didn't pay them any attention. She beelined for the kitchen, her panic rising.

She needed a way to assess what was happening to everyone. A neutral method, one they wouldn't need much power for. She needed to see how bad the damage was, what exactly they were dealing with.

In the kitchen, the tap had turned itself on again, the sink filling with brown, sulfur-smelling liquid.

"No," she whispered as her Cups power failed her. She shut it off quickly, then dove into the supply closet.

She opened her mouth to cast a summoning spell for the right box but stopped herself. She heaved a box of cleansers out of the way and then another until she found what she was looking for.

"There you are," she growled.

By the time she made it back to the living room, all of her sisters were visibly shaken. Some were crying. Others simply holding each other, their eyes rimmed in red.

"Tears won't help us. We have to help ourselves," Scarlett said firmly. She wasted no time circling the girls, box in her arms. "Go on," she urged everyone. "Take one. All of you."

Her sisters traded glances that ranged from angry to fearful. But everyone obeyed, reaching into the box for a sparkler, one by one. The same sparklers they used at the Kappa rush party each year, to determine who among the new rushes had Raven potential.

Scarlett waited until every girl in the house had taken one, herself included. Then she met her sisters' gazes, one by one, and prayed she was wrong. "Light them," Scarlett commanded.

Scarlett looked around the room with growing horror.

Not a single spark appeared in the whole room.

The Ravens' magic was gone.

CHAPTER TWENTY

Vivi

Hardly any of the Kappas slept that night. Most of the Ravens stayed up, scouring the grimoire for any hint to why the séance had gone so terribly wrong. Reagan blamed Scarlett for leading the group in an untested spell. Etta defended her but looked uncertain. Bailey grew frustrated when no one wanted to try a countercharm she'd read about—probably because it'd been discovered in the pocket of a corpse—and when Mei tried to get everyone to stop fighting, she ended up just making everyone shout even louder. And eventually, Scarlett went quiet, looking like the life had been drained from her.

Around two a.m., Vivi finally stumbled upstairs to try and sleep, which came in fits and starts. In the disorienting daze between wake and sleep, she allowed herself to believe that it'd all been just an awful dream, and that everything would be back to normal in the morning. But when Vivi staggered downstairs a little after dawn, Mei and Jess were still sitting at the kitchen table where Vivi had left them a few hours earlier.

"Any updates?" Vivi asked, her voice hoarse and ragged. Over the past few months, her magical powers had become a part of her, as natural and essential as the air in her lungs. Without them, she felt hollow and exhausted, as if someone had drained most of the blood from her body, leaving just enough to keep her alive. Barely. Reagan had spent the entire night in the bathroom, overcome with cramps and nausea.

"Doesn't seem to be," Mei said grimly. Without the magic for glamours or the energy for makeup, Mei looked pale, tired, and strangely vulnerable. "Any change with you?"

"No." Vivi shook her head, wincing from the effort. The first thing she'd done when she woke up was try to cast a simple levitation spell—one of the first she'd learned—but she hadn't been able to lift her phone from her nightstand.

With every passing minute, dread sank deeper into her bones. What would happen if they never got their magic back? She'd just been starting to get a handle on the grimoire and had only barely begun exploring the depths of her power. How could she go back to the way things were before? How could any of them?

She poured two mugs of coffee and trudged into the living room, where a few of the girls had fallen asleep, too distraught, worried, or exhausted to make it to their own rooms after their emergency gathering last night. Perhaps it was Vivi's imagination, but all the plants looked wilted, as if the life had been sucked out of them as well. The window seemed dustier than usual, and when Vivi lowered herself onto the couch, she noticed that the bottoms of her feet were covered in dirt. The charms that kept the house clean and tidy were clearly wearing off.

"What time is it?" Hazel asked, pushing herself up into a seated position.

"Almost eight." Vivi extended one of the mugs toward her. "Want some coffee?"

Hazel accepted the mug and took a long sip. "Thank you." She looked around the room. "Where's Scarlett?"

"I don't know. I haven't seen her. I'm sure she's . . . working on a plan right now," Vivi said, praying it was true.

"Dahlia never would've let this happen," Etta murmured from the couch as she stretched her arms over her head then rubbed her eyes. Vivi felt a flicker of indignation on her Big's behalf, but before she could say anything, Scarlett herself appeared in the doorway.

"No," Scarlett said wearily. She didn't just look tired, she looked defeated. "She wouldn't have. But I'm afraid Dahlia's gone. You're stuck with me. Unless any of you want to come up here and take my place right about now."

"What about your mom?" Reagan asked, slipping past Scarlett to join Etta on the couch. She was followed by Ariana and Bailey, who slumped on the floor. "Could she help us?"

Vivi stifled a bitter laugh. It was lucky for Reagan that Scarlett didn't have her magic, or else Reagan would spend the rest of the day picking maggots out of her hair.

"I'll assume that's a rhetorical question," Scarlett said icily.

"Not really." Reagan crossed her arms. "She's the head of the Monarchs. Maybe this has happened before. Or maybe they can help us fix it, at any rate."

"Oh, a few of them wrote in the spell book!" Ariana piped up. "We can read that and see if there's any mention of lost magic."

Scarlett's jaw clenched. She pointed to Ariana and Sonali. "After this meeting, you two get reading." Then she glared at Reagan. "As for calling in the alumnae, we will only consider that as a *last* resort. Do you have any idea what would happen to us if we admitted we lost our powers?"

"To us or to *you*?" Hazel said under her breath.

"We're given a lot of freedom here," Scarlett snapped. "We have our own house, we decide our own rules, govern ourselves. We cast whatever spells we want. Pool our strength between each other. Care to take a guess what will happen if the alumnae council decides we aren't capable of wielding this much responsibility?" This time, the room remained silent. After a moment, Scarlett nodded. "Didn't think so. Now, I'm going to give each of you assignments. We're going to figure this out. There's a chance the magic reacted badly with some recent spellwork. Think back to recent spells you cast, to anything unusual since we came back from winter break. We still don't know if someone did this to us—or if we did this to ourselves."

Vivi froze as a new wave of icy fear seeped through her. She still hadn't told Scarlett what she'd seen in the mirror last night. Someone knew about the talisman and was trying to send Vivi a message about it.

Or punish her for what she'd done.

A lump formed in Vivi's throat.

I need the grimoire.

Vivi rose to her feet. She barely even remembered deciding to move. She just started toward the stairs, the grimoire the only thought pulsing in her mind. *It will have an answer. It must.* She made it halfway across the living room before Scarlett's voice stopped her.

"I didn't dismiss you yet."

"I'll only be a minute," Vivi called over her shoulder. "I, uh . . . just need to grab something from my room. I think it might help."

"Sit. Down," Scarlett hissed.

Startled, Vivi fell back into her seat, wondering if perhaps Scarlett's magic had suddenly come back, because she felt utterly powerless to resist her command.

"You are *forbidden* from opening that book again. Do you understand?"

"What?" Vivi asked, cheeks flushing with embarrassment and frustration. "Why? There might be something in there that can help us."

"That book may have been the reason we lost our magic. We can't risk making things worse." The other girls exchanged glances Vivi didn't know how to read. Did everyone think that this was all her fault?

"Fine," Vivi said flatly.

"Go get it. I know you took it to your bedroom."

Her cheeks burned even hotter. Who the hell did Scarlett think she was, reprimanding Vivi in front of all the other girls? The grimoire was what had allowed Vivi to throw the most successful party in Kappa history. Just because Scarlett had messed up last night didn't mean the book itself was dangerous. "I'm not lying to you, Scarlett. You don't need to monitor my every move."

Scarlett's face hardened, and Vivi braced herself for whatever cruel words Scarlett was clearly preparing to throw her way. But then she took a deep breath and said, "Okay, fine. Just bring it to me later, all right? I'm going to lock it in the office. It'll be better for everyone that way."

The girls stayed in the living room for another hour, arguing about what they should do next. When it became clear that they weren't making any progress, Scarlett ordered everyone back to their rooms to rest. "We'll think more clearly once we've gotten some sleep. Let's reconvene this afternoon."

As they drifted out of the living room, Ariana stepped up next to Vivi and said softly, "No one thinks any of this is your fault."

"Yeah, I *know*," Vivi said tersely, then sighed. "Sorry, I'm just . . ."

"It's okay." Ariana gave her a sad smile. "We all are."

~

Back in her room, Vivi flopped on her bed and reached for the grimoire, tracing her finger along the cover. Just the weight of it in her hands felt comforting. Over the past few weeks, it had allowed her to unlock powers she didn't even realize she had. How could she just pretend none of that had ever happened? Especially now, when the situation was so desperate? She knew the grimoire contained the information she needed; she could sense it.

It didn't matter how angry Scarlett would be. She *needed* her magic back. Like oxygen, like air. She'd do anything to regain it.

I'm powerless without it.

Her heart sped up, and she pressed a hand to her chest, remembering the way it felt when Tiffany had cursed her. Remembering the horrible, wrenching sensation, pain like ribs snapping in her breastbone. Her heart going wild, frantic.

It beat that way now. She could hear it in her eardrums, feel it banging against her temples.

Without magic, she couldn't fight back. She couldn't defend herself from witches like Tiffany, from the Henosis talisman's power. She was going to be trapped again, going to lose everything, *die*.

Tentatively, she opened the cover and started flipping through the delicate pages, but soon fatigue took over, and when she felt her eyelids begin to droop, she tucked the grimoire under her pillow, turned onto her side, and gave in to sleep.

It felt like no time had passed when someone knocked on her door, startling her awake, but from the bright light streaming through the window, it was clearly past noon.

"Vivi?" Ariana called from the hall. "Are you in there?"

"Yeah," Vivi said, sitting up and rubbing her eyes. "I'll be down in a minute."

"Um, I think you should come down now." She sounded hesitant. Almost apologetic. "It's Mason. He's at the front door."

Vivi's gaze drifted to her phone. It was still plugged into her bedside table, where she'd left it that morning when she stumbled downstairs to meet the other girls. Even from here, she could see all the missed calls on the screen.

"Fine, I'm coming." She paused in front of her mirror, one hand raised. A habit, these days, to cast a glamour on herself before she went out. At the last second, she remembered. *No can do.* She resorted to pausing in her bathroom and splashing water on her face instead. It did nothing to quell the swollen, bloodshot look in her eyes. But at least some of the flushed red had faded from her cheeks.

Downstairs, the living room meeting had dispersed. Sonali had the alumnae book in her lap and was paging through it, Ariana beside her. A few other girls had hefty tomes perched on chairs and coffee tables. Still more, from the sounds of it, were hard at work in the kitchen; something was bubbling ferociously on the stove.

Vivi wove through her sisters toward the front door.

On the front porch, she found Mason sitting on the porch swing, his knees spread, head bent over them, shoulders sagging. He looked so sad that for a moment, she forgot about the chaos back in the house, forgot about her own fears and her lost magic.

Her heart throbbed.

"Mason?" She took a step closer. "What happened?"

When he raised his head, his eyes were clear, though rimmed in red. He looked almost as distraught as her. As if he hadn't slept a wink all night. But he'd seemed fine when they kissed good night after the party . . .

Vivi frowned. "You okay?"

"What do you think?" His voice came out harder than she expected. Razor-edged. "I just spent two hours explaining my career plans to my parents. Alone. Where the hell were you, Vivi?"

All at once, she remembered. Brunch. At his parents' house. This morning. The one she *promised* him she'd attend to help defuse the tension and support him.

Her lips parted. "I . . ."

"No." He shook his head. "You know what, I changed my mind. I don't want to hear another ridiculous excuse." His expression shifted from anger to hurt. "Last night you said you *loved* me. Then this morning you didn't even care enough to pick up your phone."

Something snapped in her chest. "We were dealing with something, okay? I'm sorry, but you're not the only one with problems."

"Oh, yeah?" He shoved to his feet and flung his arms wide. "So what are those problems? Huh, Vivi? What's so important that you keep blowing me off, treating me like I don't matter at all? Your precious social chair status, is that it?"

"It's not about the *status*. I have responsibilities—"

"To Kappa. Oh, yes, I know how many *responsibilities* they give you."

"What's *that* supposed to mean?" She bristled.

Mason paced back and forth across the porch. "You've been using Kappa as an excuse for weeks now. And I got it, I understood. Even when you stood me up, I saw how stressed you were, so I forgot about it. I *believed* you when you said you wouldn't do that to me again."

"I didn't mean to."

"You never do, do you?" His shoulders slumped. All at once, the fight went out of him. Without the anger, he just looked . . . sad.

I love you, Vivi. Was it only last night that he'd whispered those words? It felt like a lifetime ago. As if it had happened to another person.

"The reunion's over," Mason said. "I thought once we got past that, things would change. That after what we said to each other last night, you'd actually be here for me. But it hasn't even been a *day* since your big party, and already you're so busy you can't answer a phone call?"

"Mason . . ." What could she say right now? She had a vow to uphold, Kappa's secret to keep. This was bigger than just her. Her sisters' safety depended on it.

"I'm sorry," she whispered.

He shut his eyes and winced. He looked like she'd just sucker punched him. And maybe she had. She wished she could take the words back. She wished she could explain, tell him everything.

But wishing wouldn't change anything. Not without her magic.

When Mason met her gaze again, he looked older, somehow. Wearier, too. "I can't do this anymore. We're done." He waved a hand at Kappa House as he stormed off the porch. "I hope you figure whatever this is out."

She held her breath as she watched him go. But no matter how much she wanted to, she didn't call for him to stop.

CHAPTER TWENTY-ONE

Scarlett

Scarlett's mind wandered to an episode of her favorite childhood show as she watched Jess and Hazel page through *The Encyclopedia of Curse-Breaking & Removals,* only half paying attention to their murmured conversation. The characters on the show were witches who had lost their magic to a bad witch who had stolen it with a spell. Somehow, they managed to undo the spell and punish the offending witch before the last commercial break. Minnie had teased her about watching the show; it was nothing like how real witchcraft worked. The spells were inaccurate, and there were cartoonish special effects, like giant plumes of purple smoke when a spell was cast. Minnie had said, *You know real magic is never easy.* Scarlett knew, but she'd found it comforting then, and she longed for it now — a time when any problem could be solved in an hour or less.

"What about this one?" Hazel asked Jess.

Jess shook her head. "That spell is for spider removal."

Scarlett looked away from her sisters and out the window. This wasn't a television show. This was real life, and no matter how long it took, they would have to fix this themselves.

Scarlett took a deep breath. First the mixer, then the attack on

Bailey. Not to mention Jackson's love spell. And now this. Were they all related? Was someone truly plotting against them? All she'd done was lead her sisters into worse and worse situations this semester. And now they were utterly defenseless.

Her chest ached. Whoever planned this attack, Scarlett had to hand it to them. They were a terrifyingly effective opponent.

She jumped when someone touched her shoulder.

But it was only Etta, holding out a steaming mug. Scarlett almost asked what type of brew it was before she remembered. "Just tea," Etta said with a sigh. "And . . . sorry. For what I said earlier, about Dahlia."

Scarlett accepted it and blew on the steaming liquid, her eyes on the common room once more. "It's okay. Really. I get it." She caught more than a couple people glaring her direction, until they noticed her watching and quickly snapped back to their work. All except for Reagan, who continued to outright glower. "Am I being a total dictator?" she asked quietly.

Etta hummed under her breath for a moment. "Well, I understand *why*."

Scarlett groaned. "I have no choice. If we tell the alumnae council what's happened, they'll be all over us, especially after we lost Spring Fling privileges and nearly exposed our magic at the welcome mixer. Even if we *got* our magic back, they would impose all kinds of sanctions, barely let us use it."

The senior shrugged. "I said I understood." Then she cut Scarlett a sharper glance. "But don't pretend this is completely altruistic.

We both know you'll be the first one on the chopping block if this gets out."

Before Scarlett could reply, Etta swept away to deliver tea to the rest of the girls. Her heart sank.

She couldn't help thinking about what Xavier said at the bar the other night.

Was she only doing this to prove herself to her mother and to show up her sister? *Would* she have wanted this presidency if they hadn't come before? It made her jaw clench.

She could feel the whispers and stares on her back, like spiders crawling on her skin. She needed to be alone. Scarlett stood up abruptly and escaped to the back garden.

She felt . . . empty, without her magic. Wrung out. Who was she, if not a witch? For as long as Scarlett could remember, she'd known about her power. She'd studied how to better herself, how to perfect her spellcraft, how to be the best witch she could become.

She'd never even considered what her life would be like without it.

She tilted her head back to face the sky. What would Minnie think if she could see Scarlett now?

Bitterness crept in as a deep sense of longing to bury herself in Minnie's arms consumed her. *She'd probably tell me to quit feeling sorry for myself and get to work.* This snapped Scarlett out of her sense of self-pity. She owed it to her sisters — and to Minnie — to figure this out.

Scarlett weighed her theories. The grimoire must have had

something to do with it. The magic they'd cast using it had felt wrong: powerful and impossible to control. *Wicked magic?* whispered that voice in her head. Scarlett shuddered.

However, the grimoire didn't explain the glamours that backfired at their first party, Bailey's meltdown on the lawns, the strange fights that had sprung up around campus.

If someone was doing this *to* them . . .

Her first thought was Cait, the only other person on campus who Scarlett knew for a fact had used powerful magic recently. But a love spell was one thing. A curse to steal the powers of the strongest coven in the country?

That was something else entirely.

Yet who else on campus *could* it have been? It would have to be a fellow witch. It could be a fellow Kappa . . . but Scarlett banished the thought from her mind. Their coven had had enough betrayal for one year. She'd only consider that as a last resort.

Or maybe it was someone new to Westerly, someone who had been getting close to Kappa.

She straightened. For the first time since last night, she thought about Xavier watching her speech. The way he'd seemed awake, almost paying attention, when he should have been distracted along with the rest of the nonmagical dates in attendance.

And then there was the time she'd tried to read his mind. All she'd found was a blank wall. She'd thought her Swords spell had simply failed, but maybe not. Maybe Xavier knew enough magic to shield himself.

Maybe . . .

"Hey, can I talk to you?"

Vivi stepped into the garden, startling Scarlett out of her reverie. One glance at her Little made her forehead scrunch with worry. "Of course."

She'd never seen Vivi like this. Fists balled, face flushed, the whites of her eyes spidered with red. Like she'd been crying. Or fighting. Or maybe both.

"Are you . . ." Scarlett trailed off. Of course Vivi wasn't okay. None of them were.

But Vivi seemed to be taking the loss of their magic even harder than the rest.

"Mason just broke up with me." Vivi squeezed her eyes shut.

Scarlett's eyebrows shot upward. Last she'd checked, Vivi and Mason were doing well. Great, even. Just last night at the dance, Scarlett had seen them together, happier than ever. It was awkward, at first, thinking about her former love being her Little's current one. But it had gotten less awkward as time wore on. So much so that the idea of them breaking up seemed odd too. "What happened?"

Vivi stared past Scarlett at the forest, her gaze narrowed.

It was a beautiful day. Sunny and warm, with a faint scent of spring blossoms on the breeze. Somehow, it only soured Scarlett's mood more. It felt like the whole world was mocking them. Enjoying the Ravens' downfall.

After a moment, Scarlett cleared her throat. "If you don't want to talk about it . . ."

Vivi shook her head. "No, it's fine." She squinted back toward

Kappa House. "I just realized that it doesn't actually matter. Not in comparison to the rest of this."

Scarlett blinked. "You're allowed to be upset about more than one thing at once, you know. And you're allowed to talk to me about Mason."

Vivi crossed her arms. "I didn't come out here to talk about boys." She spun toward Scarlett, her gaze intense. "I . . . need to tell you something."

"Yes?"

The silence stretched. Wore thin. Scarlett got the distinct impression her Little was having an internal battle, though about what, she hadn't the faintest.

Finally, Vivi sucked in a deep breath. "I saw another . . . *vision*. At the party. I was off by myself near the mirror illusion, and the whole thing changed. First I saw myself wearing the Henosis talisman."

Scarlett's heart nearly stopped.

"And then I saw this old farmhouse up on a hill, surrounded by ravens. It looked so familiar . . ."

"You think someone was messing with your head?" Scarlett frowned. None of the Kappas would joke about that. They all knew how serious the Henosis talisman was. But nobody besides the Ravens even *knew* about the talisman.

Vivi shook her head. "It felt like someone was trying to tell me something, actually. Like they wanted me to come there. It was freaky, but . . . not wicked."

"It is hard to tell if something, or someone, is wicked," Scarlett said grimly. She would know. "Wickedness can feel alluring." Scarlett gazed out over the forest and suppressed a shiver. "So what are you suggesting, Vivi? That we try and find the house from your vision? Even if you wanted to, do you know how many old farmhouses there are in Georgia alone?"

"There was a sign." Vivi took a deep breath. "Lone Willow Farm. I looked it up, and . . . there's a place near here. Twenty-minute drive. The pictures online match what I saw in the mirror."

Scarlett hesitated. They *could* go. It wouldn't take long just to drive past it, even if they didn't venture inside. But still . . .

"If this *is* a message from whoever has stolen our power, wouldn't they want us to meet them at the creepy farmhouse? Is walking into their trap without our magic a good idea?"

"No," Vivi replied bluntly. "But can we ignore a potential lead when we don't have any others?"

Scarlett pressed her lips together, considering. "We do have one other lead. Maybe two."

"Who?"

Scarlett's mouth flattened to a grim line. "Xavier. He might have been lucid when we were speaking about the spell book at the reunion. And Cait put a love spell on Jackson."

Her Little's jaw dropped. "So *that's* why he . . . Oh, God, Scarlett." She took a step closer and touched her arm. "That's why you broke up with Xavier, too, isn't it? I'm so sorry."

Scarlett swallowed hard around the lump in her throat and laughed once, bitter. "Yeah, well. Good move on my part there, it turns out."

"I hate boys." Vivi scowled and then sighed. "Okay, I don't really mean that."

"I just . . ." Scarlett tugged on the end of her ponytail. "I feel like it's my fault. If I hadn't wiped Jackson's memory . . . If he knew about witches, he might not have fallen for her trap."

"No. No way. You were protecting Kappa," Vivi said. "You didn't have a choice. And besides, it's Cait's fault. She's the one using magic to mess with someone's mind, *control* them." For a split second, something flickered across Vivi's expression. Doubt, maybe, or fear. Then the anger flooded back in. "We have to stop her."

"How?" Scarlett spread her hands. "We have no magic, not anymore. And if Cait's the one behind all this . . . I mean, what if she has all the strength of the Ravens now?"

Vivi chewed on her lower lip. "Is there anything we can do to help Jackson?" she asked.

"Not until we get our own magic back," Scarlett said, hating the way that sounded. Hating the thought of leaving Jackson trapped a moment longer. But she didn't have a choice. Yet again.

Vivi straightened, fists balled. "Let's check out the farm first. If it is a trap, then we will know who our enemy is. If it's nothing, then it's nothing, but at least we'll know."

Scarlett nodded. "All right. I'll grab the car. And let's tell someone where we are going just in case. Meet me around front in—" She broke off and sniffed at the air. It smelled smoky all of a sudden. Almost as if . . .

"Fire!" Reagan shouted from the front porch. Scarlett and Vivi took one look at each other and sprinted around the side of the house.

By the time they arrived, Etta and Hazel were already aiming the garden hose at it. Flames licked across the hogweed bushes at the edge of their yard.

The bushes Etta had so carefully planted as a protection spell for Kappa.

Between the other girls, they quickly subdued the small fire. But as Scarlett surveyed the blackened and charred remains of the plants, she couldn't help but note with a pit in her stomach: one more magical defense system for their house was gone.

CHAPTER TWENTY-TWO

Vivi

Vivi and Scarlett drove in silence for most of the way, both of them absorbed by their own thoughts. From her assured movements and the set of her mouth, it was clear that Scarlett had shifted into get-it-done crisis mode.

Vivi just wished she could say the same thing for herself. With every passing hour, she felt more nauseated and twitchy, as if she were going through magic withdrawal. Her fingers itched to cast a spell, but no matter how many times Vivi muttered tried-and-true words, the crackling energy of magic never came.

It still seemed highly likely that they were walking into some kind of trap by answering the summons to Lone Willow Farm, but at this point she wasn't sure what other option they had.

"You okay?" Scarlett asked, shooting a quick glance at Vivi before turning her attention back to the road. They'd just turned off the highway and were driving along a shady road lined with large oak trees. The houses here were much larger than they were in the city, with wraparound porches and enormous velvety green lawns.

"I'm fine," Vivi said automatically. "Or whatever fine means, given the circumstances."

"We're going to figure this out. I promise."

Vivi wished she could find her Big's confidence comforting, but the truth was they were in way, way over their heads. "I know," she said, hoping the words sounded more convincing to Scarlett than they did to her.

The road widened as the quaint suburbs turned more rural, with the houses spread out at much longer intervals. After another few miles, Scarlett slowed the car and squinted at the numbers on the mailboxes. "It should be one of these . . ." she said, looking from the GPS to the house they were passing.

Vivi leaned forward to help. "Number forty-nine?" She pointed at a gated driveway up ahead between two brick pillars. They couldn't see much beyond it, just a tree-lined drive, the boughs so long and overgrown they nearly touched the pavement.

The gate stood wide open.

The girls traded uneasy looks. "This is how horror movies start," Scarlett said.

"Do we want our magic back or not?" Vivi asked wearily.

"I didn't say I wouldn't go." Scarlett turned into the driveway and gripped the steering wheel more tightly. "Just, if we die in here, remember that I called it."

"If we die, I'll make sure you get full credit."

The driveway curved through a yard that looked as unkempt as the trees. Grass swayed knee-high or taller, and weeds ran rampant along the driveway, which itself had cracked and split in places.

Then the house came into view.

It looked just like it had in the mirror: a tall, Victorian farmhouse that appeared almost like a top hat—or perhaps a crown—perched on a steep hill. Vivi shuddered slightly; she wished she knew who —or what—had summoned her here and what they wanted.

"The horror movie vibes intensify," Scarlett said briskly, as if this were all par for the course for her. As though she regularly drove up to creepy, abandoned-looking houses that appeared to people in mirrors. Perhaps she had. Scarlett had grown up among witches and magic; her idea of "normal" was very, very different from Vivi's.

Scarlett parked the car, and after a moment's pause, the girls exchanged glances and both climbed out.

As they approached the porch, Vivi stopped and grabbed Scarlett's arm. "I'm not sure this is a good idea."

"And you're just realizing this *now?*" Scarlett asked, annoyed.

"Please tell me you know jiujitsu or something," Vivi said. She tried to sound jokey, but the truth was that, without magic, they were both incredibly vulnerable.

"No jiujitsu," Scarlett said with a sigh. "I took Krav Maga for a few years when I was younger. My parents are big believers in women being able to defend themselves, with or without magic."

Vivi managed to smile through her growing dread. *Of course* Scarlett knew Krav Maga.

They made their way up the uneven wooden steps and onto the porch, which groaned under their weight. Vivi shifted from side to side, just in case too much pressure on one floorboard sent them crashing through.

Scarlett brushed a few cobwebs from a doorbell, then rang it without hesitation. Somewhere deep inside the house, a bell tolled, low and deep as a church tower.

"Not ominous at all," Vivi said grimly.

"Will you relax? There's no reason to freak out unless—" Scarlett cut herself off as the door creaked open.

By itself.

They exchanged another look, longer this time. "It seems like they're expecting us," Scarlett said with forced glibness. "Shall we?" She stepped inside, and Vivi followed, her heart thudding so loudly, it drowned out the creaking floorboards beneath her.

The foyer was dark and shadowy despite the midday sun outside, and it took a moment for Vivi's eyes to adjust. The peeling, faded wallpaper must've been beautiful once—pale tea roses on a dove gray background, and the heavy brass coatrack and umbrella stand spoke to the house's former glory. It all should've given off major haunted house vibes, but while the air had the heavy, almost smoky quality that built up after years of spellwork, it lacked the acid, metallic scent Vivi had come to associate with wicked magic.

"Come look at this," Scarlett whispered. She was staring at a small oil painting of a raven perched at the top of a church steeple. Vivi stood next to her and leaned in for a closer look. The raven's glossy black feathers were rippling ever so slightly, as if rustled by a faint breeze. Coincidence?

Silently, Vivi and Scarlett moved from the foyer into a hallway paneled in dark wood. More paintings lined the walls, mostly portraits of formidable-looking women in various historical costumes, including some Vivi thought she recognized from similar portraits at Kappa House. There was a Black woman with gold jewelry and an emerald turban, and a white woman in seventeenth-century Dutch garb. Like the raven painting, most of these had small glamours woven into the paint so that jewelry glittered or trees in the background swayed.

As they made their way down the hall, the portraits grew more modern. "Oh my God," Scarlett said as she stopped in her tracks to stare at a large, full-length portrait of a beautiful woman in a pink cocktail dress. "That's my mom. And I think that's the dress she wore at Homecoming the year she was Kappa president."

"Do you think this house belonged to a Kappa?"

"Or someone who's weirdly obsessed with us."

"Not *everyone*'s obsessed with you, Scarlett," Vivi teased.

"Oh yeah?" Scarlett nodded at a painting at the end of the hall. "Then how do you explain that one?"

Vivi shot her a quizzical look and walked over to the painting in question, then jumped backwards with a sharp gasp. It showed two girls standing in front of a gray Victorian farmhouse, a Black girl in a cream sweater dress and a white girl in jeans and a gray cardigan.

It was Scarlett and Vivi.

Vivi glanced down at her gray cardigan and shivered. "How could someone have painted this in five minutes? The paint doesn't even look wet."

"Hello?" Scarlett shouted suddenly, sending a startled Vivi leaping to the side. "Hello? Is anyone here?" Her voice echoed for a moment, then there was silence.

Except it wasn't quite silent. There was a faint, rhythmic creak coming from the walls, as if they were expanding and contracting.

Almost as if the house were breathing.

And she could have been imagining it, but Vivi thought she could sense a soft thud under the floorboards and couldn't help but think about Daphne's favorite short story, "The Tell-Tale Heart."

"Hell-ooo," Scarlett called again. "Anyone home?"

"Let's keep looking," Vivi said, and motioned for Scarlett to follow her through an open door into what seemed to be a large sitting room. A grand circular staircase swept up the middle, and cobwebs laced the banister. There was another portrait on the far wall, larger than the ones they'd seen in the hall. It was an oil painting of a stern-looking elderly white woman in a high-necked black dress with a lace collar, her mouth set in a disapproving frown.

Most of the furniture was draped in white sheets, and the few uncovered pieces were coated with a thick layer of dust. "It doesn't look like anyone's been in here for *years*," Scarlett said, wrinkling her nose.

"I'm not sure about that." Vivi pointed to a silver tray atop a low, round table that had been set for tea. Steam unfurled from the teapot, and there was a platter of freshly baked pastries.

"Okay, *what* is going on?" Scarlett crossed her arms and looked around. "I don't have time for this Beauty and the Beast crap." She cleared her throat and shouted, "Will whoever brought this tea in five minutes ago PLEASE come back?"

There was a long moment of silence and then, somewhere in the distance, a faint echo of laughter.

Both girls jumped.

"So there *is* someone here," Scarlett said, whipping her head from side to side.

The same laugh came again, but this time, from a completely different direction. The hairs on the back of Vivi's neck rose as she turned to follow the sound and found herself facing the portrait of the old woman again. But this time, she wasn't frowning.

She was smirking.

"Who do you think that is?" Scarlett asked, moving closer to examine the gold plaque on the bottom of the dusty, gilded frame. *"Agata Templeton,"* she read. "That name sounds really familiar but I can't quite place it."

"I think she was the one laughing," Vivi said quietly. The pulse Vivi had felt beneath the floorboards was growing louder, but this time, it seemed to be in the wall. "Can you feel that?"

"Feel what?"

"I'm . . . I'm not sure, exactly. It almost feels . . ." She trailed off, unwilling to say the words aloud. *Like a heartbeat.*

Vivi took a few steps toward the vibration, toward an ornate wooden writing desk against the far wall. As she inched closer, the pulse thrummed louder until it almost seemed to be coming from inside her.

A huge leather book lay on the desk. It seemed to be some kind of old almanac, and it'd been opened to a map of Savannah, though it had to be from decades ago, when it was still a small, sleepy port city. Vivi leaned in and saw a large inset in the bottom right corner—a detailed close-up of the Westerly College campus. There was Faculty Row, and there Hewitt Library and Taylor Hall, but other buildings were unfamiliar, and there were stretches of green-sketched lawns where today freshman dorms and the science wing stood.

"This was Westerly in 1858, one year after its founding," Scarlett said, pointing at a date in the corner. "Look at the woods." She gestured to a thick forest surrounding campus. The woods were far smaller now, just a stretch of trees out behind Kappa. But back in the day, it had been a veritable forest. And right in the center of it, between drawings of fat oak trees and branching willows, someone had drawn a dark blue circle with a seven-pointed red star in the center.

The same symbol that had been on the Henosis talisman.

A chill ran through Vivi. There was something written in tiny script under the symbol, and she grabbed the antique magnifying glass next to the book to take a closer look. "It says *Hadesgate*," she read. "What do you think that means?"

"Are you sure?" Scarlett looked startled.

Vivi handed her the magnifying glass. "See for yourself."

Scarlett hesitated, looking genuinely frightened for the first time since they'd arrived. "It's an old word for a spot where the veil between our realm and the next has worn thin."

"What are you talking about? What other realm?"

Scarlett shot her a withering look. "Where do you think magic comes from? Our spells and glamours are just little trickles compared to the ocean of magic churning just beyond the veil."

The words "just beyond the veil" sent goose bumps down Vivi's arm. The old Vivi, the one who'd written off Daphne as a charlatan and her tarot clients as desperate rubes, would've scoffed at such a phrase. But that was before Vivi had learned that witchcraft was real and witnessed the terrifying power of wicked magic. At this point, it seemed like anything might be possible. "Okay, but what does this have to do with us?"

"I'm not sure. I'd always heard rumors about a Hadesgate on Westerly's campus. That it's why there's so much magic in Savannah. But this is the first time I've seen any evidence of it."

"But it might not be a bad thing, right? It's just a source of magic?"

"Magic isn't the only thing that can pass through a Hadesgate," Scarlett said grimly.

Vivi pointed to the star again. "The gate seems like it would've been in the middle of the forest back in 1858, but most of the woods are gone now." She leaned in for a closer look and squinted, then turned to Scarlett. "Do you maybe think . . ."

"That those are the woods behind Greek Row? Yeah, I do."

"So that means this gate might be near Kappa House."

Something clanked behind them, and both girls spun around. The items on the silver tea tray were rattling, as if stirred by invisible hands. A moment later, the teapot rose in the air, hovered for a few seconds, then tipped and began to pour steaming liquid into one of the delicate china cups on the tray.

"Of course this is happening," Scarlett said under her breath. With an almost practiced motion, she walked over and reached for the cup just as the tea reached the cup. Feeling slightly dazed, Vivi followed suit, although her arm was shaking too hard to hold the cup steady, and tea sloshed over the rim.

"Now what?" Vivi asked. "You're not really going to drink this, are you?"

"I'm not leaving until I find out what happened to our magic, and if this is the game I have to play, so be it. If this person wanted to hurt us, they would've done so already." She took a sip of the tea, paused, then exhaled. "Seems to be fine. Drink up."

Vivi watched Scarlett drain her tea with a speed that would've horrified Marjorie Winter, then followed suit, ignoring the scalding heat. When Scarlett had finished, she held up her cup and squinted as she examined it. "I knew it. We have to read the tea leaves."

Vivi shot her a skeptical look, but then she peeked into her own cup and yanked her head back in surprise. There was clear shape at the bottom of her cup. "Are you seeing what I'm seeing?" Vivi whispered.

"I'm not sure. Is that . . ."

"The Henosis talisman," Vivi finished. Even when rendered in damp tea leaves, the shape was enough to send chills down the back of her neck. She was about to lower the cup when the talisman seemed to explode, and the dark brown leaves began to shift and spin, forming a new image. At first, it looked like a man's face, but as the leaves settled, other details emerged. Horns sprang from his head, and his mouth twisted open in a gruesome scream, his parted lips revealing bared snake fangs instead of teeth.

Vivi jerked back. "What *is* that?"

"It's a demon," Scarlett said faintly. She jerked her head up from the cup to look Vivi in the eye. "Oh my God, when we destroyed the talisman . . ."

"We what?" The pulsing from the walls was growing stronger; it was so loud now, Vivi could barely hear her own thoughts. "Scarlett, when we destroyed the talisman, we did what?"

Scarlett ignored Vivi and whipped around to face the portrait. "Did you trap a demon in the Henosis talisman?" she barked.

The woman in the painting nodded. The smirk was gone — her lips pressed together into a thin line, her eyes wide with fear.

"And . . ." Scarlett swallowed and briefly closed her eyes. When she spoke again, her voice was trembling. "Did we let him out again?"

"No," Vivi whispered. "No, that's impossible." But even as she spoke, the painting shifted again. Her eyes closed as her mouth opened, lips wrenched apart in a silent, twisted scream. A cry of agony. Of horror.

Scarlett stumbled back onto the couch and buried her head in her hands. But Vivi was frozen in place, one terrible truth echoing through her brain. She and Scarlett had unleashed a *demon,* a monster that was coming for them.

And without their magic, they were doomed.

CHAPTER TWENTY-THREE

Scarlett

"Here's something." Scarlett turned the book in her lap so Vivi could read it, too.

They'd left the house in a hurry and come straight to the library at Kappa. If their enemy really was a demon, then Scarlett had a lot of reading to do. After all, demons were supposed to be a thing of the past, dealt with a long time ago by more powerful witches than her. When she was young, Eugenie used to read aloud from eighteenth-century demon-hunting manuals to scare her. She'd run crying to Minnie's room after, and Minnie would let Scarlett sleep curled up next to her.

She wished more than anything she could do that now.

"Demons have plagued witches for centuries without known cause." Scarlett pointed to the first paragraph that had *demon* in it.

As always, Scarlett marveled at how dispassionately her ancestors had written about the things that threatened them. The witches who penned this left out an important part: what it must have felt like being hunted. Maybe they were braver than Scarlett and her sisters. Or maybe terror was just so damn commonplace.

Vivi leaned in. "Demons require a host to pass through the veil and into the human realm," she read. "They can take any form by force, but a body offered willingly is the best . . . Hang on." Vivi looked up, eyes wide. "Does this mean what I think it does?"

Scarlett's frown deepened. "It means the demon is someone on campus. Someone who looks human."

Vivi chewed on her lip. "*Any*one? How can we tell who it is?"

Scarlett flipped through the surrounding pages, then checked the book's index. That paragraph was the only mention of demons. "I don't know." She groaned and leaned her head back on the couch, staring up at the ceiling. "Even my mother's never seen one, as far as I know. Nor have any of the living alumnae."

Beside her, Vivi drew in a sharp breath.

Scarlett glanced over. "What?"

"Well . . ." Her Little hesitated. "You're not going to like it."

Scarlett groaned. "I don't like *any* of this. What's one more piece of bad news?"

"We could call your mom."

Scarlett sat bolt upright in the chair. "Vivi, I told you—"

"I know, I know. If we go to the council, they'll freak out and put all kinds of strict sanctions in place . . . But last semester, after what happened with Tiffany, remember how Marjorie was afterward? My mom, too. They wanted to help us."

"Then let's call *your* mother," Scarlett grumbled.

Another pause, while Vivi considered. "We could try Daphne, but I'm not sure this is her area of expertise. She left Kappa before she'd even graduated, remember? She spent the last twenty-odd years running *away* from the Ravens' history. I'm not sure she'd be the best resource."

Scarlett breathed out a slow sigh. As much as she hated to admit it, Vivi *did* have a point. And they didn't need to involve the entire council. Just Marjorie.

The very thought of admitting to her mother how bad things had gotten made Scarlett nauseous. But if swallowing her pride would protect Kappa and her sisters, then she had no other choice.

"Okay," she said, finally. "But I'm going to need moral support for this one."

Vivi reached over to squeeze her hand. "I'm not going anywhere, Big Sis."

Marjorie answered on the first ring, almost as if she'd been expecting a call. "Scarlett," she said. "I hope you're calling with good news for once."

Scarlett and Vivi traded grimaces. "Not exactly." Scarlett cleared her throat. "I was wondering if I could ask you for more detail about . . . about the Henosis talisman." If Scarlett had read the leaves right, the demon had been released when they destroyed it. Maybe if they knew who created the talisman and how, they could put the demon back.

"I told you everything you need to know about that accursed thing last semester," Marjorie snapped. "Or have you already forgotten?"

"No, no, I know. It possessed your friend and made her attack you. But do you know where it came from originally? Who made it?"

"I thought we had put all this unpleasantness behind us. You have more important things to focus on right now, Scarlett. A president can't spend all day wallowing over past mistakes; she needs to be looking forward, to the future."

Vivi rolled her eyes, and Scarlett flashed her a small, grateful smile. Dealing with her family *was* easier with a friend.

"Anything you can tell me about the talisman, or about the Hadesgate—"

"What did you just say?" Marjorie's voice suddenly dropped low and dangerous.

"The Hadesgate." Scarlett blinked at her phone. "The one that's rumored to be somewhere on Westerly's campus . . ."

"I don't want you anywhere near that thing, do you understand me? There are forces at work much too advanced for college girls to meddle in."

Scarlett's heart skipped a beat. "You know where it is." She shut her eyes, remembering the map they saw. It had been in the middle of the forest, somewhere along what was now Greek Row. Slowly, a horrible suspicion dawned. "Mama, is it *in* Kappa House? Is that why the house has so much power?"

"What did I just say? This is ridiculous. I've given you an order. Stay away from it."

Scarlett bristled. But then . . . *Swallow your pride,* she reminded herself. She made this call for a reason. "Mama, this is serious. I think there's something really wrong on campus. The Ravens are in trouble."

A long pause. Finally, Marjorie sniffed. "Scarlett, I've already told you everything I know about that cursed gate. But if you like,

I can speak to the Monarchs about stepping in. It will involve a thorough investigation into the matters at hand, including your recent . . . probation. The council may find it necessary to find a suitable replacement of Kappa leadership. Is that what you want?"

Scarlett's voice came out small. "No, ma'am."

"Very good." Then she hung up.

Scarlett stared at the screen, openmouthed. "Unbelievable."

Vivi reached over to squeeze her shoulder. "Sorry. That was . . . Damn."

Scarlett had thought, after last semester, she and Marjorie were on better footing. That at the very least her mother would help if Scarlett truly needed it. But Marjorie Winter had just made it clearer than ever: the Ravens were on their own.

Scarlett tightened her fist around the phone. "Well. At least we learned one thing." She looked over at Vivi. "If I know anything about my mother, the Hadesgate is in this house."

∼

Scarlett should've known all along.

She and Vivi stood at the top of the basement stairs and gazed into the dark.

It made a lot of sense. Kappa House had so much power — the rooms that glamoured themselves to match the whimsy of whoever entered. The strong wards all around the property.

Plus, Scarlett remembered the boiler and the heat waves she'd felt pouring off it, the last time she came down here to fix the water. Those whispers that she'd heard, far louder than any water backed up in a pipe could truly explain . . .

It was the Hadesgate. Right beneath their noses.

Other alumnae had to have known. But none of them bothered to tell the current Kappas. *More secrets. Back to haunt us just like always.* Scarlett balled her fists.

"Together?" Vivi asked, nearly startling Scarlett straight out of her skin.

She kept her expression calm. "Together."

She turned on the basement light. It flickered to life, casting a dim yellow glow over the staircase.

They moved forward. One step, then another. With each one, her breath came faster, and her eyes darted to take in the basement. She braced herself for the heat wave, the whispers they'd heard last time.

But so far, it looked normal. Mundane, even. Just the water heater in one corner, the rarely used laundry machines in another. Unless they regained their magic fast, Scarlett had a feeling they'd need to start figuring out how to do real laundry.

God. Scarlett hadn't done laundry in . . . ever?

"So . . . are we going to talk about the whole someone-on-campus-is-a-demon thing?" Vivi asked.

Scarlett hesitated on the bottom step. "Well, let's see. As far as I can remember—and this is from children's stories, so big grain of salt—demons love to sow discord and chaos wherever they go. They feed on it. Plus, they'd have magic, just like a witch. So it still could be Xavier or Cait. Anyone else?"

Vivi side-eyed Scarlett. "*Cait?* You really think a demon would bother casting a love spell?"

Scarlett frowned. "Maybe not. But she has more magic than she did before. We can't ignore that. And the other Thetas have all been acting really out of character this semester," Scarlett mused. "There's Maria, of course. She does seem like the type."

"I don't know. Tim keeps going on and on about Maria's heart of gold," Vivi said. "It doesn't seem like a demon would go through the trouble of being a good girlfriend."

Scarlett tilted her head. "Hang on. Didn't one of the other Thetas see you doing magic?"

Vivi winced. "Rose. She's a freshman."

"So she's new to campus too. Suspicious."

Her Little looked torn. "She seems nice, though. Wouldn't a demon be . . . I don't know. Evil?"

"Not if it needed to lure people in or something." Scarlett started to pick her way across the basement toward the boiler.

They needed to figure out what the demon wanted. What its goal on campus was. It couldn't just be stealing the Ravens' magic and causing a few fistfights. There had to be an endgame . . .

With every step closer to the boiler she took, the air grew hotter and thicker around her.

"Do you hear that?" Vivi asked suddenly.

At first, all Scarlett heard was the steady drip of water somewhere in the distance. Probably a pipe in the corner with a small leak. *Drip, drip, drip.*

Reflexively, she flinched and glanced up, afraid another pipe was going to burst and douse her in sewage again. But there was no groaning or gurgling like last time. And the lights remained lit, a steady, ugly yellow. "Should I call the plumber?"

Vivi shook her head. "Not that. The other sound."

Scarlett had to hold her breath—hold her entire body still, in fact—to hear it. But then she did. Like a distant roll of thunder far, far away. A low vibration, so steady it almost seemed like white noise, part of the background. Except now that she was listening . . . was it getting louder?

Beside her, Vivi gasped and leaped backwards. Away from the boiler.

"What?"

"The heat." Vivi pointed.

Scarlett could see it now. A shimmer in the air between her Little and the water heater. Like heat waves on the pavement of a hot summer day. She reached out a hand, tentative. Her fingers warmed. Then got hotter, so hot it felt like touching a stove. She yanked her hand away, wincing.

"We should go."

At that same moment, the ground beneath their feet heaved.

Vivi screamed and grabbed her arm. Scarlett stretched out a hand, reflexively reaching for her Cups magic. But of course, no answering power surged inside her.

The rumbling grew louder. Almost deafening. A painfully loud bass note she felt in her chest, her fingers, her scalp.

With a tremendous cracking sound, a deep crevasse split the basement floor between them. Vivi scrambled backwards, but

Scarlett was too close. She felt something seize her around the ankles, pin her in place. She shrieked, reached out to grab on to something, anything.

Vivi caught her wrists and yanked.

Scarlett looked down and immediately wished she hadn't. A thick plume of smoke had wrapped around her legs, gnarled and knobby, almost like a blackened tree root. Only it moved, snaking further up her calves toward her thighs, squeezing tighter as it went.

She pulled herself toward Vivi, and Vivi yelled through gritted teeth. They both leaned away with all their might, and finally, Scarlett felt a snap. A give, and she flew into her Little, both of them crashing to the floor.

As they landed, the room . . . changed.

The ground was thick, black sludge, and the ceiling dripped with branches like the one that had tried to strangle Scarlett. Twisted, gnarled roots and tree limbs as far as the eye could see in either direction, like a dead forest. And above it all, a sky so pitch-black Scarlett thought she could trip up into it and be lost forever . . .

She squeezed her eyes shut. The floor rumbled once, twice.

When she opened her eyes again, it was gone. The basement was back, Vivi still lying beneath her, panting. Scarlett scrambled to her feet and helped Vivi up. Together, they turned.

Beside the boiler, a large crack had appeared in the cement floor. As they stared, a single curl of smoke escaped it, drifted toward the ceiling, and dissipated.

Both girls took one look at each other and raced for the stairs.

They didn't speak until they'd sprinted back upstairs, slammed the door, and locked it behind them.

"Did you see that too?" Vivi finally asked, leaning against the door, her voice quivering. "The . . . the roots, and the black sky?"

Scarlett could only nod, her throat tight.

"I saw that once before." Vivi sucked in a breath. "At the Thirsty Scholar, after that bar fight. For a second, the whole pub looked like it was in another world or something. A dead one."

Scarlett grimaced. "Maybe it *was* a dead world. A world on the other side of the veil. The world that the demon wants to create." She thought about the whispers she'd heard like voices calling out from somewhere beyond.

Vivi swallowed hard. "What do we do now?"

Scarlett straightened her shoulders. Tried her best to put on a presidential face. "Now?" She glanced at her Little. "Now we find this demon. We have three possible three suspects over at Theta and one mysterious boy . . ." Scarlett got an idea. "Vivi, how would you feel about cozying up to Theta?"

CHAPTER TWENTY-FOUR

Vivi

Vivi forced herself to take a calm sip of coffee as she listened to Tim tell her about that morning's brutal early practice. She hadn't been able to stop trembling since leaving the basement and would've given anything for one of Mei's nerve-steadying brews, but in the twenty-four hours since they'd lost their magic, the Ravens' herbs had all withered. Vivi wasn't certain whether any of the Thetas had anything to do with the Kappas' missing magic, but she was sure as hell going to get to the bottom of it. She'd invited Rose for cupcakes in town, but they weren't meeting until five. Vivi had felt too twitchy and unsettled to do anything productive, let alone study, so she'd texted Tim to see if he wanted to meet her for coffee at the Grind. He'd arrived still sweaty from practice, and grateful for the iced vanilla latte Vivi had waiting for him.

Behind the counter, a server dropped a tray with a clatter, and Vivi flinched, sloshing her coffee.

"Are you okay?" Tim asked, surveying her with a frown. "You seem kinda jumpy."

"I'm fine," Vivi said, suppressing a bitter laugh. She certainly wasn't fine, but trying to explain it to Tim would only make her problems far worse. For the first time since joining Kappa, Vivi wondered what her life would've been like if she hadn't been initiated into a secret world of witches and magic. She tried to imagine a world where her problems concerned messy roommates and tough midterms, not vengeful demons and portals to other realms.

"Did you stay up too late studying?"

"Yeah, something like that." She needed to change the subject. As if summoned, a gray-haired Black man in a tweed jacket appeared at the table. "Professor Moore," Tim said, rising to his feet to shake the man's hand. "How are you?"

"I'll be better when you boys trounce Athens Tech this weekend," Professor Moore said with a smile. "How's the defensive line coming along?"

"Best we've had in years."

"Glad to hear it. I'll be rooting for you."

Tim nodded. "Thank you, sir."

As Professor Moore walked away, Vivi shook her head incredulously. "That's the *third* person who's come up to you since we've been here. Doesn't it get exhausting, having to be so available all the time? It's like you're a celebrity."

"Sometimes, I guess. But then I remember that I'll be a total nobody again after I graduate, so it seems silly to complain about it now."

"No plans to play professionally?"

He shrugged. "It's been a long time since a Westerly player made it to the NFL. I'm good, but I'm not, like, a once-in-a-generation talent. And honestly, I don't think my heart's in it. Might be time to try something new, you know? Actually . . ." Tim paused to take a long sip of his iced latte, "I'm actually a little jealous of you, being a freshman and everything. You have so much time to experiment, figure out what you really want."

"I guess so." Tim was right in theory. But so far, battling vengeful witches wielding wicked magic and tracking down demons hadn't left her with a whole lot of time to experiment with anything another than trying not to die. It was a nice thought, though. Imagining what her life at Westerly might be like when she could focus on normal college things.

"I'm serious," Tim insisted. "Take the weirdest classes you can find."

"I'm already taking a history class called God and the Devil in Colonial America. Right now, we're studying accounts of seventeenth-century exorcisms. It's actually pretty interesting—"

"Sorry," Tim cut in, looking at his phone. "It's getting late. What time did you say you were meeting Rose?"

"Five. I guess I should get going." She paused. "Do you think it's weird? That I'm hanging out with a Theta?"

"Not at all! I'm glad you're getting to know some of them. And I'm really excited for you to spend time with Maria." Tim smiled. "I think you'll be pleasantly surprised by how well you get along."

~

It was twilight by the time Vivi reached the bakery, and the warm light in the windows gave the store a cozy glow. She could see Rose at a table inside, typing on her phone while her foot tapped with nervous or excited energy.

It had been surprisingly easy to lure Rose out for a coffee date. All Vivi and Scarlett had done was stage a loud argument in the dining hall. Then Vivi had stormed off, right past a table of gawking Thetas. After a quick nudge from Maria, Rose had practically leaped out of her chair to follow Vivi and ask whether everything was okay. Vivi had shaken her head wearily and then asked if Rose wanted to meet up later. "I'd love your advice on something," she'd said.

They ordered their cupcakes and made small talk while they waited for the server to bring them over. In spite of herself, Vivi found Rose easy to talk to as they discussed possible majors, classes they liked (art history) and ones they hated (the statistics requirement). But Vivi didn't lose sight of her mission, and while she'd never been a good actress, it was time to give the performance of her lifetime.

"It's just not fair," Vivi said with a sigh after she'd turned the conversation to her Big. "Scarlett puts *so* much pressure on me. I'm only a freshman, and I have other things going on in my life too. Doesn't she get it?"

Rose nodded sympathetically and picked up her own drink, a cloyingly sweet-smelling spiced chai latte. "So what else *is* going on?"

Part of Vivi felt a little guilty, taking advantage of Rose like this. Then again, if Rose had stolen the Kappas' magic, Vivi wouldn't feel bad about *any* trick she pulled in order to get it back.

"Well . . ." Vivi hesitated, unsure how much of the truth to reveal. "My boyfriend and I just broke up—"

"Oh, God, you poor thing." Rose stretched a hand across the table to clasp Vivi's.

The kindness in her voice was enough to break through Vivi's defenses. She'd mentioned her breakup as a bonding technique, a way to create a sense of connection with Rose. But the hurt was far too raw and fresh for Vivi to harness it like that, and the merest touch was enough to a release a new wave of crushing pain.

She blinked a few times, trying to regain her composure. Now was not the time to fall apart. "Anyway. I just wish Scarlett understood how I felt." She was mortified to feel her throat closing up, the words difficult to force through.

"Can you talk to anyone else in Kappa?" Rose asked.

Vivi shook her head. "There's no one I can be honest with." The lie felt immensely disloyal to her wonderful sisters, any of whom would've dropped whatever they were doing if Vivi needed them. But then again, the Kappas all had much bigger problems to deal with at the moment. Scarlett had called a house meeting for tonight to brief the other girls about the demon that had escaped through the Hadesgate.

On top of all that, Vivi was torn about what to do with the grimoire. She had only *just* started to understand how to work the spells. It was big, powerful, world-altering magic, magic that was all hers, magic she could work without even the need for her sisters' strength. With it in her grasp, she had finally started to feel *safe* again. Scarlett had banned her from using it, but Vivi wondered if it might hold the key to getting their magic back.

"I'm sorry you're going through that." Rose frowned for a moment, before her face brightened, like the sun breaking through the clouds. "Hey, I have an idea that might cheer you up, if you're interested?"

Vivi cocked her head. "What is it?"

"Well." Rose leaned forward on her elbows. Her excitement was contagious, in spite of Vivi's mood. "Theta has been planning the Delta/Theta mixer for *weeks*. It's going to be the best party of the year. Why don't you come? That is, if you Kappas are allowed to go to other sororities' parties."

Vivi hesitated. Scarlett wanted her to get close to the Thetas and ferret out their secrets. But she had also warned Vivi, repeatedly, to be careful. Vivi didn't have her magic anymore—and she felt empty without it, powerless and exposed. And even if she found the demon, neither of them had any plan for vanquishing it without their magic.

Her chest tightened once more, the familiar pressure against her rib cage bringing her back to Tiffany, the woods, the knife.

This Theta party could be the perfect opportunity for Vivi to learn what they were really up to. But it might also be incredibly dangerous.

Rose, sensing her hesitation, waved a hand. "If you can't make it, don't worry. I shouldn't have asked. Y'all have so many rules at Kappa, I don't know how you handle it. People thought we were the super intense ones." She laughed again, the sound just a touch hollow.

"Are you kidding?" Vivi forced a bright smile. The longer she held it, the more real it started to feel. "I'd love to come. That might be just what I need: a break from real life."

And a chance to find out if you or your sisters are who we think.

Rose's expression brightened. Unlike Vivi's, her grin looked genuine, both pleasant and surprised at once. "Oh, awesome! That'll be so great."

In spite of herself, part of Vivi hoped Rose would prove innocent. She seemed like someone Vivi could've been real friends with in another context, not someone who'd join forces with an ancient demon to wreak havoc and steal the Kappas' magic.

Then again, if Rose were involved, she could be *using* influential magic now, to make Vivi like her, trust her.

A familiar outline in the bakery's doorway caught her eye, and Vivi's heart lurched as if thrown violently off balance. It was Mason, scanning the bakery for an empty seat. He had his leather messenger bag slung over one shoulder—papers sticking out of the pockets as usual—but that was the only normal aspect of his appearance. Dark stubble covered his generally clean-shaven face, and there were faint shadows under his eyes. But the real difference was his posture. Mason always moved with energy and confidence, no matter the situation or how many heavy books he lugged with him. Except now his shoulders were slumped, and as he took a few steps forward for a better look at the seating options, his movements seemed slow and labored, weighed down by a burden no one could see.

She froze, torn between a desire to slink down into her seat and hide, and an urge to spring from her chair and throw her arms around him. Then his gaze settled on her, and his body went rigid, his face creasing with pain. Shame and guilt churned through her. She hated seeing Mason in pain—and there was nothing she could do to make it better. Especially right now, when that pain was her fault.

"You okay?" Rose asked, surveying her curiously. "You sort of disappeared there for a second."

"I'm fine!" Vivi said with exaggerated cheer, and she forced herself to focus on Rose. "So, what time is the party?"

Rose beamed. "Tomorrow night, nine p.m., but everyone will be at least half an hour late, so don't be on time."

Perfect. What she wouldn't give to perform a spell right now to peer into Rose's head and see what was really going on inside it. *God, I miss magic.*

It was like being suffocated, like losing a limb. If going to this Theta party could bring her one step closer to getting it back . . . then there was only one possible answer.

"Great," she said, and felt a guilty little twist at the way Rose danced in her chair, genuinely excited. "What's the dress code?"

Rose waved a hand. "No dress codes. We aren't trying to be like Kappa anymore. That's what you want, isn't it? Something different."

For a moment Vivi could have sworn she *smelled* magic. Drifting in the air between them, a whiff of perfume. It made her breath catch, every nerve ending in her body spark. She was on the right track. Rose had something to do with all of this, she knew it.

Whatever it took, Vivi was going to find out.

"Sounds perfect." She smiled and ignored the twist in her stomach when she thought about her Kappa sisters. "Something different is exactly what I want."

Rose looked down, momentarily distracted by the phone in her lap, and Vivi took the opportunity to look back at Mason again. But he was already gone.

CHAPTER TWENTY-FIVE

Scarlett

Scarlett walked into the living room of Kappa House expecting to find a room full of her sisters mourning their magic. Instead, she was greeted by Jackson.

She ran a hand through her hair. She could feel it was a mess, but there was nothing she could do about it. She didn't care; he was here.

"What are you doing here?" she asked.

He didn't say a word. He pulled Scarlett to him and brought his lips to hers.

She let herself melt into the kiss. Jackson was back. The spell was broken.

But something was wrong. The kiss was hard instead of soft. His lips were cold. She pulled back, and Jackson began to chuckle.

His face began to melt, his gorgeous brown skin giving way to blood and skull.

His skin began to reform. It was paler. His features remade themselves into Xavier's.

"I had to see for myself . . . Just an ordinary little helpless girl. You're nothing special without your magic."

His face continued to melt, and his mouth gaped open. Skin peeled away to sinew and bone—

Scarlett screamed herself awake. Her chest heaved, and she bolted upright, slicked in sweat. Her room flooded back into view, her sheets drenched. *Just a nightmare.* Across the bedroom, her curtains fluttered in a faint breeze where she'd left her balcony door cracked open to the humid evening. She'd thought a nap might make her feel better, but it did just the opposite.

It brought back memories of the thing grabbing her in the basement, the crack in the floor shaking like the whole world was about to come apart at the seams.

Scarlett had always thought she understood the shape of the world, as well as her place in it. She was a witch. Magic existed, and she was one of a select few with the power to wield it.

But this . . .

Demons. Gates to other realms . . . This felt beyond her abilities, even when she'd been at her strongest. Never mind now, when she was of little more use than a random nobody picked from the crowd.

She had nothing. No magic. No defenses. No power.

Scarlett stared at her empty palms. Her nail polish had chipped in several places. A crack ran along the edge of her thumbnail, and the nail beds were red-raw, picked to pieces. A nasty habit she normally avoided. One she must have restarted in her sleep. Now she couldn't even glamour away the evidence.

Downstairs was a whole house full of normal girls like her. And beneath them, a gateway to hell. Some president she was. How was she supposed to lead them out of this?

The unease that had been growing in the pit of her stomach for a week clawed its way up the back of her throat until she tasted bile. *I can't do this.*

She didn't know how to fix this. How to track a demon, let alone defeat it.

But she knew one thing. She owed her sisters the truth.

House-wide meeting reminder, she wrote to the all-Kappa group text. *Downstairs in 15.*

Then she rolled out of bed to start getting ready. It took a lot more effort these days. She longed for even a hint of her former abilities. A spell to wipe away the bags beneath her eyes, at least.

Instead, she had to battle her nightmares the old-fashioned way — with a hefty dose of concealer.

By the time she headed downstairs, the rest of Kappa House was already waiting for her.

Silence fell as soon as Scarlett entered the common room.

She moved toward an open seat on the couch beside Mei. Across the room, Reagan and Sonali huddled on one settee with Ariana at their feet. Etta leaned against the door frame with steaming mugs in hand, Juliet and Jess were sprawled on the carpet, and Bailey was sitting close to Hazel, who was braiding her hair. Scarlett noticed Vivi wasn't in the room — she must still be out with Rose.

"Thank y'all for coming." Scarlett glanced around the room. Her sisters' expressions ranged from exhausted to — in Reagan's case — angry. Hazel surprised Scarlett by glaring almost as fiercely.

She looked away. *They have every right to be mad. I've failed them.* But she would find a way to make it right. "I called you here because Vivi and I have learned something pretty . . . disturbing. And y'all have a right to hear it too."

Mei reached over to take Scarlett's hand.

She squeezed back, grateful. "First . . . I'll assume some of y'all have heard of the Hadesgate?"

The girls exchanged uneasy looks.

"I thought that was a rumor," Reagan cut in.

"So did I." Scarlett's mouth flattened. "Until Vivi and I found it in the basement."

"Hold up." Jess straightened. "My mother would have told me if it were real, let alone in this house."

"Same," Sonali murmured, glaring at the floor as if she could see through it to the gate below.

"You're not alone." Scarlett sighed. "I don't know if the alumnae all know about the Hadesgate—it seems like the founders at least must have, to build this house where they did. But for whatever reason, they kept it to themselves."

"So you just *stumbled across* something that's been hidden since this sorority was founded?" Reagan scoffed.

"I didn't say that." Scarlett resisted the urge to snap. She took a deep breath. "There's more. The gate is weakening. Someone on campus has been trying to open it."

"Who would do that?" Jess asked. "Any witch worth her cards knows opening the gate would destroy all of Westerly's campus."

"Maybe even the whole city," Juliet added.

"That leads me to our second discovery." She picked at a hang-nail absently. "Last semester, when we destroyed the Henosis talis-man, we . . . released something. A demon."

A couple of the older girls gasped. Scarlett noticed Juliet tight-ening a protective arm around Jess.

But some were nodding, as if this explained things. "I have been noticing a lot of strange stuff on campus," Mei murmured. "Some of the sweetest people you'll ever meet fighting with one another . . ."

"That fire." Etta's expression darkened. "The one in my hedges. If the demon wants to get to the gate, it will need to destroy all of Kappa's self-defense systems first."

Scarlett nodded. "And making sure the Ravens lost their magic was a pretty ingenious first step."

Reagan squared her shoulders. "What's your plan, then? How do we stop it?"

Scarlett hesitated. This was the part she hated to admit. But good leaders put their people before their own pride, right? "I . . . don't have one yet."

Reagan shook her head. "Of course not."

"Do you have any idea who it is?" Bailey asked.

"We have some suspects. But we still don't know how to regain our power or defeat the demon if we find it," Scarlett admitted. "The research y'all have been doing on regaining lost magic—"

"Reading a bunch of history books isn't going to do shit," Rea-gan interrupted. "We need to take action."

Scarlett spread her hands. "If you've got suggestions, I'm all ears."

"You don't have *any* ideas?" Sonali bent forward, her normally picture-perfect dark ringlets hanging in limp clumps today.

"Maybe another house-wide spell," Juliet said.

"With what magic?" Hazel muttered.

Bailey raised a hand, as if this were a classroom. Scarlett nodded at her. "So . . . *now* can we ask the alumnae for help?"

Marjorie's dismissal echoed through Scarlett's thoughts again. "I talked to my mother. It . . . didn't go well. Marjorie told me we need to solve this ourselves."

"Hang on." Reagan straightened. "You order all of us to stay silent, command us not to speak to our own mothers, and then you go and do whatever you want instead? Typical."

"I never *commanded* you—"

But Reagan was already shoving to her feet, one hand on Sonali's shoulder. "That's it. I'm done. I joined Kappa to learn from y'all, to get stronger and better at my craft. But if we're just going to roll over and die, I'm leaving."

Scarlett stared. "You can't be serious."

Reagan crossed her arms. "If this sorority is failing to give us what we need, there are other options on campus."

Scarlett actually laughed. "You think any of the other sororities can help you with *this*? We're the only coven on campus—"

"We *were* a coven," Reagan shot back. "I don't know what we are now, thanks to you."

The words cut deep. Probably because they were the exact ones Scarlett had been thinking herself for days on end.

She rose, fists balled. "If you don't like the way I run things, then fine, Reagan. You know where the door is. You've been doing nothing but argue and undermine me all semester—"

"She wouldn't need to if you had a plan," Etta butted in.

That sent all of Scarlett's anger right out of her. Her shoulders slumped. Not Etta too. Etta was a senior here, one of the girls Scarlett had looked up to her whole time in Kappa. She'd been almost like a second Big Sister to Scarlett. Scarlett had always sensed that Etta never felt valued enough in the Kappa hierarchy. Even though Dahlia relied on Etta's potion skills, there was only room for Dahlia at the top. Scarlett had wanted to correct that, but Scarlett had a gnawing feeling in her gut that she had failed big time.

"I'm sorry." Etta raised her chin. "But Reagan is right. Things have changed. Even *with* our magic, this would be an untenable situation, but without it?" She shook her head. "We *need* to get our magic back—and I'm not sure you're the person to help us do it."

Don't go. She wanted to say it. But the words dried up in her throat. She felt deflated, like all the wind in her lungs had been magically sucked out.

Reagan nodded at Etta. Then looked down at Sonali. "Anyone else?"

Sonali considered Reagan for a long time, and then, to Scarlett's relief, shook her head. The relief was short-lived, though. Scarlett watched with growing horror as Bailey and Hazel both stood, too. Followed Reagan up the hall.

Nothing like this, as far as Scarlett knew, had ever happened at Kappa. Ravens didn't *leave* the sorority. Women were desperate to get *into* this house, not out of it.

"Good luck," Etta, the last to leave, told Scarlett. "I get the feeling you're going to need it."

And then she was gone.

Scarlett stared after their retreating backs until the front door slammed. Only then did she turn to look at the remaining girls. None of them had even defended Scarlett.

She sank back to her seat and put her head in her hands. "If anyone else wants to go, I won't blame you," she said, voice muffled by her palms.

Mei touched her back. "No way. I'm staying."

Jess and Juliet exchanged sideways glances. "Us too," Jess said. And then, more firmly: "But they do have a point. Just . . ." She glanced at her girlfriend again. "Are you sure we can really fix this?"

She looked around the room. What felt like half her sisters were gone in minutes. This was another nightmare—one she couldn't wake up from. Her mouth felt dry. She pressed her hands together, to stop them from shaking. *You are Scarlett Winter. Act like it.* She lifted her head, voice hard as she could make it, shoulders ramrod straight. "We have to. Whether they know it or not, all of Westerly is in danger. If we don't stop this, no one will."

CHAPTER TWENTY-SIX

Vivi

B y the time Vivi trudged up the steps to Kappa House, all she could think about was curling up in her bed and taking the longest nap in history. Between the disturbing trip to Lone Willow Farm, the chilling exploration of the basement, and her performance at the bakery with Rose, Vivi couldn't remember ever being this exhausted. She paused by the front door, waiting for it to recognize her and swing open as usual, but of course, this time it didn't budge. The magic had been leached out of Kappa House just as fully as it'd drained from the blood of the Ravens. With a sigh, Vivi fumbled for her keys and, with an unpracticed hand, unlocked the door.

From the moment she stepped inside, Vivi could tell that something was seriously wrong. It felt like walking into a tomb. From the drooping houseplants to the dust that had inexplicably gathered on every surface, the house seemed filled with an air of gloomy neglect. She poked her head into the living room where, at any given point in the day, at least two of her sisters would be lounging on the couches, studying, chatting, or practicing magic. But this evening, there wasn't a soul in sight.

Vivi wandered into the kitchen and found Mei sitting where

she'd left her that morning, albeit in a different outfit. "What's going on?" Vivi asked. "Where is everyone?"

"I'm not sure I even know where to begin," Mei said in a flat voice Vivi didn't recognize.

"I'll start," Sonali said, rubbing her eyes as she sauntered into the kitchen. "It's clear Scarlett has no plan about how to deal with this demon, and when people called her out on it, she got all defensive. So a few of the girls left."

"What do you mean, left?" Vivi asked.

"Reagan announced that she was sick of being bossed around by a failed witch and said that she'd had enough. She left and Bailey, Hazel, and Etta went with her."

"Like, they went for a walk?"

Mei shook her head. "No, like they said they didn't want to be a part of Kappa anymore."

"What?" Vivi said, looking incredulously from Mei to Sonali. "That makes absolutely no sense. If they were upset about losing their magic, why would they walk from their coven? They're pretty much guaranteeing they'll *never* get their magic back."

Mei shrugged and stirred her tea listlessly. "I know it's a pretty extreme reaction, but they're scared and frustrated. Like the rest of us."

A surge of indignation made Vivi's cheeks flush. The Kappas had no idea what Scarlett was doing for them—she was, quite literally, moving heaven and earth to get their magic back. How could Reagan and the others give up on Scarlett so quickly? Their disloyalty was truly staggering. "It's only been, like, twenty-four hours," Vivi said. "How could they jump ship already? It doesn't make any sense! How is *that* going to help us get our magic back? Are they just giving up on being witches?"

Sonali shrugged. "Maybe they'll form their own coven. Listen, I'm not saying I agree with them, but you have to admit that Scarlett isn't inspiring much confidence right now. She claims to be working on it, but won't tell us anything about it. So either she's *lying* or she doesn't trust us. She's not a president, she's a tyrant."

"I know how it looks," Vivi said, rubbing her temples. "But we just need to keep doing what we've been doing, researching magic that can help us. There's so much information in this house, in our library. We'll find an answer somewhere."

Sonali stared at Vivi critically for a long moment. "So come join us in the library, then. We're looking for similar records of lost magic."

"I'll be there in a few," Vivi said. "I just need to shower first."

She hurried out of the kitchen and bounded up the stairs, buoyed by a force even more powerful than the crushing exhaustion. Her fingers had been itching for the grimoire all day, but the urge had become overwhelming. She sensed it contained the answers they were looking for; it'd had answers for nearly everything else.

Vivi opened her door, flipped on the light, then staggered back in shock. She'd only left that morning but her room looked like it'd been abandoned for years. Cobwebs covered the window, blocking the fading light, and the tops of her desk and dresser were covered with dust. Her heart pounding, she walked over to the vase containing the flowers she'd cut from the garden just yesterday and gently ran a finger along the withered petals, turning them to dust.

The glamours that had kept Kappa House clean and beautiful hadn't vanished when the Ravens lost their magic.

They'd rotted.

Vivi wandered around her room in a daze, heartbroken over the loss of her sanctuary, the first time she'd ever had a bedroom that'd truly felt like home. She picked up her hairbrush, then yelped and tossed it aside when she saw something crawling among the bristles. Seeing her room like this felt like walking into her own tomb; she half expected to find her desiccated remains in the armchair.

She dusted off the tarot deck she'd left on the dresser, as useless as playing cards now. When she had first joined Kappa, they'd seemed so mysterious, so intriguing. The keys to magic, right at her fingertips.

But now she knew there was more effective magic out there. Spells that didn't require chants or tarot cards or herbs. Just pure force of will.

And blood.

Her fingertips tingled. She could have sworn she'd caught that scent again, the same way she had sitting across from Rose.

Vivi lifted her mattress, sputtering as a cloud of dust engulfed her face. She reached for the grimoire and opened it greedily, turning to a random page. It didn't matter which spell she performed; she just needed to know whether her magic still worked.

But then she remembered an entry she'd found the other day,

and the frenzy of voices in her overtaxed brain fell blissfully silent, one thought ringing clear as a church bell on a still, snowy evening. A sense of calm stole over her, and she carefully turned the pages until she found the page with the illustration of a hand mirror.

Oftentimes we waste precious time and energy searching for answers that lie within ourselves. There is no greater truth than the magic which seeks to flow through a powerful witch. But first, we must remove the obstacles to knowledge. We must cut through fear, peel back doubt, and drain away the arrogance that clouds true wisdom. Magic is in the air, but you must be willing to let it in.

Magic. In the air. Crackling just within reach, so close she could taste it. Vivi reached for the silver dagger on her desk. It was normally just for show, a symbol of Swords magic. Now the sharp tip gleamed, calling her name.

The grimoire would be their savior. The key to regaining their magic, their power.

Vivi tightened her hold on the knife. The handle fit perfectly in her palm. It felt right, holding it. The feeling of helplessness—powerlessness—waned just a little as she clenched it even harder.

The scent got stronger. Herbal and sharp, right below her nose. The air around her seemed to spark and thrum. If she opened her mouth, she could *taste* the power.

Before she had time to think better of it, Vivi dragged the blade across the back of her arm.

She gasped at the spark of pain, the hot rush of blood. She

dropped the knife, raised shaking hands, her fingers outstretched, ignoring the blood that continued to trickle down her arm, gathering at the point of her elbow to drip onto her bedroom carpet.

Show me what I want to see, she thought, or maybe she said it out loud. She couldn't be sure. Her bedroom felt half real, half illusion right now. As if she could stretch out one arm, wrap a fist in the fabric of the world, and rip it in two.

As if the world were a veil, paper-thin. Hers to destroy, if she wanted.

Yes. The whispers were quiet at first. A hushed hiss. The trees outside, scratching against the window, perhaps. Or maybe a rustle of paper in her bedroom.

But then they grew louder. Closer. They seemed to be coming from the mirror.

Slowly, Vivi turned to the mirror atop her dresser. In the dusty surface, she could just make out her reflection. But this Vivi wore a long white dress that fluttered around her ankles. On her head sat a crown, gold and heavy. She looked like a goddess, some Greek statue out of myth.

"The world is dying," she said, and her voice was both Vivi's voice and *not,* someone else, some*thing* else speaking with her tongue. "But you do not have to."

Not-Vivi twisted her palms together, and Vivi felt a wave of magic, power so strong it nearly bowled her over. Not-Vivi conjured up a beautiful scene: a villa high on a hill overlooking the ocean. And then, onto the veranda of the house, the sun dappling his skin gold, stepped Mason. He shaded his eyes. Called out to her.

Not-Vivi stepped forward and wrapped her arms around his waist. Mason smiled, his old, dimpled smile, the one Vivi hadn't seen in weeks. He bent to kiss Not-Vivi, and the other girl turned away, caught Vivi's eye. The trees around Not-Vivi swayed and twisted in unnatural ways. The branches almost looked like arms reaching, trying to grasp something. The hissing got louder and louder until it was roaring in Vivi's ears.

Vivi fell back onto the carpet, gasping. Her bedroom had returned, normal again, save for the fresh, ugly red bloodstains next to her. "Shit." She pushed the knife away. What *was* that?

The Hadesgate. The other demons. *They* all *want out.*

And yet the magic had been there. She'd felt it. Tasted it. Maybe if Vivi tried again, used the grimoire magic somewhere else, away from the Hadesgate, then—

Someone knocked at the door. "Vivi?"

It was Scarlett.

Scrambling, she leaped to her feet and kicked the bloody knife under the bed. She grabbed a blanket, draped it over the stain on the floor, and rushed into her bathroom. "One minute!" she called, as she turned on her sink, scrubbed at her forearm.

"Are you okay?" Vivi spun around to see Scarlett standing in her room, staring at Vivi in concern.

"Yeah, fine," Vivi said breathlessly. "Just washing some of this gross dust off my hands. Is your room like this, too?"

"Maybe not quite as bad," Scarlett said. "I can help you clean up, if you want."

"It sounds like you've had enough for one day. I can't believe Reagan and the others walked out."

"This never would've happened if Dahlia were here." Scarlett's head fell into her hands, and it sounded like she was holding back tears. "What if we *never* get our magic back? What happens if I'm responsible for the end of Kappa?"

"It's been *one* day, and we already have lots of leads. We'll figure this out, I promise." Vivi recapped her conversation with Rose and told Scarlett about the invitation to the Theta party. "I'll be on the lookout for anything strange, but I'm starting to think that Rose might not be our main suspect. Is there anyone else we should be looking into? What about your friend Xavier?"

Scarlett raised her head. There was an expression on her face Vivi couldn't quite read. "I don't think . . . I mean . . . yeah, you're right. I'll see what I can find out."

"We've faced worse than this," Vivi said, nudging Scarlett's shoe with her own. "We're Kappas—we can handle anything."

The words sounded thin even to her.

CHAPTER TWENTY-SEVEN

Scarlett

X*avier.*

The next morning, Scarlett put on a thicker layer of makeup and some designer clothes. If she was about to stalk Xavier, she wanted to make sure she used every weapon she still possessed.

Assuming demons were as thrown by girls in tight dresses as college guys were. If not, well . . . it never hurt to look good anyway.

While she got ready, she searched for more information about Xavier online. All that turned up were a couple of social media accounts, barely active, and a single old photo of him in New York City, tagged with some friends. None of whom she recognized.

What guy her age posted this little online?

She couldn't find mention of him at Vanderbilt either, which seemed suspicious. There should at least be enrollment records out there somewhere, right?

The sooner she talked to Xavier, the sooner she could figure out if he was their culprit. If he was the one behind all this, Scarlett wouldn't stop until she defeated him. Won their magic back. With or without all of her sisters behind her.

First, however, she needed to *find* him. A call to the registrar got her his class schedule, since the girl working the front desk owed Scarlett an old favor. But he didn't have any classes right now.

She scrolled through his social media again, but he hadn't posted since last week. Then Scarlett paused. On the most recent post, there were seven comments. Five had all been left by the same Gamma girl, one whose number Scarlett still had saved from a Gamma/Kappa mixer two years ago. The girl was nice enough, but she crushed a little too hard on cute guys around campus.

Scarlett texted her. *Hey. Any idea where Xavier might be? I've got some homework to give him.*

Kappa's clout on campus had fallen, but not all the way. A few minutes later, a reply appeared. *He's usually on the green with a few guy friends around now, before his calculus class later.*

Unnerving. But also useful, so Scarlett would take it.

She gave herself a last once-over in her bedroom mirror—which had new, ugly streaks across the glass that she could not clean off no matter how hard she tried. She looked as good as she could expect without glamours. With one last sigh, Scarlett headed out, every step in the heels she'd chosen bringing with it a little jolt of pain.

She'd had no idea how much she'd used magic in her day-to-day life before, until she lost it. Who knew heels hurt this badly?

Still, she powered through. To judge by the appraising looks she got from a handful of frat guys passing on her way toward campus, it was worth the effort.

When she reached the main greens, however, Scarlett stumbled to a halt, an entirely fresh type of pain jolting through her. She didn't know what she'd expected, but it wasn't this. Xavier was sprawled in the center of the lawns, homework arrayed around him, along with a group of PiKa brothers and, right smack in the center of them all . . .

Jackson.

She hadn't seen him since the reunion when he blew her off, furious at her for touching the crystal around his neck. But that had been the love spell talking. She'd seen his true face in Vivi's glamoured mirror. The horrified scream he wore.

Her chest tightened painfully.

She'd told him she would save him. She'd *promised*. And now what was she doing? Dressing up to flirt with another guy in front of him?

She prayed that wherever the real Jackson was, he wasn't awake in there. *Please let him be oblivious.* It would be so much worse, otherwise.

Finally, Scarlett's heart rate slowed enough that she was able to take off across the lawn, her legs flashing in the sun. She'd had a plan of approach, a whole speech mentally drafted to lure Xavier back in. But the sight of Jackson had knocked it all straight out of her head.

As she drew closer to the cluster of boys, she recognized another familiar face lounging between Xavier and Jackson. *Tim.* Scarlett hadn't seen him without Maria in ages. When they first started dating freshman year, Tim had a social life of his own, but lately he seemed attached at the hip to his girlfriend.

He looked more relaxed somehow, now. Happier. He had his head tipped back, and he was laughing, a contagious, happy sound.

The motion made something flash from beneath his V-neck shirt. A silver chain. Exactly like the one Jackson wore.

Scarlett stumbled on a knoll in the grass. Had *all* the Thetas cast love spells on their boyfriends, then?

"Oh. Scarlett." Xavier noticed her first. He shaded his eyes and stared up at her, his expression not exactly one you'd call friendly. Still, his gaze traveled up and down her figure, so at least she knew the outfit she'd selected was doing the trick. "Can we help you?" he asked, his tone cold.

"Actually . . ."

Across from Xavier, Jackson struggled to his feet. "I'm late for class." He waved at Tim, not even acknowledging Scarlett. "Catch you later, man?"

"I'll see you at the party. Assuming Cait lets you off the leash long enough to say hey." Tim smirked, and Jackson laughed.

Something about that laugh. It didn't sound like his. It was all wrong. The pitch was strained. How had she not figured out he was spelled sooner? He had stopped acting like Jackson when she had met him for their date. She was just too hurt to see it.

Scarlett knew she needed to stay on task, to focus. She had to get magic back, had to save her sisters. But Jackson was right here, and she could picture his expression in the mirror again, how scared he'd looked.

"Excuse me," Scarlett said to Xavier, already turning away. Trailing after Jackson, even as every instinct in her screamed to go back, finish the mission.

I need to reassure him first. If Jackson was awake and aware in there, she couldn't leave him trapped. Not without some kind of hope to cling to.

Jackson walked fast. Too fast for Scarlett in these heels. After a moment of hesitation, she reached down and slipped them off. Scarlett Winter had never gone barefoot in her life, but she did now, jogging across the lawns, heels in one hand, to catch up with him.

"Jackson." Finally, she drew near enough to catch his elbow. Yank him to a stop. "Jackson. Wait."

He stopped, albeit reluctantly. The corner of his lip turned up in a sneer. "If it isn't my stalker again. Take a hint, Winter."

"That's not you talking, and I know it." Scarlett dared a glance around the greens. But the rest of the students outside were all engrossed in their own conversations or asleep with their textbooks spread across their laps, enjoying the warm, sunny afternoon.

Still, she lowered her voice anyway. Old habits. "I know what Cait did to you," she said, low and urgent. "I'm working on reversing it, okay?"

Jackson rolled his eyes. "All Cait did to me is teach me what *real* love can be like, okay, Scarlett? Nothing like your idea of it. There's no lying with Cait."

Scarlett froze, her heart stuttering in her chest. Did he remember? But . . . "Jackson, if I ever lied to you, it was only because I had no choice. There are forces at work here, forces bigger than me or you—"

"You realize you sound insane, right?" His lip curled.

"I'm trying to tell you something, okay? However strong this hold she put on you is, it's only artificial. There will be a way to reverse it. I just need to find out what Theta's doing, how they got so much stronger all of a sudden."

"What's your problem with Theta, huh?" Jackson wrenched his arm from her grip. "You're always on about how bad they are, always trashing my girlfriend. From where I'm standing, it just looks like plain old jealousy."

She scoffed.

But he kept going. "You Kappas think you're so high and mighty. Always in charge, running this school. Well, I have news for you. There's a new leader in town." Jackson glared, his eyes suddenly intense. Sharp enough to send a trill of fear down Scarlett's spine.

Jackson had always known how to look right through her. But this . . . this was something different.

Could one tiny love spell really explain *this* level of hatred? Or was this the demon talking?

Jackson lowered his voice, and Scarlett held her breath, afraid to move. Afraid to hear this—yet afraid to miss his words, too. "As for Theta?" he murmured. "They'll teach you Ravens what you really are. Nobody at all."

He pushed past her, then, so hard she nearly stumbled. But Scarlett didn't move. Could hardly think through the rapid beat of her pulse.

She had to fix this. *Now.* Because she had a bad feeling that if she waited much longer, the Jackson she used to love would be gone forever.

CHAPTER TWENTY-EIGHT

Vivi

Theta House thumped with music so loud that Vivi could hear it from a block away. The walk from Kappa House had taken longer than expected; she'd forgotten how bad she was at walking in high heels without magic. Everything about her outfit—black skinny jeans and a leopard crop-top she'd found in the giveaway pile in the Kappas' laundry room—felt a little bit off. She couldn't ask to borrow anything without raising suspicions, and while she still wasn't fluent in fashion, she knew tonight wasn't the night to flaunt Mei's glamorous vintage pieces or one of Scarlett's designer dresses. She had to look like a girl who shopped at the mall—not in her witch sorority sisters' enchanted wardrobes.

Vivi tugged on the hem of the shirt, which, without one of the glamours she normally used to tailor her clothes, didn't hit her at a particularly flattering spot. How did people live without magic? How could she ever *go back* to living without magic after everything she'd seen? It was like going from a world of Technicolor to one of muddy grays. From hearing Beethoven performed by a symphony to listening to a fourth grader play *Ode to Joy* on a toy keyboard. Life was flat, colorless, and dreadfully off-key without magic.

When she finally reached the front of the gate, she gazed up at Theta House. It was a bit of an anomaly on Greek Row. Instead of a wraparound porch, it had an arched stone walkway circling the first floor. A grand stone staircase led up to the second-story front door, more reminiscent of a medieval castle than the Greek Revival mansions and Federal townhouses that surrounded most of Westerly's campus.

The party was already in full swing. Vivi spotted revelers through upstairs windows, leaning out over turrets, red Solo cups in hand, and a surprising number of couples dotted the lawns, some locked in more amorous embraces than Vivi would have expected in public.

Carefully, Vivi picked her way across the lawn and up the white limestone steps, flecked in places with green and gray moss. The massive front door was solid wood, adorned in iron, almost like a castle portico, but once she was inside, the surroundings looked every bit the standard sorority house. The main room was decorated with whites and cream, with lots of squashy couches and armchairs clustered around a large fireplace. Vivi winced at the pink and green paisley accent pillows, one of which was embroidered with the words LIVE, LOVE, LAUGH.

A bar had been set up near the fireplace, tended by a Theta she vaguely recognized from the disastrous welcome-back party. Spencer, maybe? That felt like a million years ago, back when she'd thought messing up one stupid spell was the worst thing that could happen to her.

Her hands throbbed with the reminder of how much further

she'd pushed herself. Her cuts had healed from the alumnae reunion by now, all except for the new, deep one on the back of her forearm.

"Hi, there," Spencer said, and Vivi dragged her mind back to the present. Back to her mission. "Rose told us you'd be coming. She'll be right down, if you want to wait here."

"Sure." Vivi forced a smile, hoping the other girl wouldn't read into it. The music pulsed from every floor, so loud Vivi could feel her temples thudding in time with it. Through neighboring rooms, she spotted thick clusters of people in varying stages of drunkenness.

Once Spencer left, Vivi could slip away and search the house for any signs of stolen magic before Rose even knew she'd arrived.

She glanced at the staircase, and froze.

Maria was skipping down the stairs in a black pleather miniskirt and hot pink platform heels, with Tim a few steps behind her, his eyes glued to his phone. "Vivi!" Maria said with a grin. She practically leaped off the final step and pulled Vivi into a hug. "Rose told us you might stop by. I'm so glad you came." She wrapped her arm around Vivi's waist and then turned to face Tim. "Babe, you remember Vivi from the Kappa party, right?"

Tim's head jerked up, his expression confused. But when he saw it was Vivi, he smiled and gave her a side hug. "Hey, hey! Glad you could make it, V!"

Vivi grinned and hugged him back. "Thanks for inviting me," Vivi said to Maria. "This party is . . . something else."

The music wasn't a kind she recognized—not the old-timey jazz or classical music that she heard at Kappa's more elegant parties, or even the club music she heard on nights out in Savannah. This was some kind of deep bass, shot through with electronic beats. It seemed to vibrate the very walls, pulsate through the air around her.

This was the kind of music you could lose your mind to, Vivi thought. For the first time, the prospect sounded almost appealing. What she wouldn't give to silence the rattling in her brain right now, if only for the length of a song.

"That's what we aim for. Different." Maria reached down to curl a hand around Tim's. "It's why you caught our attention, Vivi. We can tell you're different, too."

"Oh?" Vivi raised her chin, did her best to look like a Kappa: calm, cool, collected. "In what way?"

"You know what you want, and you go for it. And you don't mind breaking a few rules to get it."

Vivi's heart began to thud. *Is she talking about magic?* "I'm not sure I know what you mean."

Maria laughed and shot Tim a look Vivi didn't know how to read. "Please. I knew the minute I saw you that you weren't like the other Kappas, Vivi." She held up a palm to stave off Vivi's instinctive protest, then her hand trailed up Tim's arm and came to rest at the back of his neck. Vivi caught a glimpse of silver tucked between the folds of his collar and felt her breath catch in her chest.

A protective sisterly feeling surged through her. Was this the love charm Scarlett had mentioned? Did that mean the Thetas *had* somehow gotten their hands on stolen magic? But, looking around the room, which lacked any defining features other than a remarkable number of red Solo cups, it was hard to believe that the Thetas had any tools at their disposal other than a Sam's Club membership.

"I'm not judging you," Maria continued. "Far from it. Here at Theta, we're more understanding. If you want something, far be it from us to deny it."

Vivi stared at her, wondering how much Maria knew or whether she'd just made a lucky guess. It didn't take a PhD in psychology to know that Kappa life wouldn't exactly be carefree during a Scarlett Winter presidency. Maria was probably referring to dress codes or curfews—not to Scarlett's shortsighted decision to ban Vivi from using the grimoire. Still, even outsiders could tell that Scarlett didn't like to be challenged.

She breathed easier when Maria pulled Tim toward the living room, into the thick of the party. "Enjoy yourself tonight, Vivi," she called over her shoulder, then gestured for Spencer to follow her.

Vivi watched them disappear into the crowd, then looked around, trying to decide where to start her search. You couldn't walk in the door of Kappa House without being bombarded by signs of magic, but witches had been living there for more than a century. Where would Vivi need to look to find it here? Would there be a grimoire in the library? Magical herbs bubbling in a cauldron in the kitchen? What would she say if someone caught her snooping? *Where's your restroom?* was a classic; she could just use that . . .

"Vivi!"

She nearly jumped a foot in the air, turning just in time to catch a clearly tipsy Rose, who flung her arms around Vivi in a tight hug. "You came!" Her pleasure was so genuine that it made Vivi's stomach twist with guilt.

"I said I would!" Vivi said with a laugh.

Rose grabbed her hand and pulled her excitedly toward the main party. "Come on, I'll give you the tour."

Oddly, apart from the modern living room, the rest of Theta House seemed much more of a piece with its castle-like exterior. Thick Persian rugs lined the stone floors, and tapestries hung along the walls to warm the space. The number of people in the house felt oppressive, even given its grand proportions. But even with what seemed like most of Greek Row packed inside, it still felt cold in here. Cold and a little bit damp, in the way that only stone buildings could get. They passed more than one oversize fireplace, lit flames roaring in their hearths.

Rose led her through room after room, talking animatedly about how the founders built Theta House in the early 1880s, but they tried to make it an exact replica of some castle they'd seen in Germany. Vivi did her best to look interested and impressed, but she was distracted by hints of a distinctive, familiar scent wafting through the air. What was it? It bothered her that she couldn't identify it. It smelled sort of like pine with a hint of something herbal. It reminded her of Etta's supplies in the kitchen, though she couldn't place which herb it was or what its scent might mean.

Vivi spotted Jackson dancing with Cait in one of the rooms, which had been cleared of all furniture and was lit solely by bright neon green bulbs along the floor, giving everyone inside a ghostly appearance.

Vivi watched as Cait draped her arms around his neck, then pulled his face toward hers with such force Vivi winced when they kissed.

Poor Jackson. Vivi knew what it felt like to be under someone else's magical control. A wave of nausea swept over her, just as it always did when she thought about being in that clearing with Tiffany.

Rose must've noticed the unease on Vivi's face, because she grabbed her arm and said, "Let's get you a drink already." Vivi followed obediently, then stopped in her tracks when a familiar flash of red caught her eye. She turned to see Reagan dancing with abandon, her long hair flying in all directions as her hips moved with the throbbing beat of the music. She was in a tight circle of Thetas and looked happier and freer than she'd been all semester. Vivi stared at her, racking her brain for an explanation for this betrayal. It was possible that Reagan had a good reason for being at the Theta party, just like Vivi did. Yet she sure as hell didn't look like someone who'd snuck into Theta House to investigate the Kappas' missing magic.

"Oh, yeah," Rose said, smiling awkwardly as she followed Vivi's gaze. "I thought maybe you knew. Reagan, Bailey, Hazel, and Etta are going to rush Theta."

"What?" Vivi said, unable to hide her shock. Rose winced slightly, and Vivi took a deep breath to compose herself. "Sorry, that came out wrong. I'm just . . . surprised."

Nothing about this made any sense. She understood they were angry at Scarlett, but how would betraying the rest of their sisters help them get their magic back? Unless they knew something that Vivi didn't, something she and Scarlett only suspected . . .

"No, I get it. I know things are happening quickly. But it's like Maria always says, 'You're only in college once, so do it right.'"

"How profound," Vivi said, unable to keep the sarcasm out of her voice. Luckily, Rose didn't seem to notice and motioned for Vivi to follow her into the kitchen.

It was a large room with stone walls that seemed charmingly out of place with the sleeker, modern stainless steel appliances. Vivi looked around curiously, scanning for signs of potion-making or other evidence of witchcraft, but nothing caught her eye amid the liquor bottles and plastic cups covering every surface.

"Here you go!" Rose handed her a cup filled with bright purple liquid. Vivi examined it suspiciously, convinced it'd be something vile like vodka mixed with Hawaiian Punch. She took a small, tentative sip and then smiled with relief. It was delicious—a sweet, sugary mix with a hint of fresh berries and mint.

"Good, right?" Rose said, looking pleased.

"It's amazing. What's in it?" Vivi took another sip, longer this time.

Rose winked. "Trade secrets. Can't tell you unless you wind up joining Theta." Her smile faltered. "I mean. Not that I'm pressuring you, or anything. I just . . ." She trailed off, her cheeks reddening. "Shoot. I told her I wouldn't push."

"Told *who?*"

"Maria." Rose shifted her weight from side to side and fiddled with a lock of hair. "She's in recruiting mode. She wants to get more girls to join. But I told her, you're my friend, I don't want to *make* you do anything. Although I would love it if you did." Rose's face brightened again. "We'd have so much fun being sisters!"

Vivi arranged her lips into a conspiratorial smile, even as she recoiled inwardly. *I already have sisters.* That was why she was here. To break whatever spell or curse had robbed the Kappas of their magic and restore their power.

"It *does* seem like you have a lot of fun here. Can I see more of the house?"

"Sure!" Rose bounced in place with excitement.

Rose led Vivi upstairs, then paused on the landing to face her. "Most of the common areas up here are fine, but you can't go down the bedroom halls, okay?"

"Of course." Vivi waited until they were nestled in one of those common areas, browsing some communal bookshelves—mostly self-help and celebrity memoirs, nothing that looked like a grimoire—before putting on a sheepish smile.

"Is there a bathroom I could use?"

"Oh, sure." Rose pointed out the door down the hallway, near the corridor that led to the second-floor bedrooms. "It's right there. I'll wait for you here."

Vivi ducked into the bathroom, waited a minute, then peeked around the doorjamb. Rose had already pulled out her phone, her attention focused entirely on the screen. As quickly and quietly as possible, Vivi snuck back into the hall and darted around the corner, her heart racing.

If the Thetas really do have magic, is this a good idea?

If they caught her sneaking off somewhere she didn't belong, Vivi would be defenseless. They could put a spell on her, make her as meek and pliable as Tim or Jackson.

Or worse.

But if Vivi didn't find a way to get the Kappas' magic back, she'd be weak and vulnerable for the rest of her life. And so, with one last furtive look around, Vivi hurried down the nearly pitch-black hallway, toward the bedrooms.

The layout was more difficult to navigate than Kappa House; the corridors all seemed to twist and turn in on one another. But after a few closed doors, something caught her eye. Down a quiet, dark hallway, lit only by the glow from her cell phone screen: one of the ornate wooden doors was decorated in hot pink ribbons. A little balloon beside it said ROSE in bright red glitter.

Vivi glanced back up the darkened hall. She wasn't sure how long she could pass off being in the bathroom for. What would she do if Rose came looking for her? Or worse, if one of the other Thetas came upstairs to their room and found her lurking?

Vivi pressed her ear to the wood, held her breath and listened for any hint of motion within, just in case Rose had a roommate, or if another Theta had popped in to borrow something. After a moment, when nothing stirred inside, Vivi reached down and tentatively tried the knob.

Locked.

Glancing over her shoulder once more, Vivi knelt and withdrew a bobby pin from her hair, and set to work on Rose's lock. She'd done this more than a dozen times before—Daphne Devereaux had a habit of locking her out of the house by accident, so Vivi had needed to master breaking and entering at a young age.

Rose's door proved no match for Vivi's latchkey kid skills, and with a faint click, it swung inward, creaking ominously the whole way. With a wince, Vivi reached out to catch it and glanced over her shoulder again, praying none of the neighboring bedrooms were occupied, then flicked on the light.

It took a couple seconds of blinking for her eyes to adjust, even though Rose's overhead light was dim, covered by a gauzy blue veil that cast eerie shadows across the canopied four-poster bed.

Along the far wall, Vivi spotted a huge standing mirror, like something out of a fairy tale, with garlands of ivy draped over it. Then she turned to scan the bookshelves, then froze.

Someone had placed a number of objects on the windowsill: a wooden bowl with a pentacle carved into it, a silver knife, a pile of crushed powdery herbs. It was a makeshift altar, from the looks of it.

Magic.

Every nerve ending in Vivi's body lit up with desire. She *wanted* it. She could practically taste it and inhaled greedily, desperate to absorb the aftereffects of whatever spell Rose had been casting.

This was the proof she'd needed. Exactly what she'd been looking for: Theta had magic.

Reagan, Etta, and Bailey must've figured this out somehow. And while Vivi still couldn't forgive their betrayal, at least their actions now made sense.

Vivi pointed her cell phone at the altar and snapped a couple of pictures as quickly as possible. Every creak and shift in the house made her nerves jump. *You got what you came for, Vivi. Go.*

Yet she couldn't drag her eyes from the altar. Magic was right here. So close.

She took a step forward, feeling almost as if she were in a trance. *Get out of here,* a faint voice screamed from the back of her brain, but her body had ideas of its own.

She sank to her knees beside the altar, then extended her arm until her hand hovered inches from the knife.

Some sixth sense told her that if she tried to perform a grimoire spell right now, here in this house, *it would work.*

Vivi picked up the knife. She could still hear the thrum of the party below, but it seemed distant now, a world away. Here, in this stranger's bedroom, the only thing that mattered was the power that pulsed in the air, hung around her heavy as mist.

She raised the knife to her forearm and rested the cool metal against her skin. One cut. One flash of pain, and she could have it again. Her own magic.

Rose is going to come looking. Any second now, she'll come in.

But Vivi could fix that. She could fix all of this; she just knew it. All she needed was a little blood, some sharp pain, and—

A clank behind her made her breath catch in her throat. *The latch. Shit.*

Vivi dropped the knife and whirled around just in time to see the door swing inward, framing the shadowy outline of a girl in the doorway with her arms crossed, her head tilted to the side.

Vivi leaped to her feet. "I'm so sorry," she blurted. "I . . . I got lost, and the door was open, so I thought . . ."

The girl in the doorway clicked her tongue. Not Rose.

Maria.

The president of Theta smirked. "Don't bother with excuses, Vivian. I've been watching you."

Vivi swallowed hard. "I'm sorry," she repeated, slower this time. "Please don't throw me out. I was just curious."

"There's no shame in curiosity. In fact, I respect it." Her gaze drifted past Vivi, and came to rest on the altar near the window. "As you can see, Kappa isn't the only . . . *special* house on campus. Here at Theta, we reward those like you. Girls who take initiative. Girls who fight for what they deserve." Maria extended a hand, palm turned up. Inviting. "Join us, Vivian, and we can give you what you want."

The air in Rose's bedroom crackled with energy. *Maria's* energy. It was the first time Vivi had felt magic since losing her own and the sensation was intoxicating. At that moment, she felt like she'd do anything to feel that power transfer to her.

She stared at the other girl's outstretched hand. Everything in her yearned to reach out. To grab it.

"I . . . I'm not . . ." she stammered. *Say yes,* her mind screamed. *Say it.* But her tongue refused to unstick from the roof of her mouth for some reason. Latent, misplaced loyalty, perhaps. She thought about the girls waiting for her back at Kappa House. She had come here to help them. *Join Theta, and you can.* But she couldn't make her body obey. She wasn't a traitor like Reagan.

"I'm sorry. I shouldn't have come here." Vivi started for the door.

Maria extended an arm to block her, and Vivi slid to a halt, bracing herself for an attack. She could do it, Vivi knew. Maria could force Vivi to do whatever she wanted right now.

But then Maria's expression softened, and she dropped her arm from the door and stood aside to let Vivi go by. "Sleep on it," Maria said sweetly as Vivi brushed past her into the hallway. She hurried toward the staircase. But she didn't move fast enough to escape Maria's final words. They chased her down the hall, echoed in her ears.

"When you decide to come back, we'll be waiting."

CHAPTER TWENTY-NINE

Scarlett

After her disastrous attempt to cozy up to Xavier on the green, Scarlett knew she'd need to up her game. Or better yet, catch him solo, where his friends couldn't prove a distraction. But this time she had a plan.

Minnie had always taught Scarlett that magic leaves a trace. Even those without much magic of their own could detect it, if they knew where to look, and how. One such location was right on campus. The perfect place for Scarlett to lure Xavier.

As long as she could talk her way back into his good graces.

Being able to get her hands on his schedule from the girl in the registrar's office had been easy. There was some satisfaction in that. Kappa still held sway in Westerly's social hierarchy, even if they were no longer the uncontested queens of campus. And even if Scarlett didn't have magic at her disposal anymore.

The trickier part had been catching Xavier actually *in* one of his classes. As far as she could tell, he skipped more often than not. It took her ages before she finally caught up with him again, this time in the hallway of Taylor.

The second they made eye contact, he froze, his expression hardening.

But magic or no, Scarlett was still a Raven. She knew how to get what she wanted. She strode closer, her coyest smile curling the edges of her bright red lips. "You're a hard guy to find, Xavier."

His eyes narrowed ever so slightly. "Last I checked, you didn't want to."

"Listen." Another step closer. His gaze dipped to take her in before he could catch himself. "I didn't mean to upset you at the dance. I haven't really gone out with anyone in a while, not since a big breakup last semester." All true.

"I saw you chase after him like a puppy dog."

"Who?"

"You know who."

Scarlett took a deep breath. The only way to sell a lie was with a little bit of truth. "I did. But only to get some closure. Only to tell him that I have a new plan now, one that doesn't involve him."

"But it involved me?"

"Only you."

He softened, his eyes wide, as if he wanted to believe her. She had him. "You have a strange way of showing it."

"You aren't like anyone I've met before. Most guys are a little intimidated by me, but you . . . You're a force. I guess I just . . ." Her lashes lowered artfully. When she looked up again, she let her vulnerability show. "I got nervous."

And she was, actually. Though probably not in the way he assumed.

I'm nervous you might be a demon terrorizing our campus.

He searched her face. Whatever he saw must have convinced

him. Finally, his shoulders relaxed a fraction. "I didn't mean to snap," he said. "When you said you wanted to be friends, I was just taken aback. I don't like playing games." He frowned. "My family makes me do that enough."

"I'm sorry I made you feel that way." She pressed her lips together. "I know how that feels. Being forced to play games. I don't like it, either." She looked away, at the side door of the building. Then she let her expression brighten, as if an idea had only just come to her. "Here." She extended a hand. "You want to see a real piece of my history? I'll show you something."

Xavier hesitated. She could see the warring emotions on his face. Curiosity and stubbornness battling it out.

She kept her hand outstretched. Waited patiently until, just as she predicted, Xavier's curiosity won. He took her hand, and she wound her fingers through his, ignoring the faint spark in her veins at his touch. Pleasure mixed with fear.

He could be the one we're looking for.

Then again, he could just be Xavier. A cute transfer who arrived on campus at exactly the wrong moment, about to be caught up in a mess he couldn't possibly understand.

There was only one way to find out.

"If this is some kind of Greek hazing thing, I swear . . ." Xavier grumbled while she led him toward the western edge of campus, where the school's old graveyard began.

Scarlett kept her hand firmly wrapped around his, however, and that playful smile on her lips. "Trust me," she called over her shoulder. He didn't pull away.

She knew her way through the graveyard by heart. She'd led enough Raven rituals in here. And before Scarlett had gotten into Westerly, she'd come here with Minnie.

Minnie had been the first one to bring her to the tomb she was walking toward now. "This is where it all started," Minnie had said. The name on the tombstone, Pearl Johnson, had stood out in block granite lettering, Gothic and imposing. Easy enough even for Scarlett to read at seven.

"You mean the Ravens?" Scarlett had asked. She'd already known who Pearl Johnson was. That she had founded the Kappas, the group that helped her mother perfect her magic, and which, one day, Scarlett and her older sister, Eugenie, would join, too.

Marjorie Winter believed in schooling her girls early.

Minnie had laughed. "No. Pearl wanted her tomb built here, but this site is older than the Ravens. Older than the country, even, and whole civilizations before it." Minnie had knelt then, and pressed a hand to Pearl's tombstone.

She had beckoned Scarlett forward, smiling. "Feel it," she'd said. "It's called a ley line."

Scarlett had stretched out a hand, obedient, and flattened it to the stone.

It was the first time she could ever remember sensing magic. She'd felt it surge through her body. Waves upon waves of energy, a lightning spark that ignited her. She'd gasped, pulled her hand back. Then laughed and touched it again. Savoring the sensation.

She'd known then: she wanted to grow up just like her mother and Eugenie. Just like Minnie. She'd wanted to be strong.

Scarlett remembered the scene with such clarity that tears stung the backs of her eyes as they wove past the elaborate tombs of the Savannah elite and the older, moldering tombs of those less fortunate.

Behind her, Xavier hesitated. "Is this your idea of a scenic date spot?"

"You wanted me to open up." Scarlett paused and faced him. "One of my earliest memories happened here. With Minnie."

The hesitation melted from Xavier's features. "Who was Minnie?"

"My caretaker, growing up. But honestly, she was more like a mother to me than my own mother." The gravel path crunched under her feet.

Pearl's tomb was at the back of the cemetery, near the forest. They had to duck beneath Spanish moss to reach it. It was still daylight, but this far into the shaded part of the cemetery, it looked dim.

"Minnie taught me so much about my own history. About traditions, too. Like this one." Scarlett glanced over her shoulder, smiling. Then she brushed aside the last clump of moss to reveal Pearl's tomb.

Xavier grinned back. "I thought you promised me this wasn't a hazing ritual."

"It's not hazing if it's something positive, right?"

The top of the tomb was a statue. Originally, Scarlett thought, it was meant to be an angel, but its wings had long since fallen off, and its face had decayed. All you could make out now was the outline—a shadowy, veiled woman, hands clasped, head bent.

Xavier stared at the name and the dates. "And who was *this?*"

Scarlett's smile widened. "I thought you said you looked up Kappa's history. Did you fail to read about our founder?"

"Oh, right. Of course." Was it her imagination, or did his smile suddenly seem forced? "Guess I forgot her name."

His face had gone paler than usual, his mouth a thin, tight line.

Scarlett stepped forward and brought one hand to rest on the edge of the tomb. It didn't feel like last time. No overwhelming surge of energy, no rushing river of magic. But she sensed *some*thing. A tiny jolt, as if she'd just shuffled across a carpet and touched a metal doorknob.

Minnie had been right. Even non-witches could sense magic at the ley line. Which meant . . . "The story goes that Pearl never married," Scarlett said. "Wasn't the type. But she did have paramours, over the years." She turned and caught him staring, at her this time.

She widened her smile. "Everyone who wooed her had great success in life, even after their affairs ended. Rumor has it, any guy wooing a Kappa girl can achieve the same luck. All he has to do is touch this stone."

Xavier raised an eyebrow. "Your nanny brought you here to tell you how to seduce future boyfriends?"

Her face flushed. "That's not what it's about."

"Right." He stuck his hands in his pockets. At that moment, a ringtone interrupted, a bright, jaunty song, entirely out of place in the quiet of the graveyard. Xavier drew the phone out, looked at it, and silenced it without answering.

"So?" Scarlett prodded. "Don't you want to see if it works?" If he touched the stone at the same time as her, and he possessed any magical strength at all, she would feel it. The rushing surge, like the first time she'd come here.

Xavier shifted from side to side. Then he checked his phone again. "I'm not really big on superstition."

"Oh, come on." Scarlett tried to keep her voice light and teasing, but she couldn't help the note of desperation that crept into it. "No harm in a little extra luck either way, right?"

"I don't believe in luck," Xavier replied, with a withering expression. "Neither should a girl as smart as you."

Why was he hesitating? Did he have something to hide after all? Maybe he sensed the ley line here. Maybe he knew what she was trying to do.

Scarlett let her hand fall away from the stone. "It's just a fun tradition, that's all."

"Don't love traditions, either. I get enough of those forced on me as it is." He was backing away. She was losing him.

Scarlett strode toward him. She crossed her arms and gave her best teasing smirk. "What's the matter? Scared of one little tombstone?"

He laughed once, sharply. "Please. It'll take a lot more than that to frighten me, Scarlett." The way he stared at her then was a challenge. *I know what you're trying to do, and it won't work.*

Her pulse thudded against her temples. She wanted to grab his hand. Force him to touch the stone. Better yet, if she went for him, would he use magic to defend himself? Reveal once and for all who he was—*what* he was?

She held back, though. She couldn't be sure. He could just be who he seemed: a cocky transfer who disdained traditions.

"You wanted to see something real from my life, Xavier," she said.

"Exactly." He gestured at the tomb, dismissive. "This isn't that. This is some game you're playing, *yet again*. I want no part of it." With that, he turned on his heel and disappeared through the swaying fronds of moss.

It didn't take her long to find Xavier again. She'd have recognized his gait anywhere, even from a few hundred yards away.

He knew more than he'd admit—that much was clear from the way he'd backed off from the tomb. And what he said. *This is some game you're playing.*

Whether he was the demon himself or just working with whoever stole Kappa's magic, Scarlett didn't know. But she was pretty sure whoever's side Xavier was on, it wasn't hers.

She followed him the long way back to campus, on side roads. She kept her distance, just in case he looked behind himself. But he never did.

With every step, her pulse beat a little faster.

Was following him alone a good idea? The horror stories Eugenie used to torture her with as a kid came rushing back now. Tales of demons that feasted on pain and misery; others of demons who enjoyed toying with their human prey, playing tricks and mind games. There had been one in particular, about a demon who drove a young witch in Salem so wild with visions of hellfire and brimstone that she wound up confessing to witchcraft, betraying several of her coven along with her.

Scarlett shivered.

They were almost to Greek Row. *You're probably just reading into this.* Xavier was most likely just going home to PiKa to complain to his brothers about Scarlett's idea of the world's crappiest date.

Yet some instinct kept her following.

Near the turnoff for PiKa House, Xavier paused. Glanced to the side. Scarlett barely had enough time to dive behind a tree trunk before he looked back. But she was far enough away, half hidden by the shadow of the trees, that he didn't seem to notice her.

Still, this time she counted to five before starting after him again.

When they reached Greek Row, Xavier walked right past PiKa. She lingered near the front porch of Gamma, figuring she could invent an errand if he turned back around again.

But Xavier just walked straight to the end of the street, and climbed up a familiar stone staircase. *Theta.*

Scarlett watched from a distance as he rapped on the door. A slim, short figure opened it. A girl, though she couldn't tell which Theta. She pulled Xavier into a tight embrace, and then they both disappeared into the house.

Scarlett stared, her mind reeling with possibilities.

CHAPTER THIRTY

Vivi

Vivi crashed on the couch in the Kappa living room. She couldn't face an entire night alone in her gloomy bedroom, a dusty memorial to her dead magic. The other girls' rooms had also suffered from the fading glamours, but none seemed quite as dramatic as Vivi's. The couch was comfortable, mercifully, but Vivi tossed and turned all night. She couldn't close her eyes without hearing Maria's voice whisper, *Join us, Vivian, and we can give you what you want.*

When you decide to come back, we'll be waiting.

Maria had made it clear the Kappas weren't the only witches at Westerly. But there was no way the Thetas could've had magic this whole time. Not only would the Ravens have felt the presence of another coven on campus — magic always left a trace — but Scarlett told Vivi that Maria had failed to light a sparkler at their Kappa rush.

Which meant Maria's magic was brand-new.

Vivi shuddered as she remembered what Tiffany had done to steal other witches' magic — the violence and the pain and the bloodshed. Was Maria committing similar monstrous acts? If a demon had been imprisoned in the talisman, was it *his* magic

Tiffany had been using in the first place? And what was required to unleash it?

Vivi sat up, shivering, and pulled her knees to her chest under her blanket. Without its protective spells, the old house was damp and drafty. Although, objectively, Vivi knew that it couldn't be colder than fifty degrees outside, she felt a chill sinking into her bones. It seemed like she'd never be warm again.

She thought longingly of the crackling magic she'd felt radiating from Maria. Vivi shouldn't trust the Theta president. She *knew* that. Yet just the thought of having her magic back, of being able to command the elements again, was enough to battle the despair and exhaustion calcifying inside her. But even that couldn't compare to the thrill she felt as she imagined returning her sisters' magic. Vivi hated seeing the Kappas wander around the house like ghosts of their former selves.

Jess was considering resigning from her leadership role at Westerly's student newspaper—a demanding role that didn't require magic but that Jess felt too exhausted and defeated to tackle. Mei's millions of followers were beginning to lose interest in her without the lure of new content, and there was a haunted look in Sonali's eyes that made Vivi's heart break.

If you had your power back, you could help them too, argued the other voice in the back of her mind. The one that seemed to be growing louder and louder lately. She could save the Ravens. Proving her worth to Scarlett and her sisters once and for all by being the one to rescue their magic from Theta.

After all, Scarlett had told Vivi to cozy up to Theta. Wasn't the next logical step for Vivi to do just that? She could be a spy. Their woman on the inside. She was a Kappa through and through, and that meant doing whatever it took to save her loyal sisters. And to keep Reagan, Etta, Hazel, and Bailey from going too deep.

When the sun began to peek through the dusty windows, Vivi let out a long sigh and reached for her phone, surprised to see a new text. Maybe it was from Mason; he sometimes sent her sweet messages when he was up late studying.

The painful reality cut into her like a knife. No, of course the text wasn't from Mason.

She winced as she remembered the look on Mason's face right before he walked away. The whole time she'd known him, he'd been nothing but kind, patient, and understanding. And the one time he turned to *her* for support, the one time he'd truly needed her, she hadn't been there for him.

The text was from Ariana asking Vivi to meet her for breakfast in the greenhouse whenever she got up. Vivi smiled through her exhaustion. Hanging out with Ariana always made her feel better, no matter what else was going on. Without bothering to change out of her pajamas, Vivi tiptoed into the hall, careful to avoid the creaky floorboards lest she wake the rest of the house.

To her surprise, Ariana wasn't the only person waiting for her. The small glass table in the central patio of the greenhouse had been set up with three chairs on one side of the table and one on the opposite. Almost like an interview. Ariana, Sonali, and Jess sat together, surrounded by the dense, lush ferns the older girls grew here.

Vivi couldn't see any signs of food. Just a tea tray and a steaming mug already waiting for her beside the single chair, across from the rest.

"What's going on?" she asked, her voice still thick with restless sleep.

"It's an intervention," Jess said, cutting straight to the point.

"What?" Vivi stared at them, aghast. Sonali looked deeply uncomfortable, sitting ramrod straight. Ariana just seemed resigned, her mouth a grim line.

"You haven't been acting like yourself," Ariana said. "We're worried about you."

"Of course I haven't been acting like myself," Vivi snapped. "None of us have. How can we, when part of ourselves has been *stolen from us?*"

"We're just as upset about this as you," Sonali said. "But none of *us* have been sneaking off to hang out with rival sororities in the meantime."

Vivi's stomach churned. "That's not what happened."

"Oh, really?" Jess held up her phone. It was open to a Theta girl's Instagram account and showed a photo of Vivi and Rose huddled in the Theta kitchen, drinks in hand, both of them laughing. "Then how do you explain this?"

"We were busting our asses in the library all night and day, working under *your* Big's orders—which we disagree with, anyway—and you're what, partying?" Sonali said.

"I'm sure there's an explanation." Ariana shot Sonali an imploring look, as if they'd discussed this already and agreed to give Vivi a chance to defend herself.

"Yes, there is," Vivi said icily. "I was over there *looking for clues*. I didn't do anything wrong!"

"Why didn't you tell anyone first?" Jess asked, in full investigative journalist mode. "If you suspected Theta, shouldn't you have told us?"

"What does it matter?" Vivi said, indignation mixing with incredulity. This was so outrageous, it had to be some kind of joke. "I was trying to help us and you're acting like I'm the traitor. What about Reagan and Etta and the others? You know, the ones who *actually* betrayed Kappa."

Jess flinched slightly. Watching Etta leave had been a blow for her. But then she composed herself and continued her interrogation. "They're not hiding anything. We know they left Kappa. But I have to admit, I find your secrecy troubling, Vivi."

The unfairness of it was almost too much to bear. Vivi was the one who had done the work. They thought sitting around the library was difficult? Try walking into the enemy witch's lair and coming back out unscathed. She'd stood in front of Rose's altar and seen magic again. *Felt* it. Her sisters didn't understand what that was like.

"You don't understand," she said, pushing her chair back and rising to her feet.

"Then explain it to us," Ariana said, pleading.

Sonali scoffed. "She's not going to admit anything. She's Scarlett's little apprentice; she doesn't think she needs to explain herself to any of us peons."

"I'm out of here," Vivi said. She wasn't going to waste any more time when she had actual work to do, real leads to follow in the quest to get their magic back.

Sonali stood to block Vivi's path.

"What the hell are you doing?" Vivi asked. *"Move."* But then Jess rose from her chair to stand beside Sonali.

"Get out of my way."

Vivi tried to shove past them, but Ariana grabbed her arm. "Please, Vivi, we're trying to help you."

"Help me? What does that mean?"

"Last semester, I failed to notice when something was wrong with my Big Sister," Ariana said softly, stepping toward Vivi. "I don't want to make that same mistake again."

Vivi felt claustrophobic. They weren't giving her space to even *breathe.* "What the hell are you talking about?" she spat, jerking her arm away a bit harder than she meant to. "Tiffany was using wicked magic to kill other witches. I'm trying to help us get our magic back."

Ariana didn't respond. She was just staring at Vivi, wide-eyed. *She's scared,* Vivi realized. Under all the bravado and the posturing. Her friend was scared. *For me?* she wondered. *Or of me?*

"Talk to us, please," Ariana said finally, her voice barely above a whisper. "You aren't acting like yourself. I know there's something going on."

Vivi looked from Ariana to Jess and Sonali, who were standing with arms outstretched, palms open. Instinct had kicked in, and their bodies had prepared to cast protective spells, drawing on magic they no longer possessed.

They're all scared of me.

"No, you tell *me* what's really going on," Vivi said, her voice starting to shake. "You called me here to trap me, didn't you? You think I'm going to pull a Tiffany and start killing you all to steal your power?"

Sonali shot Jess an anxious look before turning back to Vivi. "We're not saying it's your fault. You and Scarlett didn't know what would happen when you destroyed the talisman. But if something did go wrong, we're here to help. To make sure you don't end up hurting anyone . . . or yourself."

Vivi stared at her, uncomprehending, until it clicked and she let out a harsh, bitter laugh that echoed through the greenhouse. "You think *I'm* the demon? Oh my God . . ." She paced in a small circle, shaking her head. Everything she'd done so far had been for these girls, whom she'd called sisters. She'd wanted to help them. *Save* them. She'd risked her *life* for it, going up against a rival sorority with magic on their hands, all for her fellow Ravens.

This was how they repaid her? With an ambush. Accusing her of masking a hidden evil.

"Vivi, listen—" Ariana started.

"Don't worry." Vivi cut her off. "You have nothing to fear from me. Because I'm out of here." Before anyone could try to stop her again, she wrenched the greenhouse door open and slammed it behind herself so hard the glass rattled in its panes.

It didn't matter what they thought of her. She was going to get their magic back, and then they'd fall to their knees, begging for her forgiveness.

Not that they'd deserve it.

~

It started raining the moment she stepped outside. Vivi instinctively raised a hand, a motion that used to repel water, before she remembered. Without her Pentacles magic, she had no control over the elements.

For now.

But she'd have her power back soon enough.

Vivi pulled her jacket tighter around her shoulders and hurried up the street, past all the other Greek houses with their clapboard siding and peeling letters, until she reached the only other noteworthy building on the block.

Theta House looked even larger than she remembered from the party. In daylight, its towers seemed to reach higher, the stone steps steeper and slick with rain at the moment. She took them two at a time anyway, eager to get started now that she'd decided on this path once and for all.

Before she reached the top step, the front door swung inward on its own, something that might've troubled, or at least surprised, Vivi before but now only confirmed that she was making the right choice.

Vivi crossed through the entryway, her footsteps echoing on the marble floor, bouncing off the high stone ceilings. She stood for a moment, unsure what to do next as water dripped from the hem of her rain-soaked jeans onto the floor.

Her eyes widened as the little puddles dried up and evaporated all on their own. It had only been twenty-fours since she'd last been in Theta House, and the new witches had clearly already stepped up their game.

Next to the front door stood a coatrack, empty except for a single fluffy white towel.

She glanced around the empty hall again, then shrugged and lifted the towel to pat off her hair and shoulders. She buried her face in it, inhaling the scent of lavender and honey. There didn't seem to be anyone around, but Vivi could see a fire crackling in the living room, and the intoxicating warmth was enough to draw her inside.

There was no sign of last night's revelry—not a Solo cup or stained couch cushion in sight. But while that alone should've been a sign of magic at work, Vivi couldn't quite reconcile the Shabby Chic slipcovers and cheesy throw pillows with witchcraft.

Someone cleared their throat behind her, and Vivi spun around to see Maria watching her with a bemused half smile. She had said Vivi would choose this. And she was right.

Slowly, Vivi reached out to replace the towel on the coatrack, keeping her eyes on Maria the whole time, then squared her shoulders to face her. "So how'd you do it?" she asked.

"Do what?" Maria said coyly.

Vivi crossed her arms. Although it was very clear that Maria knew all about the Kappas and witchcraft, pride made it difficult for Vivi to say the words aloud. She needed Maria to break first.

"I don't need to play games with you," Maria said. "I don't need to prove anything. I have everything you want."

"If that's the case, then you're hiding it *really* well. Cute pillows, by the way," Vivi said in a tone she wouldn't have been able to pull off before spending time with Scarlett. "You're the one who seems to want me to join Theta so badly. How do I know you can actually give me what I'm looking for?"

Maria snorted. "Fine, then. But be careful what you ask for." She snapped her fingers, and the couch burst into flames.

Vivi almost sprang back but caught herself just in time. She couldn't show any weakness around Maria, any sign that she was impressed or intimidated by Maria's newfound magical abilities. Any fire witch in Kappa could've performed this trick in her sleep. Except that the smell was wrong. Behind the scent of smoke and burning fabric, Vivi could detect hints of something overly pungent and sweet, like rotting fruit. Like . . . stolen magic?

The flames grew higher and more erratic, and for a moment, Maria's face looked pained, as if it required all her strength to keep the fire from spreading to the rest of the house. Sparks singed Vivi's skin, and her eyes began to water. The burning throw pillows rose slowly into the air, hovered for a moment, then exploded into balls of dark ash. But instead of falling to the ground, the ash swirled and formed back into pillows, though they were now black instead of pink and green, and instead of LIVE, LOVE, LAUGH, they were emblazed with the words GLAMOUR, HEX, CURSE.

Despite herself, Vivi laughed. "You got me," she said.

"So," Maria prompted. "Are you in?" She snapped her fingers again, and the flames vanished, although the couch still looked singed. Vivi would have to teach her a better way to cast the spell.

"I'm in."

CHAPTER THIRTY-ONE

Scarlett

Scarlett crouched in the bushes next to PiKa House, feeling like a stalker. But how else was she supposed to figure this out? None of the Thetas were about to spill the beans to Scarlett about Xavier. She'd tried waylaying one of them, Spencer, at the dining hall that morning, only to receive the world's rudest brush-off in return.

Scarlett had been texting Vivi all morning asking to chat so they could strategize. But her messages went unanswered. Vivi must be busy with her own recon mission. After the Theta party, Scarlett had gotten a brief, cryptic text. *On the right track. More tomorrow.*

Scarlett just hoped whatever Vivi was out finding today was easier than Scarlett's own mission. She shuffled in place to ease the cramps in her legs.

She knew this hiding spot well—back in the day, she'd snuck off here with Mason a couple of times, during PiKa parties when they'd wanted a little more privacy. It was hard to spot anyone in this narrow alcove, and it had a good view of the front porch.

So far, half a dozen PiKa brothers had streamed past her, either on their way back home or headed out on the town for the evening.

Most of them, to judge by their slicked-back hair and the

cologne that wafted in their wake, probably had plans to barhop downtown or seek out one of the many parties going on across Westerly's campus.

Of course, Theta would probably be the most popular destination. A fact that rankled at Scarlett almost as much as the mud she was slowly sinking into.

She shifted on her feet, drawing them back out of the loam, and leaned against the house with a sigh.

So far, no signs of Xavier.

He must still be inside. He had no classes today. She'd confirmed via a casual run-in with another PiKa brother that Xavier was back at the house. She'd been staked out here ever since.

She listened to a couple up the street arguing, another guy somewhere inside PiKa cursing. The whole campus felt antsy. Like a powder keg waiting to blow.

She couldn't help but think about the Hadesgate. Was it causing all of this angst and anger? Pitting people against each other?

Her feet throbbed, even in sensible flats.

What she wouldn't give for just a *little* spell. Something to lure Xavier out here. *Or one to heal my blisters.*

She held her breath as the PiKa front door opened again. Then she braced herself for disappointment—for one of the other PiKa brothers to stride up the walkway, the same way they had a dozen times already.

But a moment later, she caught a glimpse of Xavier's telltale sloped shoulders. *Finally.*

She continued to hold her breath as he crossed the street. She watched him check over his shoulder, and for a heart-pounding instant, she ducked, convinced he'd spotted her. When she dared to peer out through the bushes again, he was walking away, toward Westerly's main campus, with a bag slung over one shoulder.

Off to a library to study?

Or off to lure some other unsuspecting students into his trap?

She was about to find out.

Moving fast, she hurried up the front steps and into PiKa House. She already knew which bedroom must be Xavier's. After all, it was the same bedroom Mason had vacated last semester. The room they'd spent most of their relationship sneaking up to.

Somehow, even though they'd only broken up at the start of this year, that already felt like another lifetime. Another Scarlett entirely.

One who still had all her magic, she couldn't help thinking.

But she'd learned a lot last semester. She'd found other kinds of strength. She had to remember that.

Scarlett took the stairs two at a time. She didn't have an excuse prepared, but she was fairly sure that her status as Kappa president would still buy her some forgiveness if a PiKa brother caught her snooping around. If Xavier returned faster than she expected, though . . .

She'd be quick.

Scarlett let muscle memory guide her to the third door on the second floor. *Locked.* Luckily, she'd installed a failsafe for Mason their sophomore year, when he kept locking himself out. She knelt and tapped on the loose molding next to the floorboards.

Sure enough, a piece of the wooden molding came free, and tucked behind it was the spare key she'd had made.

Trying not to feel too smug just yet, Scarlett fitted the key into the lock. They might have changed it when Xavier moved in.

But it turned smoothly, and she let out a breath of relief. Quickly, she stepped inside and latched the door behind her.

At first, it looked like any other dorm room, if suspiciously neat for a college guy. The bed was precisely made, the desk looked like an Apple store in miniature, and the only textbooks she could see were stacked on the bookshelf in alphabetical order.

Xavier was definitely different from the other PiKa brothers. Even Mason, although he'd been tidy, usually had half a dozen history books lying face-down all over his room, ready for him to snatch up for reference whenever he needed.

Still, nothing about the room stood out as immediately suspect. Scarlett started with the bookshelf. The textbooks were all for classes she recognized. Econ, calculus . . . In fact, the shelf was so normal—no scuffed edges on the textbooks, no novels or pop-sci to read for fun—it started to seem weird.

What student kept their textbooks looking like they were still on the shelf at the bookstore?

On the desk, Xavier's computer hummed in idle mode. Scarlett tapped on the screen, and the password prompt arose. Once again, she would have done just about anything for her magic. A glamour spell could have made her fingerprint look like Xavier's, and she'd be able to unlock this.

Instead, she dug through his desk drawers. She had a feeling a guy as organized and competent as Xavier wouldn't keep anything so obvious as a password book lying around, but you never knew.

She found his daily planner, but it was illegible, the writing cramped and not even forming full words. She squinted at it for a full minute before it clicked. She'd seen writing like this before: her mother's law office notes. *Shorthand*. Marjorie had learned it in school, though nowadays with computers to rely on, nobody taught it anymore (something Marjorie complained about ad nauseum).

Why would a guy Xavier's age learn shorthand, let alone use it in his school planner?

Squinting, Scarlett tried to read it. A few pages back, on the date of the alumnae reunion, he'd written *Scrt*. Was that about her? Scarlett? She couldn't read the rest. Half the letters were just lines pointing in various directions.

She snapped a photo of the page.

She went through the rest of the planner, but she couldn't find anything that looked like a computer password.

She was placing it back in the drawer when something else caught her eye. A camera, resting next to the planner.

Glancing over her shoulder at the door—PiKa House was still quiet—Scarlett slid the camera out and turned it on. The first thing on the screen was a photo of her. She sucked in a sharp breath, nearly dropping the camera.

It had been taken the day she'd tried to talk to Xavier on the lawns. In the picture, she stood with Jackson, arguing with him.

Jackson was scowling, pulling away, and she was trying to reach for his arm.

So Xavier had been watching her too. That whole time.

Her heart sped up. Suddenly, the silence in PiKa House felt too conspicuous. If Xavier came back and caught her, could she scream? Was anyone else home? Would any of the guys hear her and come?

She swallowed hard. *It's fine, you saw him leave.* He'd been in his room all day. He wouldn't rush straight back.

Still, she eased up out of the chair as she continued to flip through the camera photos.

She found pictures of all the Ravens. Mei sunning herself on the lawn out back of the house. Etta coming out of a shop downtown with bags on her arm. Juliet and Jess holding hands across a restaurant table downtown, clearly out on a date night. Hazel running along the river, the sun just starting to rise.

And Vivi, huddled with Rose at the bakery. Vivi again, at the alumnae reunion. Except she didn't look right, she didn't seem happy and exuberant the way Scarlett remembered. In this photo, she wore a tense, stressed expression. And her arm . . . She was *bleeding*.

When had Vivi injured herself at the reunion? Scarlett didn't remember that. But if there was one thing these photos proved —besides that Xavier was *not* your average frat guy—it was that Scarlett had missed a *lot* going on around her. Add that to her growing pile of failures as president.

A floorboard creaked overhead. Gasping, she shoved the camera back into the drawer, slid it closed. Then she froze in the middle of Xavier's bedroom, holding her breath, pulse pounding.

Another creak, and then she heard a distant laugh. A guy's voice. Just another PiKa brother in his own room. Her shoulders relaxed a fraction.

Hurry up.

She needed more. These photos were disturbing, but he could just be your typical creep. Not necessarily a demon. She needed more than those photos.

Scarlett needed proof Xavier was working with wicked magic, proof that he knew about the Hadesgate, the Henosis talisman. She squared her shoulders and scanned the room. The computer was clearly a bust—hacking wasn't going to happen. Scarlett knew her limits.

Closet first. It was as neat as the desk and the bookshelf: all of Xavier's clothing hung in neat rows. He had about ten of the same shirt and only two pairs of jeans—dark and light wash. A leather bag hung on the side of the closet, and Scarlett's heart leaped. But it only contained pens and a pack of chewing gum.

Did demons chew gum?

She shook herself, put the bag back, and shut the closet doors.

Bed next. She pushed back the covers, scanned around it. Then she knelt on the carpet—she was pretty sure he'd steam-cleaned it, to get a dorm room carpet this spotless—and peered underneath. A couple of plastic storage cartons caught her eye. She slid one out and froze.

Through the plastic cover, she could see a stack of what looked like books. But these were different from the ones on the bookshelf. Older, the covers unlabeled leather.

She cracked the lid open and pulled the top book out. Flipped open the cover, and immediately almost dropped it.

The title page was set in an old-fashioned font, in stylized letters, but still easy enough to read. *Detecting Signes of the Wytch*.

Bile rose to the back of Scarlett's throat. She needed to get out of here — but she also needed evidence of what, exactly, Xavier was doing. She pulled her cell phone out again and snapped a picture of the cover page, then flipped to the table of contents. *Elementes of Wicked Magick. Varietals of Wytches and Theyr Weaknesses.*

Finally, near the bottom: *Methodologies of Wytch Elimination*.

She took another photo, then reached for the next book in the stack. They were all like that. No actual grimoires on how to use magic, but maybe a demon didn't need to learn magic use. Maybe he just needed to know how to find witches and . . . steal their powers? Or *eliminate* them?

Her throat felt tight, her hands clammy. She was about to load all the books back into the container when she spotted one more item lying at the bottom.

A long, thin stiletto dagger. Adrenaline flooded through her.

The markings along the blade and wrapped around the handle were all runes her mother had taught her to read, practically before she'd learned to read English. It had been the very first lesson she'd learned, the day her mother explained that she was a witch.

If you ever see these marks, anywhere . . . She could hear her mother's voice as though it was yesterday in her memory. *Run.*

Scarlett staggered to her feet without even bothering to close the container. The room fuzzed around the edges as panic gripped her.

Xavier wasn't a demon. Those books made sudden, terrible sense, all at once. So did the photographs, the way Xavier had focused on the Ravens, stalking all of them.

He's a witch-hunter.

Scarlett didn't bother to hide her tracks. Instinct took over. *Get out of here, go, go, go,* her brain screamed. She bolted toward the door and wrenched it open. The hallway outside was dark, the lights overhead flickering. Had it been this dim when she first came upstairs? Or had something changed?

She took a step, and the floorboards creaked beneath her. She froze, glanced around. But all of the other bedroom doors were shut. She couldn't hear anyone upstairs anymore either. No comforting distant voices of other PiKa guys chatting away.

You're okay, she told herself. *It's just one staircase.* Then she'd be home free. Kappa was right across the lawn. She'd run there, tell her sisters. They'd figure this out together.

First, she needed to move.

She stuck to the edges of the hallway, where the boards made less noise. Ran on tiptoe toward the staircase. Every few steps, she checked over her shoulder. The house was dim, empty. Only the flicker of the lights for company.

Her phone buzzed.

It was Marjorie.

She turned off her phone.

Finally, she reached the steps and took those two at a time, practically sprinting. She didn't care if another PiKa saw her and wondered what was going on. She just needed to escape. Get back out into fresh air, where she could clear her head.

She hit the ground floor and raced for the front door. Wrenched it open, ready to fling herself out of the house, toward freedom.

Instead, she ran straight into the witch-hunter himself.

CHAPTER THIRTY-TWO

Vivi

I t seemed as if Vivi would be joining Theta immediately. After she told Maria that she was in, her new president led her upstairs, where it seemed the other sisters were waiting for her. As she skipped up the stone steps, Vivi inhaled deeply and smiled as the familiar, slightly smoky scent made every nerve in her body tingle. She felt jolted back to life, fully awake and alert for the first time in days.

As Maria led Vivi into the common room, the Thetas greeted her with cheers and applause, Reagan and Bailey loudest of all. Vivi's chest flooded with warmth. It was all so different from Vivi's first foray into Kappa, where she'd needed to earn her place and prove her worth to Scarlett and the older girls, again and again.

Yet Vivi couldn't shake the sensation that something just seemed a little . . . off. Looking around the common room was like peering into a funhouse-mirror version of Kappa; it was undeniably magical but just the slightest bit off-kilter. When Spencer ran over to give her a hug, Vivi saw that she'd glamoured her long blond hair into a dark bob, like Mei sometimes sported. But unlike Mei's smooth, glossy locks, Spencer's hair had a fuzzy quality — like an old-fashioned TV stuck between channels — and when she moved,

Vivi caught flashes of blond trying to break through. But that made sense, given how new the Thetas were to magic, and part of Vivi looked forward to helping them. For once, she'd be the skilled, experienced one.

"It's going to take us a little while to organize your initiation ritual," Maria said. "Why don't you make yourself comfortable in the meantime? Rose can show you your room."

Rose practically leaped at the chance, grabbing Vivi's hand and pulling her toward the staircase with such enthusiasm that Vivi felt a heady rush of guilt about her behavior at the party.

"Hey, I'm really sorry I disappeared the other night. And I shouldn't have gone into your room without permission—"

"No need to apologize." Rose cut her off with a smile. "Maria explained everything. If that's what it took to convince you to join us, I'm happy you did it." She led Vivi down a pretty hallway lined with dark blue floral wallpaper. She waved a hand, and a door at the end of the hall blew open. "Your room," Rose said, clearly proud of what she'd just done.

"Nice one." Vivi grinned, but she couldn't tamp down the envy curling serpentlike around her stomach. She felt like someone on the brink of starvation forced to watch a cake-eating competition —her urge to perform magic was a physical ache. She needed it to feel like herself again, to protect herself from the darkness she could sense closing in.

"Go ahead and get settled. We'll call you when it's time," Rose said warmly, before backing out and shutting the door.

Maria had assigned Vivi a room in one of the four turrets that rose over the main house. It boasted a fireplace, a stone balcony even larger than her Juliet balcony at Kappa, and ceilings so high the dim overhead light barely illuminated the details of the wooden rafters.

It felt colder than Vivi's room at Kappa, too. As if the stones leached all the warmth from the air, though she supposed that was what the fireplace was for. But she'd be able to fix that with a snap of her fingers, once she had her magic back. Yet as she settled onto the bed, she felt a sudden pang of homesickness. She didn't want to use her recovered magic to fix this room—she wanted to break whatever curse had settled over Kappa House and restore her sisters' powers so everything could just return to normal. Well, not normal, exactly. If Vivi was the first to regain her magic, and if she used it to help the other Kappas, they'd never be able to look down on her or doubt her again.

Vivi knew she should stay on guard until the Thetas proved they'd hold up their end of the bargain and give her magic back. Yet she couldn't help but *want* to trust them. Scarlett had sent Vivi into danger all alone—and instead of danger, Vivi had found nice, welcoming sorority girls. Girls who didn't act like she was less than them because she didn't know how magic worked.

In the en suite bathroom, Vivi found luxuriously fluffy towels and an array of designer bath products with scents that reminded her of brewing-potions: thistle, rose, mugwort, and lavender. She spent longer than usual in the shower, relishing the steamy warmth.

The Kappa House plumbing had been acting up the past few days, and there'd been hardly any hot water. When she emerged, she noticed a change of clothing draped over the armchair: black jeans with a vinyl sheen and a black T-shirt. It wasn't her usual style. But then, Vivi had come here precisely because she didn't want to be herself anymore.

She wanted to be someone else. Someone stronger. Someone unafraid.

She pulled on the jeans that skimmed every curve as if they'd been tailored to her body, and slipped on the black top that hugged her tight.

The girl in the mirror looked like a Bond girl, dangerous and mysterious. Vivi hardly recognized herself.

She liked it.

She imagined how Mason would react to seeing her in this out-fit. Would he realize what a mistake he'd made letting a girl like Vivi go? What would he do if he saw her dancing with her new sisters at a party, her hips swaying, her head thrown back as she lost herself in the music? Would he be so overcome with longing that he'd be willing to give her a second chance? Not that Mason went to that many parties. If Vivi wanted him to see her in this outfit, she'd have to wear it to the library . . . at nine p.m. on a Friday, as that was when Mason "did his best thinking."

Vivi felt a pang of sadness as she thought about all the times she'd snuck coffee and candy to him inside the rare books room, how Mason's face would light up whenever he saw her, even if it'd only been a few hours. How would they ever get that back? How could she repair everything she'd ruined?

Fifteen minutes later, Etta and Bailey came to fetch Vivi and bring her back down to the common room. "Are you excited?" Etta asked as they walked down the hall. She was practically bouncing on the balls of her feet and seemed uncharacteristically giddy. "You've made the right decision, I promise."

"Yes, definitely," Vivi said. "So how long did it take your magic to come back?"

Etta and Bailey exchanged knowing smiles. "We're not supposed to talk about that until you've been initiated," Bailey said in a serene voice Vivi didn't quite recognize. Even when she was in a good mood, Bailey always seemed a little tightly wound.

"You're going to be really happy here," Etta said, grabbing Vivi's hand. "The girls are all so nice and welcoming. It already feels like I've been a Theta forever."

Bailey nodded vigorously. "And Maria's the best. You're going to love her. She actually *likes* it when someone offers advice. She always says the best ideas come from unexpected places."

"That sounds great," Vivi said, thinking again about how different this all felt from pledging Kappa with its judgment and presumption, from the invitation that'd arrived without an RSVP card to the sparklers that only lit for the worthy. Everything she'd learned from the Kappas was predicated on the idea that you had to be *born* a witch; the magic was bestowed rather than earned. But what if there was a better way? Shouldn't magic be available to anyone willing to work hard and use it for good? The Thetas might be magic novices, but they seemed eager to use their newfound powers to make Vivi feel welcome and included.

But as she followed Etta and Bailey down the stairs, Vivi realized she might have underestimated just how strong the Thetas had grown already. In the hour or so since she'd left, the ground floor had been transformed into a completely different world. Instead of the foyer she'd entered earlier today, she found herself in a copse. Trees lined either side of the hall, and grass made a velvety emerald carpet underfoot. Here and there among the grass and tree trunks, she spotted mushrooms and lichen, small night-blooming flowers that seemed to glow in the low light.

A faint breeze tickled the nape of her neck, and she shivered, rubbing her arms in the cool air as her breath fogged in front of her face.

A hooded figure appeared at her elbow, so suddenly that Vivi jumped.

The hood shadowed the figure's eyes, so all Vivi could see were round pink lips. Rose, she thought. Maybe. Or another Theta girl. "Are you prepared, initiate?" she asked with a smile. She produced a bright pink rose from her robe and handed it to Vivi.

Vivi squared her shoulders. She wouldn't let Theta theatrics intimidate her. "I'm ready," she said, proud of how steady her voice was.

"Follow me." Rose's midnight black cloak hissed faintly where it trailed over the grass.

Vivi followed her up the hallway, unable to resist the urge to reach out and let her fingers brush against the tree trunks as they walked.

It all felt so real. The grass, the bark of the trees. It even *smelled* like a forest—damp and earthy. The scent made her crave her Pentacles magic so intensely, her stomach nearly grumbled. Her hunger for it was overwhelming. No, not a hunger. A *need*.

She was so close to power now. So close to being whole again. *Safe*.

Ahead of Rose, the hallway-turned-forest widened into a circular space. Fat mushrooms ringed this clearing, luminous and gray, like chunks of the moon fallen onto the grass. When Vivi tilted her head back, she couldn't see the ceiling, or any of Theta House. All she saw was a clear sky and a fat, full moon. And stars. Millions upon millions of stars, like a thick galaxy blanket laid over the room.

It took all her effort to tear her gaze from that ceiling.

More hooded figures awaited. All of Theta had come for her initiation, and they now stood in a circle, heads bowed. Rose joined the circle, and the figures parted. One of the taller members, distinguished from the rest by a crown of spiky thorns, waved Vivi forward, into the center.

She couldn't tell who anyone was. She assumed the one with the crown was Maria, but none of these details seemed to matter, now that she was so close to getting what she craved.

Vivi could almost feel the magic reaching out to her, waiting to flood back into her veins where it belonged. Without magic, Vivi was defenseless, just another girl without a home or purpose, drifting through life the way she had before she came to Westerly. Only magic could protect her from wicked people like Tiffany. From the even worse demons that haunted this campus.

She thought about the Hadesgate under Kappa, the way it had trembled and seized, trying to suck Scarlett in. She couldn't fight that without power. And whether the Ravens were angry with Vivi right now or not, they were in danger. She couldn't leave them defenseless.

With Theta's strength, Vivi could save Kappa and stop the demon hell-bent on destroying them.

Vivi approached with her head held high. Once she reached the center of the circle, the figures closed ranks around her.

"Initiate," said another voice. Maria, this time. But when Vivi turned to look for the president, she couldn't tell whose mouth was moving, which figure had spoken. The voice seemed to come from everywhere and nowhere at once. "In joining us today, you pledge yourself—mind, body, and soul—to this circle. From this night forth, our power is your power. Your power, ours. We are one."

"We are one," the others repeated. The circle seemed to speak as one, and Vivi could feel the vibrations from their voices echoing in her chest. "We are one. We are one . . ."

"If you agree to our terms, then take up your cloak. Pledge yourself, as all those present have pledged themselves before." The crowned figure tilted her head, and Vivi followed her gaze and saw a dark robe puddled on the ground. Vivi paused, then walked over to scoop it up, leaving her rose in its place. She flung the heavy fabric over her shoulders, and let out a faint sigh of relief at the protection it gave her from the chill in the air.

"Repeat the binding after me," the crowned Theta said. Except that the crown wasn't made of thorns, she realized. They were bones—antlers from some massive creature. A deer, perhaps, but a very, very old one. Faint streaks of red stained the base of the crown.

"My power is your power," the crowned Theta said.

"My power is your power," Vivi repeated.

"My body, your body. My will, your will."

"My body, your body." The words flowed out of her faster. "My will, your will."

"In blood, we seal this pact, as all of our pacts before yours have been sealed, Vivian Devereaux." The crowned figure produced a tarnished silver chalice and a blade. Vivi watched as, one by one, each figure in the circle stepped forward. They offered a single finger, and the crowned figure pricked it. Then one by one, each Theta tilted her hand to let a drop of blood fall into the goblet.

Finally, the crowned one pricked her own fingertip, added another drop to the cup.

The chalice began to glow dark red as if lit from within by a dying star.

Vivi extended her arms and accepted the cup, bracing for the stench of blood. But when she held the chalice under her nose, it didn't smell coppery the way she'd anticipated. It smelled *sweet*.

"Drink," the crowned one commanded. "And be your whole self again, witch."

Vivi's heart trilled at the sound of the word. *Witch*.

She raised the cup to her lips and, without hesitation, swallowed the liquid down. She waited for the familiar buzz of energy to return to her skin, but nothing happened.

"I . . . I don't think it worked," Vivi said, dread and disappointment clawing at her stomach.

But Maria only smirked and extended her arm, palm turned up. A moment later, a small, dancing flame appeared in her hand. "Try it," Maria said.

Vivi hesitated, wondering if she should try a Pentacles spell first. That was how Kappa had worked. Start with the magic you can do best and work your way up.

But this wasn't Kappa.

She didn't have her tarot cards; she'd been given no spells to memorize, no exercises to do.

Maria held out a hand. Between her fingertips, a thin needle glittered. "I believe you already know how this magic works. All it takes is a little pain. A sacrifice for what you want." Maria winked. "Who do you think left you that grimoire?"

Maria gave me the grimoire? How is that possible? But the sparks of confusion were quickly extinguished by her raw, desperate need to perform magic, an urge that overpowered all other concerns. Vivi took the needle and shut her eyes. She thought about the flames dancing along Maria's palm. She wanted that. The power, the heat.

Vivi scrunched her forehead, gritted her teeth, and jabbed the needle into the center of her thumb.

Flames leaped from Vivi's fingertips, rising straight up toward the ceiling, so high that a few of the other Thetas jumped backwards, some of them laughing.

Vivi wriggled her fingers, and the flames shifted and danced in midair. One licked so close to her face she felt it sear her cheeks, her skin turning pink. With a wild grin, Vivi snapped her fist shut, and the flames winked out of existence.

"Welcome to Theta," Maria said, beaming. "You're one of us now."

CHAPTER THIRTY-THREE

Scarlett

S carlett froze, rooted to the spot. Xavier had one hand clamped around her wrist, albeit not tightly. More like he was steadying her. But it would be so easy for him to twist her arm around from this position, pin her against the wall. He was bigger than her, and stronger. Plus, she'd lost her magic.

He filled the door, his gaze darting from her face to the darkened staircase behind her. Her heartbeat picked up.

"Oh! Xavier." She tried to sound casual, but her voice was shaking too much. *Damn it.* "I was just heading out." She tried to twist her arm free, but Xavier held on.

"I just got a security alert," he said. His tone was light. Almost conversational. "Someone was in my bedroom."

Shit. She should have known. Of course a witch-hunter would have security alarms. They had everything to hide. "That's . . . unfortunate," Scarlett managed.

"Yes." His eyes were dark. Unreadable pools. "And now here you are. Sprinting out of PiKa House."

Scarlett took a deep breath. Then she screamed.

Or tried to. Xavier was faster. He clamped a hand over her mouth, so the sound came out muffled. Scarlett tried to push free, and Xavier swung her around, pinning her back against his chest. "What were you doing?" he demanded, his voice low now. No longer joking. Dangerous.

She was so close to the exit. She could kick the door frame. Maybe one of the other PiKa brothers would hear it and come to her rescue.

Her lips felt hot against his palm. Too hot. She thrashed again, and this time he let her go. But he didn't move from the doorway. Lanky though he was, he managed to block the exit easily, one hand planted on either side of the frame.

"Let me go," she said. She'd meant it to sound in control. Menacing. Instead, her voice trembled and cracked.

"You're the one who broke into *my* bedroom," Xavier pointed out. "If anyone has a right to make demands here, I think it's me."

"If you don't let me go, I'll . . ." Scarlett hesitated. Winced.

Xavier lifted a single eyebrow and smirked. "You'll what, curse me? I'd love to see you try, but I'm fairly certain you couldn't even light a sparkler right now if your life depended on it."

Her cheeks flushed. Her whole *body* flushed. How did he know about the sparklers? Hell, how did he know *anything* about the Ravens? She'd seen his photographs of her sisters out on the town, or on the lawns, but . . . They were so careful, so private. They had been for generations.

Until you came along and screwed everything up, murmured a voice at the back of her head. One that sounded suspiciously like her mother.

Scarlett had never been confronted like this before, by a complete outsider. A dangerous one at that. Every instinct in her screamed to do what she'd been taught for her entire life: deny, deny, deny. "I don't know what you're talking about," she said, too slow. Her voice sounded wooden. Fake.

Xavier barked out a laugh. "I think we're past that now, Scarlett." He took a step into the house. Toward her.

Scarlett mirrored him, backing up until her calves bumped up against the banister of the staircase. *Where the hell is everyone?* The busy fraternity house picked tonight to be empty? "So . . . what happens now?" she asked, her voice still hollow.

He nodded at the steps. "Let's talk in my room."

She crossed her arms. "I'm not going anywhere with you, witch-hunter."

Xavier groaned and glanced around them, as though afraid someone had overheard. He took another step closer, and she balled her fists. Her self-defense skills might be rusty, but she wasn't about to go down without a fight.

Before she could move, though, Xavier extended his hands again, both of them, palms out, as if he were trying to calm a spooked horse. "I'm not a witch-hunter, Scarlett."

"Bullshit," she spat. "I saw the knife. I know what those symbols are." Her mother had taught her about men like him. Men who despised witches for their magic, who believed they were unholy.

They carried knives like that. The blades were enchanted to repel magic, so they could get past witches' defenses. Murder women like Scarlett, like her family.

But then Xavier said softly, "I'm here to kill the demon."

Scarlett perched on the edge of Xavier's bed, poised to run for the door at any moment. She still didn't trust him. This could all be a trick, to worm his way beneath her defenses before he struck.

She watched him touch the knob to his bedroom and murmur something under his breath. An instant later, the knob glowed a faint blue.

"So who was playing who? I am an idiot . . ." Scarlett said as he turned to her. "None of it was real. You getting close to me, all the crap about your family."

"The two things aren't mutually exclusive. I was playing you, but that doesn't mean I didn't like it—like you," he said softly. His eyes met hers and something inside her rose, but she pushed it down. "Scarlett, there was no other way," he added quickly.

She glanced at the glowing doorknob again, which finally faded.

"I didn't realize witch-hunters dealt in magic," Scarlett commented, her lip curled. Her gaze drifted to the hunter's blade again, still lying on the floor where she'd flung it earlier in her panic to escape.

Quickly, while his back was turned, she reached out with a leg and toed it closer to herself. Within reach, if she needed it.

She didn't trust him.

"I thought y'all viewed using magic as evil. A stain on the natural order." Scarlett gazed at his back until Xavier finally turned around.

He looked exhausted. He had deep rings under his eyes, which were nearly as bloodshot as her own. Unlike her, he didn't take a seat. He leaned against the wall beside his desk, one leg kicked up behind him. "I told you, Scarlett. I'm not who you think I am." His eyes dropped to the knife under her sneaker. He nodded at it. "Keep that for now, if you want. If it makes you feel safer."

She kept her eyes on his, bent down to snatch it up. Dagger in hand, she turned the blade over, so the runes caught the overhead light. "These symbols defuse magic. Make this blade impenetrable to spellcraft. Why would you have it if you aren't hunting witches?"

Despite the fact that she was the one holding it, the dagger still made her skin crawl. She couldn't help it. The instinct ran deep, even if she no longer had her magic. Her mother had taught her early on to avoid this. Fear it.

"It works on *any* magic, Scarlett. Not just witches." He bent forward, his dark eyes even more intense than usual. "We've been tracking the demon you released ever since the Henosis talisman shattered. His name is Typheus, although I doubt he's going by it these days."

"We?" Scarlett shuddered, thinking about more hunters like him. Then she tightened her grip on the blade. "How do you know about the talisman? Or any of this. Those pictures on your camera. You've been following me, and the other Kappas . . ."

Xavier shut his eyes and pressed a thumb to the bridge of his nose for a moment. "I know how it looks. But you aren't the only one with a family dynasty, Scarlett." When he opened his eyes again, he looked . . . older, somehow. More weathered. "My family are guardians. Tasked with preventing the Hadesgate from opening and unleashing hell on earth. By whatever means necessary."

She looked from Xavier to the blade and back. Everything her mother ever told her about witch-hunters ran through her mind. They used knives like this, yes. And tricks to lure witches into lowering their defenses.

But she saw Xavier cast that spell on the doorknob to lock themselves in here. A witch-hunter would die before they used magic themselves.

Which meant, just maybe, he was telling the truth. "Say I do believe you," Scarlett began slowly. "Why were you following my sisters, if you're after this . . . Typheus?"

Xavier frowned. "I'm sure you know that demons take human form on this side of the gate. They're also capable of using magic. So, when I learned what Kappa really was . . ."

She scoffed. "You think he's one of *us*? That's impossible. I've known these girls since long before the Henosis talisman shattered."

Xavier's frown deepened. "Typheus isn't just any demon. He specializes in memory. He can alter your mind, insert himself into past memories. Make you believe he's been here all along."

Scarlett shivered. "Even the strongest Swords witch I know couldn't convince an entire campus full of people they remember a person who never existed."

"Which gives you an inkling of just how dangerous Typheus is. He could be anyone, male or female," Xavier said. "Worse, he wants to open the Hadesgate. It's the source of his power. Right now there's only a trickle. Imagine what he could do with a flood. Not to mention the rest of the demons contained behind it."

"Well, you're the guardian." Scarlett crossed her arms. "I assume you know how to stop him?"

Xavier winced. For the first time since they walked in here, he no longer looked so sure of himself. "Everyone thinks that power comes from what you had. The magic. The bond between sisters. But there is another power, an opposite power. There is a power in lacking . . ."

"What do you mean?"

"There is power in wanting, in hunger, in not having. That is where a demon's power comes from. He feeds on all that want. And a college campus is the perfect place for him. Every disappointment, every girl or guy who feels left out or second best, who feels hurt. He sucked all that in and when he had enough of that, he came for what you and your sisters had—real power. And he took it. If this goes on much longer, I fear he'll be too powerful for anyone to stop."

"So what do we do?" she asked. It pained her to have to ask, to not know, to have to depend on a witch-hunter for survival.

"I . . . have an idea. Theories. Nobody in my family has gone up against a demon in over a century, though, and my great-great-grandfather's journals are a bit outdated for a modern fight." This time, they both frowned. "The one thing working in our favor is that he can't open the gate all on his own. He needs the blood of whoever sealed the gate the last time. Plus a full coven of witches, bound to his will."

Scarlett ran her tongue along the back of her teeth. "Well, lucky us. Because right now, last I checked, there's no longer a coven on campus."

Xavier stared at the ceiling, then his balcony windows. Anywhere but at her. "That's . . . not exactly accurate."

Scarlett bent forward, elbows on her knees. "You know what happened to the Ravens' powers, don't you." It wasn't a question. She shoved off the bed, knife still in hand.

Xavier didn't even flinch. "I believe that Typheus gave your magic to Theta. If I'm correct, he will have offered it as a reward. For agreeing to obey him."

The words hit Scarlett like a punch. She'd suspected, of course, but hearing it confirmed . . . Knowing it was her own tainted magic that cursed Jackson and poor Tim, Maria's boyfriend. Not to mention countless others, if Theta kept going. "He wants them to open the Hadesgate for him."

Xavier nodded. "If my theory is correct, Typheus will be posing as someone high up in the Theta hierarchy. Maybe even at the very top."

Maria. Heat rose to Scarlett's face. But she'd known Maria for years.

Except . . . *Typheus isn't just any demon. He specializes in memory.*

"I can't believe this." She clenched her fists. Thought about Tiffany and the way she'd tried to do the same thing. "But the stolen magic won't be as effective," Scarlett said slowly. "He didn't kill the Ravens; he can't have completely bound our powers to the Thetas. It must only be a temporary spell . . ."

"Yes." Xavier hesitated. "But, with a few former Kappas having joined the Theta ranks now, their powers will be more than enough."

Scarlett flinched. She thought about Reagan and the rest. Their betrayal still hurt. But if they were under this demon's sway, too . . .

Then she scowled at Xavier again. "So all that time you were flirting with me, trying to get close to me—that was just a bid to get at Kappa, wasn't it? That's why the second we lost our strength you ditched me and starting hanging around Theta."

Xavier studied the floor now, his face flushed. "That's not the *whole* story—"

"Oh, so what else should I add? The fact that you knew why I lost my power and you didn't even bother to *warn me?* My whole sorority is in danger!"

"I didn't know if you were under his spell yet or not! Hell, I didn't know if you *were* him." Xavier took a step toward her. He was a head taller, but she had the knife. And yet somehow, she still felt he had the upper hand. They hovered inches apart, both breathing hard. "It was real, Scarlett. Everything I told you about me was true. Everything I said about my family is true."

"Except for the fact that yours has hunted mine for centuries."

"We don't hunt. We keep the balance between the supernatural and the natural. And only when things are unbalanced do we step in. You and your sisters are not the problem here. I am not here for you. You were just . . ."

"Collateral damage?"

Xavier sighed. "This is what my family does. It's what they've always done. And I have always been happy to serve. When I met you, I wondered what it would be like not to be on the edge of life and death all the time. To just be."

"Xavier—" she began, but the words died in her throat. She wondered what that sort of life would feel like, too. Life and death had become the norm recently. But to put a stop to this—to get her magic back—she'd do anything.

"There's more." Xavier glanced at the window. "Before you broke in here, I was staking out Theta. They performed a ritual tonight, a big one. Strong enough even I could sense it."

"To do what?" Dread pooled in her stomach.

"I don't know." Xavier met her gaze. "But the last person I saw going inside before they started . . . was Vivi."

Her breath caught. *No.* Scarlett had ordered her Little to go to Theta. She'd asked her to worm her way into their good graces. She'd knowingly sent Vivi there, without backup, without magic, all alone.

Just like last time, whispered a nasty voice. When Scarlett let Tiffany take Vivi. When Scarlett's ignorance nearly got Vivi killed.

When was the last time Vivi had texted? Scarlett had been trying to reach out, but she hadn't heard back, not since Vivi texted to say she'd gotten home from Theta's party.

Scarlett fished for her phone now, panicky.

Xavier watched her. "Scarlett, I——"

He never finished that sentence. The floor lurched beneath them, throwing Scarlett against the wall and sending Xavier tripping across the bed frame. They heard shouts up and down the street, and when they both ran to the window, lights had come on all up and down Greek Row.

Underfoot, the ground continued to tremble. And far away, Scarlett heard a faint, horrible cracking sound.

Only it wasn't coming from Theta.

She looked at Kappa just as the ravens on the rooftop all burst into flight at once, their caws so high-pitched the hair on her arms rose.

Something was wrong. *My sisters are in danger.*

"We have to go." Scarlett reached over to shove the knife into Xavier's hands. For better or worse, he knew how to use it better than she did. "Now."

CHAPTER THIRTY-FOUR

Vivi

"Follow me, girls," Maria called as she beckoned them toward the stairs that led to the Theta House basement. They were going somewhere. An adventure, Maria had said, and Vivi hadn't bothered to ask questions. She was too busy savoring the power surging through her veins. It was better than a drug, better than being reunited with an old friend. It felt as if a severed limb had miraculously regrown, returning with even greater strength.

She felt drunk with happiness.

And with magic.

She couldn't go more than a few minutes without performing some kind of spell. Now that she had her magic back, she clung to it fiercely. Vivi snapped her fingers, and her fingertips began to glow. She admired them for a moment, then wiggled them in the air until tendrils of light started snaking around her wrists and then up her arms. She shook her arms, and the tendrils grew leaves that curled up away from Vivi's skin, fluttering slightly.

"Oooh," Rose said admiringly as she fell in step next to Vivi. She reached over to touch one of the leaves, but before she could make contact, they'd transformed into moths that took flight in a cloud of flapping wings. Rose giggled and spun around, then shrieked playfully as the moths became larger and more corporeal, growing fangs and hairy pointed ears.

"Come on," Rose said, grabbing her hand, and Vivi let her new friend pull her along, down the steps of Theta House into their basement.

Halfway down the staircase, Vivi paused and released Rose's hand. There was something she was supposed to do, wasn't there? Something she'd come here for. But it was difficult to remember now. Her brain felt fuzzy, incapable of thinking about anything but magic. "What's wrong?" Rose tugged on her arm.

"I . . . I'm forgetting something. Something I was looking for."

"Don't be silly. Everything you need is right here."

She was right. Of course she was. Vivi started to walk again and asked, "Where are we going?"

"It's a surprise," Rose whispered. "Trust us."

"This is the best part," declared Spencer from behind, before she jogged past to catch up to Maria at the head of the procession.

The basement of Theta looked nothing like Kappa's. There was no huge, creepy boiler or cracked floors. No scary gate trembling underfoot. It was furnished, complete with tapestry wall hangings and a stone floor to match those above. Maria's footsteps echoed as she strode along in her high heels. No one seemed to know or care where Maria was leading them. There was no tension, no doubt. Everyone was just happy to be together. It was a nice feeling, being a part of something greater than herself, a small piece of the whole.

I felt that once before, she thought. *But when? With who?*

It was hard to think straight. She felt drunk, except the room didn't spin. It was only the laughing, fun part of being drunk. None of the bad parts.

She caught a flash of Reagan's red hair and glimpsed Etta talking to Maria.

See? she told herself. *Your sisters are here too.* They'd all seen what Vivi saw. That Theta had the right idea after all.

That's right, a voice whispered on the edge of her thoughts. Who was that? Cait, maybe? Or Maria? Vivi couldn't tell. Either way, she didn't care. *This is real sisterhood,* it continued. *There's no fighting, no drama . . .*

Vivi nodded. She liked this. Having other people in her mind, keeping her company. It made her feel less lonely than she'd been at Kappa lately, with all those secrets to keep from her sisters.

My sisters . . .

Rose squeezed her hand. "We're your sisters now," she said, even though Vivi didn't think she'd said that out loud.

Though maybe she'd just forgotten.

She shook the thought off, giving in to the group's festive mood. Up ahead, Maria brushed aside a tapestry, revealing the entrance to what seemed to be a dark, narrow tunnel with dirt walls. Around her, the Thetas giggled and whispered with excitement. "Where do you think it leads?" she heard someone ask. But Vivi felt certain she'd seen this tunnel somewhere before.

Kappa initiation. This was part of the network of tunnels that ran under Savannah, the one she and the other freshmen had used to get from Bonaventure Cemetery all the way back to Kappa House.

"Do you know where we're going?" she whispered to Rose.

"We'll find out when Maria shows us," Rose said with a shrug, then pulled Vivi forward, into the tunnel, plunging them both into darkness.

Vivi blinked and waited for someone to conjure a flame for light, but the Thetas plowed ahead, laughing as they stumbled their way forward, clutching each other for balance. The tunnel itself wound around and around, until Vivi lost all sense of direction. But it didn't matter. She knew what she needed to do. To follow Maria, wherever she led.

She didn't want to ask questions. Didn't need to.

This was what sisterhood should feel like. True camaraderie, all of them united in one purpose. Kappa House had never felt like this. The girls at Kappa were divided; they all had different opinions and argued among themselves.

None of the Thetas questioned anything. They just smiled and went with the flow. Life was so much simpler this way. Let someone else decide. All Vivi needed was access to magic and she'd be happy.

Vivi stretched out her palm and closed her eyes to concentrate. The ground began to tremble slightly, and a moment later, knobby tree roots burst through the tunnel's dirt walls in response to her call. She extended her fingers, and the roots unfurled, stretching toward her like bony hands, reaching, yearning. Almost as if the earth itself was trying to speak to her, trying to remind her of who she was. A Pentacles witch.

But no, that was the old her. Her old powers. Now she was so much more.

Vivi lengthened her step to catch up with Rose, then gasped as she stumbled and nearly fell. When she glanced down, she saw a root tangled around her ankle, clutching her almost like a claw. Rose grabbed Vivi's elbow to steady her, and followed her perplexed gaze down to her ankle. Rose snickered then wriggled a fingertip. The root loosened its grip, allowing Vivi to kick her foot free.

That was strange, some part of her noted, but it felt far away. A million miles from anything and anyone who mattered.

We're the only ones who matter now, whispered a voice in her head. One that felt like both her own and yet not hers at all.

"We're almost there," Maria singsonged from the head of their procession. The girls all around her grinned at one another. Cait, Spencer, Deylin, Rose, the former Ravens, and the other girls Vivi didn't know yet, whose names she hadn't even learned, and yet who she already felt she knew.

She'd shared their blood after all. Their power.

Maria stopped in front of a solid dirt wall. They must've taken a wrong turn, gone down a dead end. But then she raised a hand, and in unison, the girls standing behind her did the same. The wall began to crumble, sending dirt flying in all directions. Vivi brought her arm up to shield her face as the ground started to shake, and for a moment, she worried the tunnel itself might be collapsing. But then she noticed the dirt shifting and reforming into columns, until what used to be a crude dirt tunnel had transformed into a wide open cavern, supported by pillars spaced at even intervals.

It reminded Vivi of excavated ancient ruins, like those

archaeological sites in Rome or Greece. That might have been why it took her so long to register the other details, like the boiler at the far end of the newly reconstructed cavern.

But she recognized the crevasse in the ground. The deep crack glowed from within, lit with hues of amber and firelight. She'd seen that before, but when?

Realization crashed over her like a wave of icy water, sweeping away the fogginess in her head. Suddenly she knew where she was. Why they'd come here.

They were underneath Kappa House. In the same basement she'd descended into with Scarlett a lifetime ago. They'd been investigating the Hadesgate, still unsure if it was myth or fact until the pit opened up and those black tendrils of smoke tried to drag Scarlett inside.

Vivi's heart raced as she remembered what she'd seen next: the muddy ground, the stark burnt tree limbs, and the black void overhead. But then the image disappeared, and with it, the bracing clarity.

She blinked, trying to dispel the haziness that seemed to be settling over her like a heavy blanket, and turned her attention back to the basement. The crevasse seemed wider now, pulsing with firelight. Someone had warned her about this, but she couldn't remember any of the details.

And now it looked so warm. Inviting, almost.

"Welcome, ladies," a smooth, deep voice said.

Another figure stepped out from the shadows. Vivi stared at him, startled. She knew this person's face. At least, she thought she did. Certain features seemed familiar—the dark hair, the sharp jaw, the deep brown eyes, but they were arranged in a manner she didn't recognize. The mouth she'd always seen curled into a friendly smile was now twisted into a mocking sneer. The warm eyes had turned cold, like dying embers in a pile of ash.

It was Tim.

Why was he here? And why did he look so strange? She wanted to ask him, but for some reason, the thought of those eyes fixing on her made her blood run cold. Then she noticed the necklace peeking out from his shirt and a new wave of fear rose within her.

The Henosis talisman.

But that was impossible—she and Scarlett had destroyed it. And even if they hadn't, how the hell would it have ended up around her brother's neck? The bizarre incongruity was enough to jolt her to speak. "Tim? What are you doing here?"

"Vivi." Tim's smile widened. "So glad you could join us tonight. You're the special guest I needed. Isn't that lucky?"

"So lucky," the Thetas responded in unison. Vivi jumped and looked around, trying to catch one of her new sisters' eyes. But they were all staring straight ahead at Tim, their expressions blank.

Something was very, very wrong, but her head was spinning, and she couldn't figure out exactly why the hair on the back of her neck was standing on end. They shouldn't have come here. The pit had attacked Scarlett the last time she and Vivi had come down to the basement. And Tim was standing too close to it now.

"Tim, get away from there," she pleaded. "You're going to get hurt."

As if in response, the pit rumbled, shaking the walls of the basement. But this time, it didn't sound like an earthquake.

It sounded like laughter.

Run, Vivi. The instinct welled up from deep inside her. Somewhere deeper than magic, either Theta's or Kappa's. But she couldn't move. She could barely breathe.

"Oh, I'm not the one you should worry about," Tim said as he stepped toward Vivi. "I've heard much of your power. But no one seems to see your *pain*. Poor, lonely Vivi. She always wanted a big family. She always wanted to be *normal*. It was all too easy to pretend to be your long-lost brother to get you to trust me."

Pretend to be your long-lost brother. The words slammed against her with such force, they almost knocked the air from her lungs. "I . . . I don't understand," she said hoarsely. "Who are you?" She wrenched her head from side to side, desperate for an explanation, but the Thetas were standing still as statues, transfixed by Tim.

"Who am I?" Tim repeated, amused. "There aren't enough words in your pretty little head to understand *what* I am. I am older than time but constantly born anew. I am the anguished cry for help that's met by empty silence. I am the sorrow of a solitary death. I am remorse, I am envy, I am fear. I am the unnamed dread that settles in your bones."

As she stared into his eyes, she saw them shift. The pupils expanded, darkened the irises and the whites. There was something enchanting about those eyes. Something impossible to look away from.

Something that wished her harm.

"I won't let you kill me," Vivi said. This time she wasn't going down without a fight. She reached for her deepest reserves of magic, opening the floodgates. Her fingertips sparked and flames worthy of Reagan's Wands magic shot up to her elbows.

Tim only laughed again. "Kill you? No." He stepped closer until she could feel his breath on her skin. "I want you to join me. If you think the trickle of magic you've been using your entire life is powerful, Vivian, imagine what lies beyond this gate."

Another curl of smoke escaped the cracks in the ground, and when Vivi breathed in again, she smelled it. Sharp, smoky, and *strong*. The power emanating from the ground here was like nothing she'd ever sensed before. Wild, deep magic, the kind that spanned centuries, defied death and time and space.

The air shuddered with it. Vibrated until every hair on her body stood on end. She tasted copper at the back of her tongue, her sisters' blood or maybe just her own. She knew if she extended an arm, she could make anything she wanted happen. Anything at all.

"You sense it, don't you?" Tim whispered. Only he didn't look like Tim anymore. His features were shifting. The antlers sprouted first, straight from his skull, bursting out like tree roots and curling upward, the edges tinted with blood. Thorns jutted from his forehead and matted his hair as his face elongated.

It was monstrous and beautiful all at once. Part of her wanted to flee, and part of her felt like she'd never be ready to look away.

"You understand what we could do. Together." His voice was everywhere. In her head, her chest. It echoed through her body, and beside her, the other Thetas shivered, as though they felt it too.

"Yes," she whispered. Or tried to. Her lips didn't move, but she heard herself anyway.

He smiled. His teeth had gone sharp at the edges, pointed. "Then help me let them out."

Them.

At the word, sounds began to leak out of the Hadesgate behind him. Low and susurrous at first, like a thousand whispers at once. But it grew louder, sharper, until Vivi could hear individual voices in the chaos, cries and screams, some louder than others, all demanding the same thing.

Free us. Free us.

"For too long, my siblings have rotted away in their prison. You understand what that's like, sisters. You all know what it's like to be forgotten, cast aside. Second best, considered nothing at all to the rest of the world."

Murmurs of agreement rippled through the basement. More than a few Thetas cast dark glances at the ceiling of their little underground cavern, up to where Kappa House sat over their heads.

Vivi could understand their resentment. Sympathize, even. Kappa *had* lorded their strength over the rest of Westerly, hadn't they? They'd been so exclusive, so particular about who joined the Ravens. They had hoarded their strength, all for themselves.

Not like Theta, who welcomed Vivi so easily. Theta never demanded she prove herself, leap through hoops just to earn her place.

Scarlett had acted so high and mighty when she'd still had magic at her fingertips. Even Vivi had, in the past—she could admit that, now that she'd torn herself free from Kappa. She'd sacrificed everything to join that house, to fit in, and why? For magic?

She could have magic anytime. Anywhere. It was like her mother had always told her. There was more than one way to be a witch.

Now Vivi was finding out firsthand what other paths she could walk, if she dared.

"Help me release my brothers and sisters tonight," the demon that used to be her brother said, "and you shall be rewarded above all others. *You* will be the best. No more playing second string, no more fighting tooth and nail for everything you want. It will all come as easily to you as the magic I granted you." He snapped his fingers.

Every other girl in the room lifted her hand in unison and imitated him. The snaps echoed throughout the cavern.

Vivi raised her fist too. A spark of warmth flooded from her fingertips down her arm, up and through her entire body.

"I needed each and every one of you to open the Hadesgate." He met each of their eyes in turn. "You are essential. Necessary." He ended on Vivi last, so that it seemed like he spoke only to her when he opened his mouth next. "Will you help me?"

It was not a demand. More a plea. And Vivi could *feel* his desperation. His eagerness to be reunited with his lost brothers and sisters, who were trapped in that terrible realm beyond the Hadesgate. She thought about how she'd felt when she'd discovered she had a brother. Even if that had been a deception, his joy in meeting her had seemed genuine. Same with his request now.

It was so simple, his desire. He wanted brotherhood again. He wanted strength in numbers. He wanted his power augmented by more siblings, and wasn't that the same way Theta worked, the same way Kappa worked? How could Vivi deny him such a simple, pure request?

"*I need you, Vivian,*" he repeated, in that same echoing voice that thrummed through her entire body.

She was the last key in the lock. It felt good to be wanted—to be *needed* for this.

So Vivi smiled at the demon, soft and reassuring. "Tell me what to do," she whispered.

Beneath her feet, the ground gave a hard shake. It sounded, for a moment, like thunderous applause.

CHAPTER THIRTY-FIVE

Scarlett

S carlett could only remember one earthquake in downtown Savannah before, and it had been mild, barely even noticeable unless you'd been in a high office building at the time.

This . . .

This is no earthquake.

She and Xavier sprinted from PiKa along with a spill of brothers, everyone talking over one another, concerned and confused. In the distance, fire truck sirens blared. Scarlett ignored it all.

"They're at the gate," she said. Which meant Typheus had cleared the last hurdle in his quest. He had a coven of witches, and now . . .

Vivi. Vivi is in there.

Scarlett broke into a run, Xavier keeping pace easily. Together, they vaulted up the front porch two steps at a time and threw the front door open so hard it crashed against the wall. Nobody shouted or asked who was there. Her heart rose into her throat. Panic pulsed through every limb. She sped through the hallways, past the portraits of Kappa alumnae of old. They all seemed to glare at Scarlett, reproachful.

You let us down, she could practically hear them whispering. *You led your sisters straight into danger.*

Scarlett reached the basement door and hesitated. A black cloud of smoke poured out from beneath the door and the keyhole. The handle glowed red-hot, and even from a distance she could see the warp of heat haze around it. She wrapped a fist in her shirt to turn it. Even so, the metal stung the palm of her hand, left angry red marks on her fingertips.

She ignored the pain and peered down the basement steps. Clouds of smoke hovered in the air, so thick they obscured whatever waited below.

Xavier tapped her shoulder. "Let me go first." He brushed past her, knife in hand. Scarlett took one last deep breath of clean air, then plunged into the smoke after him.

The moment they entered the cloud, Scarlett felt a surge of emotion rising through her body. Pure, white-hot *fury*.

She was angry. At everything she'd been forced to put up with, everything she'd gone through last semester. At her sisters for fighting each other right now, when they should have been coming together. She was angry at Theta, at Typheus, hell, even at Xavier and Vivi.

She shouldn't have had to deal with this. She should have been able to lead Kappa in a normal semester, the way all her predecessors did. It wasn't *fair*.

Something brushed her hand. Xavier's fingertips. It called her back to herself, reminded her where they were. What she needed to do.

She kept moving, down the stairs, one hand on the railing

beside her. For the first few steps, she couldn't see a thing, and her eyes watered. Her lungs started to burn, starved for air. But then her feet hit dirt, and her vision cleared a little. Through teary eyes, she spotted a bright red glow in the distance and heard voices.

Chanting.

In front of her, Xavier stopped dead and gestured. She froze too, then followed his lead as he ducked behind a nearby shelf.

On the far side of the basement, she spotted the same crack that had tried to swallow her whole the last time she'd been down here. It had widened in the past few days. Gotten deeper, too. She couldn't see the bottom from where she and Xavier stood. But she could hear sounds coming from it—horrible, inhuman howls.

It was the source of the light, too, a red hue that lit all the Thetas ringed around it from below.

In its glow, Maria and her followers no longer looked human. Their teeth seemed longer and sharper, their eyes wild and dark. The whites had vanished, swallowed end to end by pitch-black pupils. She spotted Reagan and Hazel, and her heart clenched like a fist.

And there, on the far side of the circle, her mouth moving along with the rest as they chanted in some ancient, impossible-to-decipher language . . . *Vivi*.

Scarlett couldn't help it. She gasped.

Which made the hooded figure at the center of the circle raise its head and sniff the air in her direction. *Typheus*. It had to be. Between the crown of jagged bone on its head, and what looked like a dagger in its hand, wet with its own blood. Its eyes, like everyone else's, had gone pitch-black. But beneath the hood . . . Scarlett froze.

Beside her, Xavier cursed.

"Tim," Scarlett breathed. His face was horrible now, distorted and inhuman, yet recognizable.

Scarlett remembered Maria and Tim getting together two years ago, remembered whole details of their courtship. Hell, she would have sworn she and Mason had gone on a double date with them, back before Maria turned sour on Kappa.

"I should've known," Xavier murmured. Xavier, who she'd seen hanging out with Tim on the lawns, chatting comfortably. Typheus had been so close to them, all this time. Worming his way into their memories.

Lies. It was all lies.

Or was it? Typheus murmured *inside her head.* Across the basement, his gaze locked on Scarlett's.

Xavier grabbed her wrist and tried to drag her backwards toward some boxes in a corner to hide. But Scarlett was done cringing and hiding.

She rose to her feet.

Somewhere in the back of her mind, she heard Xavier curse again. Felt the swish of air as he crept away from her side. She barely noticed his absence. She had eyes only for the monster in front of her.

"You stole my sisters," Scarlett called out. Her voice made the rest of the Thetas take notice, and their heads whipped around to glare, all in unison, like some sort of multiheaded monster. It unnerved her. But one look at Vivi was enough to remind her why she'd come.

Typheus laughed. It sounded like several different people all cackling together, voices entangled. "Your sisters came to me of their own accord," he said, his voice raspy now. "Didn't you, Vivian?"

He gestured, and Vivi stepped forward, fists balled at her sides. "He's right. I wanted this, Scarlett. I'm a Theta now. We're the powerful ones. And there's nothing you can do to stop us."

"Show her, Vivian," Typheus whispered. "Stop your former sister. Prove yourself to us."

"Vivi, *don't,*" Scarlett cried.

Vivi raised her hand. Scarlett felt the ground beneath her tremble, and she reached out to grip the shelf to steady herself. But it wasn't a shelf anymore. She screamed as her hand brushed something scaly and wet.

Snakes exploded from the shelf and wrapped around her wrist, her ankles. She screamed and jerked backwards.

Across the basement, Vivi laughed. The rest of Theta joined in, their voices pitched high, gleeful. "You thought Kappa was strong, Big Sister?" Vivi called. "You have no *idea* what I'm capable of now." With that, her Little clenched her fist, and Scarlett cried out as the snake around her wrist sank its fangs into her forearm.

She tried to run, but stumbled and fell to her knees. Her ankles were caught, wrapped tight in snakes that were squeezing her calves, tighter and tighter. She started to lose feeling in her toes, her legs tingling as they went numb. Her arm burned, and she could feel the venom from the snake burning its way through her veins. Toward her heart.

Scarlett met her Little's gaze through a haze of red. "Stop, Vivi. This isn't what you want."

"You don't know what I want," this horrible, twisted version of Vivi screeched. "You don't know *me*, Scarlett. I was just another soldier for your little army."

"That's not true, and you know it," Scarlett shouted. She felt another stab of pain as the snake bit down again, and she gritted her teeth against it. "Remember Tiffany? Remember how we fought her? *Together.* We can do that again."

The world was going hazy around the edges. Blurring. The venom. She tried to lift her head, but it was so hard to focus. Her gaze kept zooming in and out, like a bad camera lens. She thought she saw something, though. A shadow, behind the hooded figure of Typheus. She frowned, watching it with confusion.

"Oh, I remember." Vivi took a step forward, and Scarlett dragged her attention back to her Little, away from that shadow. "I remember how powerless I was. How she almost destroyed me. I'll never go back there; I'll never be weak again."

"So prove it," Scarlett spat out, even as her lungs started to burn, her chest heaving with each breath. "Prove how strong you are now. *Stop him.*"

As she said the words, the figure behind Typheus leaped. She spotted a flash of something bright and metallic. *Xavier.* Scarlett realized it at the same instant the demon did. She watched, barely able to keep her head upright, as Xavier sank the demon blade into Typheus's back.

Or tried to.

Typheus moved faster than lightning, faster than Scarlett would have believed possible. One instant he was there, the perfect target, and the next he was gone, vanished—no, not vanished, he was *behind* Xavier.

Xavier swiped the knife through empty air, his head whipping back and forth, searching for the demon. He didn't know, he couldn't tell.

"Xavier," she tried to yell, but her voice choked in her throat. All that came out was a strangled groan.

Xavier looked at her then. Just as Typheus wrapped one hand around either side of the guardian's head, and snapped his neck.

Scarlett screamed.

Xavier's body crumpled to the floor, the knife clattering uselessly, inches from the Hadesgate.

The pit yawned wider. She could see things around the edges now. *Hands* clawing at the dirt of the basement floor. Reaching up and out. The Thetas' chanting started up again, louder this time. Beneath it all, Typheus laughed, gleeful.

"You're too late, little Raven," he whispered, and Scarlett couldn't tell if he was speaking aloud or only inside her head. "Your and your sisters' reign over campus has ended. I have to thank you, though."

She gasped for air. Fought with all her might to raise her head again, to at least glare at him. She wanted to move, to crawl toward the circle, but her limbs felt like they were made of lead. Rooted to the earth beneath her, on all fours.

"You made it very easy for me. You had so many enemies on campus already." Typheus reached out to ruffle Maria's hair fondly, where she stood at his side. When he pulled his hand back, a trickle of blood ran down Maria's cheek, from where his nails, slowly elongating, had scratched her. "I barely had to do anything. The Thetas all but bent over backwards to pledge their lives to me. All I promised them was a taste of Kappa magic. And now I have enough power to unlock the gate, to let my brothers and sisters loose on your pathetic little world."

"Vivi." Scarlett's voice came out a whisper, a breath. She couldn't tell if her Little was listening anymore, or even if she could hear her, from that distance. She struggled through the red haze closing in. "You're . . . stronger than him. Fight . . ."

She couldn't see her sister anymore. Couldn't see the Thetas, or the pit. But she could hear them. Hear the chanting. Hear the demon's laughter. Then the darkness closed in, and she pitched forward into it.

CHAPTER THIRTY-SIX

Vivi

Scarlett sank to her knees, staring in horror and revulsion at the snakes twisting themselves around her arms. She made a halfhearted attempt to shake them off, then shrieked as the snakes hissed and rattled angrily, tightening their hold.

Vivi had never seen her Big so vulnerable, and the thought was enough to make her laugh with pleasure. Her magic was back with a vengeance, and no one would doubt her power ever again.

"You've done enough already," Vivi singsonged in a mocking tone, recalling Scarlett's cold dismissal the night of the Alice in Wonderland party. "Trust me, Scar, you haven't seen anything yet."

"Vivi? Why are you doing this?" Scarlett gasped, her eyes wide with fear and pain.

She deserves it, whispered a voice at the back of Vivi's mind. *After everything she's done to you, everything she put you through.*

But as Vivi watched Scarlett struggle to raise her head, another thought forced its way through.

She fought for you.

Back in the woods, when Tiffany was about to drive a blade through Vivi's heart, Scarlett had arrived just in time to confront her best friend and save Vivi. She'd knowingly risked her life, well aware of Tiffany's twisted new powers, and nearly died for it. And yet here she was, doing the exact same thing again. She'd come down here unarmed, without even the slightest bit of magic to protect her. Why?

For me.

Confusion warred with the anger flooding Vivi's veins. Anger was easier; anger was simple. All you had to do with anger was give in, let it fill your heart and drive your fists.

But underneath the anger, other emotions were swirling. Looking past the hurt meant delving into guilt and fear and all kinds of unpleasant emotions Vivi would much rather ignore.

She wrenched her gaze from Scarlett to find herself staring at the boy her Big had brought with her, Xavier. Or rather, the boy who had once been Xavier. He was very clearly dead, his neck tilted at a horrible angle, his eyes open and completely blank. The knife he'd wielded glittered near his lifeless, outstretched hand, inches from the edge of the pit. One more shake of the earth, and it would tip into the pit, lost forever.

As Vivi watched, the blade seemed to glow faintly. A light blue haze among the shades of red and amber.

Scarlett had stopped struggling at this point. The poison was working its way through her body, and soon she'd be as cold and still as Xavier, two perfect corpses. Prom king and queen of the dead. Her eyes had fluttered closed, and she was mouthing something Vivi couldn't hear. Perhaps she was performing her own last rites or whispering farewell to the family she'd never see again.

But then her voice rang through Vivi's head, a sound far louder than a dying girl could possibly produce.

You're so strong. Stronger than him. Remember who you are.

"Good work, Vivi," the demon purred. "Now finish it."

Vivi's arms buzzed with a surge of crackling magic, but she wasn't summoning her own power — she could feel the demon's magic streaming into her like a river. Her body began to quiver, as if her human bones were too delicate to contain the forces rattling through her. She could do anything with this kind of power. She could tear a towering tree up from the roots. She could reduce a building to dust. She was hurricane. She was death and destruction and renewal. But it was *his* magic. She had to carry out his orders or lose this feeling forever. How could she go back to flesh and blood after tasting the ancient magic of the eternal? She'd be weak, powerless. Just another waiting victim. Anyone could hurt her.

"Finish it. *Kill her.*"

Vivi knelt down and pressed both palms to the earth, preparing to curse Scarlett again.

Then she wrapped a fist around the handle of Xavier's knife.

The moment she touched the handle, her vision cleared.

Remember your sisters. A weight she hadn't even noticed flew off her chest. She gasped and felt like she was taking her first breath of fresh air in days.

When she lifted her head again, the basement looked brighter. Sharper. She could see things clearly now.

Remember the Ravens.

Scarlett was still on her knees, surrounded by the Thetas, who were slowly turning to look at Vivi, their faces twisted in fury as they bellowed the guttural words of the spell the demon had taught them.

This wasn't right. This wasn't the kind of magic Vivi had wanted.

Tim raised his arms to finish his spell. He wasn't looking at her just now. He wasn't looking at any of them. He was gazing down at the ground, at the widening pit at their feet. Claws stretched out of its depths, many-fingered and scorched black. They were attached to long arms, far too long to belong to humans. Too bent at horrible angles, with more joints than any animal Vivi had ever seen.

For a split second, terror rooted her to the spot. The animal part of her brain screamed at her to run, to flee for her life. But then she saw Scarlett collapse to the ground, her twitching limbs finally gone still.

No. The word tore through Vivi like a wild animal released from a cage. She had to do something. She had to stop this.

Slowly, as if through molasses, Vivi lifted her arm, the blade glinting in her palm.

It was hard to move. Invisible forces pulled at her limbs, and voices in the back of her mind screamed at her to stop, to chant along with the Thetas. *We're so close,* they hissed. *We can't stop now.*

Vivi forced herself to think about Scarlett coming down those stairs to find Vivi, to save her, against all odds.

She thought about the rest of Kappa upstairs, oblivious to what was coming. She even thought about the Thetas ringed around her, these girls she barely knew, but whose blood she'd shared and who were caught up in a web of power they didn't understand. Girls who had been turned into soldiers for a monster's army, without their knowledge or consent.

She rose unsteadily and took a slow, painful step forward. Heat flared from the pit, searing her skin and stinging her eyes. She gritted her teeth and tightened her fist around the dagger.

"Hey, Tim," she spat.

The demon turned at the sound of her voice. His face barely looked human anymore, the last shreds of Tim falling away into cat-slit pupils and a too-wide mouth. Still, there was just enough humanity left in him for a look of surprise to register as she summoned every ounce of strength she had and drove the blade into his heart.

That almost comical expression of surprise stayed on his face. His eyes jumped from the knife up to Vivi's and back as he cursed and spat in a language she didn't recognize.

The ground lurched suddenly, throwing her sideways into Rose as the Thetas staggered and fell backwards.

The spitting, hissing demon reached up and fumbled for the handle of the knife in his chest. The moment he touched the hilt, his hands began to sear, filling the basement with the stench of singed hair and burnt skin.

The demon's mouth opened, and he let out an earsplitting, high-pitched scream. Vivi backed away in horror as his hands *melted*.

His arms followed, dripping to the ground in thick globs like candle wax. He opened his mouth to scream again, but it came out a horrible gurgling sound instead, just before his face collapsed in on itself.

He sank inward, an inch at a time, until all that remained was a steaming puddle on the floor, the black cloak smoking above it.

Someone cried out in anguish. Maria. Vivi whipped her head around just in time to see the Theta president sprint forward toward the puddle. "No!" Vivi caught Maria's arm before she could touch what remained of her boyfriend.

Maria screeched, her nails raking across Vivi's face. But around her, Vivi could see the other Thetas were starting to emerge from the spell, blinking and shaking their heads before gasping in shock and terror at the scene around them.

"What did you *do?*" Maria screamed. Her sorority sisters were beside her now, pulling her backwards.

Rose wrapped her arms around Maria and whispered, "It's okay . . . You're okay."

Once free of Maria, Vivi spun around to face the Hadesgate. If anything, it was *wider* than before. But she couldn't worry about that now. Not until she'd tended to Scarlett. Vivi sprinted over to where Scarlett lay on the ground. Reagan had cradled her head in her lap while Etta and Bailey muttered spells over her, tears streaming down both of their cheeks.

Vivi felt for a pulse and found one, although it seemed sluggish, and fading. Scarlett's chest still rose and fell, but her breath rattled with every intake. Cursing, Vivi looked back at the Thetas, who were stumbling away from the edge of the Hadesgate. As she watched, Xavier's limp body fell over the edge and vanished into the depths.

"We need everyone!" Vivi shouted. "All of the Ravens. Now!"

With a nod, Reagan gently lowered Scarlett's head to the ground and sprinted for the stairs with Etta, shoving past the frightened Thetas trying to find their way.

Vivi reached for her magic. But she couldn't access the power that had flooded through her just minutes earlier—it'd vanished with the demon. Nor did she have the easy flick-and-wave magic of Theta anymore.

She shut her eyes and reached deeper. She could sense the earth, the hard ground under her knees, the roots and worms and life stretching out from where she knelt.

That was when she heard her magic calling to her.

She heard the wind rustling the leaves in the woods behind Kappa House.

She felt the cold stones by the creek, rubbed smooth by the eternally flowing water.

She smelled the damp dirt after a heavy rain.

She watched plants unfurl from the ground. They were a part of her, and she was a part of them. Despite it all, Vivi was still a Pentacles witch.

She held both hands over Scarlett's chest, just over her heart. She hadn't cast a spell like this in so long, and her tarot cards were upstairs somewhere, lost in the melee of Kappa House.

It doesn't matter. The magic is inside you.

She closed her eyes again. "I call to the Queen of Earth," Vivi said, her voice steady and strong. "Show us your power over death and rebirth." She heard a creaking sound nearby but she didn't dare open her eyes to check. "I call to the Queen of Earth," she repeated, louder. "Show us your power over death and rebirth."

She felt her body drawing magic up from the ground, directing it toward Scarlett. Somewhere in the back of her mind, she could see the trees behind Kappa House begin to sway. The plants in the garden burst into a frenzy of color, then dried and withered, sacrificing themselves to the Pentacles witch who needed their power. But no matter how hard she pushed, it wasn't enough. The poison had already done its work.

"No, Scarlett, please, no," Vivi said as tears filled her eyes. *"Please."* Why couldn't she do this? Why wasn't she ever enough?

Then she felt something, like a whisper brushing past her cheek. Before she could even turn to look, she smelled it—the scent of other magic.

Kappa had come after all.

Vivi opened her eyes to see Etta, Hazel, and Bailey standing over Scarlett as Reagan tore down the stairs with the others in tow.

Mei looped her hand through Vivi's as Ariana caught Vivi's left hand. The rest of her sisters knelt, one by one, until they formed a ring around Scarlett. The Hadesgate rumbled ominously behind them, yet no one turned, no one so much as batted an eye. They braved danger for their sister.

The same way they always would.

Vivi tightened her grip on both Mei's and Ariana's hands. "I call to the Queen of Earth," she chanted, and this time her sisters joined her, their voices rising up to the ceiling, echoing back against the throb of the pit. "Show us your power over death and rebirth."

Scarlett's chest went still, and there was a long moment of silence.

Vivi held her breath, too, and felt her sisters doing the same around her, all eyes wide, fixed on their sister. Their leader.

Come on, Scarlett, Vivi silently begged. *Wake up.*

CHAPTER THIRTY-SEVEN

Scarlett

S carlett wore a white dress that reached all the way down to her ankles. She stood at the edge of a vast body of water. It licked her ankles, bringing with it the scent of salt water, so heavy she could taste it. The sky overhead hung somewhere between night and day.

Twilight, which cast the ocean waves before her in a milky white hue.

There was a boat out in the water. It had a dark wooden hull and a name she couldn't read scrawled on its side. She took a step toward it, and the water swelled up to her calves, tickling the backs of her knees.

"Scarlett."

That voice. Her chest tightened. She hadn't heard it aloud in months, and yet she would still know it anywhere. "Minnie." She whirled, and the dress flared out around her, floating on the gentle waves like sea foam.

The woman who had all but singlehandedly raised Scarlett stood barefoot on the sandy beach, wearing a dress Scarlett recognized. It was the one Minnie always wore to church on Easter, her special-occasion outfit. Scarlett's mother had offered to buy her a replacement, but Minnie always refused.

This one still works just fine, she always said, a hint of reproach in her voice that Scarlett had secretly thrilled at. She loved it whenever Minnie stood up to her mother. Whenever she pointed out that money and power and style weren't *everything,* whatever Marjorie Winter might claim.

But the Minnie waiting on the sand looked years younger than when Scarlett had last seen her. No sign of the illness that had ravaged her body in later years showed on her unlined face or in her broad smile. That was when Scarlett realized.

"I'm dead, aren't I?" she asked.

Minnie's smile softened. The look she gave Scarlett was one she'd seen a million times growing up. It was a look that said, *You know this answer already.*

"That depends on you," Minnie murmured. "You can choose what path you set your will to now."

Scarlett's heart wrenched. She wanted to be with Minnie. Wanted to embrace her again. But . . . *I have so much life to live.* She had work to do. A legacy to uphold. And . . .

In the distance, she heard voices calling her name. Familiar voices. Vivi, Mei, Etta . . .

My sisters are waiting, she said. Or maybe she only thought it. She couldn't tell. She opened her mouth wider to try again, and—

Scarlett gasped.

It burned like hell. Her chest, her lungs, her whole *body* felt like it was on fire. Her eyes flew open. Minnie, the beach, the sand, the ocean, they were all gone. Instead, she was lying flat on her back on hard ground, a dozen faces peering down at her with varying levels of fear.

She latched on to the first person she saw. "Vivi." Her voice came out a croak.

Her Little let out a strangled sound, somewhere between a laugh and a sob. Then her arms wrapped around Scarlett's shoulders, enveloping her in a tight hug.

Scarlett groaned. "Ow."

"Oh, God, I thought we lost you." Vivi gasped against her neck.

Scarlett's memory returned in fits and starts. Xavier's body crumpling lifeless to the floor. The demon Typheus raising a hand toward Scarlett, and at his side, Vivi imitating him, her eyes pitch-black. The snake's venomous fangs, sinking into Scarlett's wrist.

"This is really sweet and all," murmured Jess from somewhere nearby. "But we still have a pretty big problem over here."

With Vivi's help, Scarlett pulled herself up to her knees, then staggered to her feet. "The demon . . ." Too slow, she remembered whose face it had worn. "Tim?" she amended.

Vivi shook her head, looking relieved. "Dead. And our magic is back," she added with a glance at their sisters. "But . . ." She gestured.

That was when Scarlett turned to see the Hadesgate. It still pulsed a deep, angry red. It had widened to swallow nearly half the basement so far. The boiler had ripped from the wall and tipped into it, and gallons upon gallons of sulfurous, stinking water poured from it.

The far wall behind the boiler had begun to crack and splinter too. Overhead, Kappa House groaned as its supports shook.

Scarlett swallowed hard. "Ravens." Scarlett's voice went hard. Her sisters straightened, standing shoulder to shoulder with her, all facing the pit. "If you still trust me—"

"Just tell us what to do, dammit," Reagan barked. Etta snorted, and Mei nudged her.

"We all screwed up, okay?" Etta met Scarlett's gaze. "You didn't do any worse than the rest of us."

"I'm your president," Scarlett muttered. "I should have done better."

"So do it now," Vivi said softly, and reached over to squeeze Scarlett's hand.

She squared her shoulders. Time to save the house. To save Savannah—maybe save everyone. *You can do this.* Minnie's words echoed in the back of her mind. *You can choose what path you set your will to.*

This was just another spell. That was all.

She grasped her sisters' hands. A sharp cawing sound broke her attention for an instant, and she glanced upward to see the ravens from the roost circling overhead, flitting between the basement rafters, as if drawn by the power down here. Or by their sisters' need.

She smiled. Then she focused on the Hadesgate once more.

"I call to all the Queens, to the mighty four," she intoned, and her sisters echoed it. "Seal this gate forevermore."

The Ravens' magic crackled around their heads, sparked at their fingertips. When Scarlett inhaled, she felt it sting her lungs, painful and yet reassuringly familiar at the same time. *Her magic was back.* She was a witch again, *herself* again.

And yet . . . she was more than that, now. Because she'd learned that even without magic, Scarlett Winter was still a fighter. She'd still charge headlong into the fray for a sister, without a chance in hell at winning.

She smiled. Without magic, she was a warrior. *With* it? The Hadesgate didn't stand a chance.

"I call to all the Queens, to the mighty four. Seal this gate forevermore." She shouted the words, her sisters echoing them.

The ground under their feet groaned and roiled. The walls buckled. Electricity crackled overhead, shooting along the pipes and power lines of the house. Something burst in the corner, and the water from the boiler began to jolt with electricity, firing sparks as it poured into the depths.

As it fell, it hissed and steamed.

Then pieces of earth began to break off from under them and join the waterfall.

Somewhere above, glass shattered. She heard wind howling down the steps toward them, rushing toward the Hadesgate as well.

"I call to all the Queens, to the mighty four. Seal this gate forevermore."

The water seemed to rush faster. Harder. *My Cups magic,* she realized, just as the gust of wind picked up, whipping their hair into their eyes. The earth pitched at the Pentacles' command, too. Every element joined in.

Fire arrived last. A lick of flame from the pit rose and twisted around on itself, like a snake swallowing its own tail. It bent backwards, arced along the length of the crevasse.

"I call to all the Queens, to the mighty four," the Ravens bellowed. "Seal this gate forevermore."

With one final groan and shudder, the water, earth, air, and fire all converged at the heart of the Hadesgate. The two halves of the basement floor rose an inch and then crashed together.

The house continued to shake overhead, and water kept pouring from the busted boiler. Only now it ran over a smooth, unbroken floor. No crack in sight. Just a puddle forming rapidly under their feet.

Scarlett didn't realize she was gasping for breath until Vivi's hand came to rest on her shoulder and her Little's voice whispered close to her ear. "It's okay. It's done."

The Hadesgate was closed once more.

CHAPTER THIRTY-EIGHT

Vivi

The first thing the Ravens did with their newly restored powers was to repair the house, fixing the shattered windows, the electrical damage, and the basement floor. It was slow going, though. Even the most experienced witches struggled to properly calibrate their magic, which felt wild and unruly, like riding a skittish mustang instead of a powerful, obedient show horse.

"Well, that didn't quite go according to plan," Hazel said with a laugh as she stepped back to survey the wall she'd just cleaned. The spell had worked, but in addition to scouring the smoke and debris, it had pulverized the framed pictures and stripped the paint, leaving bare plaster behind. She shook her hands, as if her fingers were still hot from the effort.

"You're still doing better than I am," Ariana called from across the living room where she was struggling to repair a pane of broken glass. The cracks were gone, but for some reason, the glass had turned deep purple.

"It's pretty. Just leave it," Mei said from the top of the ladder, where she was carefully replacing a busted light fixture. At first, she'd tried to levitate, but instead of hovering in the air, she had kept shooting painfully into the ceiling. Her hair was still on point, though. She'd gone for long auburn waves today, and the old sparkle had returned to her eyes from a combination of good spirits and some deftly applied glamours.

For a while, Vivi was all too happy to throw herself into the work, but she couldn't ignore the pit of unease in her stomach. She still hadn't spoken to Scarlett, and the tension between them seemed to grow by the minute. Vivi called to Bailey to spot Mei's ladder, then headed up to Scarlett's office, where she found her Big using a spell to sweep up shards of glass. She looked tired and a little sweaty, but otherwise unharmed from the previous night's events. Yet the sight wasn't enough to push aside the lingering horror in Vivi's mind as she thought about the horrible spell she'd cast. The way she'd followed the demon's orders and nearly gotten Scarlett killed.

"Hey," Vivi said, hovering in the doorway. "Do you have a sec?"

Scarlett paused in the middle of sweeping and brushed her hair back from her forehead, slicked with sweat. "Of course." She gestured for Vivi to take a seat in the green velvet armchair.

Vivi nodded, but before she even made it to the chair, she spun around to face Scarlett and blurted, "I'm so, so sorry. I can't believe I almost—"

"Vivi—" Scarlett leaned against the edge of her desk and rubbed her head.

"I should never have abandoned Kappa. I should have talked to you before I went and *joined* Theta to get my magic back, I—"

Scarlett held up a hand, cutting her off. "And *I* should never have asked you to go there in the first place. Not alone like that, with no magic."

Vivi shook her head. "That doesn't excuse that . . . that spell I tried to perform," she said vaguely, unable to say the words aloud. *The spell that was meant to kill you.*

"You were under Typheus's influence. You saw what he made those Thetas do."

"I was just so scared of not having any power. Of being defenseless, like last time . . ."

Scarlett paused for a moment, then sighed and crossed the room to place a hand on Vivi's shoulder. "We both made mistakes. I was so focused on being the most impressive president Kappa had ever seen, I didn't realize when y'all needed my help."

Vivi thought about the past Kappas, including the ones responsible for sealing Typheus in the Henosis talisman. "I don't know," Vivi said, cracking a faint smile. "In the end, we did banish a demon instead of foisting him on future generations."

"But I lost us Spring Fling, nearly exposed witchcraft to all of Westerly, lost us our magic entirely, and oh yeah, then almost allowed a portal to hell to be opened in our basement. Great track record."

"Key word there being *almost.*" Vivi stood up and faced Scarlett. "Scar. The best leaders don't look showy on paper. The best leaders are the ones who show up for their people when they're needed. Leaders make sacrifices for their people. And whatever mistakes you've made, you showed up for me. You ran into *actual hell,* with no magic, to save me. That's a leader."

Scarlett finally smiled back. "I guess if you want to put it like that . . ."

"I do. And . . ." Vivi drew a slow breath. "I really am sorry. For hurting you."

"I know." Scarlett paused, momentarily lost in her own thoughts. "You made the right decision in the end, though. That's more than some people have done."

When the silence got too heavy, Vivi extended a hand, pinkie out. "Let's make a promise. From here on out, we ask for help when we need it. No more shame, no more trying to do everything on our own to prove ourselves." Vivi grimaced. "We're sisters."

The corner of Scarlett's mouth twitched. Then she raised her hand and hooked a pinkie around Vivi's in return. "Sisters," she agreed. "But I disagree with you on one point. The *best* leaders work as a team." She raised an eyebrow. "So what do you say? You still with me, social chair?"

Vivi grinned back. "Always."

∽

Scarlett left to help Jess with a tricky busted pipe, and Vivi drifted out into the garden to try calling her mother. The withered plants were already starting to blossom again, and Vivi inhaled deeply, relishing the clean, herbal scent of the Ravens' magic. When she felt sufficiently centered, she pressed the dial button on her cell phone. Despite the hour, Daphne actually picked up. "Hello?" she said groggily. "Is everything okay, sweetheart?"

At the sound of her mother's voice, tears prickled Vivi's eyes, though she wasn't even entirely sure why. A combination of pride, relief, and exhaustion maybe. "Is everything *okay?*" Vivi repeated with a weak laugh. "I don't even know where to begin . . ."

She did her best to give an overview of everything that had happened. Although it'd only been a few hours since they'd defeated Typheus, it seemed like a lifetime ago, as if she were describing events from a terrible but fading dream.

"Oh my goodness . . ." Daphne said hoarsely. "I'm so sorry, honey. What an awful thing for you girls to face on your own, especially so soon after everything with Tiffany." Her voice cracked and Vivi could imagine the pain on her face. "I can't believe I let you down again."

"It's okay," Vivi said. And she meant it. "We ended up handling it."

"Of course you did. You're an incredible witch. I'm so proud of you."

"Thank you." She felt a little surge of pride, but it wasn't enough to overpower the question still tugging at her. "But why me? Why did Typheus need *my* blood to open the gate?"

Daphne hesitated, and for a moment, Vivi worried she was going to deflect as usual. "We come from a long line of witches, honey. If I had to guess, I'd say that whoever opened that gate the first time was an ancestor of ours. Someone whose blood you still carry."

Vivi thought back to the portrait at Lone Willow Farm. "There was a woman—sort of," Vivi said. "Her portrait warned me and Scarlett about the demon and the Hadesgate."

"That's old, powerful magic," Daphne said with reverence. "The Ravens are bonded through magic. And family is bonded through blood—even after death. Any ancestor who was also a Kappa has a special ability to communicate from beyond the grave. She returned to warn you, Vivi, and I'm glad you listened."

"Me too." Vivi paused, mustering the courage to bring up the real reason she'd been so keen to speak to Daphne. "There's something else I've been thinking about. Tim and I spent a lot of time talking about our dad, and I really need to know: what actually happened with you two?" The mix of secrets and demon magic made it impossible to distinguish between truth and fiction. If Tim was a lie, was everything else he told her a lie too?

Daphne let out a long breath on the other end of the phone. "Well, honey pie, you have a right to know, of course. But there's not much to tell. Vince and I were at Westerly together. He was a big football star, and I had a bit of a crush on him. When I left school and started traveling, I passed through Vancouver. It turned out he had just moved there himself, so we met up at a hotel bar and . . . Well, that's how you happened."

Vivi had expected as much. "So he's in Canada?"

"I'm not quite sure. He and I haven't been in touch much over the years. I blamed him and convinced myself that he didn't want anything to do with us. That's why I never wanted to tell you anything about him—I didn't want you to end up getting hurt. But I see now that not telling you caused even more harm and heartache, and I'm so very sorry for that."

Vivi was quiet for a long moment as she grappled with the question forming a painful knot in her chest. "Does he even know about me?" she asked finally.

"Yes. The last time we spoke, I told him everything. He said he'd love to meet his only daughter if you ever wanted to."

Vivi let the words wash over her. *His only daughter.* "Would it upset you if I wanted to?"

"No, Vivi. You should follow your own path," Daphne said. "Besides, I did a tarot reading yesterday, and I drew the Page of Cups. Maybe it's a sign. Reaching out to your father could be the start of a rewarding journey."

Vivi smiled and shook her head.

"Maybe it is . . ."

CHAPTER THIRTY-NINE

Scarlett

"There we have it." Marjorie Winter finished writing with a flourish and passed the book to Scarlett. "Everything I remember."

Scarlett glanced down at the page and watched her mother's handwriting shift and morph with the spell, until it was indistinguishable from anyone else's penmanship in the leather-bound volume. After she had filled her mother in on everything that had transpired at the Hadesgate, Marjorie had apologized, saying that she felt like she'd been in a daze these past weeks. Perhaps Typheus had been tampering with them all. She'd spoken to the Monarchs about contributing to Scarlett's book, *History of the Ravens,* immediately to ensure the coven's future safety.

"Does this mean you're finally willing to admit I was right?"

"I'll admit it is a good idea to have an impartial record of our experiences here at Kappa. Something no outside force can tamper with." Marjorie held her daughter's gaze. "For what it's worth, you're stronger than I ever was, Scarlett."

She froze in her seat, stunned. "Mama . . ."

"I don't mean magically," Marjorie amended, and Scarlett couldn't help it. She laughed. *Of course.* Her mother grinned. "Well.

Perhaps. But no, I'm talking about your mental fortitude. Your loyalty to your sisters, your ability to do what must be done, regardless of appearances or the toll it takes on you. That's real strength, Scarlett. More powerful than any spell."

Scarlett smiled, even as her chest tightened.

That wasn't *exactly* true. She still had one task she'd been avoiding. One duty to perform for her sisters that she desperately wished she could avoid.

After Marjorie left, Scarlett lingered in the common room for a minute. Mei, her hair freshly glamoured into an enormous pouf of bright red curls, was giving Reagan tips on contour glamours. "There's a fine line between believably beautiful and a creepy uncanny valley anime girl look," Mei was saying.

Nearby, Etta puttered around the houseplants. They'd perked back up once the Ravens' power had been restored, but Etta didn't seem to want to take any chances and was showering them all with extra attention.

Jess had spread a pile of newspaper clippings around the carpet to sort. Sonali perched nearby, asking questions about different reporting styles.

Just the sight of her sisters going about their regular lives buoyed Scarlett's spirits more than any spell. She'd missed this. The easy, buzzing chatter of Kappa House on a normal day.

Someone yelped, and Scarlett jumped, only to spot Ariana hurriedly dousing a candle spell with Etta's watering can.

Well. Relatively normal, anyway.

They're who I'm doing this for, Scarlett reminded herself, with a glance at the clock over the door. And if she wanted to do this right, she needed to get a move on.

She hurried across campus and reached the library a few seconds after the last Friday afternoon bell tolled. Sure enough, as predicted, Jackson's telltale curls appeared through the window a moment later. She lingered on the sidewalk as he jogged down the front steps, and intercepted him at the base.

"Jackson."

His expression, when he met her eyes, went through a rush of emotions. Surprise, anger, and then a brief glimpse of something else, something she couldn't quite read, before he settled back into a dark scowl, one that looked so off on his normally cheerful face. "Winter."

Great. They were back to last names.

But it was better than him blanking her completely in favor of a girl he'd been cursed into falling in love with. When he started up the path toward the dining hall, Scarlett fell into step next to him. "How are you doing?"

He glanced over and held her gaze longer this time. "I'm not really sure how to answer that. Or why you're asking me, in fact."

She winced. She supposed she deserved that. "I heard about your breakup with Cait."

"You know"—he stopped dead now, and whirled to face her—"I'm not actually sure what's worse in the long run. Having a love spell put on you and losing control of your ability to decide anything for yourself . . . or being lied to by the one person who must have known what was happening all along."

Scarlett froze midstep. "Jackson . . ."

He waited for her to finish that statement. When she didn't, he folded his arms, jaw set. "Yeah. Obviously, Cait's spell broke. I assume I have you to thank for that?"

She swallowed hard. *He knows it was a spell.* Which means . . .

She struggled to formulate the right response. "I'm sorry. I should have broken it sooner. I wanted to, but it was more difficult than I expected, and . . ." She stopped herself. "What all do you remember, Jackson?"

"Enough." He scanned her up and down. After a moment, something softened. A wall he'd put up, melting. "Scarlett . . . I don't know what to think. Last semester, I felt . . ." He squeezed his eyes shut. Cursed. "I had feelings for you. I still do. But what you did to me, taking my memories like that—"

"I had to, Jackson. If you remember everything from last semester, then you remember the rules, too." She glanced around the sidewalk. But nobody else was near enough to overhear. Still, she stepped closer to Jackson anyway, just in case. "Magic has to stay a secret. For the Ravens' safety as well as everyone else's."

Jackson's jaw worked hard. He glanced up at the sky, like he couldn't bear to meet her gaze. "You think I don't realize that? After Cait . . ." His voice cracked.

"I'm so sorry." Scarlett frowned. "I can't imagine what that was like."

"Not being in control of your own body, your own mind?" He shook his head. "No. You can't." He swallowed hard. She waited for him to continue. Overhead, fluffy white clouds wheeled through an otherwise cheerful blue sky. A beautiful Savannah day. So at odds with the way she was feeling right now. Like a storm cloud sat in her chest, waiting to burst. "I told you last semester, I think it's dangerous that some people have this much control over others. I still think so," he said, finally. "Even you, Scar."

"I get that. Believe me, I do." She twisted her hands together, to stop her sudden urge to reach out to him. When she spoke, her voice sounded small. Conflicted. "I don't know what to do, Jackson."

He finally looked at her. His expression hardened. "What? Aren't you here to just wipe my brain again? Steal my memories and make me forget any of this ever happened?"

Her eyes stung. "I don't *want* to."

"But you'll do it anyway."

"I have a duty. To my sisters, to Kappa." If she'd learned one thing this year, it was that she couldn't allow herself to lose sight of that. "Believe me, if there was any way I could let you keep those memories, I would. This semester . . . it was killing me that you couldn't remember. That you had no idea what we'd been through together."

He took a step closer, and her breath snagged in her chest. "So let me remember, Scar."

"Would you promise not to ever reveal it to anyone else? Would you keep it to yourself, no matter what you saw, no matter what happened on campus—"

"You know I couldn't do that," he interrupted, his voice going softer. "Not if something like this happened again. Not if other people were in danger." As he spoke, his face tilted toward hers.

She felt herself doing the same. As she bent up toward him, their eyes locked. This was the Jackson she'd missed. The Jackson she'd fallen for. Relentless. The one who would never take no for an answer. Who had his beliefs and stuck to them. She respected it, respected *him*.

It was exactly why she couldn't place her sisters' lives in his hands.

She thought about Xavier. The enormous sacrifice he'd made in order to save them all. If he could do that, Scarlett could handle this. She could handle giving up the one person who had ever fully seen her. Understood her.

"I'm sorry, Jackson," she whispered.

He shut his eyes. For a terrifying, perfect second, she thought he might kiss her anyway. Let them both pretend, for one more moment, that everything would be fine. That they could be together. Work through this.

"It's not just the magic. I don't want to forget you, either," he murmured, the words like a fist around her heart.

"I wish there was another way." They were so close. Their mouths barely an inch apart.

Then Jackson's eyes snapped open, and he took a step back, jerky and unsettled. "Can you give me a day at least?" He ran a hand through his hair. Looked back at the sky. Pulling away from her all over again. "One more day to remember. Just . . ." His throat bobbed, the sun pooling along the perfect brown expanse of it. "I want a night to really sit with what happened to Harper. Tomorrow you can do whatever you want. Not that I have any real say in it, but . . ."

She took a slow, jagged breath. She hadn't thought of that. Of how it must feel for him to have discovered the truth of what happened to his adopted sister, only to lose it again. "One night," Scarlett said softly. "I can do that."

"Thanks, I guess." The hardness returned to his tone. "See you tomorrow, then."

He was gone before she found the words to ask him to stay.

CHAPTER FORTY

Vivi

"D o we really want to dress like we're scheduled for a court appearance?" Mei asked, eyeing the blazers, pumps, and shift dresses Scarlett had insisted the Kappa executive board wear to that day's meeting of the Panhellenic council. "We're not on trial."

"We need to prove that there's no reason for us to be on notice," Scarlett said. She adjusted her triple strand of pearls so they lay flat against her black wool dress.

"You mean, apart from opening the gates to hell and almost burning down the entire campus," Reagan called from the couch where she was glamouring her nails a vinyl black. She'd been uncharacteristically meek and quiet for the past few days, and while Vivi would never have said it aloud, she was glad to see that some of Reagan's old sass had returned.

Juliet walked over to straighten the collar on Jess's blazer. "We should think of it more as a public service," she said cheerfully. "Though I'd probably avoid bringing it up. So far, everyone seems to be buying the earthquake story, right?"

"Yes, so far," Scarlett said. "Dean Sanderson has it out for us, but even he struggles to blame us for an act of God."

"An act of a demon, you mean," Reagan said.

Some of the girls laughed, but Vivi barely managed a weak smile. It was foolish to mourn a brother who'd never really existed, but she couldn't help but feel a pang of grief amid the shame and anger that came from falling prey to Typheus. When she'd met Tim, she had feared that the idea of a long-lost half brother was too good to be true, and of course, her fears had proved correct, albeit in a far darker, more twisted way than she'd ever expected. Still, she mourned what could have been in another life. But while her grief was real, it wasn't accompanied by a sense of loneliness. After all, Vivi might've grown up an only child, but now she had a whole house full of sisters, bound by a force thicker than blood. Magic.

An hour later, Scarlett led the girls into the large lecture hall, their high heels tapping in unison on the marble floor. Vivi suppressed a smile at the flurry of whispers and admiring stares they left in their wake. The Kappas always created a minor commotion whenever they arrived on campus en masse, and it seemed as if being put on notice hadn't been enough to damage their mystique.

Out of the corner of her eye, Vivi saw Maria leading the Thetas down the aisle on the other side of the hall, clearly heading for empty seats in the front row, where the Kappas traditionally held court. In her haste, Maria had broken into an undignified half-running shuffle, which made her look even more ridiculous when compared to the elegant, poised Scarlett gliding down the aisle with her head held high.

Maria and Scarlett reached the lecture stage, turned into the front row, then stopped to face each other. It was the first time they'd met since their showdown in the basement, and Vivi was struck by how much each girl had changed. Maria looked pale and diminished, her lank hair pulled into a tight ponytail that only made her face look more drawn, as if she'd been drained of more than just stolen magic. She and Scarlett stared wordlessly, Maria shifting from side to side and shooting furtive glances at the other Thetas, Scarlett looking straight ahead, her expression serene, as if she had all the time in the world. In usual circumstances, it took a lot for anyone to challenge Scarlett Winter—even the non-magical could sense that she was someone not to be crossed, which was probably why Maria had the air of a gazelle staring down a lion. Finally, she spun around and slunk a few rows back, hissing for the other Thetas to follow her.

Vivi felt a pang of sympathy as she watched the other girls exchange nervous looks. The Thetas hadn't understood what they were getting into when Typheus seduced them. If even Vivi, a trained witch who had seen wicked magic before, had fallen for Typheus's influence, how much worse must it have been for a group of girls with no knowledge of the magical world?

Of course, Theta didn't remember the specifics of everything that had happened. Their memories had been reworked. But some things, like the terror they'd all felt upon awakening next to the Hadesgate after Typheus fell, couldn't be completely erased. Vivi had heard through the grapevine that more than a few Thetas had taken leaves of absence this semester.

Dean Sanderson strode across the stage and took a seat next to the lectern. He seemed to have aged in the month since the last council meeting. Vivi got the sense it had been a difficult month for him, too. Between the unexpected earthquakes on campus— which had damaged some important artifacts in Hewitt Library, not to mention several of the Greek Row houses—and all the council meetings they'd been holding to determine how to handle campus infractions that had cropped up, since Kappa and Theta hadn't been the only people on campus affected by Typheus's negative energy . . . the dean looked like a man at his wit's end. He called the Panhellenic council to session with a hoarse voice, and took a few enormous gulps of coffee from a thermos before he greeted the room and asked the sorority and fraternity presidents to take their seats on stage.

"Good luck," Vivi whispered to Scarlett as she rose to her feet and ascended the three steps that led to the stage. It was clear that she didn't need magic to walk in heels—she moved like someone who'd taken her first baby steps in stilettos. She sat, crossed her legs at the ankles, and listened with a polite but slightly bored expression as Dean Sanderson read the opening minutes, then moved on to a discussion about fundraising, followed by the earthquake repair plans.

"Finally, we return to the notice against Kappa Rho Nu," the dean said as he cleared his throat and looked down at his notes.

"I know we agreed not to use magic to influence anyone," Mei murmured. "But I gotta admit, it's tempting as hell right now."

"Believe me, I know," Vivi said, shifting in her seat.

Mei reached over to grip her hand tight.

"The council has found no further charges to bring against the sorority after the review period of one month. In light of this, Kappa may continue to operate as per usual, in all their previously agreed-upon capacities."

Vivi glanced at Mei. *Does that mean . . .*

Onstage, Maria's hand shot up.

The dean shot her a disparaging look. "Please wait until I finish reading my entire statement, Ms. Grimaldi."

Maria dropped her hand into her lap, practically vibrating with tension.

"Given the fact that, as Ms. Winter had previously stated, no such infractions have ever been brought against Kappa Rho Nu in the past, and given their exemplary behavior over the past month, we have decided, after a vote of the council, to return the hosting privileges for Spring Fling to Kappa."

Jess let out a *whoop,* and a few other people in the audience spontaneously applauded, a testament to the Kappas' party-planning prowess. Mei gripped Vivi's shoulder, shaking her with excitement. At the front of the room, the corners of Scarlett's mouth tightened, as if she were fighting to suppress a huge smile.

Maria, on the other hand, slumped in her seat. When Vivi scanned the crowd again, Rose had done the same, her head resting on Spencer's shoulder, the very picture of defeat.

It should have felt good, to get this event back. To have Kappa back on track for being their old selves again: the undisputed queens of campus. Yet Vivi couldn't help but think about how easy it had been for Typheus to exploit the Thetas. In part, due to the way Kappa acted. They'd always been so exclusive, so "us before everyone else." As much as Theta had gotten wrong, Vivi couldn't deny that she'd liked their more welcoming approach. The way that, for better or worse, they wanted to include everybody in their plans.

The meeting continued around them, but Vivi slipped one hand into her purse to touch her tarot cards. She fished through them until she found a Swords card, to help with the spell.

Then she concentrated on Scarlett, up on the stage.

I have an idea, she sent to her Big.

A moment later, Scarlett locked eyes with her, and nodded.

As soon as the dean dismissed the council, Vivi leaped from her seat as though electrocuted.

"Hey, where's the fire?" Mei called after her. But Vivi was the social chair; this sort of thing was her job.

She sought out Rose's pink head above the crowd and wove her way toward the cluster of Thetas. She reached them at the same time as Maria, whose shoulders sagged in defeat.

"We'll just have to try again next year," Maria was saying. "It's okay."

But it didn't *sound* all right. The Thetas looked utterly dejected. Vivi cleared her throat.

Rose noticed her first and nodded her way. The rest turned, and Maria's expression hardened. "Oh. Vivian. Come to gloat?"

"Actually . . ." Vivi glanced from Rose to Maria. "As Kappa's social chair, I wanted to ask if Theta would be interested in cohosting the Spring Fling with Kappa this year."

For a moment, nobody spoke. Then Rose broke into a huge grin. "Seriously?"

"We'll have to think about it . . ." Maria hedged. But Vivi could tell from the pleased flush on her face that she was tempted.

"It's just, I know how much the Fling means to you all," Vivi said. "And I know Kappa hasn't always been the most . . . welcoming. In the past. We want to turn over a new leaf this semester. Work *with* the other girls on campus, instead of against them."

Maria stared at her for a long moment, then smiled. "I knew you had a little bit of Theta ideals in you, Vivian."

"Oh, I'm a Raven through and through. But if you ask me, Kappa and Theta aren't as different as we think."

"Amen to that." Rose slid around her president to squeeze Vivi's arm once, quickly. "Looking forward to party-planning with you."

"Same," Vivi replied, grinning. And unlike the last parties she'd planned, where her nerves had nearly consumed her beforehand, this time, she really was excited about it.

By the time Vivi met up with the other Kappas outside, they were all on their phones, texting the good news to the rest of the house. "We're free!" Mei shouted, jumping up and down a few times. She glanced from side to side to make sure no one was watching, then shook out her long auburn waves, transforming them into a mass of short, hot pink curls that matched her platform sneakers perfectly.

"Really?" Scarlett said, with a smirk. "After all that, you're going to risk our exposure to fix your hair?"

"Oh, look who's talking." Jess gave Scarlett an affectionate jab with her elbow. "You're the one who had that potion ready to slip into Dean Sanderson's coffee if the meeting didn't go our way."

Scarlett shrugged. "A good president is always prepared. Now, who wants to go to that cute bakery in town for cupcakes? My treat."

⁓

On their way back to Kappa House, Vivi slipped off and headed to the rare books library, where she settled down on the stone steps to wait, a steaming coffee in each hand. It was twilight, her favorite time of day on campus. The sky was a deep, rich blue and the gas lamps that lined the quad were flickering to life.

Vivi took a deep breath of evening air and tried to steady her nerves, but she couldn't quite stop her arm from shaking, sloshing coffee over the lid. They'd defeated Typheus and gotten their magic back, but there was still something she had to fix before she could truly relax. A few minutes after six, Mason walked up the brick path, just as she knew he would. He always studied here for an hour or so before dinner. When he spotted her, he froze in his tracks, and for a moment Vivi was sure he was going to spin on his heel and walk in the other direction. But then he seemed to gather himself and continued forward, avoiding her eye until he was right in front of her.

"Hey," Vivi said. "Sorry, I guess I should have texted, but I wasn't sure what to say. So I figured . . ." She then held up the coffee with a hopeful smile. "I thought maybe if I brought you expensive coffee, you'd forgive me for being the worst girlfriend in history. Seems like a fair trade, right?"

Mason surveyed her with an inscrutable expression but said nothing. It was a strange, lonely sensation to feel so far removed from him. He was normally so easy for her to read, but at this moment, she truly had no idea what was going on in the mind she loved so much.

"I mean, *really* expensive," she blathered on. "I went to that place where they only brew one cup at a time and give you a nasty look if you ask for sugar."

"Thank you," Mason said, accepting the cup from her outstretched hand. She could tell he'd had a long day; his drawl grew more pronounced when he was tired.

"Look, I know you have no reason to forgive me. I know I was a jerk, and I shut you out without so much as an explanation—"

"So is this the part where you offer one?" Mason asked, his elongated vowels knocking against her heart. He looked so *dejected*. And she'd done that. She'd pushed him away—let her magic come between them. The worst part was, as much as she *wanted* to confide in him now, she still couldn't. Not about everything.

Not about her biggest, most important secret, anyway. But there were other ones she could broach.

"I almost quit Kappa. Actually, I *did* quit, for a while, and joined Theta instead."

"*What?* That doesn't make any sense. Kappa's so important to you."

"I know. It was. It *is*. But I lost sight of that for a little while.

Our first two parties of the semester were a disaster, and Scarlett was relying on me to do so much, and we were all fighting with each other. I told you I didn't want to ask for help, but that wasn't the whole story. I was . . ." She took a deep breath. "I was just so scared."

The skepticism vanished from his face, replaced by such sincere sympathy, it made a lump form in her throat. "I know it's stupid," she continued. "I know I'm fine, I survived that storm. But every time I shut my eyes at night, I'm back in the middle of it, thinking it'll be me this time, me who dies instead of one of the other girls."

"Vivi . . . I'm so sorry. That sounds awful."

"It was." She sighed. "But it's not an excuse. I know that. I should have opened up, should have listened to you when you asked me to."

He nodded and was quiet for a moment. "Sometimes asking for help is the hardest thing to do."

Vivi couldn't help but laugh a little. "Believe me, I learned that lesson."

"So you aren't a Kappa anymore?"

"Actually, they accepted me back. But I had to promise not to work myself to death, and to delegate projects to other Kappas if I get overwhelmed."

"I'm glad," he said with a smile. "Those girls are good for you. And you're good for them."

Vivi rose from the steps and inched toward him, close enough to catch his familiar scent. "The thing I regret most, though, is how I treated you. I let you down when you needed me the most. And

I know you don't have any reason to forgive me. But I promise, if I'm lucky enough to get a second chance, I won't let you down again. I promise I'll actually, y'know, *communicate* this time."

He let out a faint chuckle, which made her heart lurch with a complicated kind of hope.

She wanted this. So badly. She was going to earn him back. Whatever it took.

"Vivi . . ." Mason sighed, looking pained.

Please, she thought.

"I need a little time," he said, and it took all her willpower not to drop back down to the steps. "I have some more thinking to do."

"Right. Right, of course, however much time you need. I completely understand."

Mason's expression softened. "I'm not saying no, okay? I just . . . We'll see."

"I'll keep trying." Vivi held his gaze. "However long it takes. I'm not giving up on us, Mason."

This time, she promised.

CHAPTER FORTY-ONE

Scarlett

The woman waiting for Scarlett at the coffee shop in downtown Savannah looked so familiar that for a moment she froze in the middle of the sidewalk, feeling as though all the air had been sucked from her lungs.

Not for the first time since their battle with Typheus, Scarlett pictured the last moments of Xavier's life. Him meeting her gaze across the basement, as Typheus gripped his head in both hands. The horrible snap when his neck broke.

"You must be Claudia." Scarlett forced herself to move, to offer a hand to the woman. They shook, and Scarlett took a seat across from her at the café table. She'd gotten a message over social media a couple days after Xavier's death. His family. From the sounds of it, they'd already known what had happened to him, although Scarlett couldn't work out how. Or how many of the details they actually knew.

Claudia, in particular, had wanted to meet her.

"Scarlett Winter." Xavier's sister was his spitting image. They could have been twins. Except where Xavier had been all dangerous flirtation, his sister looked so composed she almost seemed bored.

"I'm so sorry for your loss," Scarlett murmured.

At that, however, Claudia's composure flickered. She shut her eyes for a long moment, as though recovering her calm, before she nodded. "Thank you. It's been difficult for the whole family."

"Xavier talked a lot about y'all," Scarlett said. Granted, often to say how much pressure they put on him. But Scarlett knew from experience — you could still love the hell out of relatives who asked a lot of you. "He wanted to make you proud. More than anything."

Claudia sighed, her shoulders dropping. "And he did. To the last, I'm afraid."

Scarlett reached into her purse to withdraw a slim box. She'd packed Xavier's knife into it. It felt strange having a witch-hunter's knife in Kappa House. But it felt even stranger to hand it back to someone who might very well be the kind of hunter her mother had warned her against.

They sent Xavier to help us, Scarlett reminded herself. *They're on our side.*

With a deep breath, she slid the box across the table. "You should have this," Scarlett said.

Claudia opened the lid. There was that brief flicker again, the crack in her composure. Her brow furrowed, and her eyes went glassy. Not quite tears, but . . .

Scarlett wondered if this was how Eugenie would look if anything ever happened to her. As much as they fought, they also shared so much. The same family history, same drive in life, same goals in Kappa.

After a long, quiet moment, Claudia closed the box again. "A hunter's blade goes to their successor. I already have mine. Xavier's should go to a trainee, but he hadn't chosen an apprentice yet, so . . ."

Scarlett frowned. "I don't understand."

Claudia shifted in her seat. "How much did Xavier tell you?"

"If you're worried he spilled any trade secrets, don't be." She smiled almost fondly. "Your brother was a locked book to the end."

Claudia smiled. "He was such a purist. He believed that his—our—work mattered. That he was making a real difference in the world, as difficult as our job might be at times."

"He did," Scarlett said. "He saved us all. The whole campus; hell, maybe the entire world."

Claudia squeezed her eyes shut. "I just wish I could tell him how proud I am. One more time." Then she patted the box and slid the knife back across the table toward Scarlett. "You keep it for now. Added protection. And if you meet someone you think would be worthy of wielding this, well, then . . ." Claudia dropped a business card on top of the box. "Have them give me a call."

Scarlett watched Claudia leave. And then, all at once, a knot in her chest loosened. She slid the knife back into her purse, an idea forming.

～

"I'm confused." Mei looked at the box Scarlett had passed her. "Isn't it the wrong semester for pledge votes?"

The Ravens had all gathered in the greenhouse at Scarlett's request, sitting cross-legged on a series of matching rattan poufs Etta had conjured out of overturned flower baskets.

"This isn't a pledge situation, exactly," Scarlett said. "But I want input from y'all before I move forward. I want to make sure this is something the whole house is comfortable with."

So, with a shrug, Mei withdrew a single white feather from the box and passed it along to Etta. While the box was going around, each of the girls taking out her voting feather, Scarlett carefully set Xavier's blade on the ground in the center of the circle. More than a few of the girls shuddered, even though Scarlett had already explained who Xavier was and how he'd fought on their side.

It was hard to shake the instinct that had been drilled into most of them by their parents from a young age. Hunters were dangerous.

Then again, they'd all faced plenty worse danger in the last two semesters.

"As Vivi and I told y'all." Scarlett glanced across the circle at her Little, who smiled in encouragement. "Xavier's family is looking for a new recruit."

"This is our problem why?" Reagan grumbled.

Scarlett smiled at her, indulgent. "Would you rather they choose someone random, who doesn't know anything about the Ravens and might view our magic as a threat? Or would we rather have a hand in picking his successor? Someone who knows us, someone who won't threaten Kappa's way of life." *Unless one of us goes full Tiffany again.* Scarlett repressed the thought.

"I like that idea," Etta said. "It would be nice if we could learn from the guardians, and vice versa."

"But I still don't get why the feathers," Jess spoke up.

"Well. The feathers are because . . ." Scarlett hesitated. Glanced at Vivi again, then Mei. "I have a nomination. And I'd like to hear your thoughts. Personally, I think this person will do a great job, but I might be biased. So. I wanted to put it to a vote."

And then she explained her nominee.

As she'd expected, debate broke out. Some were in immediate favor. Others raised questions that Scarlett knew were entirely fair. Questions she'd been asking herself, like: *Is this selfish? Should I be asking this?*

In the end, though, after they'd talked through every angle, Scarlett finally held up her feather. "All those in favor," she said. At the same time, her white feather slowly transformed, black bleeding across it like ink.

And all around the circle, more and more feathers did the same. The dark color spreading, until every single feather a Kappa held was raven black.

Scarlett couldn't help it. She grinned, her heart skipping a beat in her chest. "Well. That settles it, then."

CHAPTER FORTY-TWO

Vivi

Party planning was a lot easier when you had the resources of two whole sororities at your disposal instead of one. They'd opted to host the Spring Fling on a riverboat this year — Maria's father captained one, and he'd given them a very good deal.

The boat's natural facilities were impressive on their own. It had three decks, complete with an infinity pool on the top, an open-air bar on the central deck, and an old-fashioned water wheel on the bottom deck. The Kappas' magical enhancements only added to the festive atmosphere: a cascading series of lights woven through the wheel to make the water appear shimmering and golden as they sailed; soundproofing so each deck featured different music, none of it clashing or blending when one moved between levels; and this time, they'd perfected Etta and Ariana's brew to create hangover-proof alcohol. Not that anyone would appreciate that touch until the morning after, but still.

Up on the top deck, Vivi leaned against the railing to watch the Westerly students flooding onto the boat, resplendent in their Spring Fling attire. She smiled as Rose approached, carrying two plastic cups.

"Cheers to teamwork." Rose handed Vivi a cup, then tapped

hers against Vivi's. The boat had a no-glass policy, so Kappa had conceded to Theta's choice of drinkware this time. Scarlett had wrinkled her nose the first time the bartender poured her martini into one, but at least had the decency to look shamefaced when she spotted Vivi watching. Then she'd laughed and taken a sip.

"Tastes the same, after all," Scarlett had admitted, with a smile that lifted Vivi's spirits.

Vivi felt a similar thrill as she listened to the guests' murmurs of surprise and appreciation as they stepped aboard. "We ended up making a pretty great team, didn't we?" Vivi said.

"Definitely," Rose said. "Though I wish y'all would've let us help with the finishing touches. Those lights must've taken you *ages!* How'd you do it?"

Rose sounded completely sincere, but Vivi couldn't help but scan her for a sign — a glint in her eyes or a trace of a knowing smile — any hint that she knew how the Ravens had created such a spectacular effect. But her friendly, open face revealed nothing. The memory charms had worked perfectly.

None of the Thetas remembered ever having magic.

It was for the best, of course. It'd have been cruel and frankly dangerous to leave the Thetas with the memory of Tim's deception. But Vivi couldn't help but feel a slight pang of pity for her new friends. Losing your magic was the hardest thing in the world, whether you remembered having it or not.

"Is Mason here yet?" Rose asked, leaning over the rail to scan the crowd.

Vivi shook her head. "No, and I'm not sure if he's coming. He had a family thing tonight he didn't think he could miss."

Rose reached over to squeeze Vivi's arm. "He'll come around."

"Maybe." She and Mason had seen each other a few times since their conversation outside the library. Their outings hadn't felt platonic, exactly—last week, Vivi had accompanied him to a history department social hour, where she'd met his adviser in person and felt a thrill of pride as she listened to the esteemed professor gush about Mason's research. But while he'd treated her like his girlfriend at the event, introducing her to his fellow history majors and the grad students he'd worked with, he didn't initiate any sort of physical contact all night. When he'd dropped her off, Vivi had walked up the front path feeling even lonelier than she had after their breakup. She understood that she had to win back Mason's trust, but the uncertainty was killing her.

Vivi spotted Bailey, Ariana, Sonali, and Reagan waving to her from the bottom deck. "I should see if they need me for anything. I'll find you later?"

Rose saluted with her cup, and Vivi wound her way down the stairs and through the growing crowd to join the other freshman Kappas.

"This all looks *fantastic*," Vivi said, admiring the oyster bar and seafood tower that had somehow sprung up in the last twenty minutes. "Thanks so much for all your help. I hope it wasn't too much work." She'd divvied up all the spellwork this time to make sure she didn't get in over her head.

"For the millionth time, we *want* to help," Sonali said with a smile. "That's the whole point of being Ravens. We work together."

"Even if we have to do it with Thetas sometimes," Ariana said, looking around the deck with exaggerated suspicion. It'd taken her a few days to recover from the sting of watching her sisters walk out, even if they'd been under the influence of demon magic. Yet despite her posturing, Vivi knew Ariana was warming to the Thetas. She'd even spotted her having lunch with Spencer a few days back.

"Vivi," Reagan said, and elbowed her in the side.

"Ow, what?" Vivi glared at Reagan, then turned to follow her gaze. A familiar tousle of curls sent her heart lurching against her rib cage. Mason had stepped aboard and was already scanning the crowd.

"Good luck," Reagan whispered as Vivi set off, excitement and worry churning in her stomach. She'd hurt him so badly, he had every right to decide he wasn't ready to give her another chance. Yet as she watched him weave through the crowd in a blue seersucker suit that matched his eyes, giving a warm smile to every familiar face, Vivi knew that she would never be satisfied just being friends.

She smoothed her skirt one last time before she reached his side. "I'm glad you came," she said, pausing a moment before she gave him a slightly awkward hug.

He grinned. "Me too."

She bit her lip nervously, grateful to once again have lipstick fixing spells at the ready. "I . . . I wasn't sure if you would." She didn't care if it made her sound needy or vulnerable. She was done trying to hide her emotions from him.

"To be honest, neither was I." He slid his hands into his pockets and rocked back and forth on his heels.

"Oh." The admission landed like a blow, but she forced herself to nod. "That's fair."

"What?" He looked startled. "I just meant that I wasn't sure if I'd be able to get away in time."

"Oh," she said again, though this time the word slid out with a sigh of relief. "I just thought . . . Never mind."

"My adviser really liked you, by the way," Mason said, clearly eager to change the subject.

"That's nice to hear. I was afraid she'd somehow see into my brain and know that in fifth grade I Googled 'who is the king of America?'"

"I'm sure she would've been impressed by your precocious show of curiosity." He paused. "Did you really Google that?"

Vivi shrugged. "That's what happens when you switch elementary schools too many times. You never learn how the American Revolution ended."

"All the more reason for you to come with me to that conference in Boston."

A spark of hope ignited in her chest, sending a current of excitement through her veins. "The one this fall?"

"Yes, assuming you don't have plans six months from now."

"Is that how long you need to do your thinking?" Vivi asked, feeling suddenly bold.

"I've done enough thinking," he said quietly, and took her hand. "I want you in my life. I need you."

"So are you saying . . ." She trailed off, too afraid to release the words fluttering on her lips lest he crush them.

He bent his head and kissed her softly, then brought his hand to her cheek. "I'm saying that I love you and I want us to be together."

The surge of relief and joy came so fast and quick, Vivi was almost thrown off balance. "I love you, too," she said, rising onto her toes to kiss him back. When they finally broke away, he was grinning. Those damn dimples. She could never get sick of watching him like this, openhearted and happy.

"I promise not to be a secretive, flaky weirdo." She squeezed his hand and leaned into his side.

He wrapped his arm around her waist and pulled her closer. "You can't promise not to be a weirdo. That's one of the things I love about you."

"What are some of the other things?"

"Well . . ." He looked around the boat. "You throw a hell of a party, for one."

"That doesn't count." She crossed her arms and smiled.

"You look extra adorable when you pretend to be angry," he said, then kissed the top of her head. "Does that count?"

"Fine, but you have to tell me the rest later."

"Sure. After I tell you the story of the first king of America, though."

"Stop it!" She pretended to hit his arm. "I should've never admitted that."

"Once upon a time, in a kingdom called Georgia, there was a beautiful princess who stood up all her dates—" He cut himself off with a laugh as Vivi pulled him onto the dance floor and arranged herself in his arms.

Whatever else happened, whatever else came their way, Vivi would make sure they faced it together now. Side by side.

CHAPTER FORTY-THREE

Scarlett

Congratulations, sis. I hear this party isn't half terrible. The text from Eugenie actually made Scarlett smile — which might have been a first. She'd been making more of an effort with her sister the last couple weeks, ever since meeting Xavier's sister.

It was an up-and-down road so far. But they were making progress, she thought. Slow, painstaking progress, but still. Progress.

Mei slid an arm around her waist. "So, spill. Who did you wind up bringing as your date?"

Speculation over that had been all over the house for days. Scarlett hadn't exactly helped the rumor mill, since she'd avoided the question every time. Now, though, she couldn't dodge any longer.

"I didn't bring one."

Mei actually did a double take, her lips parting. "You're joking."

"What's wrong with going stag?" Scarlett tossed her hair, curled for the occasion, over one shoulder. "I don't need a guy on my arm to enjoy myself."

Mei raised both hands in surrender. "No, of course not. It's just . . . I never thought I'd see the day you chose to, that's all."

She hadn't, actually. But she wasn't about to admit in front of everyone that her date had turned down her invitation.

She understood why, of course. She didn't blame him. But it still stung.

"Drinks?" Scarlett asked. "I'm going for a refill."

"Please." Mei passed over her cup — Solo cups, honestly, what was Theta thinking? Although Scarlett had to admit, on the riverboat, which swayed gently underfoot as they took to the water, chugging slowly away from the Savannah docks, it did make a little more sense. She'd hate to have to work up a spell to keep every single glass object on the boat shatterproof for the entire night.

Scarlett wove between patrons on her way to the bar. She was just about to cast a quick spell to speed her way to the front of the line, when someone brushed her elbow.

"I can fill those, if you'd like."

Her heart skipped a beat. "Jackson." Her eyebrows rose. "I thought you weren't coming."

He wore a catering uniform, which gave her pause. She held out her cups, and he poured a healthy dose of champagne into each before he answered.

"I couldn't come as your date," he said slowly, "because I'd already agreed to work tonight."

"Still saving up for that road trip?"

His head bobbed. "For Harper's sake. Even if it'll be harder, once I forget the truth about her again. I still want to go. I promised her."

She swirled the champagne in her cup, not drinking it yet. "You could have told me, you know. About tonight."

She'd texted to invite him. He'd left her message on read. She'd also texted him to say they needed to talk. He hadn't even *read* that one.

"I know." He sighed. "I guess I just . . ." He paused. Glanced over his shoulder at the surrounding crowd. "Um. I figured, the next time we talked, it would be when you'd come to . . . well. Drug me again."

Ah. "You realize I don't need to be near you to do that, right?" Last time she had used a potion, but there were other memory-altering spells.

Kappa was getting awfully skilled at those lately.

His eyes narrowed. "Gee. Comforting."

"I'm just being honest." She shrugged.

He set the champagne on another waiter's tray as they passed, and crossed his arms. "So is this it, then? Is my time up?"

"Not necessarily," Scarlett replied.

He frowned, and only now did she notice how bloodshot his eyes were. "What do you mean? I thought you told me you had no other choice."

His voice rose, and Scarlett couldn't help it. She raised a hand to cast a distraction spell, to divert the eyes of the other Westerly students pressed close on all sides.

Jackson flinched when she moved. "Scarlett, don't—"

"I'm not casting this on you," she hissed. "I'm just trying to contain this conversation." She gestured at the crowd. Everyone's eyes were averted now, fixed on their own cups or conversation partners.

Jackson turned and stared. "Hey. Hello!" Jackson waved a hand before the closest couple's noses. Neither one reacted.

When he turned back to Scarlett again, he looked reluctantly impressed. "It's not fair. One group of people having so much power. No one else even knows you can do this. You must see that there's an imbalance here."

"I do," Scarlett said, and Jackson blinked, taken aback. He'd probably been expecting her to argue. It made her smile, just a little bit.

This was the right decision. This was why wiping his mind had felt so wrong last time. Because Jackson was *exactly* the right person for this assignment.

Slowly, Scarlett reached into her purse and withdrew a thin box. "Open it," she said.

Unlike the Ravens, who had all flinched reflexively at the sight of Xavier's blade, Jackson reached out with wonder to trace the hilt. "This is gorgeous. Where did you get it? It looks seriously historic." Then he squinted at her. "You didn't rob a museum, did you?"

She laughed. "No, this was acquired a hundred percent voluntarily." She took a deep breath. *Here goes.* "An opening has come up for someone who thinks the way you do. Someone who wants to ensure the safety of both the magical and the mundane worlds." She pressed her lips together for a moment. "It's not an easy job. The last person who wielded this, he . . ." Scarlett winced. "Died. In the line of duty."

Jackson watched her closely. "Xavier?" he guessed.

Scarlett blinked. "How did you . . . ?"

"When I was still under Cait's spell, Tim talked about being suspicious of Xavier. Not trusting him. Then, when the news came out about Xavier dying in that car accident the same night my spell broke . . . Wasn't exactly hard to piece together. Xavier was trying to stop Tim, wasn't he?"

Scarlett nodded. "He gave his life to save everyone on campus."

Jackson slipped the knife from its box and hefted it experimentally in one hand. "But he wasn't a witch, like you?"

"No. He was a guardian. All of his family are." Scarlett passed Jackson the card Claudia had left her. "They've offered to train you, if you want to become one too. They'd teach you how to stop demons like Tim, or anyone else who goes too far in their pursuit of power."

"Even a rogue witch?" Jackson lifted an eyebrow.

Scarlett hesitated. "Even a witch, yes, if . . . if someone else ever started to act like . . .." She didn't need to say Tiffany's name. He remembered now. In so many ways, that was a relief. But maybe it was selfish of her, to hope he'd stay. To hope he'd put himself in harm's way just to remain part of her world. Scarlett cleared her throat. "You don't need to decide right away. Take some time, think it over. Weigh the risks."

Jackson placed the knife back into the box and shut the lid. "Would I get to keep my memory? If I said yes."

She nodded again. "But make sure you really want this, Jackson. Memories aside."

Jackson slid the business card into his pocket. When he looked at her again, a hint of a smile played at the corners of his mouth. "Let me guess. You give all the boys you like some sort of life-endangering quest before they're allowed on a date with you."

Scarlett snorted. But she didn't disagree, either, which made Jackson laugh.

"You Kappas are impossible."

"And dangerous. You just all but said as much yourself." She took a step closer, gaze fixed on his. "Which is why we need someone to keep an eye on us. For our safety, and for everyone else's."

"Tell me this isn't just a ploy to convince me to kiss you again, Winter," he said, and his words sent a thrill through her veins, a spark that kindled in her rib cage.

This was what she'd been missing all semester. Their banter, Jackson's way of saying what she didn't expect anyone to be uncouth enough to voice aloud. "Well . . . it's not *just* that," she replied, and his grin widened.

"You really are a bad witch." But he was laughing as he said it.

She took a step toward him, and he mirrored her, their chests brushing, every inch of her body on fire at being this close to him again, after so long apart. "Does this mean you'll be my guardian?" She lifted an eyebrow.

Something crashed in the distance. She looked up to see the fireworks starting, exploding out over the river in bright golden streams. Around them, the other partygoers oohed.

Jackson, however, never took his gaze off her.

"Game on," he murmured. Then he bent his head down, and finally, *finally* kissed her. As she sank against him, her arms sliding up his arms to wrap around his neck, Scarlett had the strangest sensation. Like falling and being caught all at once.

Then someone jostled her shoulder, and they broke apart, breathless.

You two lovebirds are missing the show, Mei admonished, whispering in Scarlett's head. With a wide grin, Scarlett grasped Jackson's hand and pulled him through the crowd toward the prow of the ship.

Her sisters closed rank around them, welcoming Jackson as easily as if he were one of their own. She caught Vivi and Mason standing near the edge of the group. Vivi lifted her eyebrows, a silent question.

He said yes, Scarlett reassured her.

Vivi's smile widened. And to judge by the way her Little leaned her head on Mason's shoulder, he must have forgiven Vivi, too.

Jackson wound his arms around Scarlett from behind, his chin resting on her shoulder. "What have I gotten myself into?" he whispered, breath hot on her skin.

She looked back at him, smirking. "Don't tell me you're afraid of a few sorority witches."

He laughed and kissed the nape of her neck. "Oh, I think everyone should fear y'all. Because I'm pretty sure there's nothing you can't do."

Vivi and Mason moved in closer to stand next to them. Scarlett took Vivi's hand and squeezed it. Her Little beamed back at her.

Jackson was right. With her sisters at her side, she was unstoppable. They all were. Together.

The night sky exploded with bright colors all around them, and her chest swelled. Scarlett knew there was nothing in the whole world that was better than this feeling.

It was magic.

ACKNOWLEDGMENTS

Thank you to the team at Alloy, who've made my writerly dreams come true, including Sara Shandler, Josh Bank, Les Morgenstein, Romy Golan, and Joelle Hobeika. Extra thanks to Lanie Davis and Laura Barbiea, whose storytelling instincts dazzle me at every turn, and to Emilia Rhodes, whose insight and intelligence inspire me to be a better writer *and* a better editor.

I'm very grateful to the whole team at Clarion Books, especially Liz Agyemang, Tara Shanahan, Sammy Brown, Julie Yeater, and everyone who worked so hard to help the Ravens take flight.

A very special thank-you to the talented Ellen Goodlett, who made invaluable contributions to this book. And my deepest thanks to my witchy sister, Danielle Paige, who dreamt up Kappa Rho Nu and brought so much magic into my life.

And finally, thank you to all the readers who've joined us on this journey. Your tweets, reviews, comments, words of encouragement, and gorgeous Bookstagram posts have been the highlight of a deeply strange year, and I'm so very grateful to have you all in our coven.

Kass Morgan

There are so many kinds of magic. And I am so grateful for all the magic in my life. Kass, sitting next to you at that panel all those years ago was kismet. I am so glad to have you as my sister writer witch. You didn't just accept my invite to the sorority, you brought your own magic and made us and the Ravens unstoppable. Love you, friend.

To my family: my love, Chris Albers, I would still cross any room to get to you. Andrea, Daddy, Sienna, and Josh, your love is magic; it's made me who I am.

To my beloved second families: Annie, Chris, Fiona, and Jackson Rolland; Lauren Dell and Sandy and Don Goodman; Stephen Mcpherson and Tina Sloan; Jill Lorie and Tony Hurst. To Bonnie Datt . . . dresses are magic and so are you! To Daryn Strauss, my brilliant, prolific friend! To my friends Carin Greenberg, Josh Sabarra, Michele Wells, Kami Garcia, Frank Lesser, Sasha Alsberg, Leslie Rider, Paloma Ramirez, Jeanne-Marie Hudson, Megan Steintrager, Lexi Dwyer, Lisa Tollin, Sarah Kagan, Kristin Nelthorpe, Leslie Kendall Dye, Crystal Chappell, Melissa Salmons,

Laura Wright, Jordan Vilasuso, Sasha Mote, Chris Lowe . . . and so many more . . . my life is more charmed for having you all in it.

And to my dear Emily Williams! Thank you for being the Ravens' social chair and my personal touchstone!

To our loyal and trusted team at Alloy who helped bring our witches together, Sara Shandler, Josh Bank, Les Morgenstein, Romy Golan, and Joelle Hobeika. And especially Lanie Davis and Laura Barbiea for their editing spells.

To our Clarion Books team, Liz Agyemang, Tara Shanahan, Sammy Brown, Julie Yeater, and especially our editor, Emilia Rhodes, for shepherding our sorority on the page and off to bookstores with such fierce support.

And to Ellen Goodlett, who is definitely a Raven and a friend.

And finally, to our ever-growing coven of readers, who have given our witches so much love. Thanks to everyone who picked up our book, who gave it a shout or drew some art. We've missed getting to see you in person. And I cannot wait for our virtual hugs to be real ones again. Munchkins, you've given me so much magic. May your own magic find you!

Danielle Paige

WANT MORE?

If you enjoyed this and would like to find out about similar books we publish, we'd love you to join our online Sci-Fi, Fantasy and Horror community, Hodderscape.

Visit hodderscape.co.uk for exclusive content form our authors, news, competitions and general musings, and feel free to comment, contribute or just keep an eye on what we are up to.

See you there!

HODDERSCAPE
NEVER AFRAID TO BE OUT OF THIS WORLD

 @Hodderscape 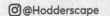 @Hodderscape   /hodderscape